The Russian Short Story

A CRITICAL HISTORY

TWAYNE'S CRITICAL HISTORY OF THE SHORT STORY

William Peden, General Editor
University of Missouri-Columbia

The American Short Story before 1850
Eugene Current-García, Auburn University

The American Short Story, 1850–1900
Donald Crowley, University of Missouri-Columbia

The American Short Story, 1900–1945
Philip Stevick, Temple University

The American Short Story, 1945–1980
Gordon Weaver, Oklahoma State University

The English Short Story, 1880–1945
Joseph M. Flora, University of North Carolina-Chapel Hill

The English Short Story, 1945–1980
Dennis Vannatta, University of Arkansas-Little Rock

The Irish Short Story
James F. Kilroy, Vanderbilt University

The Latin American Short Story
Margaret Sayers Peden, University of Missouri-Columbia

The Russian Short Story

A CRITICAL HISTORY

Charles A. Moser, Editor
George Washington University

Twayne Publishers • Boston
A Division of G. K. Hall & Co.

The Russian Short Story
A Critical History

Published in 1986 by Twayne Publishers
A Division of G. K. Hall & Co.
70 Lincoln Street, Boston, Massachusetts 02111

First Printing

Printed on permanent/durable
acid-free paper and bound in
the United States of America

Book design by Barbara Anderson
Book production by Elizabeth Todesco
Copyediting supervised by Lewis DeSimone

Typeset in 11 pt. Garamond
with Perpetua display type
by Compset, Inc., Beverly, Massachusetts

Library of Congress Cataloging in Publication Data

Moser, Charles A.
The Russian short story.

(Twayne's critical history of the short story)
Bibliography: p. 196
Includes index.
1. Russian fiction—19th century—History and criticism. 2. Russian fiction—20th century—History and criticism. 3. Short stories, Russian—History and criticism. I. Title. II. Series.
PG3097.M67 1986 891.73'01'09 86-14865
ISBN 0-8057-9360-7

Contents

Chronology

1830 *Tales of the Late Ivan Petrovich Belkin* (Pushkin) written. "The Test" (Bestuzhev-Marlinsky).

1831 *Tales of the Late Ivan Petrovich Belkin* (Pushkin) published. *Evenings on a Farm near Dikanka,* vol. 1 (Gogol).

1832 "Ammalat-Bek" (Bestuzhev-Marlinsky). *Evenings on a Farm near Dikanka,* vol. 2 (Gogol).

1833 "The Frigate *Nadezhda*" (Bestuzhev-Marlinsky).

1834 "Queen of Spades" (Pushkin).

1835 *Mirgorod* (Gogol). *Arabesques* (Gogol). *Three Tales* (Pavlov).

1837 "Egyptian Nights" published (Pushkin).

1840 *A Hero of Our Time* (Lermontov).

1842 "The Overcoat" (Gogol).

1844 *Russian Nights* (Odoevsky). "Andrey Kolosov" (Turgenev).

1845 Almanac *Physiology of St. Petersburg* (Nekrasov).

1846 "The Village" (Grigorovich).

1847 "Anton Goremyka" (Grigorovich). *The Hunting Sketches* (Turgenev) begins to appear.

1848 "White Nights" (Dostoevsky).

1850 *Diary of a Superfluous Man* (Turgenev).

1852 "Mumu" (Turgenev).

1855 Alexander II ascends the throne. "Yakov Pasynkov" (Turgenev).

1856 Crimean War ends. *Sketches from Peasant Life* (Pisemsky). *Sebastopol Tales* (Tolstoy).

1857 "The Little Hero" (Dostoevsky). *Provincial Sketches* (Saltykov).

1858 "Asya" (Turgenev).

1859 "Family Happiness" (Tolstoy).

1860 "First Love" (Turgenev).

1861 Emancipation of the serfs. "An Old Man's Sin" (Pisemsky).

1863 "The Cossacks" (Tolstoy). *Seminary Sketches* (Pomyalovsky). "Lodging for the Night" (Sleptsov).

1864 *People of Podlipnaya* (Reshetnikov).

1865 "Lady Macbeth of the Mtsensk District" (Leskov).

1866 *Mores of Rasteryaev Street* (Gleb Uspensky).

1868 "The Sentry Box" (Gleb Uspensky).

1870 "King Lear of the Steppes" (Turgenev). "Eternal Husband" (Dostoevsky).

1873 "The Enchanted Wanderer" (Leskov). "The Sealed Angel" (Leskov).

1876 "A Gentle Creature" (Dostoevsky).

1881 "The Lefthander" (Leskov). Alexander III ascends the throne.

1883 "The Red Flower" (Garshin). "Makar's Dream" (Korolenko). "Klara Milich" (Turgenev).

1886 *Death of Ivan Ilych* (Tolstoy).

1887 "The Sentry" (Leskov).

1888 "The Steppe" (Chekhov).

1889 "The Kreutzer Sonata" (Tolstoy). "A Boring Story" (Chekhov).

1892 "Ward Six" (Chekhov).

1894 Nicholas II ascends the throne.

1895 "Master and Man" (Tolstoy). "Chelkash" (Gorky).

1897 "Peasants" (Chekhov).

1899 "Twenty-six Men and a Girl" (Gorky).

1900 "Lady with a Lapdog" (Chekhov).

1902 "The Abyss" (Andreev).

1904 "Red Laughter" (Andreev).

1906 "The Bush" (Bely).

1907 *The Axis of the Earth* (Bryusov).

1911 "The Bracelet of Garnets" (Kuprin).

1913 "A Provincial Tale" (Zamyatin).

1914 Outbreak of First World War.

1915 "The Gentleman from San Francisco" (Bunin).

1916 "Light Breathing" (Bunin).

1917 The February and October revolutions.

1920 *The Past* (Pilnyak).

1922 *Stories of Nazar Il'ich, Mr. Bluebelly* (Zoshchenko).

1923 "The Emery Machine" (Slonimsky).

1924 "The End of an Ordinary Man" (Leonov). *Stories* (Gorky).

1925 *Diaboliad* (Bulgakov).

1926 *Red Cavalry* (Babel). *Unholy Tales* (Zamyatin). "Tale of the Unextinguished Moon" (Pilnyak). *Tales from the Don* (Sholokhov).

1927 "Epifan Locks" (Platonov).

1931 *Tales from Odessa* (Babel).

1934 Union of Soviet Writers established.

1941 German invasion.

1942 "The Flag" (V. Kataev). *Tales of Ivan Sudarev* (A. Tolstoy).

1946 "Adventures of a Monkey" (Zoshchenko). Zhdanov purge.

1953 Stalin dies.

1956 Almanac *Literary Moscow* (Paustovsky). "Levers" (Yashin).

1961 Almanac *Leaves from Tarusa* (Paustovsky).

1962 "Halfway to the Moon" (Aksenov).

1963 "Matrena's Homestead" (Solzhenitsyn). *The Villagers* (Shukshin).

1966 "Constellation of the Goatabix" (Iskander).

1967 "Money for Maria" (Rasputin).

1968 *The Carpenter Tales* (Belov).

1973 "Sweet Woman" (Velembovskaya).

1976 "The Departing Monakhov" (Bitov).

1978 "Pasha" (Soloukhin).

1979 Almanac *Metropol* (Aksenov).

Introduction: Pushkin and the Russian Short Story

This history of the short story in Russian literature begins in 1830, not merely because the choice of that point enables us to set the volume's chronological boundaries at a mathematically pleasing 150 years, from 1830 to 1980. More important is the fact that in 1830 Aleksandr Pushkin—Russia's finest poet and the source of much of modern Russian literature—dedicated a large part of the autumn season (which a cholera epidemic compelled him to spend at his country estate) to the writing of the *Povesti pokoinogo Ivan Petrovicha Belkina* (*Tales of the Late Ivan Petrovich Belkin*), published the following year under the initials "A. P." That small volume has since become arguably the most important single collection of what we would now call short stories in Russian literature, and therefore it is appropriate that this study should derive its inception from it.

Tales of Belkin, like so much of Pushkin's work, both summed up the literary achievement that had preceded it and laid the groundwork for the subsequent development of the short story up to the work of Anton Chekhov (a plausible contender for designation as the greatest master of the genre in all of world literature) and even beyond, through the Soviet period and down to today. That is no mean accomplishment for a collection of but five tales with a brief introduction, and it is a measure of Pushkin's genius.

Eighteenth-century Russian literature was dominated by poetry and a well-developed system of poetic genres. Prose existed, but it was held in scant respect and only gradually came into its own at the end of the century and in the early nineteenth century. In his own career Pushkin recapitulated that transition from poetry to prose: indeed, *Tales of Belkin* marked such a shift not only for Pushkin personally but for Russian literature generally. To be sure, Russian literature had known short prose narrations beginning at least from around 1770, but they had scarcely coalesced into a genre until the appearance of stories by Nikolay Karamzin (1766–1826) in the 1790s and early 1800s, stories crucial to the formation of the sentimental school, the chief prose school in Russian literature before the advent of romanticism. This school was a very literary one in the sense that it derived its sustenance more from literary traditions than from real life. As Peter Brang concludes in a detailed study of the prehistory of the Russian short story, the sentimental short story dealt almost entirely with love affairs ending in tragedy, betrayal, or the thwarting of marriage.[1] Thus Karamzin's most famous story, "Bednaia Liza" ("Poor Liza," 1803), conjoins this tradition to the popular theme of love across the divisions of social class. It narrates the love of a peasant girl for a young man of the gentry: she drowns herself when he betrays her, and he suffers the pangs of remorse for the remainder of his life.

It required some time for literary theory to take proper cognizance of such a phenomenon as the developing short story and to work out appropriate terminology for the prose genres. The famous literary handbook compiled by Nikolay Ostolopov in 1812—a very good one for its time—lacked entries for *roman* (novel) and *povest'* (tale), even though Ostolopov wrote short stories himself; and his entry for *skazka* (which today means "folktale") spoke only of verse forms. Nikolay Grech, perhaps the leading literary theoretician of the early nineteenth century, in a textbook that first appeared around 1820 dealt with these genres still only in terms of poetry.[2] It was difficult for literary critics to liberate themselves from the neoclassical ways of thinking.

Still, prose narrations required names of some sort as they began to appear. In the eighteenth and early nineteenth centuries a prose narration was ordinarily called a roman, less often a povest', and occasionally a skazka. Initially the word *rasskaz,* now the standard term for "short story," denoted a manner of narration, not the narration itself. It was apparently used in this latter sense for the first time in 1818. But within a decade or so it had displaced the word *skazka* as the designation of a brief prose narrative in general, although it was retained in the meaning of allegorical or fantastic fairy tales, like the political satires Mikhail Saltykov-Shchedrin cast in this form in the 1880s. *Roman* still designated a long prose narration, and *povest'* survived as an elastic term denoting a narration of intermediate length.[3] Indeed, it remained the dominant designation of works we would call short stories for some time into the nineteenth century.

Actually there is a fairly close parallel between English and Russian terminology at this period. As Karl Kramer has formulated it, "historically the term *povest'* bears the same relation to the term *rasskaz* as the English word 'tale' bears to 'short story.' Both *rasskaz* and 'short story' acquired specifically literary meanings very late in the nineteenth century."[4] And indeed, as Kramer points out, we need only recall Poe's *Tales of the Grotesque and Arabesque* or Hawthorne's *Twice-Told Tales,*[5] and we feel historically comfortable in translating *Povesti Belkina* as *Tales of Belkin.* Indeed it took Ivan Turgenev until 1881 to separate from the corpus of his writing six works—including *Fathers and Sons*—which he then denoted *romany* rather than *povesti,* the designation he had previously given them. To us it is quite clear that the *Belkin* tales are short stories and *Fathers and Sons* is a novel, but their creators originally used the same Russian term—*povest'*—to designate both of them.

In any case, Pushkin designed his *Belkin* tales as experimental works. Experiments are by no means always successful, of course, and the experimenter runs a greater risk than usual of being misunderstood by his contemporaries. Pushkin was no exception to that rule. When the *Belkin* tales first appeared semianonymously in 1831, and then again under Pushkin's full name in 1834 with the addition of "The Queen of Spades," the critics either ignored or disparaged them. Thus a reviewer for one of the major contemporary journals, *Moskovsky telegraf* (Moscow telegraph), read them as no more than unsuccessful attempts by Pushkin to arouse his readers' interest with essentially uninteresting narrations and declared that as a short-story writer Pushkin fell far short of the standard set by a Washington Irving, for example.[6] In sum, the *Belkin* tales might have passed with virtually no notice at all had it not been known that Pushkin was their author.

The extent of the initial failure of *Tales of Belkin* can be gauged from the words of Vissarion Belinsky, the most outstanding critic of the nineteenth century in Russia and the first to pay proper notice to the rise of the short story narrative form in Russian literature. In his article of 1835 "O russkoi povesti i povestiakh g. Gogolia" (On the Russian tale and the tales of Gogol),[7] the critic declared that the povest'—which he defined as a "chapter torn from a novel"—had swept almost all before it. Had he lived at that time, Belinsky exclaimed, even Juvenal would have written tales rather than verse satires, "for if there are ideas of a time, there are also forms of a time." The povest' was not only the literary form of the day; it was also, he said, the form that suited Gogol uniquely, "a literary genus [*rod*] which is just as necessary and inevitable for him as the tale for Balzac, the song for Béranger, the drama for Shakespeare." For our purposes, however, it is especially interesting to note that when Belinsky traced the history of the povest' in Russian literature, he found its source in certain works of the 1820s by Aleksandr Bestuzhev-Marlinsky; it had then been developed further, he went on, by Vladimir Odoevsky, Mikhail Pogodin, Nikolay Polevoy, and Nikolay Pavlov until it blossomed in the works of Nikolay Gogol. One name is conspicuously missing from this literary genealogy: that of Aleksandr Pushkin. Even the perceptive Belinsky did not recognize the importance of the *Belkin* tales.

Today there is still some disagreement among scholars of Russian literature over the aesthetic worth of *Tales of Belkin*. Indeed, in his contribution to this volume, Victor Terras, like the critic of the *Moskovsky telegraf,* declares them to be of interest only because Pushkin wrote them. Scholars in the Soviet Union, on the other hand, are virtually obliged to regard them very highly, and some have exaggerated their intrinsic literary value. I consider them worthwhile pieces in and of themselves, but it is indisputable that in historical perspective these experimental works successfully encapsulate the tradition of earlier shorter prose works and also foreshadow the future development of the genre in a remarkable way. Thus, a general discussion of the Russian short story may profitably take *Tales of Belkin* as its foundation, for the seeds of its future in 1830 lay precisely there.

The retrospective elements of *Tales of Belkin* are less important for our present purposes, but still we may begin with a few words about them. Pushkin was always highly conscious of his immediate and more distant literary antecedents. He often chose epigraphs from other writers, and many of those he selected for the *Belkin* tales were taken from poets. Thus in a symbolic way he transformed poetry into prose, realizing that the great age of poetry was ending and that nineteenth-century Russian literature would be preeminently a prose literature. So the epigraph to the entire work came from Denis Fonvizin (1745–92), playwright, satirist, and wit, a man close to Pushkin's heart and one who worked almost wholly in prose even though he was entirely of the poetic eighteenth century. In this special way, then, Pushkin recapitulated the literary development preceding him, renewing it for his own purposes.

Pushkin's renewal of old tradition is very visible in his choice of plots for the five stories. Going back to the medieval tradition of the short narrative, he sought no particular originality in his plots; but he did provide them with unexpected twists. "The Stationmaster," for instance, is a reworking of the tale of the prodigal son. But here the prodigal child is a daughter, and the moral and material disasters the father unhappily expects his daughter to suffer are instead visited upon him. "The Peasant Miss" recasts the situation—by then trite—of peasant girl in love with gentry boy: in this case the seemingly insuperable conflict between social classes proves illusory, and the happy couple are united in marriage. In the *Belkin* tales, then, Pushkin quite openly toyed with literary conventions. In "Poor Liza" Karamzin had proclaimed his distress at the necessity of describing a real-life tragedy, and sentimentalist readers actually visited the pond where Liza was supposed to have drowned herself; but the reader of Pushkin's tales had no doubt that he was reading a literary work intended primarily as entertainment.

The more important aspects of *Tales of Belkin,* however, chart certain major lines along which the genre would develop after Pushkin: they helped define the future.

To begin with, we should note the obvious fact that the *Belkin* tales are written in prose and only in prose, except for certain poetic epigraphs. This provided a major impetus in the direction of prose and away from poetry, although it was not obvious to everyone at the time that there could or should be a strict demarcation between the two. Pushkin had called his own *Eugene Onegin* a "novel in verse," and it is his poetic masterpiece: Soviet scholars who regard it as the foundation of the nineteenth-century Russian novel must overlook the fact that subsequent novels were written in prose. In theory at least, the short story might have developed as a genre that combined prose and verse. Pushkin himself contributed to such a mixed genre with his fragment "Egyptian Nights," a stimulating work but one in which the prose serves primarily as a setting for two of Pushkin's best poems; and in 1848 the poet Karolina Pavlova published "A Double Life," in which the heroine's thoughts are given in verse. But this hybrid genre did not develop, and writers turned ever further from poetry as the century proceeded. At the beginning of his career Gogol dabbled in poetry but then abandoned it in favor of poetic prose; Ivan Turgenev, who began his career in the 1840s, did something similar. By the end of the century we find writers like Vsevolod Garshin and Anton Chekhov who worked entirely within the prose tradition, displaying no interest in writing poetry at all.

In the second place, all the *Belkin* tales are of similar length, and all are extremely brief. Although it may seem trivial, brevity is in fact the defining feature of the short story. Russian literary theoreticians did not seriously turn their attention to the short story as a genre until the rise of the formalist school in the 1920s, but when they did they necessarily emphasized the short story's very shortness. Boris Eikhenbaum, for example, in an article of 1927 on O. Henry as a short-story writer, pointed to "small dimensions" as one of the genre's two defining features;[8] and M. A. Petrovsky, in an extensive article the same year on what he chose to call the novella rather than the rasskaz, wrote much the same thing. "The novel [roman] and the short story [novella], taken as concepts," he said, "are two types of organization of narration. The relationship between them is the relationship between the extensive and the intensive, the expansive and the concentrated."[9] In saying this, the critics merely codified in critical language that which the genre's practitioners had long known: the physical dimensions of the narration in large measure define the character of the short-story genre in its purest form.

Anton Chekhov made some instructive observations on this subject in his personal correspondence, speaking out of his experience with extremely brief stories like the humorous ones he wrote at the beginning of his career in the early 1880s. In 1886 he sent his brother Aleksandr a six-point prescription for the genre that distills his views on it. Two of the six points are clearly linked to brevity:

> 1) Absence of long-winded tirades of a political, social and economic nature; 2) thorough-going objectivity; 3) truthfulness in the description of characters and objects; 4) total brevity; 5) daring and originality; keep away from clichés; 6) warmth of feeling.[10]

Some time later, in another letter, Chekhov dealt with the question of brevity as interconnected with objectivity, a central feature of his artistic approach: he believed brevity and objectivity were in fact closely connected. Referring to his work "Vory" ("Thieves"), he wrote:

> In order to depict horsethieves in 700 lines, I must constantly speak and think in their tones and feel in their spirit, for if I were to add a lot of subjectivity the images would spread out and the story would not be as compact as all short stories should be. When I write I count on the reader entirely to fill in the subjective elements missing in the story.[11]

Chekhov thus argued that there could be no space for subjectivity in a brief story: there was room only for the objectivity he valued so highly.

And if that is so, then three of the six points Chekhov formulates in his letter of 1886 are directly or indirectly tied to the principle of brevity.

Maksim Gorky, whom A. Ninov calls the fountainhead of the Soviet short story,[12] also saw brevity as central to the essence of the genre. Speaking before the First Congress of the Union of Soviet Writers in 1934, he said writers should learn from short stories, "for the short story teaches us to economize on words, to arrange our material logically, to make our plot clear and our topic plain."[13] Of course, not all writers—and especially those within the Russian tradition—adhered to the ideal of brevity. When we think of great works of Russian prose, we tend to recall vast narratives reaching even beyond the novel to what Soviet critics like to call the "epic novel," works that seek to encompass an entire epoch of signal historical change, like Tolstoy's *War and Peace,* Mikhail Sholokhov's *Quiet Don,* or any of Aleksandr Solzhenitsyn's major novels, not to mention his projected series beginning with *August 1914.* But the history of Russian literature includes masterful practitioners of the short-story genre who wrote remarkably brief works: many of the best works of not only Chekhov but Isaak Babel or Mikhail Zoshchenko in the Soviet Union of the 1920s run to no more than three or four pages of print, yet are heavy with content. In this area Pushkin set the standard; in *Tales of Belkin* he exemplified his realization that the short story in its pure form must be brief.

In Boris Eikhenbaum's theoretical article of 1927, the second characteristic of the short story is the "surprise ending" ("siuzhetnoe udarenie v kontse").[14] In his view, the novel as a form naturally incorporates delays, false endings, and the like. Consequently, Tolstoy simply "could not" end *Anna Karenina* with Anna's sudden suicide: he had to add a final section, for he was writing a novel, not a short story; it is the short story that by its nature concentrates its energies upon the ending. It is worthy of note that, in two instructive pages launching a discussion of O. Henry, Eikhenbaum contrasts *Anna Karenina* as representative of the novel form with *Tales of Belkin* as the embodiment of the short story.

And indeed in this respect Pushkin's experimental tales are exemplary. Three of the five stories ("The Blizzard," "The Undertaker," "The Peasant Miss") end extremely abruptly; the conclusion to "The Blizzard" is clearly designed to strain the reader's credulity to the utmost. "The Shot" ends almost as suddenly, although its final sentence serves as a condensed epilogue. Only "The Stationmaster" is narrated at a relatively leisurely pace and concludes with something in the nature of an epilogue. Some one hundred years after Pushkin the prominent Soviet writer Aleksey Nikolaevich Tolstoy, in a theoretical treatment of the short story, expanded on the question of the surprise ending. He argued that at the end the anecdote—which is at the core of the short story—had to display an element of either the unexpected or the fated: in the first case we have a "situation comedy," in the second a "tragedy."[15] Tolstoy also agreed that the short story is "a most difficult form of art" and that brevity is essential to it, brevity achieved through "the concentration of material, the selection of the most essential things." One of Tolstoy's most interesting formulations holds that "architectonically the short story must be constructed with a comma followed by 'but'"[16] There is always a "but," introducing something unexpected and very possibly unwelcome, at the conclusion of the short story in its purest form.

It would be impossible to enumerate all the Russian short stories adhering to the formula of the abrupt and/or surprise ending, from Gogol's "Nose," in which a wandering nose suddenly returns to its owner's face; through Nikolay Leskov's "Lady Macbeth of the Mtsensk District," with its sudden murder and suicide by drowning; through Chekhov's "Grasshopper," where a wife suddenly realizes what she has lost in her husband's death; down to Babel and the brutally abrupt endings of his *Red Cavalry* tales (one of Babel's models was the greatest practitioner of the abrupt ending in world literature, Guy de Maupassant, and one of his finest short stories bears that name as its title). For our purposes, again, the important point is that Pushkin established that formula in *Tales of Belkin,* and strikingly so, in ways that disconcerted contemporary readers and that still retain the capacity to astonish us today.

Pushkin's reshaping of traditional plots, his brevity, his emphasis upon the abrupt and unanticipated ending—all these have to do with the structure of the narration. Another structural element in the *Tales,* though less often remarked on, proved important in the development of a branch of the short story—the sketch, or *ocherk.* The seeds of this genre are to be discovered in the central work of the *Belkin* cycle, "The Undertaker," with its generalizations on the subject of undertakers as an occupational category, and especially in "The Stationmaster," which opens with an essay on the character of the typical stationmaster.

Thanks in part to the impetus Pushkin provided, the sketch became perhaps the leading shorter prose genre of the 1840s. In that decade a favorite literary form was the "physiological sketch," which supplied in artistic ways a semisociological description of certain occupational and social classes. Dmitry Grigorovich's "Peterburgskie sharmanshchiki" ("St. Petersburg Organ-Grinders," 1845) described several variants of the organ-grinders of the capital treated as an urban subclass. In the mid-1850s Aleksey Pisemsky did something similar for subcategories of the peasantry in his *Ocherki iz krest'ianskogo byta* (*Sketches from Peasant Life*). In the mid-1860s Pisemsky undertook a more controversial effort with his *Russkie lguny* (*Russian Liars,* 1865), a psychological and sociological investigation of the prevaricator; he held that one could make a rough assessment of the "level of intellectual, moral, and even political development of a country" by analyzing the things about which the people of that country lie.[17] The young radicals of the 1860s displayed a strong interest in the artistic depiction of an unlovely reality through the sketch with a powerful political thrust.

Defining the sketch as a genre in Russian literature is no simple matter, but the American Slavist Deming Brown has done as well as anyone in treating this question.[18] The sketch as it exists within the Russian tradition, he believes, deals with social reality directly: it must have an "'eye-witness' quality," and (the most essential element) "the narrator [must] be identified closely with the author himself." In its early history the sketch was fused most thoroughly with the short story in Ivan Turgenev's *Zapiski okhotnika* (usually translated *The Hunting Sketches* [1847–52], although the Russian *zapiski* means "notes"). Events in this cycle are narrated through the consciousness of the hunter, who comments explicitly or implicitly on the "typical reality" he is observing—so that narrator and observer are here indeed one. A number of the *Sketches* are nearly plotless, which fits with the idea of the sketch as a snapshot of reality, though others incorporate a plot line. In any case *The Hunting Sketches* are of such merit that one can certainly agree with A. Ninov's formulation that "Turgenev reformed the Russian short story on the basis of the genre of the lyric sketch" even if one cannot accept his view that this cycle defined "the major tradition of the Russian short story" well into the twentieth century.[19]

The "lyricism" of *The Hunting Sketches* was mostly Turgenev's personal contribution: one finds little enough of it in the sketches of the 1860s. The sketch assumed renewed importance, however, following the Revolution of 1917 and the social upheaval it brought in its train. At that time the paths of journalism and literature converged. Mikhail Zoshchenko wrote many of his brilliant satirical short stories of the 1920s on the basis of direct observation of life, but he also claimed to have derived up to 40 percent of his topics from the newspapers.[20] And occasionally even a suppressed lyricism might reappear: Ninov is right in remarking that "Babel joined the prose poem with the old-fashioned physiological sketch,"[21] even though Babel describes some of the most ghastly scenes in world history, scenes in which lyricism would seem theoretically totally out of place.

The controversy over the relationship between the sketch—which purports to deal with contemporary social reality and lays claim to a certain documentary validity—and the short story—at bottom a work of fiction the author is pleased to have his reader recognize as such—derives from a vigorous dispute over the relative value of art on the one hand and social justice on the other. Pushkin's first allegiance was to literature, and for him his experimentation in *Tales of Belkin* with the development of a prose language and the techniques of multiple narration was important in ways it could not be for those who believed literature should deal directly with social reality. In his old age Tolstoy was among the latter, although he remained too much the born artist to take no interest at all in problems of form. And so in 1903 he wrote in his diary: "In a conversation about Chekhov . . . I realized how he has moved form ahead just as Pushkin did. And that is a great contribution. Except that he has no content, just like Pushkin."[22]

No doubt both Pushkin and Chekhov would have taken strong exception to Tolstoy's belief that they lacked content had they known about it, but it is also true that they were very much interested in problems of language and narration, which had no direct connection with social problems. Pushkin was a born poet, but as time passed he turned with dedication to developing a language for Russian prose: "The years incline us to stern prose," he wrote in *Eugene Onegin* as he approached thirty. Thus in *Tales of Belkin* he set out to provide illustrations of that spare language in which he believed prose should be written and to set the standard for succeeding generations. The prose of the *Tales* is indeed "stern" and unadorned. Pushkin employed as few adjectives as possible while giving heightened prominence to verbs and nouns; his clauses and sometimes his sentences became almost choppy as he sought to create a prose that would be transparent to the eye of the beholder.

At the same time he worked to simplify his language, Pushkin moved to complicate his narration through the use of multiple narrators. The entire cycle is supposedly narrated by Ivan Petrovich Belkin, a young landowner of no special literary gifts; but each of the five constituent stories is reportedly told to him by another narrator. Both "The Blizzard" and "The Peasant Miss," tales of requited love, are recounted by a young lady and therefore should reflect a feminine point of view; "The Undertaker" is narrated by a shopkeeper, a man on the same social level as his subject; "The Shot" is told by a military officer, with a considerable additional layer of narration by the two major characters; "The Stationmaster" is passed on by a civil servant who travels a great deal. Each of these narrators takes a different approach to his subject and also—at least theoretically—employs a different narrative style. Pushkin may not have succeeded wholly in differentiating his narrators' individual styles, but here he was moving in even less explored territory than some of the other experimental facets of *Tales of Belkin*.

Though Pushkin may have been in principle correct in his creation of a simplified prose language as a model, he was unsuccessful in practice: for the most part the language of Russian prose did not follow the trails he had blazed. The 1830s were a period of triumphant, even excessive, romanticism; and Pushkin's closest disciple in the short story was Gogol, whose ebullient prose style was the polar opposite of his. To be sure, no one could match the brilliance of Gogol's style either, but it was somehow more appealing at the time than Pushkinian spareness. Lermontov wrought something of a synthesis between these two styles in *Geroi nashego vremeni* (*A Hero of Our Time*) of 1840. He wrote the sort of prose a good writer might conceivably emulate without doing violence to himself, so that half a century later Chekhov would urge the detailed study of Lermontov's prose upon anyone who wished to write Russian well. To be sure, there have been scattered individuals who found Pushkin's theory persuasive. Zoshchenko, for instance, told a group of Soviet listeners around 1930 that "we must interest the masses in literature. And for that we must write clearly, briefly and with all possible simplicity."[23] And he did endeavor to write simply himself, although very colloquially as well. There were those like his contemporary Babel who even in the Soviet period could maintain that content was of little importance for literature. "I can write a short story about washing underwear," he told Konstantin Paustovsky, "and it will read like Julius Caesar's prose. It's all a matter of language and style."[24] But Babel's own style was ornate and difficult. He could in no way accept the linguistic simplicity Pushkin advocated for prose.

Pushkin's narrative experimentation in the *Tales* yielded unexpected fruit. Of the five stories in the collection, three are narrated in the third person, and two ("The Shot" and "The Stationmaster") in the first person. The latter two stories are also of interest as exercises in overlapping narration: in "The Shot" there are first-person narrations by two characters within the frame narration, and in "The Stationmaster" a further first-person narration within the first-person narration. These successful overlapping first-person narrations in time were transformed into a central device of the Russian short story called *skaz,* or a first-person narration cast entirely in the words of a character, frequently from the lower classes, who may employ unliterary forms: it is as if the partial narration by old Samson Vyrin in "The Stationmaster" had been expanded to encompass the entire tale. The device of skaz is fused with a genius for pure narrative in the short stories of Nikolay Leskov. Leskov's stories, sometimes quite lengthy, are tours de force of linguistic brilliance replete with scarcely translatable puns and allusions imbedded in a story of purely narrative interest that scarcely supports any psychological or ideological interpretation. In the early twentieth century Aleksey Remizov continued the skaz tradition, as did Mikhail Zoshchenko in the Soviet Union of the 1920s.

Finally, in *Tales of Belkin* Pushkin approaches his group of stories not as individual pieces but as a cycle. For all their disparate subjects, Pushkin conceived them as a whole, wrote them as a whole, and published them as a whole, linking them formally through the mild personality of Ivan Petrovich Belkin. *Eugene Onegin,* a "novel in verse," and the prose cycle *Tales of Belkin* together laid the foundation of the nineteenth-century Russian novel in prose. Lermontov's *Hero of Our Time* may be viewed either as a tightly knit cycle of short stories or as a novel. Like the *Belkin* tales, it is bound together by an individual personality, this time a much more powerful one, though some of the stories were written and even published before Lermontov conceived of the work as a whole. Gogol's *Dead Souls*—certainly a novel by our standards but subtitled a poem by its author—displays elements of a cycle in its first several chapters, in which the hero Chichikov pays visits to one local landowner after another. Turgenev prepared for the short novels that made him famous not only through individual short stories but also through the cycle *The Hunting Sketches.* The Russian novel did not spring forth in all its classically voluminous glory until the appearance of Goncharov's *Oblomov* in 1859; that was followed by Dostoevsky's great novels of the 1860s and Tolstoy's *War and Peace* of 1869 (even Tolstoy had improved his budding reputation in the mid-1850s with a cycle of Sebastopol stories). Even during the novel's heyday, however, authors like Mikhail Saltykov-Shchedrin wrote novels more accurately viewed as extensive short-story cycles: thus his most famous novel, *Gospoda Golovlyovy* (*The Golovlyovs*), was written and published in the late 1870s more as a cycle of short stories than as a novel. Cycles of tales have retained their prominence in Russian literature to the present, as in Babel's *Konarmiia* (*Red Cavalry,* 1926), or Varlam Shalamov's powerful *Kolyma Tales* (probably written in the 1950s and early 1960s), describing in the dispassionate Chekhovian tradition the inhumanity visited upon Soviet prisoners in the gulag of the far North.[25] Here again Pushkin traced the path of the future through his cycle *Tales of Belkin.*

Of course, Pushkin influenced the subsequent development of the Russian short story in other ways as well, and not only through *Tales of Belkin.* "The Queen of Spades" (1834) similarly had a considerable impact on the future course of Russian literature. Taking our cue from the English critic John Bayley, who remarks that its "conclusion, compressed to the verge of parody, is that of a novel,"[26] we might regard the entire work as a compressed novel, even though it is clearly an independent short story in its external form and has a surprising and certainly very abrupt ending. Perhaps we might define "The Queen of Spades" as a quintessential povest', a form truly intermediate between the short story and the novel.

Finally, we might note briefly Pushkin's predilection for the romantic genre of the "fragment." A good example of this is "Egyptian Nights," which breaks off in such a way that we can only conjecture how it might end. Whether intentionally or unintentionally, Pushkin left so many fragments among his prose writings that they might almost be considered to form a subgenre of his narrative prose. One of Gogol's early stories, "Ivan Fedorovich Shpon'ka i ego tetushka" ("Ivan Fedorovich Shpon'ka and His Aunt"), is in the form of a fragment. However, the vogue of fragments passed into history with Russian romanticism, and they have played little or no role in the development of the short story since.

The body of this volume consists of a more detailed historical view of the development of the Russian short story from 1830 to 1980. An introduction of this length can do no more than sketch the broad outlines of its development, with special attention to those writers—Pushkin, Gogol, Turgenev, Leskov, Chekhov, of course, Babel, Zoshchenko—who have been key figures in that history, although only one or two of them confined themselves entirely to the genre. Until the rise of the formalist school in the 1920s, literary critics devoted little attention to the theory of the short story, and it is only very recently that scholars and literary critics have begun to write at all extensively on the topic both in the Soviet Union and in the West. Perhaps in fact we were better off when we had fewer theoreticians and more superb practitioners of the short-story genre, writers whose guiding principles we could derive from their fiction or from scattered comments in their correspondence, as I have tried to do in this discussion of Pushkin's legacy to the history of the Russian short story in the 150 years that have elapsed since *Tales of the Late Ivan Petrovich Belkin* first appeared.

Charles A. Moser

George Washington University

THE RUSSIAN SHORT STORY 1830–1850

The National and International Background

The year 1830 is a watershed in the history of Russian literature. It marked the end of the golden age of poetry and the ascendancy of prose fiction, short fiction in particular. Aleksandr Pushkin turned to prose in 1830. His friend, the Decembrist revolutionary Aleksandr Bestuzhev, had been more active as a poet and critic than as a writer of prose fiction before the rebellion of 1825. After receiving permission to publish again, he began a new and brilliant career in 1830 under the pen name "Marlinsky" and soon was Russia's most popular storyteller. Nikolay Gogol, the first major literary figure to write nothing but prose, launched his meteoric career in 1831, and several other writers emerged at approximately the same time. Vladimir Dal published his first short story in 1830, and Aleksandr Veltman in 1831. Mikhail Pogodin published a book of short stories in 1832, Nikolay Polevoy in 1833, and Nikolay Pavlov in 1835. The critic Vissarion Belinsky (1811–48) registered the unstoppable march of the short story (povest') in a major survey article of 1835.

The reasons for this development were manifold. Popular taste in western Europe had swung toward prose in the 1820s. The prose of E. T. A. Hoffmann, Sir Walter Scott, Maturin, Balzac, Dickens, Hugo, and the members of the French phrenetic school, such as Jules Janin, Fréderick Soulié, and Alphonse Karr, replaced the poetry of Byron, Thomas Moore, Southey, Goethe, and Schiller as standard fare of the Russian reading public as well, and by the end of the 1830s Russians were reading the social fiction of Eugene Sue and George Sand.

There was now a growing market for prose fiction. Larger numbers of literary journals appeared, and more started up every year than went out of business. In Moscow alone six journals were published in 1830, and three years later both Moscow and St. Petersburg had this many. To be sure, most journals did not last very long: *Literaturnaia gazeta* (The literary gazette, 1830–31) went out of business, and *Moskovskii telegraf* (The Moscow telegraph, 1825–34) and *Teleskop* (The telescope, 1831–36) were closed by the government. But some survived, attracted enough permanent subscribers, and became profitable: *Biblioteka dlia chteniia* (The reading library, 1834–64), *Sovremennik* (The contemporary, 1836-66), *Otechestvennye zapiski* (The national annals, 1839–84), *Moskvitianin* (The Muscovite, 1841–56), and others. Many short stories also appeared in almanacs, such as *Severnye tsvety* (Northern flowers, 1831), *Novosel'e* (The housewarming, 1833–34), *Fiziologiia Peterburga* (A physiology of Petersburg, 1845), *Peterburgskii sbornik* (Petersburg miscellany, 1846), and *Literaturnyi sbornik* (Literary miscellany, 1848). In several instances, writers now published collections of their short stories, with or without a frame to tie them together: Pushkin's *Povesti Belkina* (*Tales of Belkin,* 1831),Pogodin's *Povesti* (*Stories,* 1832), Polevoy's *Mechty i zhizn': byli i povesti* (*Dreams and Life: Real Stories and Fiction,* 1833–34), and others.

The initial tendency of Russian prose fiction of the 1830s was decidedly romantic. A variety of genres existed, and most writers practiced all or at least several of them. Most romantic tales emphasized plot, and many were essentially expanded anecdotes, like Pushkin's "Pikovaia dama" ("The Queen of Spades," 1834). The Gothic tale, which had appeared even before 1830, as in "Lefortovskaia makovnitsa" ("The Poppyseed-Cake Woman of Lefortovo," 1828) by Antony Pogorelsky, flourished in the 1830s.

The Walter Scott–type historical novel and novella also found adherents in Russia. The tales of Hoffmann inspired Russian imitators to produce *Künstlernovellen,* featuring an artist's conflict with society or with himself, as well as stories, sometimes fantastic or utopian, dealing with themes of romantic philosophy, such as the question of man's place in nature or the destiny of mankind. The French phrenetic school found immediate imitators, particularly since a tradition of tales of high and criminal passion, escape and pursuit, abduction, violence, and murder had existed in Russian chapbook literature since the eighteenth century. Among the early imitators of the phrenetic school were Mikhail Pogodin (1800–75) whose "Vasil'ev vecher" ("St. Basil's Eve," 1832) is a perfect example of the genre, and Nikolay Gogol (1809–52), several of whose Ukrainian as well as St. Petersburg tales of the 1830s have obvious "phrenetic" traits, as the Soviet scholar Viktor Vinogradov has demonstrated.[1]

There is considerable transfer from the Byronic verse epic to the prose tale of exotic adventure, often set in the Caucasus, of which Bestuzhev-Marlinsky was the prime exponent. The interest in folklore and native culture generated by the romantic movement led to the development of a folkloric prose genre, either patterned after the folk tale or based on folk legends and traditions. Veltman is considered the main representative of romantic folklorism, but Vladimir Odoevsky (1804–69), Vladimir Dal (1801–72), and others contributed to this genre. Regional and dialect tales, Ukrainian in particular, also made their appearance, as several major authors were from the Ukraine: Gogol, of course, Orest Somov (1793–1833), Antony Pogorelsky (1787–1836), Grigory Kvitka (1778–1843), and Evgeny Grebenka (1812–48).

Along with these genres whose world was once or twice removed from immediate reality, there developed the more realistic "society tale." It had several subgenres. The most common of these was the novella of love and intrigue, often culminating in a duel or some other tragic denouement. As a rule, it implicitly condemned the spiritual emptiness, the emotional cruelty, and the prejudices of society. The diary or confession form was common, too, often with a strong undercurrent of an oppressed individual's protest against the forces that would not allow the person to develop his or her personality. Here George Sand's influence was great, and several woman authors wrote stories of this type. In some instances the society tale turned into outright social satire, as in some works by Odoevsky, Pavlov, and Vladimir Sollogub (1813–82). The Western influences that helped generate the Russian society tale were Bulwer-Lytton, Balzac, Musset, and, of course, George Sand.

The society tale, with its occasional pretense of refinement and gentility, invited parody. For example, "Neobyknovennyi poedinok" ("An Unusual Duel," 1845) by Aleksandr Kulchitsky (1815–45), a typical adherent of the natural school, begins with one young man challenging the other to a duel over a young lady they are both courting. That is followed by an account of their courtship and then the comic denouement: neither of the combatants owns a pistol or is able to obtain one. Besides, it develops that the young lady really does not much care for either of them. Parodic versions of the society tale were also produced by Osip Senkovsky (1800–58), Ivan Panaev (1812–62), Mikhail Markov (1810–76), and Nikolay Verevkin (1813–38).

Almost simultaneously with the flowering of the romantic tale, there developed what Belinsky in his article of 1835 called "the tale of real life." It was eventually identified with the natural school, a label used—sarcastically at first—by Faddey Bulgarin in a review of *Petersburg Miscellany* printed in 1846 and then generically by Belinsky and others. Gogol's "Old-time Landowners" and "Memoirs of a Madman" (both 1835) were for Belinsky the harbingers of a new beginning in Russian literature, one he warmly welcomed and vigorously championed.

The natural school developed under the influence of the French phrenetic school, Dickens, Balzac, and the French *roman-feuilleton* with a social tendency. Its most characteristic product was the physiological sketch, a plotless or nearly plotless description of a particular ambience of Russian society, such as "The Organ-Grinders of St. Petersburg" (1845) by Dmitry Grigorovich (1822–99) or Dal's "A Janitor of St. Petersburg" (1845). This genre, too, was of Western origin, with Balzac's physiological sketches and Dickens's *Sketches by Boz* exerting major influences on it.[2]

The natural school flourished until the early 1850s (Tolstoy's early stories had much of the physiological sketch about them) and developed several other characteristic genres. The "tale of a poor clerk," of which Gogol's "The Overcoat" (1842) is the most famous instance, appeared in at least forty different versions.[3] In some the author satirized the imperial bureaucracy; in others he injected a definite overtone of social protest. The social novella, dealing with injustice and inequality, was at its most poignant in such abolitionist (antiserfdom) tales as "The Nameday Party" (1835) by Pavlov and "The Village" (1846) by Grigorovich. The antiserfdom story overlaps with the simple *Dorfgeschichte,* presenting the life of the Russian peasantry for its human or ethnographic interest, sometimes in the peasant's own idiom, as skaz[4]—as in some of Dal's stories.

Another favorite of the natural school was the "story of a superfluous man," exposing the empty, idle, and parasitic existence of the Russian landed gentry. Thus, "Poslednii vizit" ("The Last Visit," 1844) by Petr Kudriavtsev (1816–58) depicts an educated young landowner who can find no way to apply either his talents or his goodwill to anything constructive. Other examples are Panaev's "The Onager" (1841) and "Actaeon" (1842), and, of course, Turgenev's *Diary of a Superfluous Man* (1850).

The natural school develops a specific style whose principal trait is a tendency to fuse the narrator's point of view with that of his subject, though often retaining a certain amount of ironic tension between them. Specifically, the narrator tends to adopt certain speech mannerisms of his characters. In connection with this tendency, self-conscious verbal stylization ("grimacing"), a somewhat forced humor, hyperbole or litotes, and various types of catachresis (pointedly "false" usage) are common in works of the natural school.

Such opponents of the natural school as Bulgarin and Senkovsky attacked it for making "peasants, janitors, cabmen, etc." the heroes of their stories in such settings as "slum tenements, the refuges of hungry beggars, and often all kinds of immorality." In fact, writers of the natural school consistently lowered the social (and often even the moral) condition of their subjects to a level previously unheard of and, moreover, infused their stories with compassion for the social underdog. The critic Apollon Grigorev (1822–64) created the label "the school of sentimental humanitarianism" for the many writers who exhibited this attitude, singling out the young Dostoevsky as the most remarkable among them.

In spite of Belinsky's energetic advertising of the new school as one of "the poetry of reality" (the term *realism* was used for the first time by Pavel Annenkov in an article for *Sovremennik* of January 1849), most of its work still displayed romantic traits, even if they dealt with rural or urban low life. Thus, Dostoevsky's stories of the 1840s feature lyric intermezzi, romantic irony (as when blatant literary allusions create a subtext that deconstructs the realism of the plot), ample use of symbolic detail, and familiar romantic themes, such as the doppelgänger, picturesque madness, the romantic dreamer's clash with reality, or the artist's conflict with society.

Pushkin and the Short Story's Beginnings

The prose of Aleksandr Pushkin (1799–1837), which for the most part enjoyed little success in his lifetime and much of which appeared only after his death, is now the subject of much scholarly and critical analysis. The general view of today was first stated with great conviction by Apollon Grigorev, who held that Pushkin's prose was just as important as his poetry and that it was the foundation on which much of the prose fiction of succeeding generations was built. This is particularly true of Pushkin's short stories in *Tales of Belkin* (1831) and "The Queen of Spades" (1834).

Povesti pokoinogo Ivana Petrovicha Belkina (*Tales of the Late Ivan Petrovich Belkin*) contains five short stories with an editor's preface citing a letter solicited by the editor from the late Belkin's neighbor to obtain some information about Ivan Petrovich. The preface also suggests that Belkin was not himself the author of these tales but merely their collector. We thus encounter a multilayered mystification: the editor, though he signs his preface "A. P.," is not Pushkin speaking in his own voice, but the mocking parody of a literary entrepreneur, whose affected erudition and bonhomie are unmasked by the crudity of his style and the absurdity of his unctuous moral pronouncements. The neighbor's letter is essentially skaz, anticipating Gogol, as it features inadvertent digressions, comic nonsequiturs, and contradictions between intended effect and actual message. The stories, in turn, reflect the personalities of their alleged authors, but at the same time parody certain directions then apparent in Russian prose fiction. In creating his imaginary narrators, Pushkin was following the practice of Walter Scott, Washington Irving, and other Western writers then in vogue.

"Vystrel" ("The Shot"), told by a "Lt. Colonel I. L. P.," has all the qualities of a romantic version of the classical novella. There is a single, well-focused plot line, in which everything gravitates toward "the shot." The hero, Silvio, a Byronic figure, gratuitously provokes a duel with a hated rival, a handsome and brilliant young count. The count misses his shot. Seeing that his adversary is unafraid to die, Silvio reserves his own shot. Years later, upon hearing that the count has recently married and may value his life more highly, Silvio goes back to claim his shot. He humiliates his adversary by offering him a second shot before taking his first. When the count misses again, Silvio spares his life, satisfied with the humiliation he has inflicted upon him. The narrative structure of "The Shot" is, however, intricate: we hear, in turn, the narrator, Silvio, again the narrator, the count, and once more the narrator. Also, there are different vantage points: the first shot is separated from the second by a number of years. "The Shot" has been interpreted as a parodic deflation of the Byronic hero, whose whole being is obsessed with the memory of a single traumatic experience, but it is a fine short story even in a straightforward reading.

"Metel'" ("The Blizzard"), told by "Miss K. I. T.," relates the incredible tale of Marya Gavrilovna, a country miss, who agrees to elope with her sweetheart, Vladimir. She barely makes it to the church in a blizzard, while he loses his way for hours. In the meantime another traveler, Burmin, accidentally enters the church and is taken for the bridegroom. On a lark, he goes along with the deception, marries a woman he does not know, and then continues his journey. The bride, dazed by the anguish of the drive through the blizzard and the long wait, manages only to exclaim "not him!" after the marriage is concluded. She then returns to her parents and tries to forget her misfortune. A few years later, Burmin accidentally meets Marya Gavrilovna, falls in love with her without recognizing her, and confesses that he is legally a married man. Having heard his account of that night in the blizzard, she exclaims "So it was you!" as he flings himself at her feet.

"Grobovshchik" ("The Undertaker"), told by "B. V., a steward," is a comic grotesque. Prokhorov, an undertaker, attends a party given by another artisan, gets drunk, and has a nightmare in which a whole host of his customers pay him a visit. The story contains some Gogolian traits in its black humor, contained in such phrases as "a dead man can't live without his coffin," or "only those [of the dead] stayed at home who were by then really incapacitated."

"Stantsionnyi smotritel'" ("The Stationmaster"), told by "A. G. N., titular councilor," gives a parodic twist to the familiar sentimental theme of the innocent peasant maiden seduced by a dashing nobleman. Dunya, the stationmaster's daughter, runs off to St. Petersburg with Minsky, a rich and handsome young officer, leaving her father heartbroken. He tracks down Minsky in St. Petersburg and begs him to return his daughter, but to no avail. The disconsolate stationmaster returns home, takes to drink, and soon dies. But the story ends with Dunya, now a beautiful lady and mother of three, visiting her father's grave—so perhaps his conviction that she would end badly had been unjustified.

The last story, "Baryshnia-krest'ianka" ("The Peasant Miss"), told by Miss K. I. T., is a Russian version of the hackneyed theme of a young nobleman in love with a peasant beauty who turns out to be a young lady dressed in peasant garb.

Tales of Belkin met with only a lukewarm reception from contemporaries, who saw the stories as passable entertainment, but unworthy of Pushkin's genius. Today the *Tales* are viewed as a parodic anthology of early nineteenth-century prose fiction. Contemporary critics did not see them thus, and even now critics who accept the *Tales* as parodies see "The Shot" and "The Stationmaster" as original masterpieces, though parodies as well. The general view now is that Belkin was created as a satire on Pushkin's literary adversaries. This clashes with the nineteenth-century opinions of Grigorev and others, who saw Belkin as an epoch-making prototype of the "new Russian man," the "meek" Russian returning to his "native soil." Nor does this interpretation square well with the notion, advanced by some critics, that the two protagonists of "The Shot" are, like Mozart and Salieri, expressions of two aspects of Pushkin's own personality. Dostoevsky's response to "The Stationmaster" in his own novel *Poor Folk* (1846) seems to stem from a straight reading that ignores any parodic element. In short, perhaps *Tales of Belkin* has received such extraordinary attention largely because Pushkin wrote it. Generations of scholars have discovered in these tales meanings not detected even by otherwise perceptive contemporaries. It has been demonstrated that every single motif in the *Tales* has literary antecedents. An element of parodic deconstruction, like that seen in the *Tales,* was a common feature of the romantic tale, E. T. A. Hoffmann's and Washington Irving's in particular. If *Tales of Belkin* had not been written by Pushkin, the stories would hardly stand out significantly among their competitors.

"Pikovaia dama" ("The Queen of Spades"), first published in 1834, was an immediate success. Tschaikowsky's opera (first performed in 1890, only one of several stage versions) made it well known internationally. The story is told by a third-person narrator who neither renounces nor insists on his omniscience. The narrative features frequent changes of point of view with several flashbacks. The first of these launches the plot. A young officer, Tomsky, tells his friends about the secret of a winning three-card series which a notorious adventurer revealed to Tomsky's grandmother sixty years ago. Among the listeners is Hermann, a young officer in the Corps of Engineers. A commoner of modest means, Hermann likes to watch card games, but he himself never gambles. The narrative then shifts to the old countess's house, where Tomsky casually meets Liza, his grandmother's companion. For some time Hermann has been courting Liza, who desperately seeks a way out of her humiliating situation. When Liza allows him to come to her room one night, Hermann hides in the countess's chamber instead and threatens the old woman with a pistol to extort from her the secret of the three cards. She dies of fright, however. Three days later Hermann has a nocturnal vision of the deceased countess, who gives him three cards: three, seven, ace. Hermann goes to a gaming house and stakes his entire patrimony—forty-seven thousand rubles—on the series. The third evening he stakes everything on the ace. It wins, too, but Hermann discovers to his horror that the card in his hand is not an ace, but the queen of spades, in whom he recognizes the old countess, whereupon he goes mad and ends in an asylum.

"The Queen of Spades" has been overinterpreted even more than *Tales of Belkin.* Critics have noted that it contains a wealth of literary echoes, possibly some coded personal allusions, and certainly a multitude of numbers, mostly ones, twos, threes, and sevens, which has led some to engage in numerological speculations. Other scholars claim to have discovered Masonic and/or other symbolism in the story. Dostoevsky saw Hermann as a "colossal type," and "The Queen of Spades" as the prototype of a new genre, the "St. Petersburg tale." Hermann, whose Napoleonic profile and Mephistophelean airs emerge in sharp relief in Pushkin's text, has been seen as a forerunner of Raskolnikov and other individualistic, godless, and driven rebels of Russian literature. Boris Eikhenbaum has suggested that Hermann is no less a parody of the Byronic hero than Silvio of "The Shot."[5] More recently, Paul Debreczeny has attempted a Freudian interpretation: Hermann destroys himself because he has not measured up to his father's expectations; when he stakes his patrimony on a card, he rebels against what his bourgeois German father stood for: hard work, patience, accumulating a fortune slowly but surely.[6]

Pushkin left a number of incomplete prose works, most of which are too fragmentary to be classified as either short story or novel. The longest of these, *Dubrovsky,* first published in 1841, is structurally a short novel rather than a short story. The incomplete "Egipetskie nochi" ("Egyptian Nights"), first published in 1837, though clearly a short story, is dominated by the unfinished poem with whose recitation the manuscript ends. The introductory prose portion offers an interesting character sketch of a Russian poet and man of the world, who introduces a visiting Italian improviser who composes, first a brief ode on the poet's independence from the crowd, and then a longer work on the topic of Cleopatra and her lovers.

Bestuzhev and His Romantic Successors

Among Pushkin's contemporaries, Aleksandr Bestuzhev-Marlinsky (1797–1837) had no peer as a prose writer. Bestuzhev's career as a man of letters was interrupted by his participation in the Decembrist revolt of 1825, and he resumed publishing only in 1830, under the name Marlinsky. It is generally agreed that his later works are far superior to his early ones, and certainly they were extraordinarily successful with the public. Bestuzhev was deprived of his previously unchallenged position as Russia's foremost prose writer only by Belinsky, who in a series of essays and reviews beginning with "On the Russian Short Story and the Short Stories of Mr. Gogol" (1835) championed the natural school over the romantic school and its leading figure, Bestuzhev. Belinsky believed that while "Mr. Marlinsky was Russia's first storyteller, the creator, or rather, the initiator of the Russian short story," his stories contained "no truth of life, no reality, such as it is, for all in them is invented, all is calculated by a calculus of probability, much as happens in the making or construction of machines." Belinsky also suggested that one could see the strings and pulleys moving Marlinsky's machines. He even denied them the appellation of "ideal poetry," which he was willing to grant the tales of Hoffmann, on the grounds that they lacked "all depth of thought, fire of emotion, or lyricism." Belinsky did, however, credit Bestuzhev with being attuned to the most recent European trends, and also with erudition, intelligence, and "occasionally, excellent thoughts." He acknowledged Bestuzhev's style to be "original and brilliant, strained though it is." Everything Belinsky said was true. Bestuzhev's prose is rhetorical and highly mannered, but it has great vigor. His characters, dashing young officers mostly, use conceits, witticisms, and rhetorical flourishes in speech laced with bons mots (sometimes French), proverbs, and striking images. All this rather resembles the style of Alexandre Dumas père. Bestuzhev's narrator draws his reader into his confidence, asks questions of him, and enlightens him, freely expressing his feelings of pain, compassion, sorrow, admiration, and delight.

Bestuzhev had a great facility for learning languages and a histrionic ability to impersonate various human types, though in a rather superficial way. He was well read and widely traveled and was familiar with several ambiences: the navy, the army, life in the Baltic provinces, in Siberia, in the Caucasus. His descriptive passages are vividly interesting: a St. Petersburg food market at Christmas time followed by an elaborate cityscape that will stand comparison with Balzac's Paris or Hoffmann's Berlin ("The Test"); a storm at sea ("Lieutenant Belozor"); Caucasian landscapes ("Ammalat-Bek" and "Mulla-Nur"). Both narrative and dialogue include expressions and entire phrases from various languages: French in the society tales, English in the sea stories, and a great deal of Tartar and Persian, properly translated, in the Caucasian tales.

The structure of Bestuzhev's stories is drawn from his Western teachers, Walter Scott, Captain Marryat, E. T. A. Hoffmann. As a rule, there is a frame, which may or may not be thematically linked to the story (or stories) told. Various digressions—letters, documents, lines of poetry—frequently enter the flow of the narrative. It has been noted that in some instances the structure of Bestuzhev's stories resembles that of the romantic verse epic: a master narrative serves as a frame, allowing for arbitrary changes of both scene and point of view, as for instance in "The Cuirassier" (1832).[7]

Bestuzhev's post-1830 stories fall into four basic categories: society tales, sea stories, Gothic tales, and Caucasian stories. "Ispytanie" ("The Test," 1830) is an example of the first. It contains a fine description of a ball, with scraps of society banter and its stale witticisms ever so slightly overdone to turn them into parody. The implied social criticism is of a liberal sort. One of his women says: "This is how men are! You inveigh against us for our ignorance, but you are even more angry with us if we do acquire some knowledge." The plot is typical of the society tale. Prince Gremin asks his friend Strelinsky to test the faithfulness of his beloved, the widowed Countess Zvezdich. Strelinsky's flirtation turns into real love and he proposes to her. In the meantime Gremin has fallen out of love with the countess, but still feels obliged to challenge Strelinsky to a duel. Only the resolute intervention of Strelinsky's sister Olga, who loves Gremin, saves both. Incidentally, Bestuzhev's description of Strelinsky's courtship of Countess Zvezdich anticipates Vronsky's courtship of Anna Karenina in many specific details.

"Fregat 'Nadezhda'" ("The Frigate *Nadezhda*" [Hope] 1833), a long short story, is a mixture of society tale and sea story. Pravin, the young skipper of the frigate, has an adulterous love affair with Princess Vera N. He invites her and her unsuspecting husband to be his guests on a passage to England. When they have disembarked and he is about to continue his voyage, Pravin cannot resist seeking one last tryst with Vera. He leaves his ship in a sloop manned by ten sailors, although warned by his mate that a storm is imminent. When Pravin returns to take command of his ship, the sloop is smashed against the hull of the frigate, with loss of life in the sloop and on the frigate; Pravin himself is gravely injured. Tortured by guilt and the conviction that he has lost his honor forever, he dies after writing a last melancholy letter to Princess Vera, who also soon dies of a broken heart.

"The Frigate *Nadezhda*" is structurally complex. The rhetorical narrative, with digressions and literary allusions, alternates with letters by Pravin and Princess Vera as well as a good deal of dialogue, and concludes with a news flash from *Severnaya pchela* on the frigate's return to port and an ironic description of a brilliant ball at which the seeds of yet another tragedy may have been planted. While the conflict between love and duty is a carryover from neoclassical tragedy, its treatment here is archromantic, for the narrator's sympathy is with the adulterous lovers throughout. It is not objective retribution that kills Pravin, but his spiritual turmoil. The frame suggests that he and Vera are morally superior to most members of their social set.

Bestuzhev's other sea tales lack the psychological dimension of "The Frigate *Nadezhda*." "Leitenant Belozor" ("Lieutenant Belozor," 1831) details the adventures of a Russian naval officer stranded in French-occupied Holland who falls in love with a Dutch girl and takes her back to Russia. The story has fine descriptions of the sea and seamanship—for instance, the breakup of a British threemaster on the reefs off the Dutch coast. "Morekhod Nikitin" ("Seafarer Nikitin," 1834) is a lively story about a Russian sea captain and his small crew, who are taken prisoners by the British but turn the tables on their captors and bring the British ship back to Archangel in triumph. The tale is based on a real event of 1810. In his sea tales Bestuzhev employs many authentic marine terms and provides exact descriptions of various types of sailing ships and details of their rigging.

Bestuzhev also wrote some Gothic tales in the 1830s. As Lauren Leighton has pointed out, in these tales Bestuzhev uses most of the devices recommended for the Gothic tale in Walter Scott's "Prefatory Memoirs to the Novels of Mrs. Ann Radcliffe" (1824). He follows the example of Ann Radcliffe in showing that seemingly supernatural events have a natural explanation. Bestuzhev carefully introduces details that build up a mood of imminent danger and creates suspense by artfully suspending the plot at crucial junctures. "Vecher na Kavkazskikh vodakh v 1824 godu" ("An Evening at a Caucasian Spa in 1824," 1830) features several ghost stories told by Russian officers. In two of these, the ghost is explained away à la Mrs. Radcliffe, but one, involving a bet to shake hands with a corpse on the gibbet (described in naturalistic detail!), remains unresolved. However, the frame of the story is open: the readers were promised a sequel, but it never materialized. "Strashnoe gadan'e" ("A Terrible Fortune-Telling," 1831), a lively, suspenseful story, contains strong folklore elements, including various superstitions about divination on New Year's Eve. "Latnik" ("The Cuirassier," 1832) has an artfully constructed though quite preposterous plot, in which the frame narrative and the stories within interact to resolve the mysteries of several plot lines.

Bestuzhev is at his best in his Caucasian tales and sketches. He does not abandon his romantic style, but combines it with a great deal of topographic and ethnographic detail. His Caucasian tales are crammed with information about the customs and habits, the beliefs and the language of the peoples of the region.

"Ammalat-Bek" (1832), based on a real character, tells of a brave and honest young chieftain torn between his mountaineer loyalties and his attraction for the more civilized Russians and his friendship with a young Russian colonel named Verkhovsky. Eventually Ammalat-Bek kills his friend and then perishes himself, a traitor to the Russians but also rejected by his own people. The structure of the story is complex. The plot is advanced through third-person narrative (less rhetorical than in most of Bestuzhev's stories), letters, diary pages, monologues, and dialogue, with many descriptive interludes and other digressions. "Ammalat-Bek" is a remarkably original treatment of the meeting of a European romantic idealist and a noble savage. Bestuzhev shows that Ammalat-Bek is moved by emotions, beliefs, and values alien to a civilized European, and makes no attempt to rationalize them.

"Mulla-Nur" (1836) is a Walter Scott–type romance transplanted to the Caucasus. Mulla-Nur is a Caucasian Rob Roy, a brave and crafty outlaw, who generously rewards the story's hero, young Iskander-Bek, for having saved his life. The love story of Iskander-Bek and the beautiful Kichkene is uninteresting, but the story makes for entertaining reading nevertheless because of its local color enhanced by a wealth of Tartar phrases. The most entertaining character is the cowardly braggart and liar Hadji Yusuf, with the greedy and treacherous Mulla Sadek not far behind.

After Bestuzhev, Aleksandr Veltman (1800–70) was the most popular prose writer of the 1830s, and continued to be a leading writer through the 1840s. His fame then quickly faded.[8] Veltman was also an archaeologist, ethnographer, and folklorist, who found scope for his scholarship in his fiction. Veltman's relaxed, digressive, and playful narrative manner was less suited to the short story than to the novel, but he was extraordinarily prolific in both genres, ranging over the whole spectrum of romantic fiction: that of manners and historical, utopian, Gothic, adventure, and satirical tales. He would incorporate any kind of diction into his narrative, yet always left the door open to romantic irony as he casually shifted from one point of view to another. Many of his stories move in and out of the world of the Russian fairy tale and folk epic. With his zigzag story lines, constant changes of scene and focus, frequent digressions, ample erudition, and whimsical humor Veltman resembles Sterne and Jean Paul, both of whom surely influenced him directly. Only a few examples of Veltman's craft may be discussed here.

"Erotida" ("Erotis," 1835) may echo the real story of Nadezhda Durova, who will be mentioned later. Erotis is raised as an Amazon horsewoman by her widowed father, a retired cavalry officer. She is about to be married to G., a young officer, when the War of 1812 takes him to distant parts and he forgets her. He goes to the spa of Carlsbad to treat a war injury and there courts Emilia, a beautiful Russian lady, to whom he gives the ring he had received from Erotis. He next sees the ring when it is staked in a card game by a young Russian officer. When G. insists that the officer explain how he obtained the ring and the other refuses, he challenges him to a duel. G. kills his adversary, and only then discovers, first, that the young officer is really Emilia and, second, that Emilia is really Erotis. The frame of the story, narrated by G., suggests that the transformation of the naive Erotis into the dazzling Emilia is unconvincing and implies that G. may have made this all up on a whim. Thus the story may be read as a spoof all the way.

"Neistovyi Roland" ("The Furious Roland," 1835) is an extended anecdote, resembling the one on which Gogol's play *The Inspector-General* is based. A half-mad and drunken actor, dressed in a fancy uniform, is taken for a visiting governor-general and humored by local dignitaries as he declaims incoherent monologues from his tragic repertoire. Meanwhile the tragedy in which he should have played the lead is staged without him, its plot much improved by the air of mystery this produces. The dialogue of this story is racy and entertaining, and of course the work contains a strong element of satire.

"Alenushka" (1836) has a strange, almost surrealistic plot: it shifts from a satirical society tale into a ghost story, which at first is deflated, but then seems to pick up again. The woman the hero had loved, and then inadvertently had seen having a nocturnal tryst with another man (she was the "ghost" servants swore they had seen), seems to reenter his life as a demented beggar woman—but finally he decides that Alenushka is not the Elena he had loved, after all.

"Iolanda" (1837) is a Gothic tale of sorcery and high passion set in medieval France. "Radoi" (1839) takes place, for the most part, in the Balkans during the unsuccessful insurrection of Alexander Ypsilanti. Veltman uses his familiarity with the region, where he was stationed as an officer, to create an exotic setting, and his linguistic knowledge to add color to his dialogue by inserting Yiddish, Romanian, and Polish phrases into the text. The structure of the story is interesting in that the hero, Radoi Branković, a Serbian freedom fighter, appears only briefly and episodically until the narrator and ostensible hero learns that it is Radoi for whom his own wife has been pining for many years. In an epilogue, quite characteristic of Veltman's style, we learn more about Radoi—but are then told that the person we have encountered may not have been Radoi after all.

"Priezzhii iz uezda, ili sumatokha v stolitse" ("The Man from the Provinces, or an Uproar in the Capital," 1841) is a spirited satire on the Moscow literary world. A mediocre and very young poet from the provinces accidentally gains admission to the best Moscow society as a budding genius, but is soon discarded as other attractions appear. The story contains parodic imitations of the verse of Vladimir Benediktov, a poet who enjoyed great but ephemeral fame in the late 1830s and early 1840s.

Orest Somov (1793–1833) came to St. Petersburg from the Ukraine. Best known for his essay "On Romantic Poetry" (1823), the first attempt by a Russian to assess romanticism objectively, Somov published a number of short stories that are characteristic of the state of the art in the early 1830s. Somov wrote some ghost stories, most of them rather feeble and derivative to boot. But "Kievskie ved'my" ("The Witches of Kiev," 1833), essentially the same story as Pushkin's ballad "The Hussar," is lively and suspenseful. Unlike "The Hussar," though, it ends sadly. "Kikimora" ("The Poltergeist," 1830) is an example of romantic folklorism or ethnographism, as it simply dramatizes a Russian folk superstition. Somov also published some Russian and Ukrainian folktales.

Somov also wrote novellas of manners, which recall some of Pushkin's *Tales of Belkin.* "Roman v dvukh pis'makh" ("A Novel in Two Letters," 1832) is actually a short story consisting of two very long letters written by a young landowner to a friend in St. Petersburg. Describing his courtship and marriage to the pretty daughter of one of his neighbors, they reveal the rapid transformation of a blasé Onegin into a very ordinary Larin. The letter writer quotes liberally from *Eugene Onegin* and other contemporary works. "Matushka i synok" ("Mama and Sonny," 1833), a satirical anecdote, describes the "sentimental education" of young Valery, only son of a well-to-do provincial couple, and his abortive attempt to see the world.

Somov's style is fluent and literate, his language that of a man of the world. His narrative manner is digressive, ironic, and often stylized. It aims at wit and surprise. But Somov's inventive powers are limited, his plots not particularly interesting or well contrived, and his characters altogether schematic and lifeless.

Polish-born Osip Senkovsky (1800–58), a professor of Oriental languages at St. Petersburg University, began his brilliant journalistic career in 1830 with a Polish newspaper in St. Petersburg and from 1834 to 1847 edited and published *Biblioteka dlia chteniia,* the most successful "thick journal" of his age. A major contributor to his own journal, Senkovsky created the character "Baron Brambeus," under whose name he printed "Fantasticheskie puteshestviia barona Brambeusa" (The fantastic journeys of Baron Brambeus) and a quantity of fiction, essays, feuilletons, and criticism. Senkovsky wrote "Oriental tales" based in part on his travels in the Near East—such as "Vospominaniia o Sirii (prestupnye liubovniki)" ("Reminiscences of Syria [Criminal Lovers]," 1834)—and in part on his studies of Oriental literatures, as well as other, more readily accessible literary sources, such as "Mikeriia-Nil'skaia Liliia" ("Mikeria, Lily of the Nile," 1845), lifted from the second book of Herodotus. In his satirical society tales Senkovsky used Western authors liberally. Thus, his story "Bol'shoi vykhod u Satany" ("A Grand Outing at Satan's," 1833) was plagiarized from Balzac's "La comédie du diable" and "Neznakomka" ("The Stranger," 1833) from Jules Janin. Senkovsky, an amateur inventor and scientist, was more original in his science fiction. Altogether, his fiction has a tendency to slide into the genre of the feuilleton, as he casually takes advantage of every opportunity to make a pun, throw in an anecdote, introduce some scientific or scholarly information, and make fun of anything and anybody. As one scholar has put it, "Possessing literary talent, erudition, and an easy style, he did not, however, create fiction of lasting value."

Odoevsky and Lermontov

Vladimir Odoevsky (1804–69), the leading figure of Russian philosophic romanticism, was a man of many talents. He made a career in public service as a librarian and educator and was an amateur composer and competent musicologist. He also dabbled in science and was an amateur inventor. This background is reflected in his literary output, which is not large but of great interest and high quality.

Odoevsky's collection of stories *Russkie nochi* (*Russian Nights,* 1844), the chef d'oeuvre of Russian philosophic romanticism, is patterned after E. T. A. Hoffmann's *Die Serapionsbrüder.* The frame is that of a group of young Russians reading their stories to one another and discussing their content as well as other subjects, chief among which is the evaluation of modern civilization. Odoevsky's philosophy is close to that of F. W. J. Schelling. It rejects rationalism and positivism, and embraces intuition and creativity.

Thematically the stories of *Russian Nights* range far and wide. The lead story, untitled, though "Opere del Cavaliere Giambattista Piranesi" is its leitmotiv, resembles Hoffmann's "Der Ritter von Gluck." A Neapolitan eccentric dreams of executing Piranesi's fantastic architectural projects, believing in fact that he is himself the Cavaliere, much as Hoffmann's eccentric concludes that story by declaring that he *is* "der Ritter von Gluck," There are two fictionalized tributes to great composers: "Poslednii kvartet Betkhovena" ("Beethoven's Last Quartet") and "Sebastian Bakh." The latter develops the idea of a universal language that is the basis of all art forms. A strange character in the story is in fact composing a dictionary of the hieroglyphics of this language.

But then "Brigadir" ("The Brigadier") is an amazing preview of Tolstoy's *The Death of Ivan Ilyich:* it too starts with the funeral of what must have been a happy and successful man and then lets the dead man tell the real story of his life, a most ordinary and proper one if viewed from the outside, but in fact a sinful waste and an ugly tragedy.

The stories "Bal" ("The Ball") and "Nasmeshka mertvetsa" ("A Dead Man's Joke") are Gothic fantasies rather in the style of *The Vigils of Bonaventure* (1804). That an avowed Schellingian like Odoevsky also indulged in macabre fantasies may not be irrelevant to the conjecture of some scholars that Schelling was in fact the author of the anonymous *Vigils*. "The Ball" begins with a triumphant battle communiqué and continues with the description of a brilliant ball celebrating the victory. As the music resounds, the listener believes he hears behind each note the sound of pain, anguish, despair, and death. Finally he sees a vision of a danse macabre of skeletons, those killed or maimed in the victorious battle. "A Dead Man's Joke" describes a beautiful society lady who has abandoned her young lover to marry a middle-aged dignitary. She dreams she sees the unfortunate young man in his coffin as her carriage passes a hearse while taking her to a ball. The dream continues with the ball routed by the raging flood waters of the Neva and the faithless woman astride the coffin containing her lover's corpse. The lid snaps open and she encounters the livid features of the dead man. The lady then awakens to learn that she had fainted at the ball.

The main topic of *Russian Nights* is mankind's future. "Poslednee samoubiistvo" ("The Last Suicide") is an avowedly Malthusian fantasy: Mankind, because of overpopulation, has arrived at a state of perversion of all moral values. It finally finds the unanimity it has lacked throughout its history and uses its combined efforts and scientific achievements to blow up the globe. "Gorod bez imeni" ("A Nameless City") is another condensed "history" of modern humanity ending in ruin, one in which the optimistic economic theories of Adam Smith and Jeremy Bentham serve as targets of Odoevsky's irony.

Though the *Russian Nights* stories are invariably challenging philosophically, they are not necessarily great fiction. The whole format (the dialogues of the frame take up as much space as the stories) is geared to the development of ideas rather than plot or characters. Odoevsky's style is lively and vigorous, but it lacks an individual note. Belinsky, as always, hit the nail on the head: "Do not look in Odoevsky's works for a poetic representation of real life; and do not look for a story in his tales, for the story was for him not a goal, but so to say, a means to an end, not an essential form, but a convenient frame."

Odoevsky wrote a number of stories not included in *Russian Nights*. Most of these are totally Hoffmannesque and not very good. The most interesting, though not the best, among them is "Salamandra" ("The Salamander," 1841), an intricate tale of love and alchemy, set partly in Finland and with extensive quotes from the Finnish folk epic *Kalevala*. But there are also some remarkable pieces that, like "The Brigadier," anticipate the future development of Russian literature.

"Zhivopisets" ("The Painter," 1839) is a story of artistic failure, of a sort earlier attempted by Polevoy in a story of the same title (1833) and more brilliantly realized by Dostoevsky in *Netochka Nezvanova* (1848–49). The painter Shumsky has genuine talent, but a combination of poverty, lack of understanding on the part of his customers, and his own stubborn insistence on pursuing his fleeting visions instead of concentrating on completing his pictures leads to his failure. He dies young, leaving a single large canvas covered by many layers of uncompleted paintings.

"Neoboidennyi dom" ("The Unpassable House," 1842), done in the manner of a Russian folk legend, anticipates Tolstoy's *Tales for the People*. A pious pilgrim woman gets lost in a forest on her way to a monastery and chances upon a den of thieves. Only a boy of fifteen is at home. He gives her food and drink and directs her to the monastery. She sets out, only to return to the same house where she meets the same boy, now a man of thirty-five. She learns that he has murdered her son, but forgives him and is sent on her way once more. When she returns after another futile attempt to reach the monastery, the man, now sixty years old, has in the meantime raped and murdered her daughter. She forgives him yet again, and this time they set out for the monastery together. They get there in time for mass and meet her children whom they thought dead. The woman learns, however, that the murderer's story was true. The pious old woman lives to age 120 and dies on the same day as the robber Fedor, now a pious monk.

Odoevsky's society tales go far in the direction of the psychological novella of the age of realism. "Kniazhna Mimi" ("Princess Mimi," 1834) features a masterful character sketch of an aging spinster whose spiteful gossip causes a hideous tragedy. Her victims, though set within an ingenious and credible plot, remain schematic. "Kniazhna Zizi" ("Princess Zizi," 1839) has both an interesting heroine and psychologically intriguing plot. The heroine is devoted to a seemingly decent and attractive man. When he marries her flighty sister, she conceals her love and contents herself with the role of housekeeper and governess in her sister's household. When her sister dies, Princess Zizi finally reveals her feelings to her brother-in-law only to discover that he is a scoundrel who married her sister for her money and will use her similarly. But Princess Zizi recovers from this blow, and the end of the story depicts her as a charming and wise middle-aged woman who enjoys life.

Mikhail Lermontov (1814–41), poet and dramatist, was also a prolific prose writer in all the romantic genres. His only mature prose work, though, is *Geroi nashego vremeni* (A Hero of Our Time, 1840), now generally considered a novel. Still it deserves mention here because it developed from what were originally several short stories, three of which ("Taman," "Bela," and "The Fatalist") had previously been published by themselves. There is evidence that originally Lermontov did not view "Taman" and "The Fatalist" as part of a cycle "From an Officer's Caucasian Notebooks" (the subtitle of "Bela" in the journal version of 1839), and he had to adapt their respective heroes to the image of Pechorin, hero of the other three stories.

In some ways *A Hero of Our Time* resembles Pushkin's *Tales of Belkin.* It also has a hierarchy of narrators who provide a frame, and five stories, each done in a different manner. The stories of *A Hero of Our Time,* though, are linked by a common hero, Pechorin, whose personality is gradually revealed as each story presents further episodes in his life. Boris Eikhenbaum has suggested that in Russia, where no major novel tradition existed, it was precisely the cycle of short stories (popular in romantic literature in Russia as well as in the West) that developed into the novel. And indeed the first three great Russian novels—*Eugene Onegin, A Hero of Our Time,* and *Dead Souls*—were so composed, as were the first novels of Dostoevsky (*Netochka Nezvanova*) and Tolstoy (*Childhood*).

Unlike *Tales of Belkin,* however, *A Hero of Our Time* was acclaimed by contemporaries, and it has always retained its lofty position as a classic. Belinsky's authority—never seriously challenged by Apollon Grigorev's argument that Pechorin was an artificial creation not really anchored in Russian life—established Lermontov's hero as a generic type and a link in the chain of Russia's "superfluous men."

The lead story, "Bela," is a Caucasian romance recounted by Maksim Maksimych, an honest but simpleminded fellow officer. In the tale, Pechorin is cast in the role of a blasé Byronic hero. The story, trite enough in itself, of an innocent native girl's tragic love for an emotionally spent European is framed by a travelogue that twice interrupts the narrative. The narrative is essentially *erlebte Rede,* with Maksim Maksimych's voice filtered through the consciousness and language of a more sophisticated narrator, but Pechorin's voice is also heard, since Maksim Maksimych "quotes" him repeatedly. Still, the general agreement among Russian critics that "Bela" is a masterpiece rests upon the expenditure of a great deal of interpretive ingenuity upon what might well be considered a predictable variation on an old theme if it were not by Lermontov.

In the second story, "Maksim Maksimych," the narrator witnesses a chance meeting between Pechorin and Maksim Maksimych and offers a first character sketch of Pechorin. This tale also provides a bridge to the following stories, as the narrator comes into possession of Pechorin's notebooks. The next story, "Taman," is a masterful, though quite Marlinskian, tease: Pechorin's adventures in Taman, a small seaport in the Caucasus, involve an "unclean" house, an enticingly mysterious young woman, and an uncanny blind boy—but everything finds a prosaic resolution. "Taman," in a way, rebuts the Rousseauism of "Bela" and deflates that story's hero. V. V. Vinogradov has also suggested that "Taman" takes a parodic stab at Vasily Zhukovsky's "Undina," a poetic version (in hexameters) of Friedrich de la Motte-Fouqué's romantic tale "Undine." Pechorin, cast in the role of that story's knightly hero, does call the young woman who tries to drown him his "Undina," or mermaid.

The fourth story, "Kniazhna Meri" ("Princess Mary"), a society tale of illicit love and intrigue, ends in a fatal duel between Pechorin and his rival Grushnitsky. It is told by Pechorin himself and reveals still more of his character. Interestingly, young Grushnitsky is Pechorin in travesty, as it were, and as much of a projection of Lermontov's own personality as Pechorin. The final story, "Fatalist" ("The Fatalist"), is a conventional romantic tale of suspense, but it also lays bare the mainspring of Pechorin's personality: lacking firm beliefs or principles, he follows his impulses and, being naturally brave and vigorous, delights in any challenge, even against heavy odds. Eikhenbaum seeks a deeper meaning in "The Fatalist": it carries, he says, the message that fatalism—that is, an awareness of the iron laws of history—should lead not to passive submission but to energetic action.

The stories of *A Hero of Our Time* are generally viewed as representing a transition from romanticism to psychological realism. Pechorin became Onegin's successor in a chain of superfluous men in Russian literature, indeed, a step forward, as it were, because he is a rebel without a cause rather than an aimless sybarite. Lermontov's disciplined prose style had a considerable influence on the subsequent development of the Russian short story. Nevertheless, the stories of *A Hero of Our Time* still bear signs of Lermontov's relative inexperience in composition and plot development.

Gogol as the Early Master

The short stories of Nikolay Gogol (1809–52) encompass the whole range of the Russian short story of the 1830s and 1840s, from the various romantic genres to those of the natural school. He launched his career with a collection of stories, *Vechera na khutore bliz Dikan'ki* (*Evenings on a Farm near Dikanka,* 1831), followed by a second volume the next year. The tales made him immensely popular and became instant classics. They are loosely connected by a frame, written after the stories were finished, in which a beekeeper named Rudy Panko of Mirgorod in the Ukraine presents himself as the author and/or collector of these stories. Their rather literary style is explained post factum by a hint at a "young gentleman in a pea-green jacket" who may have had a hand in some of them. The deacon Foma Grigorevich, who tells some of the stories, is an integral part of the narrative, as is the narrator of the next to last story, "Ivan Fedorovich Shpon'ka i ego tetushka" ("Ivan Fedorovich Shponka and His Aunt"). In one instance—"Vecher nakanune Ivana Kupala" ("St. John's Eve")—three narrators are interposed between author and reader: Rudy Panko, the deacon, and the latter's late grandfather, who told him the story. The introduction of an ingenuous narrator "from the people" was a routine device of the romantic short story, with Walter Scott's *Tales of My Landlord* a prime example. It was also Scott who had made local color, folk tradition, and regional dialect routine components of fiction. Gogol's Ukrainian tales fuse colorful genre scenes (with many loving descriptions of food and drink, in particular), equally colorful motifs from Ukrainian folktales and folk superstitions, and a narrative and dialogue liberally sprinkled with Ukrainianisms. Verse as well as prose quotations in Ukrainian, taken from folklore (Gogol was an avid collector of Ukrainian folk songs), literature, and the dialect comedies of Gogol's father, appear in the text and as epigraphs to some of the stories.

The characters in *Evenings* are the stereotypes of the Ukrainian puppet theater: young cossacks are brave, enterprising, and amorous; maidens are pretty and little else; old men are foolish, drunken, and henpecked; old women are shrewish and not averse to extramarital escapades; the clergy are superstitious, gluttonous, and lecherous; and the Devil is in each and every story. The general mood is frankly Ukrainian: Gogol baits "Muscovites" lustily, along with Jews, Poles, and Catholics. The stories are a mixture of genres, styles, moods, and idioms, and there are frequent shifts of point of view. Delicate lyric passages and poetic nature descriptions alternate with ethnographic burlesque and crude vulgarisms, idyllic high style with folksy colloquialisms, and perfectly literate Russian with blatant Ukrainianisms. The underlying mood of lusty folk humor is occasionally interrupted by pensive observations on the elusiveness of joy and the transitoriness of all human concerns: a good example is the passage concluding the otherwise riotously funny lead story, "The Fair at Sorochintsy."

The plots of Gogol's Ukrainian tales range from farce and genre comedy to melodrama. In "Noch' pered rozhdestvom" ("Christmas Eve"), Vakula, the village smith, who paints icons as a sideline, angers the Devil by depicting him in most uncomplimentary ways. The Devil wreaks vengeance by stealing the moon and causing all kinds of mischief in the village. Some burlesque happenings revolve around the amorous escapades of Vakula's mother, the village witch. Oksana, Vakula's lady love, promises to marry him if he will give her a pair of shoes like the ones the empress herself wears. Vakula hitches a ride to St. Petersburg on the Devil's back to obtain the shoes and marries her. The episode in St. Petersburg presents a whimsically estranged view of Catherine the Great and her court. The story, quite long, is full of colorful folkloric and ethnographic detail, whimsical humor (mostly of the slapstick variety), spirited narrative, and racy dialogue. "The Fair at Sorochintsy," "Maiskaia noch'" ("A May Night"), "Propavshaia gramota" ("The Lost Letter"), and "Zakoldovannoe mesto" ("A Bewitched Place") display the same qualities, though in varying degrees.

The Gothic element prevails in "Strashnaia mest'" ("A Terrible Vengeance") and certain other of Gogol's Ukrainian tales. "A Terrible Vengeance" has an intricate plot split into several episodes that gradually reveal the secret of an ancient curse. The main plot features the struggle between an honest cossack warrior, Danilo, and an evil sorcerer, the father of his wife, Katerina. The latter is torn between her loyalty to her father and to her husband. In the end all three perish. The story contains many motifs typical of the Gothic tale: dungeons, a cemetery from which the dead arise, conjuring of spirits, incestuous passion, a pious hermit, the murder of an innocent babe, and so forth. It also contains beautiful lyric passages, such as a celebrated description of the Dnepr River. The Gothic elements here and in other stories by Gogol, such as "Vii" ("Viy") and "Portret" ("The Portrait"), have been traced to Western influences, including E. T. A. Hoffmann and Ludwig Tieck. However, "A Terrible Vengeance" also incorporates elements of the Ukrainian folk ballad, the *duma,* especially in the syntax and rhythm of its narrative, the structure of its imagery (triadic arrangement, negative simile), and the stylization of certain lyric passages such as Katerina's lament. Critical opinion on this and other Gothic stories by Gogol is sharply divided. Some consider them "absurd" and "contrived," whereas others view them as "psychologically profound" and "ingeniously structured."

Gogol's second collection, *Mirgorod* (1835), also in two parts, contains some of his greatest stories. *Taras Bulba,* a longish historical novella in its *Mirgorod* version, was expanded into a historical novel in 1842 and will not be discussed here. "Viy," also revised in 1842, is a Gothic tale set in the Ukraine of old. A Kiev divinity student rides an old witch to death on a frenzied nocturnal flight but discovers at dawn that the dead woman is a beautiful young maiden. Her father summons him to read the prayers for the departed over her coffin. After having barely survived two spooky nights, he falls victim on the third to the Viy, a terrible earth spirit who kills with his horrible gaze. "Viy" is a successful fusion of lighthearted genre comedy and terrifying grotesque. It has its share of lyric passages and is one of Gogol's few stories with a genuine erotic motif, though it is quickly dismissed.

While opinions vary about "Viy," "Starosvetskie pomeshchiki" ("Old-World Landowners") and "Povest' o tom, kak possorilis' Ivan

Ivanovich s Ivanom Nikiforovichem" ("The Tale of How Ivan Ivanovich Quarreled with Ivan Nikiforovich, or The Tale of the Two Ivans") are acknowledged masterpieces. The first is a *parodie sérieuse* of the Philemon and Baucis theme, explicitly mentioned in the text. A rural idyll is destroyed by the meticulous exposure of the terrible sloth, gluttony, and mindlessness—always by implication rather than open castigation—of a happily married elderly couple, and then given another turn by the touching story of their death. "The Tale of the Two Ivans" is more explicitly a satire, yet it too has concealed depths. The banality and heartlessness of the good people of Mirgorod are genuine, and what one tends to take for an absurd grotesque is simply the truth of life. "The Tale of the Two Ivans" fully develops those Gogolian elements that first appeared in "Ivan Fedorovich Shponka and His Aunt": verbal caricatures of human types, so apt as to be taken for portraits; ironic innuendo that transforms seemingly harmless banality into ugly cruelty; parody of romantic rhetoric (a foul puddle in the middle of Mirgorod's city square is described in terms of a romantic landscape); hyperbole and hyperoche masquerading as realistic description; absurd nonsequiturs and other forms of verbal clowning; and last but not least, so-called sound speech (*zvukorech'*)—that is, sequences of grotesque words and word combinations, such as lists of names and patronymics that sound absurd to the Russian ear.

Gogol's miscellany of fiction and nonfiction entitled *Arabeski* (*Arabesques,* two parts, 1835) contains three more important short stories: "Portret" ("The Portrait"), "Nevskii prospekt" ("Nevsky Prospect"), and "Zapiski sumasshedshego" ("The Diary of a Madman"), all three set in St. Petersburg. "The Portrait" is a Hoffmannesque Künstlernovelle with an involved plot combining a serious though hardly original treatment of the artist's obligation to his talent with an assortment of Gothic details, and in particular a cursed portrait with an "evil eye." The explicit message is conventionally romantic. Talent is a gift of God, which obligates an artist to seek "inner meaning" and "the higher mystery of creation" in all that he represents. Hence there are no "low" subjects, for even the lowliest is ennobled by passing through the crucible of the artist's soul; art always reflects a divine order and is therefore superior to the world from which it emerges; it illuminates and brings peace. An artist like Chartkov, hero of "The Portrait," who loses touch with reality and prostitutes his talent for gain or fame, soon ceases to be an artist.

"Nevsky Prospect" is half Küstlernovelle, too. It begins with a lively description of Nevsky Prospect, St. Petersburg's main thoroughfare, then follows the paths of two young men, an artist and an officer, who are drawn into exciting adventures while strolling there, and ends with another glance at Nevsky Prospect, as "a demon lights the streetlamps only to let everything appear not as it really is." The sensitive artist Piskarev meets a young woman of great beauty who turns out to be a prostitute. He is so shocked by this experience that he goes mad and takes his own life. The robust officer Pirogov also follows a beautiful young woman, the virtuous wife of a German artisan. Pirogov's attempts at seduction gain him a sound thrashing from Frau Schiller's husband and his friends Hoffmann and Kuntz. But Pirogov easily shakes off this indignity and that very night is seen dancing the mazurka in the best company.

"The Diary of a Madman" is a tour de force: the familiar romantic theme of a dreamer's tragic clash with a hostile world is transferred from the world of art (an early version was entitled "The Diary of a Mad Musician") into the drab ambience of a copying clerk. Moreover, Gogol retains the romantic form of the "confession," or rather first-person stream of consciousness, much as in Victor Hugo's *The Last Day of a Condemned Man.* "The Diary" creates an estranged view of life through various devices. The standard ploy of talking dogs, who convey one aspect of it, is motivated by the hero's madness. The hero, Poprishchin, who suffers the pains traditionally reserved for artists, is an ignorant, stupid, and vain fellow, a caricature of the petty clerk. The world is shown not only in terms of his madness but also in terms of his mundane everyday concerns. The story also poses a deeper existential question: how should a copying clerk, a mere cog in a soulless machine, realize his individuality? Poprishchin does it by imagining he is the king of Spain. The moral is that there is no rational way to resolve his dilemma. Gogol seeks to show the deterioration of Poprishchin's mind through the language of his notes, but with little clinical accuracy.

"Nos" ("The Nose") appeared in 1836 in Pushkin's journal *Sovremennik,* but the definitive version of 1842 contains changes and additions. The work is a comic grotesque describing the mysterious disappearance and eventual reappearance of Collegiate Assessor Kovalev's nose. The loss and recovery of a nose, as well as other anecdotes and puns featuring a nose or noses, were common subjects of eighteenth- and early nineteenth-century literature.[9] Since Russian has many proverbial sayings featuring the nose, the story is also in part a study in realized metaphor. The device of setting a miraculous or absurd event in perfectly normal, even trivial surroundings was popular in romantic literature. In "The Nose," the noseless Kovalev requests the aid of the police, a doctor, and a newspaper ad agency, which in each case results in merciless satire: real ads, for example, are if anything even more absurd than Kovalev's. The plot of "The Nose" has no key or resolution, for Gogol dropped a conclusion that announced the whole thing was a dream. Also, the plot deconstructs itself repeatedly: for example, the plot line of the first chapter, in which Kovalev's barber finds a cut-off nose in a loaf of bread, is not pursued further. One might call the logic of the plot surrealist. Yet the story is told by a third-person narrator who feigns perfect solidarity with and solicitude for his hero and in general exudes bonhomie—mock bonhomie, of course. "The Nose" is a virtuoso piece, though the tremendous amount of attention it has attracted seems excessive.

The same may be said of "Shinel'" ("The Overcoat," 1842), although this is without a doubt one of the great short stories in world literature. "The Overcoat" is yet another "tale about a poor clerk." Its hero, Akaky Akakievich Bashmachkin, has been totally absorbed in his copying for thirty years. Nothing else exists for him until his tailor tells him that his old overcoat is beyond repair and that he must have a new one. Much of the story describes Bashmachkin's heroic efforts to save the money needed for the new coat: he starves himself, quits drinking tea, walks very lightly to save the heels of his shoes. When Bashmachkin finally takes his new coat to the office, he is invited to a party to celebrate the occasion. On his way home afterward, the coat is stolen off his back. He makes a desperate effort to retrieve it, but is thwarted by a callous "important personage." Heartbroken, Bashmachkin falls ill and dies; afterward his ghost haunts the streets of St. Petersburg and steals people's overcoats, until in the end the important personage himself falls victim to the vengeful ghost.

The type created by Gogol is not new: he is closely related to Dickens's poor clerks and the *surnumeraires* of Balzac. But Gogol drives dehumanization to the limit in this little clerk, who takes delight only in the shape of certain letters and whose only love affair in life is with an overcoat. The story is told in the third person and in a lightly bantering tone, interrupted only a few times by serious moral observations. But these latter have caused many readers to interpret the work as a story of "sentimental humanitarianism," that is, compassion for the socially and intellectually underprivileged. Some critics have interpreted the appearance of the ghost as a call to rebellion against the little man's oppressors. In this interpretation, the story is a social rather than a moral satire.

In his first novel, *Poor Folk* (1846), Dostoevsky has his hero, another copy clerk, criticize "The Overcoat" as a libelous attack on the dignity of the little man. This line of interpretation developed later on. Vasily Rozanov (1856–1919) saw in Bashmachkin a veritable travesty of a human being, deprived of his soul. Boris Eikhenbaum, in his celebrated essay, "Kak sdelana 'Shinel' 'Gogolia" ("How Gogol's 'Overcoat' Is Made," 1919), presents "The Overcoat" as a comic grotesque, whose major elements are play with sound effects (iconic use of funny or expressive sound patterns), verbal clowning, and comic imagery. Other critics, like Dmitry Chizhevsky, have viewed "The Overcoat" as a serious exercise in philosophical anthropology. Bashmachkin is the subject of an experiment: reduced to the lowest level of human individuality, he has virtually reverted to a state of pristine innocence, which he then loses, seduced by Petrovich the tailor, who tempts him with the overcoat. F. C. Driessen observes that the story of Akaky Akakievich resembles the legend of St. Akaky (Acacius), a humble monk obedient to a stern elder. When Akaky died, his master, having momentarily forgotten that his servant was dead, called for him, and Akaky obediently rose from his bier, still the devoted servant. The story of Bashmachkin's life, death, and reappearance as a ghost is then a travesty on a modern saint's life.[10]

Another interpretation, first advanced by Belinsky (who applied it specifically to Gogol's comedy *The Inspector-General*), holds that "The Overcoat" is a study in human existence as it tends toward nonexistence. The hero's life is ghostlike (in the sense in which Hoffmann would speak of a "ghostlike philistine existence"), and only in death does he acquire a modicum of reality. This conception moves "The Overcoat" into the region of romantic fiction, recalling Hoffmann's "Master Flea," which generates dread precisely by reducing the normal to the subnormal. In this sense we find in "The Overcoat" shadows "linking our state of existence to those other states and modes which we dimly apprehend in our rare moments of irrational perception" (Vladimir Nabokov). The great variety of interpretations given to "The Overcoat" (only a few are mentioned here) indicates the story's depth and ambiguity. Its style and structure are difficult to define: The ghost theme, for example, vacillates between metaphor, tease, and reality. "The Overcoat" contains many false leads, dead ends, nonsequiturs, and absurdities, but a good deal of straightforward satire and unmistakable irony, too.

From Romanticism to the Natural School

The transition from romanticism to the natural school was not very smooth chronologically. Though most of the key figures of the natural school were born around 1820 and began to publish in the 1840s, some were older and began their careers in the 1830s. Nikolay Pavlov (1803–64) was among them. Born a serf, he received a good education after the manumission of his family in 1811. He worked briefly as an actor and then concentrated on writing, beginning with translations (he was the first Russian translator of Balzac) and undistinguished verse. His *Tri povesti* (*Three Tales,* 1835) brought him general recognition. Later on, Pavlov wrote other short stories and was active as a critic, polemicist, and journalist, but without much success. Pavlov's early tales, though awkwardly constructed and composed in a jerky, self-conscious manner, still contain flashes of genuine pathos and some observations with the ring of truth. Their great success was due to their social message.

Belinsky described "Iatagan" ("The Dagger," 1835) as a story "remarkable more for its details than as a whole." The critic surmised that "the author had heard an anecdotic story, made a tale from it, and not knowing the characters personally, failed to re-create their portraits correctly." The hero, an impetuous young officer in love with a charming princess, kills a rival in a duel and is reduced to the ranks. His colonel happens to be another of the princess's suitors and a battle of wills between them ensues. In the end the colonel has the soldier flogged for insubordination and the soldier stabs him with the dagger that appears in the title and serves as the story's central symbol ("the falcon").[11] The story ends with a chilling description of the preparations for the gauntlet the soldier will not survive.

"Imeniny" ("The Nameday Party," 1835), an antiserfdom story, is also clumsily constructed and even more anecdotal. The rather extensive frame is particularly implausible. The hero is a serf trained as a musician. His talent gains him admission to elegant drawing rooms where the guests are unaware of his social origins. A young lady falls in love with him. Realizing the impossibility of a consummation of their love, he reveals his secret to her and flees to become a soldier, for this is his only chance to become a free man. Having distinguished himself on the battlefield and been promoted to officer's rank, he returns to his home province, where he accidentally meets the woman he loved, now another man's wife.

The importance of Pavlov's stories lay in their distinct social tendency. His society tales feature not only consistent, though awkward, attempts at psychological motivation but also efforts to link fiction to Russian social reality.

Vladimir Sollogub (1813–82) is best known for his satirical journey "Tarantas"(1845), but he also wrote a number of short stories that were highly regarded in the 1840s. Though he came from a family of Polish magnates and belonged to high society, Sollogub cast his literary lot with the *raznochintsy*[12] of the natural school.

"Serezha" (1838) is a society tale with an ironic twist. Serezha, a young guardsman, out of boredom, attends to his neighbor's reasonably attractive daughter, who is madly in love with him. When it seems he must propose, Serezha suddenly leaves for St. Petersburg to continue his dissipated life there. His conscience bothers him, though, until four years later he receives a letter from the girl he had jilted, now happily married and trying to use him to obtain a promotion for her husband.

"Istoriia dvukh kalosh" ("The Story of Two Galoshes," 1839) is a tragic Künstlernovelle. The hero is a German musician who suffers every kind of misfortune and dies in poverty and despair. The unhappy love that forms part of the plot is trite, and the whole tale sounds derivative. An absurd frame consists of the delivery of two pairs of galoshes: one to the poor musician, one to the government official who has married the poor musician's great love. "Aptekarsha" ("The Apothecary's Wife," 1841) also has a German cast, with a plot moving from Dorpat, a German university town in Livonia, to a provincial Russian town. An elegant young baron encounters a woman he jilted when a student at Dorpat, as the wife of a fellow student, now a provincial apothecary. The baron tries to rekindle their romance and succeeds in breaking her heart.

"Sobachka" ("The Lap Dog" 1845), Sollogub's best-known story, is a ferocious satire on provincial corruption. A police chief's wife takes a fancy to a lap dog that belongs to the prima donna of a traveling ensemble visiting the town. When the actress refuses to part with her pet, the police chief closes the theater, declaring that it will reopen only when his wife gets the dog and a three-hundred ruble shawl, and he a thousand rubles. The frightened actors, faced with ruin, give in. "Metel'" ("The Blizzard," 1845) begins with a poetic description of a blizzard, which serves as the frame for a love story. A handsome young officer is stranded at a wretched stagecoach station. Among the other travelers there is a young woman of sublime beauty. The two spend the night holding hands and exchanging confidences, and at dawn they part forever. The story projects a Chekhovian mood, though Sollogub, a mediocre stylist, lacks Chekhov's impressionist finesse.

Evgeny Grebenka (1812–48) is best known as one of the founders of modern Ukrainian literature. But his Russian stories, mostly in the tradition of the natural school, are also remarkable. "Kulik" ("The Snipe," 1841), his most famous one, is set in the country. Petrushka, a handsome and literate house serf, falls in love with Masha, a chambermaid on the neighboring estate. But they cannot marry because their masters have quarreled over hunting rights. Moreover, Masha is cruelly abused by her master for having dared to become involved with Petrushka, who had said "may your master choke on this snipe" during the incident that led to the quarrel. In the end Petrushka and Masha make a suicide pact. He shoots her, is prevented from turning the gun on himself, and soon dies in prison. The story is an effective piece of antiserfdom propaganda, for Grebenka cleverly contrasts a rural idyll with the landowners' arrogant callousness. He also displays some of Gogol's stylistic mannerisms, particularly when he makes a sly pretense of solicitous solidarity with the detestable landowners and bureaucrats who populate his stories.

Vladimir Dal (Russian: Dal'; Danish: Dahl, 1801–72), the son of a Danish father and German mother, is remembered as a great Russian lexicographer, linguist, and collector of proverbs, riddles, folktales, and other folklore genres. He began his amazingly varied professional life in the navy, studied medicine and practiced it for some years, and then devoted many years to administrative service in the eastern provinces of European Russia. His manifold practical, scientific (he was also a busy naturalist), and scholarly activities are very much reflected in his fiction, consisting of long and short stories, physiological sketches, satirical tales, fairy tales, and ethnographic sketches, mostly written in the 1830s and 1840s. Under the pseudonym "Kazak Lugansky" he was one of the most popular writers of that period. Though politically conservative, he was an outspoken critic of the imperial bureaucracy and a sober observer of popular life. Stylistically, he offers greater variety than the other writers of the natural school as he ranges from sly satire and gentle (rarely bitter) irony to impersonation of various narrative voices, including peasant dialect (skaz).

Dal's ethnographic sketches anticipate such works from Turgenev's *The Hunting Sketches* as "Khor and Kalinych." For example, "Ural'skii kazak" ("A Ural Cossack," 1842) presents a thoroughly personalized biography and character sketch of Proklyatov, a stalwart Old Believer cossack warrior, fisherman, and pater familias. It ends in a moving scene. When the cossack regiment returns from the wars, Proklyatov's wife asks the first horsemen where her husband is and is told, "Further back." When she hears the same response from the next squad, and the next, she knows the truth and breaks out into a wail.

In many ways Dal also anticipates Leskov. He has a genuine knowledge of and sympathy for simple Russian people. He reproduces their language without stylizing it. He does not gloss over the dark side of serfdom as much as censorship allowed. His sympathy for the underdog is genuine and unsentimental, and he restrains his moralizing to a tolerable minimum. The story "Khmel', son i iav'" ("Drunken Ravings, Dreams, and Reality," 1843) begins with an ethnographic sketch of the life-style of Russian peasants who leave their villages to work as seasonal traveling artisans all over the country. It then tells the story of a carpenter named Stepan Voropaev who kills a robber on the highway in self-defense and then returns to the scene to empty the dead man's billfold. His conscience does not bother him much. Some time later Stepan wakes up one morning, after drinking heavily, with a recollection of having slain his drinking companion and pushed his body into a river. He remorsefully confesses his crime and is on the verge of being deported, when the "dead man" turns up. Stepan's guilty conscience had caused him to dream of a crime, and in his drunken state he had taken his dream for reality. Stepan learns his lesson and becomes a good family man.

"Vakkh Sidorov Chaikin, ili Rasskaz ego o sobstvennom svoem zhit'e-byt'e, za pervuiu polovinu zhizni svoei" ("Vakkh Sidorov Chaikin, or His Story of His Own Life and Experiences, for the First Half of His Life," 1843), a rather lengthy story, describes a freeborn orphan who, in the course of his wanderings, is made a serf by mistake and then a cantonist (soldier-settler) by yet another error, and experiences all manner of trials and tribulations. But he advances in the world and obtains a medical education and a job in the public health service, where he experiences further trials, mostly thanks to his integrity. But in the end he finds happiness with the woman he thought he had lost, and the future looks brighter. The story is told in the first person in language that reflects the narrator's character, background, and station in life. It conveys the quiet dignity and worldly wisdom of a man who knows his worth, but who is also aware of the total insecurity of existence.

Dal also wrote pieces typical of the natural school: physiological sketches, such as "Peterburgskii dvornik" and "Denshchik" ("A St. Petersburg Janitor," 1844; "An Orderly," 1845), and "tales about a poor clerk." "Bedovik" ("A Hard Luck Fellow," 1839) is the story of a poor clerk, a clumsy but honest and hardworking young man, who loses his job in a provincial town, leaves for St. Petersburg or Moscow (he can't make up his mind which), undergoes comic adventures on the way, never gets there, and eventually is brought back to a happy ending by his old benefactress, whom he meets by chance on the highway. The story has some Gogolian features. The hero indulges in a long and whimsical disquisition on the inability of Russian officials to write simply and clearly. In one lengthy passage the men at a marshal's ball are methodically likened to various animals—cats, dogs, hamsters, oxen, and so on, and the ladies to various birds. Even more Gogolian is "Zhizn' cheloveka, ili Progulka po Nevskomu prospektu" ("A Man's Life, or a Walk along Nevsky Prospect," 1843), a tale about a poor clerk whose whole life literally moves along Nevsky Prospect. The point of the story, as in Gogol, is the reduction of man to a ludicrously petty range of experience, which causes him to be utterly helpless outside his little niche in life and paralyzed with fear at the thought of leaving it. The story does have a touch of the grotesque, but is more concrete and closer to reality than "The Overcoat."

Dal's repertory extended well beyond the natural school. "Pavel Alekseevich Igrivy" (1847), a tale of unhappy love, is a psychological novella worthy of a Turgenev. Its structure is interesting. The story begins with a meticulous description of the daily routine of a middle-aged provincial landowner, apparently a rather odd and dull-witted recluse. It continues with the story of his life, which shows that he is really a noble, sensitive, loving, and capable man, whose zest for life was destroyed by several unfortunate events: the woman he loved was married off to a scoundrel who wanted only her money. When she is finally freed by her husband's death, Igrivy again arrives too late, through no fault of his own. Dal's psychology is remarkably unconventional: his villains are weak and pathetic, though their villainies have disastrous effects. The hero, though not very vividly drawn, acts in a psychologically convincing manner.

Nikolay Nekrasov (1821–78) is best known as one of the great poets of the nineteenth century and as the publisher of *Sovremennik, Otechestvennye zapiski,* and several major almanacs, such as *A Physiology of Petersburg.* Nekrasov began to write for a living when not yet twenty; much of what he wrote was hastily concocted and clearly derivative, especially such melodramatic stories as "Pevitsa" ("The Singer," 1840) or "V Sardinii" ("In Sardinia," 1842), works of the sort Dostoevsky parodied as "Italian Passions" in his *Poor Folk.* Nekrasov's humorous stories—for example, "Makar Osipovich Sluchainyi" or "Bez vesti propavshii piita" ("A Poet Lost without a Trace"), both 1840, the first a satire on corruption and nepotism, the second a mock-pathetic account of the trials of an unsuccessful poet—are rather insipid. Some of Nekrasov's serious stories in the style of the natural school are of more interest, though they display the mannerisms of that school in a particularly obtrusive way. "Zhizn' Aleksandry Ivanovny: Povest' o chetyrekh ekipazhakh" ("The Life of Aleksandra Ivanovna: A Tale of Four Carriages," 1841) records the way stations of the heroine's descent from a kept woman riding in an elegant carriage to her death as a poor washerwoman whose coffin is taken to the cemetery on a cart. In "Kareta: Predsmertnye zapiski duraka" ("The Carriage: Notes of a Fool Written before His Death," 1841) a poor clerk tries to purchase status by spending a small inheritance on a carriage he cannot afford to maintain. Rather than sell it, he smashes it up. A pedestrian again, he is run over by a carriage and loses a leg and then writes these notes to keep other fools from following his example. "Rostovshchik" ("The Usurer," 1841) is a tightly structured story with a surprise ending: the usurer's victim turns out to be his own son. When the dying man's wife comes to pawn her husband's last precious possession, a medallion with a picture of his parents, the usurer recognizes himself. He rushes to his son's bedside but arrives too late.

Nekrasov shares many features with Gogol and the natural school: a penchant for the farfetched metaphor or simile, as well as for realized metaphor, a pervasively ironic tone, frequent apostrophes to the reader, and occasional unmotivated digressions. For example, in "Dvadtsat' piat' rublei" ("Twenty-Five Rubles," 1841), the hero is likened to the owner of a sugar beet processing plant, who believes that the virtue of patience will sooner or later produce sweet and plentiful fruit. In the same story, the human heart is said to resemble an apartment building with many flats of varying quality: "The best are occupied by virtues, while the worst have ben invaded by ambition, greed, hatred, envy, sloth, etc." This metaphor is subsequently realized: for the rest of the story whatever goes on in the hero's mind is described in terms of the goings-on at an apartment house. In short, Nekrasov showed clear signs of talent even this early in his career. What prevented him from becoming an outstanding prose writer was his disdain for the artistic quality of his prose. He must have regarded fiction as primarily a source of income and, to some extent, an expression of social protest (he is clearly a very angry young man), and his poetry as the principal outlet for his artistic bent.

Ivan Panaev (1812–62), Nekrasov's co-publisher and editor of *Sovremennik* after 1846, was primarily a journalist, who also wrote short stories, essays, feuilletons, and reviews. Panaev began publishing his stories in the early 1830s, but gained real prominence as a leader of the natural school in the 1840s. His stories have an obvious social tendency: they point an accusing finger at the parasitic upper class of landowners, military officers, and bureaucrats. "Barynia" ("A Lady," 1841) has for an introduction an outright physiological sketch of the several subspecies of the Russian lady (capital, provincial, and so on). "A Lady" is the life story of one Pelageya, a St. Petersburg lady. A brigadier's daughter, she has a decent dowry, and her parents marry her off to a middle-aged civil servant who is in love with her. Pelageya Petrovna dedicates her life to idleness, living beyond her husband's means and mismanaging her household. Her only purpose in life is always to maintain the status of a lady.

"Onagr" ("The Onager," 1841) describes a harebrained, insipid young nobleman who is wasting his mother's money on high living in St. Petersburg. Just as his debts assume menacing proportions, he learns that his uncle has died and left him twenty-eight hundred serfs. The impecunious onager is transformed into a wealthy gentleman and brilliant match. He marries a beautiful and refined lady whose parents compel her to accept his proposal although she does not love him. "Akteon" ("Actaeon," 1842) continues the story of the onager, Petr Aleksandrovich, beginning with his arrival at his uncle's estate and continuing with his ruin through high living, gambling, mismanagement, and general stupidity. The message of the story is that the typical Russian landowner is simply a parasite with no redeeming virtues, such as a respect for cultural values. He is also a failure as husband and father. But this somber picture has a silver lining. Olga Mikhailovna, Petr Aleksandrovich's wife, is intellectually and morally superior to her husband. She avoids his caresses and disregards his carousing. When she by chance encounters her former music teacher, now a tutor at a neighbor's estate, she confesses to him that she despises her husband and has no motherly feeling for her young son because he reminds her of his father. Olga Mikhailovna eventually dies of a broken heart, but she clearly is a "new woman," just as the tutor is a "new man," a cultured, sensitive, but poor *raznochinets*. "Actaeon" contains some curious details. At one point the narrative is interrupted by the tutor's essay on Schubert, whose "Serenade" is a key motif in the plot. In another episode the landowner Andrei Petrovich orders a poor hanger-on of a nobleman to dance in a squat for the amusement of his guests, which anticipates a scene in Turgenev's *The Hunting Sketches* ("My Neighbor Radilov"). Another story by Panaev, "Rodstvenniki" ("Relatives," 1847), also anticipates Turgenev in its caustic portrayal of a Moscow circle of "young men, linked by *higher interests and sympathies*" and their idealist philosophy. This was a critique of the circle of Nikolay Stankevich, as are portions of Turgenev's *Rudin* (1856).

Yakov Butkov (ca. 1820–56) was perhaps the most typical representative of the natural school, even by virtue of the fact that he himself belonged to the world he described in his two volumes of stories published as *Petersburgskie vershiny* (*The Summits* [garrets] *of St. Petersburg*, 1845–46). He was a friend of Dostoevsky's during the years 1847–49 when both were regular contributors to *Otechestvennye zapiski*. Butkov's literary career ended with the Petrashevsky affair of 1849. Although he was not directly involved in it, he became suspect to the authorities and to the censors and could no longer publish much. Eventually he died in a hospital for the indigent.

Butkov's witty and pointedly literate introduction to *The Summits of St. Petersburg* presents a mock phenomenology of the city in which its inhabitants are classified according to their positions, horizontal and vertical. This introduction is, however, very close—to the point of plagiarism—to a passage in Jules Janin's *La Confession* (1830). Among the inhabitants of St. Petersburg, the "lofty people" who occupy the highest level—the garrets—have received too little attention, and Butkov proposes to rectify this situation. He suggests that while the passions and desires, hopes and ambitions of the garret dwellers are quite mundane and kept low by their dependence on those living below them, these people still have their own philosophy of life, one he translates into the language of those who occupy middle floors in the better quarters of the city.

Butkov's hero is always a poor clerk, but his stories are of two kinds: satirical or pathetic. "Poriadochnyi chelovek" ("A Decent Man," who is a cardsharp) and "Pochtennyi chelovek" ("A Respected Man," who organizes charities to line his own pockets) are in the former category, as is "Khoroshee mesto" ("A Good Position," obtained by discreetly staying away from home when His Excellency deigns to visit, and letting one's pretty wife entertain him). Butkov's pathetic tales—"Sto rublei" ("A Hundred Rubles"), "Pervoe chislo" ("The First of the Month"), and "Goriun" ("A Hard Luck Guy")—resemble Dostoevsky's early stories, but are rather more dispirited and cruel. Butkov's hapless clerks are downtrodden, meek, and dull witted. Like Dostoevsky's heroes, they struggle to maintain their identity by holding on to, or seeking a position of their own (*svoe mesto*) in the world. Their stories are recounted with an ironic detachment that causes them to appear as limp puppets on a string rather than live human beings. The automaton motif, so common in romantic fiction, is made explicit. In "The First of the Month," the narrator observes: "For a long time he had been an *automaton,* moved by need and a desire to overcome, to eliminate need—and at last he had become a *man*!"

The plot is usually developed around an insipid anecdote. In "Partikuliarnaia para" ("A Business Suit"), the hero misses his chance for happiness because he does not own a proper suit to wear to the party that may make his fortune. "Nevskii prospekt, ili Puteshestviia Nestora Zaletaeva" ("Nevsky Prospect, or the Travels of Nestor Zaletaev") describes a jobless clerk who wins an elegant carriage in a lottery and for two days tries to impersonate a gentleman. The sad stories of several other characters whom Zaletaev encounters on this spree are of similarly anecdotal nature.

Butkov's style is lively, journalistic, mannered, occasionally whimsical, and sometimes witty. His aphorisms are often poignant: "A man is not self-sufficient the way a good position is; he is an absolute nothing if he does not occupy such a position; only if by some twist of fate he should really get one, will he be something" ("A Good Position"). At his best, Butkov approaches the young Dostoevsky. But unlike him Butkov uses relatively little dialogue, and what there is is not very spirited. Altogether, Butkov writes in a transitional manner characteristic of the natural school: the subject matter and the author's social ideas are those of realism, but he has not quite found a consistently straightforward way to communicate them, and permits an unmotivated irony to discredit the authenticity of what he reports.

Ivan Kokorev (1825–53) spent most of his brief literary career with the journal *Moskvitianin,* became an alcoholic, and died in a hospital for the poor. He was the author of perceptive and entertaining physiological sketches on Moscow lower- and lower-middle-class life and some short stories. "Sibirka" (1847) is a combination of physiological sketch and novella of manners. The Sibirka was a Moscow house of detention where draftees awaited their turn to be transported to their place of service. Here Nikolay Timofeevich, a skillful painter, is saved from having to enter military service and leave behind the woman he loves when Ivan Petrovich, a drunkard shoemaker who has just lost his wife, volunteers to take his place. "Savvushka," written in 1847 but stopped by the censor, appeared only in 1852. A novella of manners set in a Moscow slum among tradespeople, beggars, and drunks, it follows the life of Savvushka, a tailor, through a series of episodes from impetuous adolescence through aimless young manhood and on to more sensible middle years and mellow old age. "Savvushka" is a quintessential natural-school story. It is rich in genre scenes and descriptions of the goings-on in a Moscow beer hall, a tailor's shop, or a tenement building. Kokorev uses proverbs liberally and lets his characters tell their stories in their own language. A simple man presents his philosophy in his own simpleminded manner, as when Savvushka meditates on divine justice and why death takes one person and not another. The basic narrative, however, like that of almost all stories of the natural school, is written in educated literary language or, more precisely, in the journalese of the 1840s. It is also laced with allusions to works of Russian and western literatures.

Dmitry Grigorovich (1822–99) was considered a major literary figure throughout his life, but now he is remembered almost solely for his short stories of the 1840s. A schoolmate of Dostoevsky's at the St. Petersburg Engineering Academy and at one time his roommate, Grigorovich launched his literary career before Dostoevsky and was instrumental in the latter's "discovery" by Nekrasov and Belinsky.

Grigorovich's stories stand midway between the sentimental humanitarianism of the natural school and the realism of the 1850s as it would emerge in Turgenev, Pisemsky, and Tolstoy. His plots are unpretentious and credible and deal with genuine problems of prereform Russia. The setting of each tale, though not particularly rich in ethnographic detail, is sufficiently realistic. For these qualities Grigorovich received high praise from Belinsky, and Turgenev would later say that Grigorovich's story "The Village" was "the first attempt to bring our literature closer to the life of the people, the first of our 'village tales.'"

Grigorovich's narrator stands above his narrative, though he empathizes with his characters in a general way. A certain self-conscious glance at the reader comes through at times, as in this apostrophe in the midst of "The Village":

> Although the narrator of this tale finds it inexpressibly pleasurable to speak of personages who are enlightened, well educated, and who belong to the highest class of people; and although he is wholly convinced that the reader, too, is incomparably more interested in these than in coarse, dirty and, what's more, stupid peasant men and women, he will pass on, nevertheless, to the latter, since they represent, alas, the main subject of his narrative.

Grigorovich's narrative is fluent and vivid. His plentiful dialogue appears authentic without excessive dialectisms. But then Grigorovich did not really seek any striking effects. His tales contain detailed descriptions of characters (the sketch, for example, of Grigory, Akulina's good-for-nothing husband, in "The Village") and genre scenes (like the rehearsal at a provincial theater in "Kapellmeister Suslikov"). Such passages recall Turgenev, though they lack his plasticity.

Grigorovich covered all the essential genres of the natural school. His physiological sketch, "Peterburgskie sharmanshchiki" ("The Organ-Grinders of St. Petersburg," 1843), subtitled "A Story," became the best-known example of that genre when it first appeared in *A Physiology of St. Petersburg* (1844). "Kapellmeister Suslikov" (1848) is basically a satire on the establishment in provincial Russia, but links the natural school with romanticism in having a talented but unappreciated musician for its hero.

Grigorovich's tales of peasant life paint a sad picture of poverty, ignorance, brutality, and mindless suffering, but contain fewer and more veiled attacks on serfdom than Turgenev's *The Hunting Sketches*. "Derevnia" ("The Village," 1846) tells the story of the orphan Akulina, whose entire life is full of suffering. Even her master's well-meant decision to marry her off adds to her misery, for her husband is a drunken brute who neglects and abuses her. The story ends with Akulina's lonely and unlamented death. The lengthy "Anton Goremyka" (1847) tells of a poor peasant who has fallen behind in his rent payments. He is finally forced to take his only horse to market to obtain the needed money. But on the way there his horse is stolen. In desperation, Anton seeks the help of his brother Ermolay, a thief. Both Ermolay and Anton are arrested and shipped off to prison, and Anton's wailing family remains behind. In "Bobyl'"("The Pauper," 1848), an eighty-year-old wayfarer is taken ill in the village of Marya Petrovna, an elderly landowner. The kind old lady wants to help him with food and medicine, but then it seems he may die very soon. A friend visiting her warns her that she will face no end of trouble if the man dies on her land. So the old man is sent on his way and the next day is found dead in a ditch, not far off, but no longer on Marya Petrovna's land. The good old lady tearfully thanks the Lord for having saved her from great grief.

Altogether, Grigorovich's stories of the 1840s form an important stepping-stone toward Turgenev's and Tolstoy's peasant tales, like the former's "Postoialyi dvor" ("The Roadside Inn," 1855) and the latter's "Polikushka" (1863). The difference between Grigorovich's art and theirs is one of execution, not of design or spirit.

Aleksandr Herzen (1812–70), the first Russian to challenge the autocracy with some success, was a prolific writer, but mostly of nonfiction. In the 1840s, while still in Russia, he published *Kto vinovat?* (*Who Is to Blame?* 1846–47), one of the first explicitly "social" novels in Russian literature, as well as short stories of similar orientation. "Doktor Krupov" (1847) is told in the first person by a physician interested in psychiatry. (Krupov also appears elsewhere in Herzen's fiction, including *Who Is to Blame?*) The first section of "Doctor Krupov" is a fine sketch of the friendship between young Krupov, the son of a village deacon, and Lyovka, the sexton's retarded son. The brutality and lack of understanding Lyovka receives from his father and the community are depicted with sensitivity and tact. "Soroka-vorovka" ("The Thieving Magpie," 1848) is one of the finest antiserfage stories. It is the tragedy of a great actress who also happens to be the serf of a rich landowner in whose theater she plays. When she refuses her owner's persistent advances, her life becomes hell and she dies miserably. Herzen tells his tale with restrained pathos and slow-burning indignation.

The Early Dostoevsky

Fedor Dostoevsky began his career with a series of short works; the unfinished *Netochka Nezvanova* (1848–49) was his first full-fledged novel. However, his two most significant works of the 1840s—*Bednye liudi* and *Dvoinik* (*Poor Folk* and *The Double,* both 1846)— though short are generally regarded as novels. These works, as well as his others of the 1840s, conveniently fit the mold of the natural school, with the exception, perhaps, of "Khoziaika" ("The Landlady," 1847), which has strong romantic elements. All these works are set in contemporary St. Petersburg. Their narrative structure and style are quite varied, but almost all of them, discounting some feuilletonistic trifles, may be reduced to a single formula: Dostoevsky drives a romantic character and/or theme to its ultimate limit by developing it in a setting of St. Petersburg low life.

"Gospodin Prokharchin" ("Mr. Prokharchin," 1846), told by a third-person narrator in the bantering tone characteristic of the natural school, is a travesty of the Pushkinian "covetous knight" motif. Mr. Prokharchin, an elderly, poor, and ignorant copying clerk, has secretly accumulated a quantity of money which he hides in his mattress. Pushkin's covetous knight in the play of the same title hoards his gold to relish the sense of power it gives him in a world where only power counts. Prokharchin hoards his rubles to gain a sense of security in a world where nothing is secure. Both sacrifice everything to their idée fixe, both live to realize how illusory it is; both leave their money behind to be squandered.

"The Landlady" describes the mad infatuation of a young scholar named Ordynov with his beautiful landlady Katerina, the wife of a sinister old man, Murin, who exercises inexplicable power over her. A tale of arson, murder, and incest (Murin may be Katerina's natural father) unfolds before the delirious Ordynov. When he regains his senses, the old man orders him to move out and the young man obeys, his heart and his will to live broken forever. Belinsky rightly said that the story was an odd mixture of Hoffmann and Marlinsky, with some Russian folklore thrown in for good measure. Later on, critics observed that the story resembled Gogol's "A Terrible Vengeance." Though artistically a failure, it contains the seeds of some of Dostoevsky's deepest ideas, such as the Grand Inquisitor theme of *The Brothers Karamazov.* It may also have an allegorical subtext, inspired by the young Dostoevsky's utopian socialist ideas: the evil old man is autocracy, the beautiful young woman is the Russian people, and the young scholar is the revolutionary who seeks to free the people.[13]

"Belye nochi" ("White Nights," 1848) is an anonymous young dreamer's retrospective diary of four summer nights. The dreamer, who has lived all his adult life in a a world of Hoffmann, Walter Scott, and romantic poetry and music, has a chance at real happiness when he meets a charming young girl on one of those enchanting white nights in St. Petersburg. But he lets his chance slip by and, no longer able to dream, faces a meaningless life in a bleak reality. The moral of the story is ambivalent: it could be a regretful adieu to romanticism, or it could also—in view of its intrinsic value as the loveliest of all of Dostoevsky's stories—be the exact opposite, an apotheosis of creative fantasy.[14]

The theme stated in the title of "Slaboe serdtse" ("A Faint Heart," 1848) is a recurrent one in Dostoevsky. The hero, another poor copying clerk, cannot stand the happiness of young love and announced betrothal, and goes out of his mind when he misses an office deadline. The unexpressed thought that it is the cruel bureaucracy that crushes poor Vasya, not any excess of happiness or gratitude, hovers over the text, particularly at its magnificent conclusion: Vasya's friend experiences a ghostly vision of St. Petersburg as a phantasmagoria which may be blown away by a gust of wind from the sea. A post-Freudian reader may be inclined to diagnose Vasya's fear as a latent homosexual attachment to his bearlike friend.

"Chestnyi vor" ("An Honest Thief," 1848) is a framed skaz narrative by a retired soldier, now a tailor. It is a sad story, whose point is that even the most abject derelict is still a human being in whose soul noble feelings may stir.

The young Dostoevsky is clearly experimenting with different styles, viewpoints, and narrative structures. He is responding, directly or indirectly, to the general approach, or to specific works, of Pushkin, Gogol, Hoffmann, George Sand, and others. He has not quite developed his own style. But even so, his short fiction of the 1840s stands head and shoulders above most of what his contemporaries, including his brother Mikhail Dostoevsky, could offer.

Women Writers

In the 1830s there appeared for the first time a sufficient number of women writers to function as a distinct factor in Russian literature.[15] This development occurred for the same reasons behind the ascendancy of prose fiction. There was the example of George Sand and other successful women writers in the West. There was the emergence of a movement for the emancipation of women, with access to education a key issue, which provided a powerful stimulus for literature written from a woman's point of view. With no occupation save that of governess open to educated women, a career as a writer was particularly attractive to them. There was now a steady demand for children's books, and some women writers, such as Aleksandra Ishimova (1806–81), specialized in this field.

The 1830s and 1840s produced no woman prose writer whose works survived very long, with the possible exception of Evgenia Tur (1815–92). Her first stories, "Oshibka" ("A Mistake") and "Plemiannitsa" ("The Niece"), appeared in *Sovremennik* in 1849 and 1850. But there were several women writers who acquired considerable reputations both with the public and with the critics of their time.

Belinsky, in a lengthy review article of 1843 on Elena Gan, while accepting the traditional notions of gender-specific traits in male and female creativity, encouraged Russian women writers to present *their* view of life, society, and morality. He suggested that women writers were relegated to a special compartment of literature, that of innocuous entertainment and maudlin edification. He also noted that Russian women writers were better educated and more literate than many of their male competitors, mostly because women writers were not as yet taking up literature as many men did, "by sheer accident and utterly unprepared," as a means of livelihood. Belinsky then pointed to the shining example of George Sand, who had freed women writers everywhere from the bonds of decorous mediocrity and enabled them to write, as men always could, challengingly, provocatively, advancing new ideas, including ideas of women's rights. In fact, the women writers of Belinsky's age gave greater promise of an emergent feminist literature than following generations realized.

Nadezhda Durova (1783–1866) was known as the "maiden cavalry officer." Disguised as a man, she had served with distinction in the tsar's cavalry from 1806 to 1816. In 1836 she published her memoirs, *Zapiski kavalerist-devitsy* (*Notes of a Maiden Cavalry Officer*). Subsequently she published a novel, *Gudishki* (1839), and a number of short stories, collected in a single volume, *Povesti i rasskazy* (*Tales and Stories*, 1839). Durova's tales are written in the romantic vein of Bestuzhev and Veltman. They usually have intricate plots, feature local color, and are told vigorously though conventionally. Durova's best-known story, "Sernyi kliuch" ("The Sulphur Spring," 1839), is a touching tale of two young lovers: he dies when, armed only with a knife, he challenges a huge bear; she loses her mind from grief. These events are set in a Cheremis village and are given an exotic air by some touches of folklore; but it is more likely that Walter Scott's *The Bride of Lammermoor* inspired the tale than any Cheremis folk tradition.

Maria Zhukova (1804–55) scored a significant success with her two-volume collection *Vechera na Karpovke* (*Evenings on Karpovka,* 1838–39). Her *Povesti* (*Tales* 1840), also in two parts, was well received too: Belinsky bestowed qualified praise on both collections. He thought Zhukova a talented writer and her stories well written, entertaining, and socially useful, though they were not "works of art" (*khudozhestvennye*) by his standards.

Zhukova wrote some historical novellas, and certain of her works are set abroad with non-Russian characters (common in Russian literature during the romantic period); but her favorite personage is the educated, soulful, but unhappy young Russian woman. In "Medal'on" ("The Medallion," 1838) she is a homely, pensive orphan who must live in the shadow of the beautiful natural daughter of her foster parents. As in other works on that theme, Maria is the more deeply talented of the two, but Sofia always wins the prize with her superficial brilliance. In "Samopozhertvovanie" ("The Self-Sacrifice," 1840), Liza, the ward of a rich countess, is in love with Minsky, a distant relative of the countess. As the family is taking the waters at Baden-Baden, the countess is carrying on an affair with a French gentleman. When the count surprises the lovers, Liza has the presence of mind to pretend that it is she, not her benefactress, who is involved in an illicit liaison. The French gentleman is so impressed with Liza's magnanimity (after all, her reputation is ruined) that he asks for her hand. She accepts, but later releases him from his promise and returns to Russia to open a boarding school for young girls.

Zhukova, like George Sand, often digresses from her narrative to discuss social issues, and especially her central thesis: that women are capable people and ought to have a sphere of activity outside the family. Her heroines and other female characters, Belinsky wrote, "are more clever, more loving, and more truthful than her male characters." Zhukova's narrative style also resembles George Sand's: fluent, at times florid, emotional, but rather facile and without much of a personal imprint. The composition of her stories is somewhat amateurish. They are not well focused, and the gaps between exposition, inserted pieces of *Vorgeschichte,* and epilogue are sometimes annoying.

Karolina Pavlova (née Jaenisch, 1807–93), a distinguished poet in Russian, German, and French, married the writer Nikolay Pavlov in 1837 and with him presided over a brilliant literary salon in Moscow. Her society tale "Dvoinaia zhizn'" ("A Double Life," 1848) has a simple and realistic plot. Tsetsilia, a beautiful and pensive young lady, has many suitors. Her well-intentioned mother arranges her marriage to an attractive young man who, while also in love with her, really wants to marry her for her money. As the reader follows the preparations for the wedding, he realizes that Tsetsilia's marriage will be unhappy and she will waste her gifts in an aimless life: the bridegroom, at a boisterous bachelor party, wagers that he will spend a night with the gypsies before he has been married a week. The structure of the story is remarkable in that the heroine's lonely meditations are given in verse, a device well motivated by the theme of a dual life: outwardly a radiant society belle, Tsetsilia has a rich inner life filled with sad forebodings, doubts about the meaning of her existence, and a yearning for higher things. Pavlova's excellent verses are in character with the heroine's feelings; her prose is elegantly fluent, though not very expressive.

Elena Gan (Hahn, née Fadeeva, 1814–42), who published under the pen name Zeneida R——va, met with instant success: some hailed her as the Russian George Sand. Several of her stories—"Ideal" ("The Ideal," 1837), "Sud sveta" ("Society's Judgment," 1840), and "Sud Bozhii ("God's Judgment," 1840)—deal with the author's own plight: intelligent and well educated, she was married to an army officer intellectually very much her inferior and had to live under the stifling conditions of garrison duty in the provinces. Her stories are a call for a woman's right to independent intellectual development and a cry of anguish over the slow death of a woman's mind and soul in a society that has no use for either. As was not always the case in the literature of that day, the heroine remains virtuous, and sexual emancipation is not one of the author's concerns.

Like George Sand, Gan experimented with exotic settings, as in "Utballa" (1838), where she utilized her familiarity with the Kalmyks of the Astrakhan region, or "Teofania Abbiadzhio" ("Teofania Abbiaggio," 1841), set in Italy. Gan shared some of the virtues, but also some of the faults, of the early George Sand. Her sincere emotionality sometimes becomes sentimentality, her fluid style rhetorical, and her sharply drawn characters stereotypes. However, when she speaks of what must have been her own experiences—the officers' wives' reaction to the appearance among them of a real writer who also happens to be the wife of a mere captain ("Society's Judgment"), or her anger at men's callous indifference to a woman's emotions and a woman's ideals ("The Ideal")—her voice rings with genuine pathos.

Avdotya Panaeva (1820–93, who used the pseudonym N. Stanitsky), the legal wife of Ivan Panaev and common-law wife of Nikolay Nekrasov, actively assisted with *Sovremennik.* She began her writing career with a story of nearly a hundred pages, *Semeistvo Tal'nikovykh* (*The Talnikov Family*), printed in an almanac of 1848. The almanac was, however, confiscated by the authorities, largely on account of Panaeva's contribution, which was declared "subversive of parental authority." Panaeva went on to publish several more novels and short stories, as well as important memoirs. *The Talnikov Family* is a family novella describing the events in a growing upper-middle-class family through the eyes of an "ugly duckling" daughter from the age of six to the day of her wedding at seventeen. The picture is a sordid one: a brutal father and an insensitive mother neglect their children, leaving them in the care of a cruel governess, or uncles and aunts who are even worse. The children survive by themselves becoming callous at an early age. The whole story is crassly naturalistic, including descriptions of cruel whippings and the vermin that infest this genteel home. The vivid narrative, though obviously influenced by Dickens, Sue, and others, has the ring of truth.

Countess Evdokya Rostopchina (1811–58), a Moscow socialite, was better known for her poetry and for her plays of the 1850s than for her short stories, though the latter are not significantly inferior to those of Pavlov, Gan, or Zhukova. "Chiny i den'gi" ("Rank and Money," 1838) is an awkwardly structured society tale. In a single long letter, Vadim Svirsky tells his sister that he has fallen in love with Vera, a beautiful Moscow debutante who reciprocates his feelings. But, he continues, her parents will not allow her to marry him because he has neither rank nor fortune. There follows "Fragments from Vadim's Diary," in which he deplores his misfortune, without, however, losing all hope. The diary breaks off with an entry about an unexpected invitation to a party at Vera's and the narrative continues in the words of Svirsky's sister, as can be gathered from the content. It tells of Vera's betrothal to Baron Hochberg, a middle-aged general, Vadim's suicide, and Vera's early death. "Poedinok" ("The Duel," 1838) begins with a physiological sketch of an army officer's life before revealing the guilty secret of its melancholy hero in familiar Byronic fashion. The story the hero finally tells resembles Silvio's in Pushkin's "The Shot," with the difference that this time the other man is killed. An innocent and soulful heroine and a gypsy woman's prophecy of doom are thrown in, the latter in a rather gauche postmortem Vorgeschichte.

This summary by no means exhausts the contribution of women writers to the Russian short story of the 1830s and 1840s. In view of the above-average quality of prose works by women writers during that time (as noted by Belinsky), it would appear to be a mere accident that no Russian Jane Austen or Charlotte Brontë appeared then.

Turgenev

Ivan Turgenev (1818–83) began his literary career as a poet and dramatist, but soon turned to prose fiction. Although he is famous for his novels, he was basically a short-story writer who felt that his novels were essentially novellas. In his early stories Turgenev experimented with various approaches, but in the very first stories of what would become *The Hunting Sketches* he found his peculiar style: a curious episode from real life is perceived through the eyes of an attentive and intelligent, but somewhat melancholy, observer.

"Andrey Kolosov" (1844), Turgenev's first published story, was already vintage Turgenev, a psychological étude of human weakness. The hero and narrator is a sensitive but weak young man, an observer rather than a participant in life. The plot, too, offers a typically Turgenevian anticlimax, The narrator observes his much admired friend Andrey Kolosov court and then abandon Varya, a pretty seventeen-year-old. He resolves to take Kolosov's place, fancying that he will marry Varya and make her happy forever. Instead he too abandons Varya, but in a much more ignoble way than Kolosov.

"Tri portreta" ("Three Portraits," 1846) is a romantic tale of passion and violence, entirely in the manner of Marlinsky, even to the point of utilizing a rather extensive frame. "Zhid" ("The Jew," 1847) also has a Marlinskian flavor, but is remarkable for its theme. The narrator, a young ensign, witnesses the arrest and execution of a Jew caught spying on the Russians besieging Danzig in 1813. The effect of the story is based on the contrast between what the Russian officer perceives as the Jew's grotesque behavior and the human anguish he recognizes in it. "Breter" ("The Bretteur," 1847) clearly derives from *A Hero of Our Time:* Pechorin is changed into an insensitive bully who compensates for his blatant shortcomings in every other respect by physical bravery, while his victim is morally upgraded—the callow Grushnitsky becomes a high-minded youth.

"Petushkov" (1848) is an unsuccessful attempt to capture the Gogolian manner: Petushkov is a variation of Gogol's Ivan Fedorovich Shponka, that nitwit perennial second lieutenant. But much as happens in the young Dostoevsky's variations on Gogolian themes, Turgenev replaces Gogol's humor with a rather unpleasant irony, which makes the tale of Lieutenant Petushkov's ruin through infatuation with a buxom bakery salesgirl rather painful reading

Dnevnik lishnego cheloveka (*The Diary of a Superfluous Man,* 1850) is Turgenev's first successful novella, and a classic of the genre. Cast in the form of a diary, or more precisely a confession (the first entry is made ten days before, the last on the day of the hero's death, as a postscript shows), it delineated once and for all the type of the Russian intellectual who, through his hypersensitivity, morbid self-consciousness, and lack of any meaningful occupation, has lost both his self-respect and his will to live. Turgenev's Chulkaturin is an important step toward Dostoevsky's antihero in *Notes from Underground* (1864). In both works the actual story is preceded by an introduction in which the hero bares his soul and looks back upon his unhappy life.

The story is that of a disastrous love affair in which the hero was involved as a young man. Chulkaturin falls very much in love with a provincial belle and hopes for a moment that he will not be rejected this time. But the lady gives herself instead to a young aristocrat, who promptly jilts her. Chulkaturin gets no credit for having challenged his rival to a duel and his readiness to marry the lady even with a tarnished reputation, and she marries a wretched underling whom even Chulkaturin had not considered a rival.

At this stage in Turgenev's writing, the superfluous quality of his hero is psychological and hardly open to a social interpretation. Chulkaturin cannot find his place in life and is fated always to be an outsider. His penchant for excessive introspection alienates him from the world around him and causes him to equate his own negative image of himself with the world's opinion of him. Clearly, Chulkaturin is no more and no less than a new variant on the alienated romantic hero (Chateaubriand's René, to be specific), placed in a drab naturalistic setting and deprived of all glamor. The development of the Turgenevian superfluous man into a sociohistorical phenomenon would take place only later.

Turgenev's *Zapiski okhotnika* (*The Hunting Sketches*) was published in book form in 1852, but most of the sketches appeared individually in *Sovremennik* between 1847 and 1850. Much later Turgenev added more pieces: "Konets Chertopkhanova" ("Chertopkhanov's Death," 1872), a sequel to the story "Chertopkhanov i Nedopiuskin" ("Chertopkhanov and Nedopiuskin"); the famous "Zhivye moshchi" ("A Living Relic," 1874); and "Stuchit!" ("It's Knocking!" 1874). Most of these works are cast very much in the mold of the natural school. Most are plotless physiological sketches of country life, combined with character sketches of peasants and landowners. The novelty and implied ideological point of the sketches and stories featuring peasants lay in their presentation as individuals encompassing the whole spectrum of human types and characters.

The first and perhaps most famous of the sketches, "Khor' i Kalinych" ("Khor and Kalinych"), paints a vivid picture of Khor's prosperous peasant household. The patriarchal Khor, though illiterate, is very clever, a shrewd businessman, a skeptic with an ironic view of life who knows how to handle people, including his nominal owner (Khor is a serf). Khor's friend, Kalinych, is literate, but poor and shiftless. A romantic dreamer, he prefers hunting and performing odd jobs to any steady work. He is skillful with cattle and bees, and occasionally heals people, too. Kalinych can sing and play the balalaika, and Khor likes to listen to him. Overall, Kalinych is closer to nature, Khor to human affairs.

Another famous story, "Bezhin lug" ("Bezhin Meadow"), describes a night the hunter spends with some peasant boys gathered around a campfire. Several of the boys emerge as sharply drawn individuals. Their conversation and the stories they tell each other reveal a rich world of peasant culture. "Bezhin Meadow," like some other pieces among the *Sketches,* also strikes a fine balance between nature description and narrative. "Kas'ian s Krasivoi Mechi" ("Kasian of Krasivaia Mecha") introduces a peasant eccentric whose free spirit, gentleness, and Franciscan philosophy of life (he upbraids the hunter for killing the forest creatures) put the gentleman hunter to shame. "Pevtsy" ("The Singers") describes a contest between two singers, a foreman and a factory hand, in a country inn: the beauty of Russian folk songs ennobles the contestants and their audience. "Biriuk" ("The Wolf") lets the hunter meet a stalwart gamekeeper who in appearance, demeanor, and character has all the traits of a tragic hero: he lives alone in the forest; the peasant community hates him because he does his job honestly; his life is in constant danger; his wife has left him with two children to care for. This "lone wolf" (so the peasants call him) is also a good man who endures his fate with dignity and without rancor, and the hunter clearly admires him.

Turgenev's landscape descriptions are among the best in the language. His peasant characters are vividly credible precisely because they are observed by a knowledgeable, but unsentimental outsider. In their precision, aptness, and expressiveness, the best of the *Sketches* are unsurpassed masterpieces. Those that deal with landowners (about half the total twenty-five) are less impressive, for the individual landowners are generally neither attractive nor interesting. The most remarkable of these, "Gamlet Shchigrovskogo uezda" ("Hamlet of Shchigry District"), is another variation on the theme of the superfluous man. *The Hunting Sketches* soon gained a reputation as a classic statement against serfdom. However, those stories that pursue a definite moral objective—ordinarily that of branding serfdom as an evil that corrupts master and serf alike—are scarcely superior to similar pieces by Dal, Grigorovich, Grebenka, and others. Such stories include, for example, "Burmistr" ("The Bailiff") and "Dva pomeshchika" ("Two Landowners").

Those few pieces among the *Sketches* that are conventionally plotted short stories—"Petr Petrovich Karataev," say, or "Chertopkhanov and Nedopiuskin"—are not particularly remarkable. Turgenev's original contribution to Russian literature revolves about the slice-of-life vignette that replaces plot development with character study and derives its emotional and structural unity from the presence of the narrator's observant and sympathetic consciousness. Mikhail Gershenzon indeed once wrote that each of the *Sketches* was in fact a projection of Turgenev's melancholy mind on the countryside and people of his home province. Turgenev's manner of projecting a lyric mood through his narrative became established in Russian short fiction, leading directly to the lyricism of Garshin and Chekhov.

Victor Terras

THE RUSSIAN SHORT STORY 1850–1880

An Overview

The critic and man of letters Pavel Annenkov, who spoke of the 1840s as the "remarkable decade," regarded the 1850s as a time of intellectual torpor. The first half of the decade corresponded with the last years of Nicholas I's reign, a time of extreme reaction and literary censorship. Nevertheless, for the history of Russian literature the decade is important because at that time certain artistic methods, with links to changes in the country's social and political life, came to the fore.

The literature of the 1850s may be regarded either as an epilogue to the natural school of the 1840s or as prologue to the new realism of the 1860s. In the 1850s there arose a new esthetic interest in the problem of reality, its functional links with man, and the nature of men itself. Literature began to deal with the confrontation between social norms and human nature, with the notion of the all-encompassing power of the times forming a major motif. The physiological literature of the 1840s had taken up the sensitive subject of the interrelationship between man and milieu: here, however, the protagonist existed in his milieu like a snail in its shell; he lived and breathed in harmony with his environment, represented it by his life, his behavior, his predilections and habits. But in the next decade reality and the individual were gradually polarized into diametrically opposed aesthetic categories, and the process of life was interpreted as the interaction between history and human nature.

Man was no longer conceived of as given, as a finished product. If an author wished to depict negative characters, he had to show how the seeds of goodness within them had been stifled by social conditions. He could no longer offer a daguerrotype of reality but had to reveal the roots of social evil and diagnose the disease itself. It was widely believed that any injury to human nature or denial of natural human needs would inevitably lead to suffering and thence to psychological and social anomalies.

During the romantic period the writer or poet was thought of as a superior being, a prophet or seer; but by the 1850s he was redefined as a "conscientious toiler of thought," as Nikolay Nekrasov put it; even the conservative critic Aleksandr Druzhinin spoke of him as a "noble toiler for the common weal." And now the writer as "intellectual laborer" also had to serve as a teacher or purveyor of information, for intellectuals stressed the idea of art as cognition.

The gradual disintegration of the natural school and the evolution of its principles generated new artistic forms that required a new objectivity and the establishment of a difference between author and hero, between author and the object he depicted. Even the direct heirs of the romantic tradition in Russian literature to a degree deromanticized their work even as they retained elements of romanticism. For example, the romantic idea of the hero as his creator's alter ego was undermined by the new rift between author and personage.

Among the prominent writers of the 1850s Ivan Turgenev was undoubtedly best at transforming the poetics of the physiological sketch, at synthesizing the romantic tradition and the physiological sketch to produce a unique blend of lyricism and idealism clothed in the sober garb of everyday life. The critic Apollon Grigorev rebuked Turgenev for "false idealization" in "Bezhin Meadow," not realizing that the Byronic elements he complained about were quite in harmony with the poetic mood of the *Hunting Sketches.* Time and again Turgenev's comments invoke universal associations to penetrate the circle of specifically peasant and even purely Russian associations in his stories.

This refraction of genre, to use the Soviet scholar Yuri Tynyanov's expression, became the guiding principle of Russian literature from 1850 to 1880. The conventional genres were replaced by hybrid ones; sketches expanded into unified cycles that defy classification; and the genre barriers were broken down even in larger works such as novels.

In the 1850s the image of the teacher became as central to literature as that of the artist in the 1830s or the government clerk in the 1840s. As author, editor, and journalist Ivan Panaev phrased it in 1855, "Russian fiction of the last few years has decided to choose as its hero . . . the teacher. . . . the teacher has become the favorite and inevitable personage of the Russian story in our time." The teacher, who represented the "heroic toil" of educated people, met the test of reality. Even if unrequited love deprived him of the happiness of which he had dreamed, the result was not suicide but moral regeneration and a spiritual explosion for the common good. Werthers were transformed into Don Quixotes.

Many stories of this time are marked by very little plot, concentrating on character analysis instead. A number of them may be termed psychological sketches with an antiromantic thrust: their underlying assumption is that it is not the will of men that guides life, or an accumulation of fatal conditions that destroys life, but rather that men are crippled by false morality and the injustice of social circumstance.

The quest for a new hero was linked to the problem of individual and national self-definition that so occupied Russian minds at that time. That problem incorporated the question of man's responsibility to society, usually framed in terms of a conflict between personal desires and a hostile social force, whether class prejudice or religious and ethical prohibitions.

The authorial presence in the new prose frequently took the form of fictional diaries, memoirs, or autobiographies, of which many examples could be cited. An insistence on authenticity and almost journalistic accuracy contributed to the flowering of the fictional memoir, as in Nikolay Pomyalovsky's *Seminary Sketches* and a number of other works. At times this autobiographical trend led to a narrowing of the gap between narrator and hero, but just as frequently there was a marked difference in point of view between narrator and hero. This division could have semantic significance, since it permitted the author to define the specific moral concepts of the milieu he was describing. That approach was, unsurprisingly, important for satirists such as Mikhail Saltykov-Shchedrin.

The artistic life continued to interest writers in the 1850s. At the center of these depictions is an internal polemic between romantics and realists on the proper relationship of art to life. In some of Turgenev's works a sympathetic appreciation of music may be a defining sign of a positive hero. Dmitry Grigorovich and Aleksandr Druzhinin wrote about painters; Leo Tolstoy and others dealt with musicians.

Another important thread in the newly democratized literature of the period 1850–80 was the depiction of the Russian serf or peasant. Although the muzhik had entered literature in the 1840s, in subsequent years he became rather the intellectual and cultural fashion. Scarcely any number of a serious journal appeared without a story, sketch, scene, or tale of peasant life, and there was hardly a writer who in one way or another did not treat the topic of nationalism as embodied in the peasantry. But where the natural school has been content for the most part with the external depiction of the peasant, Turgenev, Tolstoy, and Pisemsky turned their attention to his psychology, creating strong, original, and authentic peasant heroes. In some of his stories of the early 1850s Turgenev examines universal problems of ethics as exemplified in the experiences of the common people. In "A Landowner's Morning" of 1856, Tolstoy provides detailed descriptions of peasant huts and the half-decayed house and tiny yard of Ivan Churisenko, who nevertheless possesses intelligence and a certain dignity. Through psychological analysis and extended dialogue Tolstoy enables the reader to glimpse the inner life of a muzhik mistrustful of the master, his eternal enemy. Other specialists in the peasant theme, such as Dmitry Grigorovich, now emphasize the Russian peasant's intelligence, energy, and will as a promise of future liberation and development.

In the 1820s and 1830s the word *narodnyi* (national, of the people) was perceived as exotic. By the 1850s it was applied to the average representative of the Russian nation, not just of the peasantry, but also of the merchant class and even the gentry. But the centrality of nationality in the new literature also posed problems for writers. Such authors as Grigorovich and Turgenev even in the 1860s continued to depict the common people in a lyrically poetic manner, but a growing sense of the necessity to approach this theme in a new way engendered a powerful literary movement that left its imprint on the course of Russian literary history in ensuing years.

The 1860s were in general an exciting period in Russian cultural life. The rise of the natural sciences and the appearance of internationally prominent Russian scientists were characteristic of the decade. In music the group of composers known as the Mighty Five, including Modest Musorgsky, Aleksandr Borodin, and Nikolay Rimsky-Korsakov, came to prominence, and in 1863 a group of artists led by Ivan Kramskoy broke away from the artistic establishment and eventually founded an artistic collective called the Wanderers. So too in literature: a whole constellation of young writers appeared who in their own manner reflected the social currents, the ideals, and the disillusionments of that time. They adopted an explicitly utilitarian and didactic view of literature, which led their ideological opponents to denounce them as destroyers of aesthetics, proponents of cynicism, naturalism, or the "theory of ugliness." Nikolay Uspensky laid the groundwork for this school, to be followed by such writers as Nikolay Pomyalovsky, Vasily Sleptsov, Gleb Uspensky, and Fedor Reshetnikov.

Most of these writers were raznochintsy, or members of social classes other than the gentry, and in their writings they mirrored their often tragic personal fates: many suffered from alcoholism or insanity and many died young, sometimes by suicide or violence.

In the hands of the generation of the 1860s the sentimental maxim of the 1840s "you are my brother" was transformed into a cynical "dog eat dog" approach. The humor of the 1840s became satire, the comic, tragic. Moreover, the new writers were acutely aware of the gap between their literary views and their predecessors', and frequently had biting remarks to make on the subject.

Although the "democratic" writers of the 1860s and 1870s could not match such giants as Tolstoy, Dostoevsky, and Turgenev, they made many artistic contributions to critical realism. Despite their individual differences, these writers saw themselves not only as artists but also as combatants in the struggle for enlightenment. They believed that in itself the creation of artistic images was insufficient: they had to go on to interpret the significance of those images and comment on what they were showing the reader. Consequently their descriptive prose slipped readily into pure journalism. Today's reader must remember that these writers consciously rejected traditional aesthetics in order to follow a program of describing the new man—frequently drawn from peasants and workers—and his relationship to the old world, and to pioneer innovative prose forms for the presentation of unusual material.

Nikolay Uspensky, for instance, radically challenged the idealization of the peasantry that had been so prevalent in the 1850s: he mocked their intellectual passivity and their superstitions. The artistic means by which he depicted this monotonous world were also scanty: there is a predominant grayness in his work. And this was a tradition followed by the other democratic writers who came after him.

The most widespread form among the new writers consisted of brief sketches made up of minute and disparate scenes and descriptions. Plot recedes into the background, for the pronouncing of judgment is the author's chief purpose even though that judgment may remain implicit. Still, the presentation of the material is dramatic, and the reader has little difficulty in discerning the author's views.

Saltykov-Shchedrin considered the struggle for existence to be the paramount topic of contemporary literature, and this was indeed the basis for the plot in many works of the time. Pomyalovsky examined the social and psychological effects of this struggle upon gifted plebeians: he was the first to observe that the natural yearning of the lower classes for security was transformed into a fanatical rejection of anything that disturbed the status quo once they had attained their goal.

The social disintegration of the period after the Emancipation of the serfs by Tsar Alexander II in 1861 was also reflected in contemporary fiction. A hero may frequently be forced to break with his environment or voluntarily reject the traditions of his class and family. A member of the gentry may wish to live by his own labor and in effect become a peasant; peasants may leave their villages to become workers in the cities, on railroads and rivers, or in the gold mines.

The 1870s witnessed new social unrest in the form of a powerful movement among the intelligentsia called "going to the people." However, idealistic students and teachers who streamed into the villages for the purpose of bringing enlightenment to the masses met with ignominious defeat: the peasants themselves turned many of them over to the authorities. Still, this "populist" movement had its impact on literature: indeed in 1876 Dostoevsky termed it "the most important problem" of the day. While the populist writers continued to investigate the peasantry as a class, the real problem was that of land ownership, which in turn led to the question of the uniqueness of Russia's historical path and the Russian national character. The debate was not limited to peasant collectives but spread to encompass the national sources of Russian social organization generally in contrast with the developed societies of Western Europe.

As we have seen, the new genre of the 1860s was something between sketch and short story, a collage of pictures, fragments, with no real plot line, and often with subtitles reflecting their character ("Types and Scenes of a Village Fair" or "Scenes at a Police Precinct"). Having become entrenched in prose literature, the new genre could evolve into cycles under the umbrella of thematic unity. Mikhail Saltykov-Shchedrin and Gleb Uspensky justified their writing of sketch cycles by arguing that the classical genres of the short story and the novel had become obsolete or, at least, could not depict the numerous nuances of a social order in violent flux. Saltykov claimed that his search for more flexible forms untied his hands and brought him into more direct contact with his reader. His formulation was important for the writers of the 1870s, when democratic fiction acquired programmatic significance for the masses and the progressive intellectuals. Documentary sketches picturing various phenomena of daily life and different types and characteristics developed into broad epic canvases of contemporary reality. Thus the sketch contributed to the rejuvenation of the traditional fictional genres: the short story and the novel. This process is seen especially clearly in the fiction of writers who began their careers in the 1870s, for example, Vsevolod Garshin or Dmitry Mamin-Sibiryak.

The flexibility of the sketch, moreover, allowed it to incorporate extraliterary components, such as the greater role of the subtext, which places greater demands on the reader. The structural principle of cycles is the authorial point of view, sufficiently defined to form an inner axis on which episodes may be threaded. The authorial conception thus determined the stability of the narrative structure and could lead to the contraction of disparate sketches and episodes into a single story.

On the other hand, while such a cycle could easily grow, it could just as painlessly contract by losing episodes. Saltykov perceived this weakness in the novel-cycles of Fedor Reshetnikov and Pavel Melnikov (Andrey Pechersky). Indeed, in editing Reshetnikov's works he omitted episodes and even whole sections in the conviction that this would strengthen the structure.

To an extent these innovations that broke down the conventional structure of the short story served as a fruitful point of departure for Chekhov and Gorky: they enriched the form with new possibilities. Moreover, their open tendentiousness altered the traditional role of the narrator. The author could now emerge from behind the mask of a persona to assert his position at the structural center of the narrative.

Such is the legacy of the short story of this period to the further development of the Russian short story.

Grigorovich, Pisemsky, and Potekhin

Dmitry Grigorovich (1822–99), who began his career in the 1840s, continued to publish in the 1850s. The blueprint he developed for his stories provides the reader sentimental enjoyment without bothersome questions. Images of neat poverty are juxtaposed to pictures of heartless wealth. The nobility, moral purity, patience, and meekness of the impoverished are generally rewarded. In "Svetloe Khristovo voskresenie" ("On Easter Day," 1851) a plowman named Andrey unexpectedly acquires money, and his idyllic love for a peasant girl ends well. "Zimnii vecher" ("A Winter Evening," 1854) follows the traditions of the

Christmas story: a desperately poor family of street musicians obtains sudden prosperity by taking in an abandoned child. A beggar in "Prokhozhii" ("The Passerby") is lost in a snowstorm. When the unfeeling rich turn him away, Aleksey and his old mother give him refuge in their poor but clean hut, and in gratitude the dying beggar gives them a thousand rubles.

The predictability of Grigorovich's plots is made more bearable by the rich folklore material he inserts into them, including descriptions of various folk rites and church holidays. Colorful ethnographic material and vivid lyric landscapes also enhance the narrative. Grigorovich's landscape depictions are surprisingly factual and yet majestic. At the center of these pictures is the peasant, sculpted out of bronze and illuminated with the special light of authorial love.

"Pakhar'" ("The Plowman," 1856) ends an especially idyllic stage in Grigorovich's literary career. The gigantic image of the young plowman Savely and the iconlike description of his old father, whose saintly death is at the story's center, are imbued with lyricism and a sense of man's organic link with nature.

Although Grigorovich's stories of subsequent years—for example, "Koshka i myshka" ("Cat and Mouse," 1857) and "Pakhatnik i barkhatnik" ("The Plowman and the Man in Velvet," 1859)—use similar themes but discuss the inhumanity of serfdom more explicitly. Now Grigorovich contrasts not only specific images of the poor and the rich but classes as such: workers and idlers, or peasants and predators (the mice and the cats). Belinsky had commented that in "Anton Goremyka" Grigorovich had not really described the landowner as a type or a specific character, but simply as the author of events that befall the peasant. As if in response to this criticism, in "The Plowman and the Man in Velvet" Grigorovich describes, not just one peasant protagonist, but an entire village of peasants who express their views in open debate. Unlike Anton, they will not suffer and perish in silence.

Beginning in the early 1850s, Aleksey Pisemsky (1821–81) wrote stories about the lower classes. His *Ocherki iz krest'ianskogo byta* (*Sketches from Peasant Life,* 1856) shows a different side of their life. Pisemsky demonstrates that evil comes not only from landowners but also from the injustices wrought by the village collective council and the passions of the peasants themselves. Unlike Turgenev's narrator in *The Hunting Sketches,* who only observes without interfering actively, Pisemsky's narrator "interviews" his characters to discover what is really occurring. Since almost all the stories culminate with a crime and a catastrophe and Pisemsky's narrator is a district police officer, his duties hinge upon his investigations in a very natural way.

The *Sketches* are made up of three stories published earlier: "Pitershchik" ("The Petersburger," 1852), "Leshii" ("The Wood Demon," 1853), and "Plotnich'ia artel'" ("The Carpenters' Guild," 1855). In "The Petersburger" a rich married serf who represents himself to be a merchant "buys" a young gentry lady from her aunt. He lives with her, loses all his money, and is forced to return to the village. He is subject to the same passions that rule other peasants and indeed all other classes. "The Wood Demon" describes the kidnapping of a peasant girl by an estate manager who exploits her superstitions by pretending to be a wood demon and thereby forcing her into cohabitation. His crimes are exposed by the police officer. "The Carpenters' Guild" reads like a Russian *Phèdre.* Petr describes his stepmother's passion for him and her attempts to take vengeance on him and his wife for his moral integrity. For such behavior the stepmother is punished by a whipping and exiled. The second part of the story recounts Petr's involuntary murder of another peasant, ending with his arrest.

"Starcheskii grekh" ("An Old Man's Sin," 1861) describes a poor clerk who rises in the bureaucracy by his impeccable conduct. However, his infatuation for an adventuress drives him to embezzlement, and in the end he commits suicide. In "Bat'ka" ("Dad," 1861) a rich peasant tries to seduce his daughter-in-law and harasses his own son by setting fire to his own house, denouncing his son, and then having both him and his wife arrested, abused, and imprisoned. The father's machinations, however, are exposed in the end.

There is a great deal of ethnographic material in the short stories of Aleksey Potekhin (1839–1908): the genuineness of his familiarity with the milieu he describes comes through very clearly. His language is vivid and conversational. He certainly idealizes peasant life in his depictions (there are no contradictions in his rural paradise, where total harmony reigns), and thus it is not difficult to regard his stories as apologia for the peasant commune as a social institution. His well-known story "Tit Sofronovich Kozanok" (1852) depicts the descendants of a pious and industrious beekeeper, who prove to be morally much inferior to their ancestor. In "Burmistr" ("The Burgermaster," 1859), the excesses of the landowner's evil valet and housekeeper bring an honest and hardworking peasant family to the verge of ruin. On the other hand, the burgermaster is not only rich but generous, and persuaded that man is given money in order to share it with the poor.

Thus he gives a drunkard blacksmith a new smithy to replace his old one, which has burned down, and is even prepared to send his own son into the army instead of replacing him with someone else's son. Social contradictions are smoothed over in Potekhin's idyllic works: one literary historian called his writing a "mixed salad of contemporary morality."

Turgenev

Although known primarily in world literature for his novels, Ivan Turgenev (1818–83) made immense contributions to the short-story genre, developing a remarkable range of themes and characters in his shorter works. In an era dominated by militantly progressive literature, Turgenev's stories convey a complex sense of fatalism, faith in an ideal, and his unceasing quest for a positive hero or heroine. His lyrical prose includes magnificent landscape descriptions of the sort ordinarily found in poetry. Turgenev is a master of intense psychological analysis, blending the psychological realities of human nature with a poetic mood. For all the realistic trimmings of his stories, Turgenev was very much the heir of the romantic tradition in his day.

The 1850s saw the publication of many of Turgenev's finest short stories, including a number dealing with the peasant theme. In "Mumu" (1852) a giant deaf-mute serf named Gerasim finds an abandoned puppy named Mumu who becomes his only friend. One night Mumu's barking awakens Gerasim's owner, a capricious old lady, and she orders the dog destroyed. Gerasim obediently drowns the dog, but then returns to his village to live out his lonely life, the possessor of enormous strength and incomprehensible meekness. In "Postoialyi dvor" ("The Inn," 1852) an inn owner named Akim is betrayed by his wife and her lover and ultimately loses all his possessions as well. Although tormented by dreams of vengeance, Akim finally accepts his fate and departs to become a traditional Russian holy wanderer.

Turgenev's peasant heroes no longer resemble the wretched serfs of the past: they have the strength of will to determine their own fate. The poetry of self-abnegation is best seen in Akim, whose acceptance of his lot manifests his tremendous spiritual strength. In some ways the Akim who conquers his anger is more fearsome than Akim the arsonist: he is no less a giant than the deaf-mute Gerasim.

One of Turgenev's favorite themes—that of fatal passion in conflict with reason or duty—emerges in such works as "Faust" (1856). Turgenev expresses his tragic view of the world with special force in this work, which describes the way in which the narrator arouses the emotions of a young married woman by introducing her to literature. Stimulated by their reading of *Faust,* the heroine sets out for a tryst with the narrator, only to find her way barred by the ghost of her mother, who has always shielded her from powerful emotions. The heroine falls ill and dies, while the inconsolable hero is left with the realization that he is responsible for her destruction. The story thus sets out Turgenev's philosophy of the inevitable punishment for human happiness, a view that contrasted starkly with the morality of rational egoism advanced by the radical thinker Nikolay Chernyshevsky and the new men who would become so prominent in the 1860s.

Turgenev's lyrically elegiac voice comes through forcefully in "Zatish'e" ("A Quiet Spot," 1854), "Perepiska" ("A Correspondence," 1854), and "Yakov Pasynkov" (1855). In "A Correspondence" the young woman who authors half the correspondence confesses to a male friend that she has rejected her family's expectations for her: she will not have a conventional marriage, but rather will seek a full emotional and intellectual life. The young man, moved, declares his intention to return from abroad so that they may be joined, but then he is silent for a year. His last letter, written from his deathbed, tells of his destruction through his desperate passion for a dancer. In "Yakov Pasynkov" the narrator—who ironically dubs himself "superannuated"—voices his nostalgic enthusiasm upon meeting his old friend Yakov Pasynkov, the last romantic. Unlike the narrator, Pasynkov has lived his life nobly: true to his ideals and his only love, he dies with a vision of heaven.

In his short stories as well as his novels Turgenev sought a positive hero who could define his own place in the world. In "A Quiet Spot" and "Asya" (1858) that hero turns out to be a woman. In the first story a strong, passionate young woman is contrasted to the intelligent and talented young man she loves: he suffers from a tragic flaw in lack of will, practical intelligence, and purpose. In the end the heroine commits suicide and the hero becomes an alcoholic. In "Asya" the "reflective" Hamlet-like hero inexcusably loses his chance for happiness with Asya, an uninhibitedly innocent young woman who is strong enough to avow her love for him spontaneously. The appearance of "Asya" provided the occasion for a famous response by Chernyshevsky, in which the critic congratulated Asya on having avoided a union with a man unworthy of her and blamed the social system for creating a flabby and emotionally bankrupt male capable only of analyzing himself and not of taking any decisive action.

"Pervaia liubov'" ("First Love," 1860) beautifully portrays the first birth of passion in this narrative of a sixteen-year-old who falls in love, for the first time in his life, with the beautiful Zinaida, only to discover finally that Zinaida and his own father are engaged in an adulterous affair. One of the most poignant scenes in all of Turgenev's fiction is that in which the adolescent Vladimir sees Zinaida slowly kissing the red welt her lover's crop has raised on her arm, and begins to understand something of the intensity of passion. The story ends with the father's sudden death and the unmotivated death of Zinaida a few years later. While the death of both lovers symbolizes Turgenev's mature belief in the impossibility of personal happiness in love, the adolescent narrator's freshness moves in a unique atmosphere of charm, suspense, and mystery.

Turgenev's ingrained pessimism emerges explicitly in such stories of the 1860s as "Prizraki" ("Phantoms," 1864) and "Dovol'no" ("Enough," 1865). The first is a fantasy in which the narrator is transported through the air by a phantom figure named Ellis: together they visit ancient Rome to see Julius Caesar; they witness the wild hordes of the seventeenth-century Russian rebel leader Stepan Razin; and they survey contemporary Paris and St. Petersburg. Wherever he is, the narrator experiences only horror and disgust, and after every flight feels physically weaker. On their last flight they confront a monstrous figure that turns out to be death itself. Apparently vanquished by death, Ellis disappears into nothingness, and the narrator feels his own end approaching.

"Enough" is an even more eclectic collage of meditations, memories, and scenes. All these disparate elements, however, are imbued with the same nostalgic sadness, and at the end the narrator finally rejects every human ideal: art, beauty, love, freedom, justice.

Instead of depicting well-formed characters, Turgenev portrays instability and variability as elements of individual psychology: at any moment a person may be quite different from what he was just a short time before. What is a person's genuine self? Beneath a veil of external contentment the human heart conceals stormy passions and powerful struggles. Some of Turgenev's stories from the last period of his life—"Neschastnaia" ("The Unfortunate Girl," 1869), "Stepnoi Korol' Lir" ("King Lear of the Steppes," 1870), "Veshnie vody" ("The Torrents of Spring," 1872)—explore this problem. "The Unfortunate Girl" exhibits Dostoevskian resonances. The heroine, Susanna, not only finds herself in much the same situation as Nastasya Filipovna from *The Idiot* but also suffers from the same sort of wounded pride as she. Susanna is in effect Nastasya Filipovna while still under Totsky's tutelage. The illegitimate daughter of a rich landowner and a Jewess, Turgenev's heroine lives with her mother in the same house as her father, but without ever being acknowledged as his, which damages her psychologically. After the father's death his brother inherits the estate. Susanna and the new owner's son fall in love with each other but are brutally separated; Susanna eventually kills herself. A rebellious, spontaneous nature, always in the throes of hidden passions, Susanna's emotional intensity accompanies her on every page and at the end spills over into her suicide. But that outcome is inescapable: the narrator long before noted the spiritual torment constantly expressed on Susanna's face.

The character of the small landowner Kharlov ("King Lear of the Steppes") is equally tempestuous. This noble man foolishly deeds his small estate to his two daughters, only to find himself then entirely in their power. When he can no longer stand their cruelty he destroys with his bare hands the house in which he used to live and dies in its wreckage. Unpredictably meek despite his great size, and equally unpredictably violent, this ordinary Russian is at the same time an exceptional man.

Sanin, the hero of "Torrents of Spring," is violently attracted in turn by two heroines who are absolute opposites. Gemma represents purity, spiritual nobility, and elegance, while Maria Nikolaevna embodies will and passionate sensuality. The former offers Sanin the dream of family joy; the latter—that beautiful "serpent"—destroys all his hopes quite pitilessly. Sanin chooses Lilith over Eve, and the dark power of erotic passion compels him to become lover and lackey. In this work the woman is the predator and the man the victim.

Toward the end of Turgenev's life the romanticism that had always been part of his character emerged with new force in a series of supernatural stories. "Stuk . . . stuk . . . stuk" ("Knock, Knock, Knock," 1871), "Son" ("The Dream," 1877), "Pesn' torzhestvuiushchei liubvi" ("Song of Triumphant Love," 1881) and "Klara Milich" (1883) illustrate his ambivalent attitude toward the supernatural.

Initially Teglev, the hero of "Knock, Knock, Knock," seems a mere parody of a Marlinskian romantic. Though he appears a perfectly ordinary man except for his small green eyes with yellow eyelashes and his expression of inner sadness and arrogance, he believes that he is a "fatal" character and finally follows his destiny to suicide. Despite the realistic explanations the author provides for the series of events leading to his death, the reader still feels the sense of doom that hovers over Teglev.

That same sense of the supernatural is present in "Klara Milich," whose hero, Aratov, expects something fateful even before he learns of the suicide of Klara, who had earlier declared her love for him. Haunted by what he believes is Klara's ghost, he does not know how to react to realistic explanations of his visions. When he is discovered dead with a lock of Klara's hair in his hand, we learn that Aratov had been given Klara's diary and that the lock could very well have been left in it by Klara's sister when she gave it to him. But there is a blissful smile on his face after his death.

"The Dream" is a highly stylized work, with its mysterious villain and his silent Arab servant, strange meetings, prophetic dreams, the interplay of shadows, light and darkness, good and evil. The narrator, the story's hero, is drawn into a whirlpool of horror by investigating his mother's past. Is the mysterious baron really his father? Is he dead at the end? How much of what occurs is a figment of the boy's imagination, how much due to the inexplicable power of fate? Turgenev gives no answer in this tale, which is an unusual one for him.

Only in "The Song of Triumphant Love" does Turgenev deal openly and explicitly with magic and the supernatural. Set in seventeenth-century Italy, the work describes the enigmatic force drawing Fabius's wife, Valeria, to his friend Mutsii. With the assistance of his Malaysian servant Mutsii performs incantations to hypnotize the innocent Valeria and evidently lead to her seduction. The jealous husband kills Mutsii, but Mutsii's servant apparently resurrects him. After the two depart, the young wife senses the presence of new life within her as her fingers involuntarily play on an organ the same song Mutsii had previously performed on a strange Indian violin encased in blue snakeskin.

Tolstoy

In his first published work, *Detstvo* (*Childhood,* 1852), Leo Tolstoy (1828–1910) demonstrated that his approach to literary genres was iconoclastic. Although *Childhood* cannot be considered in any sense a short story, it was of considerable importance in indicating the future development of Tolstoy's writing. The child in this piece is no ordinary small boy: from the beginning he seeks to interpret what he sees, to judge people's relationships as well as his own actions and thoughts. As for literary method, as Nikolay Chernyshevsky noted at the time, Tolstoy was not content "with the depiction of the results of the psychological process—he is interested in the process itself and the barely perceived manifestations of this inner life, constantly changing with great rapidity and inexhaustible variety." Thus Tolstoy developed from the first the method of the interior monologue, which would serve to present the deepest and most tragic feelings and thoughts of his future heroes, as well as reflect his yearning to resolve the problem of life and death within the soul of a single individual. Finally, Tolstoy looked to the Russian peasant as the repository of much that is good in mankind, the exemplar of his major ethical principle: living for others. The only person the narrator of *Childhood* trusts implicitly is Natalya Savishna, who embodies modesty, truthfulness, and simplicity. Though silent and meek, Natalya Savishna is no submissive slave or martyr. She has her own philosophy of life, her own moral code, partly developed on her own but partly elaborated by generations of peasants who have undergone the same sufferings she has. She is one of the chief moral influences on the spiritual evolution of the young nobleman depicted in *Childhood.*

"Utro pomeshchika" ("A Landowner's Morning," 1856) developed out of an unrealized plan of Tolstoy's for a novel designed to portray an estate owner dedicated to improving the living conditions of his serfs. It tells the story of a young prince, Nekhlyudov, who, believing that the essence of life lies in "doing good," seeks to eradicate the poverty of his peasants through work and patience. The peasants, however, reject all the suggestions he makes for the betterment of their lot, until finally he understands that they do not trust him at all. For example, when he offers a new cottage in a nearby area to a peasant whose hut is on the point of collapse, the entire family pleads with him to remain where they are. When he visits a second peasant to help him straighten out his affairs, he realizes he is being lied to; he sees that a third peasant is simply lazy. Finally he realizes he can do nothing in the face of their distrust. The interests of peasant and master are too divergent, and Nekhlyudov cannot overcome the barriers between the two classes.

Tolstoy's military service provided the material for his stories of the Caucasus and the Crimean War. "Nabeg" ("The Raid," 1853) and "Rubka lesa" ("The Wood Felling," 1855) handle the well-established theme of the Caucasus in Russian literature in a peculiar way. Pushkin and Lermontov had celebrated the beauty of the Caucasus and its people; it was a central topic of romanticism generally; and in some forms it has survived down to the present day. The Caucasian literary stereotypes included dashing, fearless natives surrounded by beautiful nature. This literature portrayed war as a lofty spectacle of courage and heroic deeds, and men's emotions as stormy, unrestrained passions. In Tolstoy's stories, though, the romantic natives become Georgian peasants trying to defend their homes against the enemy; the dashing officers become ordinary Russian soldiers who do not know why they are fighting and are compelled to wage a destructive war without feeling any hostility toward the Georgians. In addition to deromanticizing the Caucasus and war, Tolstoy examines bravery as well. For Tolstoy the romantic traits of courage and virility are only facets of the integrated character of a Russian: more important features are a sense of naturalness, duty, and comradeship, along with a consciousness of unity with one's people.

The Tolstoyan hero is the soldier or simple officer who shares the life of his men. In "The Raid" Captain Khlopov, unlike the stereotyped Marlinskian officer, is not proud or snobbish, but in a moment of danger "behaves as he should," along with his soldiers. Thus in the narrator's eyes he becomes the embodiment of "genuineness and simplicity." Courage is discovered in the deeds of battle, not in words. It is Captain Khlopov and the modest Trosenko from "The Wood Felling" who are truly brave, not Lieutenant Rosenkrants ("The Raid") or Captain Kraft ("The Wood Felling"), devotees of big words and juvenile recklessness. Khlopov and Trosenko merely do their duty as soldiers. Indeed Khlopov admits he is serving in the Caucasus for double pay.

The Crimean War of 1853–55 between France, England, and Russia provided Tolstoy with material for a fine cycle comprising three stories: "Sevastopol' v dekabre mesiatse" ("Sebastopol in December"); "Sevastopol' v mae" ("Sebastopol in May"); and "Sevastopol' v avguste 1855 goda" ("Sebastopol in August of 1855") (1855–56). The axis of the cycle is people and war: war as a cruel and ugly business is the leitmotiv of each story, though it is varied in each one.

In "Sebastopol in December" the theme of national heroism is presented in a generalized way. None of the characters has either a name or a biography, but together they embody the heroic spirit of Sebastopol. In order to convey the emotional impact of the siege, Tolstoy utilizes the device of transforming the reader into his companion, whom he then accompanies and on whose reactions he comments. The narrative thus seems to emanate from the reader, who, when he arrives in the town, is astonished at how false his ideas have been and begins to understand how things really are. The narrator ultimately interprets the significance of what the reader sees, generalizes on the basis of the reader's experiences, and then presents his conclusions. But the heroes of the siege are the simple people of Russia. The narrative consists of small sketches, each of which freezes a moment in time and space, but the work is not at all static: the vignettes are presented like a panorama unrolling before the observer's eyes, and thus an illusion of motion is created.

In Tolstoy's world the touchstone of genuineness is his characters' responses to the national war effort. In "Sebastopol in May" he compares various personages. Many officers from the aristocracy are motivated by the prospect of medals and personal advancement, whereas the soldiers fight for their fatherland. Of all the officers, Captain Mikhaylov is the most positive. Now Tolstoy's people have names and characteristics; Sebastopol is populated by individuals with their own psychological complexities. The plot deals with a cliché of war literature: one's response at the moment of greatest danger in battle. By Tolstoy's logic, nothing is as we are led to believe it is: Praskukhin, who thinks he has escaped, is killed; Mikhaylov, who believes he is dying, gets off with a concussion.

The third Sebastopol story is a more concentrated narrative about two brothers. The elder, an experienced officer, simply does his duty, and dies a hero's death at the end; the younger, richly endowed with imagination and ambitions, grows morally to emerge a more mature person. In this story Tolstoy also employs the device of "making strange," or depicting what should be familiar as odd and unfamiliar. By presenting horrible details, he destroys the romanticism of war. In "The Wood Felling" the sight of Velenchuk's naked, white, healthy leg affects the narrator especially strongly: clearly Velenchuk has been mortally wounded, as his shrunken face and pallor attest, and the white leg serves as the symbol of a dead object.

In the latter 1850s and the early 1860s Tolstoy turned from psychological analysis to address ethics and aesthetics. The writer himself defined the form of the tales he wrote now when he said that a story is a work describing only one event and tracing only one idea. That one idea clearly evolves out of the narrative, and sometimes it is given at the end as a sort of authorial conclusion. Thus "Lucerne" (1857) ends with an explicit philosophical and social disquisition evoked by the simplest of stories: an itinerant musician and singer arrives in the beautiful resort city of Lucerne and endures contempt from both the rich tourists and the hotel servants, none of whom appreciates his spontaneous, delicate art.

"Dva gusara" ("Two Hussars," 1856) and "Tri smerti" ("Three Deaths," 1859) in their structure resemble parables giving direct and unadorned expression to an idea that eventually can be expressed almost in the form of an aphorism. Many years later Tolstoy would revert to this type of "philosophical tale" in writing stories for ordinary people. "Two Hussars" investigates the differing values of two generations. The father, though far from an ideal character, is a dashing and wealthy count who exhibits generosity and nobility in his dealings with women and friends. But his son, who arrives in the same town twenty years later, is a poor replacement for his father. Though as charming as the older count, he entirely lacks his father's extravagant spirit and good heart: indeed he turns out to be a spiritually petty egotist who tries to take advantage of a young girl. The story needs no interpretation: the contrast between old-fashioned morality and modern pettiness is stark.

"Three Deaths" is even more dogmatic in its outlook than "Two Hussars." Tolstoy artificially compares the acceptance of death by a rich lady, a peasant, and a tree. The lady is dying of consumption, and because she fears death so greatly she accepts the lies of her husband and her doctor even though she realizes they are lies. A peasant, lying mortally ill in a hut at the same time, dies in peace because he accepts death as calmly as he has life. And the tree falls quietly when it is cut down to provide a cross for the peasant's grave. The contrast between these three deaths is so blunt as to detract from what small aesthetic satisfaction may be derived from the story.

"Albert" (1858), though it has no real plot, is a more sophisticated philosophical and psychological story about an impoverished alcoholic musician whom the wealthy Delesov wants to "save" by caring for him. Ultimately Albert flees the unbearable restrictions Delesov's charity imposes upon him. In one sense "Albert" stems from the tradition of the popular artist story dating back to the 1840s, for Albert has links with the poor genius unappreciated by society and doomed to failure. But on the other hand Albert is not destroyed by inhumane treatment, and his sufferings do not constitute the work's chief subject. "Albert" deals instead with the question of art, reflecting the aesthetic discussions of those years. The work has to do not with an artist and his unsuccessful career but with a man who lives outside contemporary society's laws. Albert reacts to Delesov's attempts to improve his situation with active hostility. He wants only to make music before an audience of one or many, masters or servants. He worships Mozart and Beethoven, but he also loves Strauss's lighter music and plays a Russian folk song for the servants with great inspiration. Albert cares nothing for practical considerations or for social barriers: he is equally friendly toward Delesov and toward his valet. Both master and servant consider Albert pitifully weak, but he serves and loves only one thing—beauty. In this story Tolstoy deals with the special meaning of beauty, with the special relationship that develops among people when they experience true art, and with those feelings that are inseparable from true art—namely, goodness, brotherhood, and faith in man's power to overcome evil.

Tolstoy also dealt with the contemporary issue of the treatment of women in ways that were both polemical and original, as we would expect. The problems of a woman's position in her family and of her right to independence are taken up from a feminine perspective in "Semeinoe schast'e" ("Family Happiness," 1859).

The story's rather ordinary plot revolves around a seventeen-year-old girl, Masha, whose parents are dead, and her guardian Sergey, a man of thirty-six. What begins as friendship ends in marriage, despite Sergey's misgivings about the difference in their ages. The reader follows their developing closeness, succeeded by quarrels in which Masha complains that Sergey treats her like a child. They move to St. Petersburg, where they begin to grow apart as Masha becomes involved in society life; finally they go abroad. When eventually they return to their country estate, she feels that their intimacy is now a burden to her husband and blames him for having allowed her excessive freedom when she was too young to use it properly. At the end she perceives that their life together has entered a new phase: "My love affair with my husband was over . . . and a new feeling of love for the children and the father of my children laid the foundation for another, totally different, happy life which I have not yet lived to the full."

"Family Happiness" exposes family relations as a process involving the appearance and resolution of contradictions, a kind of curve of psychological states and relationships between people who experience those states. Tolstoy believes that no one discrete stage in the relationship is crucial: only the development of the relationship in its totality can be evaluated as happy or unhappy.

"Kazaki" ("The Cossacks," 1863) presents the further development and deconstruction of the romantic Caucasus theme, including the hero in love with a native girl. The title itself stresses the link with romantic thematics, but Tolstoy stands the traditional plot of the European among natives on its head: it is the Russian who appears comical by contrast with the spontaneous, freedom-loving cossacks.

In a later story, however, "Kavkazskii plennik" ("The Prisoner of the Caucasus," 1872), Tolstoy not only attacks this well-known romantic locale but also recasts Pushkin's famous narrative poem of the same name. Tolstoy's response to the demand for the creation of a "new man" advanced in the 1860s was the portrayal of the modest Zhilin in a children's story written in simple colloquial language. Unlike romantic heroes who suffered and caused others to suffer, Zhilin is simple, strong, and wholesome. A good horseman and marksman, he is strong enough to withstand cruel treatment, cunning enough to deceive his captors, and compassionate enough to risk his life for a man who has betrayed him. Zhilin is a living rebuttal of the romantic stereotypes.

Tolstoy describes Zhilin's capture, unsuccessful escape attempt, and final successful flight in simple terms and without national prejudice: Zhilin respects the customs of others and finds a common language with both women and children. Moreover, Tolstoy substitutes the theme of brotherhood and friendship for the traditional love story. He introduces, instead of a beautiful native girl in love with the prisoner, a small girl, Dina, who responds to Zhilin's kindness with devotion and helps him escape despite the fact that he is her people's enemy.

Tolstoy returns to the peasant theme in "Polikushka" (1863), describing an irresponsible drunkard and occasional thief. Polikushka sincerely repents after each of his offenses, and his owner, a rich lady, is touched by his humility. One day she decides to test his honesty by trusting him to bring some money from town. Overwhelmed by such trust, Polikushka resists drinking when he receives the money and hides it in his hat. But on the way home he falls asleep in the cart and loses the hat. He hangs himself in despair, and when his wife discovers what has happened she forgets her baby, who drowns in the bathtub. Thus in this story the author illustrates (as Turgenev did in "Mumu") the complex contradictions in the soul of the poorest serf. His perception of events constitutes the story's psychological content and engenders an intensely dramatic denouement.

Dostoevsky

Dostoevsky's prose of the later 1850s—"Malen'kii geroi" ("The Little Hero," 1857) and "Diadiushkin son" ("Uncle's Dream," 1859)—

provides curious examples of the way one genre can be redefined as another.

"The Little Hero," originally planned as a tale entitled "Detskaia skazka" ("A Child's Fairy Tale"), was reworked and given the subtitle "From Unknown Memoirs." The narrative is organized vividly and rapidly: the events of the plot develop in two days and are resolved in a finale lasting only a few moments. The three protagonists—a boy; Madame M., object of the child's first love; and a nameless cousin, the narrator's enemy-friend— are sharply delineated, while the other characters are vaguer. The theme is that one may be chivalrous at any age, and the underlying idea is the notion of the superiority of the romantic spirit over the rationalistic viewpoint of the era.

On a visit to a country estate the narrator, an eleven-year-old boy, meets the beautiful cousin and Madame M. Immediately attracted by Madame M.'s pensive expression, the child becomes her page. In a mad attempt to show off in front of her, he tries to ride an unbroken stallion and is fortunate to escape injury. But he exhibits even greater nobility when he overhears a farewell scene between Madame M. and a handsome young man and finds what is apparently the man's last love letter to her. The child has the delicacy to conceal the letter in a bouquet of flowers which he presents to Madame M., who kisses the boy passionately out of joyous gratitude and thus completes his tumultuous experience. This relatively early story displays many distinctive features of Dostoevsky's later creative approach: the work begins at a leisurely pace, gathers momentum, and explodes at the scene of the mad ride on the charger. The denouement accelerates swiftly but gently to its resolution in the full-blooded kiss.

Evidently Dostoevsky made a conscious decision at this stage to depart from traditional forms, a conjecture corroborated by the creative history of "Uncle's Dream." Though its subtitle "From the Mordasov Chronicles" suggests an extended narrative, the story in fact concentrates on one episode: the pursuit of a rich bridegroom, an old prince. The work is limited to the theme of mercenary self-interest, around which almost all the protagonists revolve.

"Skvernyi anekdot" ("A Nasty Joke," 1862) is more reminiscent of the young Dostoevsky. It describes a high official who learns that one of his clerks is being married as he passes by his house and decides that an impromptu visit from him will both gain the clerk's gratitude and demonstrate his own "progressive" views. But the visit creates nothing but hardship for his hosts. They must scramble to find money to purchase champagne for their important guest, who then ruins the gathering by collapsing dead drunk. He is deposited on the only available bed, intended for the newlyweds, and is violently ill all night. Compelled to try to consummate their marriage on a mattress installed atop a few dining chairs, the young couple collapse on the floor. The high official thereafter stays at home for a week out of shame.

"Krotkaia" ("A Gentle Creature," 1876) portrays an entire life full of dramatic conflicts and poignant situations within the confines of a short story. Dostoevsky himself starkly summarizes the plot in his introduction: "Imagine a husband whose wife is lying on a table (dead); she has committed suicide a few hours earlier by throwing herself out the window." Anticipating criticism occasioned by his polemic subtitle "A Fantastic Story," he also declares in the introduction: "I entitled it fantastic while I myself considered it to be realistic to the highest degree. However, the fantastic is truly there, and precisely in the story's very form." Dostoevsky compares himself to an unseen stenographer who records everything his hero says, but then edits the chaotic material in a way that does not interfere with its most important feature, "psychological order."

The story provides information on the heroine's background, including the desperate poverty from which she seeks to escape by marrying the hero, a former officer who is now a pawnbroker. The setting of the slums as well as the husband's perverse pride and obsessive intent to break his young wife's spirit fit the ideological, poetical, and psychological facets of Dostoevsky's literary approach in the 1860s and 1870s. But there is also a new element: the confessional soliloquy, with all its complexity and contradictory disorder, reproduces the chaotically capricious yet directed thought of the hero, who seeks to discover the true reasons for the catastrophe. He reconstructs his past and hers, including their marriage, feverishly searching his memory for various episodes and even "little traits," the terrible and the ordinary moments of life, confusing and contradicting himself but all the while moving inexorably closer to the truth. Through his morbid self-analysis he reveals his paranoid desire for revenge on society for its past injuries to him, while recognizing the absurdity and baseness of that desire. A distorted sense of honor has led him to exile himself from society into his terrible dark underground where he nurtures the idea of rehabilitation. And yet along with this somber bitterness there exists deep within him a desire for truth, love, and redemption. But for the time being he suppresses this positive desire in order to pursue his cruel but well-designed system to achieve rehabilitation after his disgraceful past through the gentle creature he has taken as his wife. She is also to be part of a future idyllic life on the southern coast of the Crimea.

The narrator, simultaneously prosecutor and defendant, refuses to accept any sentence except that pronounced by his own conscience. He rails against youth, against women, against blind chance, against the cruel irony of fate, and against nature itself, but each accusation proves to be without substance. His casuistry is refuted each time by the invincible argument lying on the table, compelling his final admission: "I have tortured her to death, that's what it is." By accepting the judgment of his conscience, the hero rises to heights permitting him to declare his great and final rebellion against the state, the law, the courts, and faith. The truth enhances, but does not redeem him: his guilt is too great for that, his loss irrevocable. But now the underground theme has acquired a new direction.

Dostoevsky returns to this theme in "Son smeshnogo cheloveka" ("The Dream of a Ridiculous Man," 1877). Here he takes the narrative to the outermost limits, the point at which "nothing matters," after which we follow the hero into nonbeing, death, until suddenly and miraculously he is resurrected to new life and happiness.

"Vechnyi muzh" ("The Eternal Husband," 1869–70) is an earlier tale of the underground mentality. Recounted from the viewpoint of Velchaninov, the former lover of Madame Trusotskaya, the narrative revolves around the tormenting struggle between him and Trusotsky, who discovers after his wife's death not only that she has been repeatedly unfaithful to him but also that his little girl Liza is in fact Velchaninov's daughter. Trusotsky comes to St. Petersburg with Liza, whom he uses as a weapon in a silent duel with Velchaninov: in their repeated encounters, their facial expressions, hysterical gestures, and incoherent words bear witness to the tormenting passions wracking each of them. The duel ends with the cuckolded husband's attempt to murder Velchaninov. The epilogue, which occurs a few years later, depicts Trusotsky once more in the role of eternal husband and Velchaninov once again as the bon vivant. But this plot summary cannot convey the emotional complexity of the work. Thus Trusotsky's former admiration of Velchaninov turns to hatred, though he realizes this only at the end, while Velchaninov is oppressed throughout by an unbearable emotional weight he cannot describe in words. After her deliberate rejection by her legal father, Liza dies of a broken heart, to the despair of Velchaninov, who had hoped to begin a new life with her. The alternating feelings of hatred and admiration that both men feel lead to unexpected reactions. Thus Trusotsky nurses Velchaninov genuinely, even devotedly, during a medical crisis, but a few hours later he is discovered with a razor poised over his rival's throat.

Finally, of Dostoevsky's short stories one should mention a brief fantastic story that appeared in 1873 in *The Diary of a Writer.* "Bobok" portrays the hallucinations of the narrator in a cemetery: he imagines he overhears conversations emanating from the graves. It turns out the corpses remain "alive" for several months after death: they can communicate with one another, and with an astonishing cynicism of expression, for now their freedom from worldly considerations permits them to express their true opinions and desires. Sexual perversion, financial manipulation, and sycophantic flattery are as widespread among the dead as among the living, and much more open in their avowal. The Soviet scholar Mikhail Bakhtin was intrigued by this work's formal originality and regarded the story almost as a microcosm of Dostoevsky's creative art. He argued that many of Dostoevsky's themes and images—including some very important ones—emerge here in vividly naked form: the notion that "all is permitted" if there is no God and no immortality; the theme of confession without repentance, of "shameless truth"; the theme of eroticism permeating the highest levels of consciousness; and the idea of the "unrighteousness" of life.

Saltykov-Shchedrin

Mikhail Saltykov (1826–89) first achieved renown with the publication of *Gubernskie ocherki* (*Provincial Sketches,* 1856–57), issued under the pseudonym N. Shchedrin. In these popular sketches Saltykov-Shchedrin attacks the excesses of power and exposes bribery, extortion, slander, and outright theft: in his world everyone from governor to petty clerk pitilessly robs the poor, though he also depicts these social parasites not as evil in themselves but as the inevitable products of an exploitative social system. In addition, a significant segment of *Sketches* is dedicated to the common people, religious wanderers, pilgrims, and prison inmates.

The sketches revolve about a vertical dissection of the provincial town of Krutogorsk, which lives its own profoundly limited life at the end of the world, as it were, for there are no roads from it leading anywhere else. Drawing on the tradition of the physiological sketch of the 1840s, Saltykov begins with a picture of a typical street fête and then introduces us to the town's history and the background of some of its leading citizens in "Proshlye vremena" ("Bygone Days"). Following that is a sketch devoted to the governor, his daughter, and local officials. Petty officials are depicted either through a collective image of the "poor toiler," as meek victims of brutal bureaucracy ("Khristos voskres" ["Christ is Risen"]), or in individual scenes: the very title of "Vygodnaia zhenit'ba" ("An Advantageous Marriage") speaks for itself. A characteristic sketch dealing with the "poor civil servant" theme is "Pervyi shag" ("The First Step"), in which the problem of boots acquires the same dimensions as Akaky Akakievich's purchase of a coat in Gogol's "Overcoat." Saltykov, however, goes Gogol one better: at the end his clerk is arrested because he has become involved in a bribery scandal. Gogol's influence is also apparent in the introduction to the book, whose lyricism mixed with ironically good-natured praise of Krutogorsk's patriarchal way of life recalls "Old-World Landowners."

The most significant elements of Saltykov-Shchedrin's artistic method emerge in *Provincial Sketches,* with dramatic scenes, monologues, travelogues, portrait galleries, and group descriptions all linked to the initial thematic plan. The free treatment of literary forms—transitions from one subgenre to another within the same cycle or even within the same story—is Saltykov's hallmark. Often he would publish a story—for example, his "V ostroge" ("In Prison," 1856)—and then develop it into a series of stories under the same title. Thus in 1857 he published "Talantlivaia natura" ("A Talented Nature") and then expanded it into a cycle entitled *Talantlivye natury* (*Talented Natures*).

In *Provincial Sketches* Saltykov employed an important satirical device he used in subsequent years, that of the zoological comparison, as when he wrote of "animallike ferocity," "a porcupine expression," or "the majesty characteristic of a turkey." The stories also exhibit in embryo his obliquely allegorical narrative manner, his "realistic fantasy," and his overuse of hyperbole, satirical nicknames and epithets, and grotesque devices. In short, Saltykov early achieved an individual but unified synthesis of fiction with journalism. After *Provincial Sketches* Saltykov was regarded as the leader of the school of literary exposure, and people spoke of the "Shchedrin school" or the "Shchedrin spirit."

Nevinnye rasskazy (*Innocent Tales,* 1857–63) and *Satiry v proze* (*Satires in Prose,* 1859–62) complete the portrait gallery Saltykov began with *Provincial Sketches.* For the first time he introduced cruel serf owners and individuals who attempt to oppose oppression, in such works as "Gospozha Padeikova" ("Mrs. Padeykova"), "Razveseloe zhitie" ("Happy Living"), and "Derevenskaia tish'" ("Rural Tranquility"). His depiction of provincial officialdom became a symbol of governmental administration generally in tsarist Russia. The cycle *Satires in Prose* is unified by the notion of serfdom's historically predetermined doom.

Satires in Prose also presents for the first time the town of Glupov (Fooltown) and its benighted inhabitants, an acid artistic metaphor for the entire tsarist regime. Saltykov would develop it to its highest point in one of his best-known cycles, *Istoriia odnogo goroda (History of a Town,* 1869–70). *Pompadury i pompadurshy* (*Messrs. Pompadours and Mmes. Pompadours,* 1863–75, derived from the name of the mistress of Louis XV) is the allegorical title of a cycle attacking the caprices of powerful provincial bureaucrats, an attack continued in *Gospoda Tashkenttsy* (*The Tashkent Gentry,* 1869–73).

Some critics have belittled Saltykov for his feuilletonistic style. It is true he employed many propagandistic elements, but they were organically fused with his artistic devices; and if a writer is to be judged by the degree to which he fulfills his intent, then Saltykov ranks very high. Unlike his contemporaries Turgenev, Dostoevsky, or Tolstoy, who sought to create psychologically convincing characters, Saltykov wished to depict his social milieu and the aggregate of conditions that constituted the prevailing social order. Indeed the radical critic Nikolay Dobrolyubov commented that the Turgenevian school of writing held that "the environment devours man," and depicted this quite well, but that the school did a poor job of describing the environment itself and its relationship to the individual. Thus Saltykov, uninterested in the nuances of character, took upon himself the task of depicting the milieu, those social types who most clearly embodied the negative features of the group or class he was investigating. He was preeminently a political satirist.

Thus if Saltykov failed to explore the psychology of his characters, it was because psychological unveiling humanizes an individual, whereas satire exposes a humanoid creature. He focused on the psychology of class behavior rather than the individual: around the central person satirized are grouped a number of satellites who offer variations and nuances of a basic type. Thus Saltykov observed his characters in the social arena, not the personal one. And when he did touch upon their personal lives, it was only in order to trace the end of a development that began outside the family domain.

The names and nicknames that form an important element of Saltykov's artistic system derive from the satirical tradition established by Denis Fonvizin, Aleksandr Griboedov, and Nikolay Gogol. His "speaking" names are usually bestowed upon carriers of negative traits like lust for power, despotism, ferocity, and rapaciousness: Zmeishchev (Snakelike), Zubatov (Toothy), Davilov (Oppressor), Obirailov (Despoiler), Krokodilov (Crocodile). A second category points to intellectual and moral limitation: Slabomyslov (Weak-minded), Negodyaev (Scoundrel), Balbesov (Idiot). A third group bear names suggesting physical characteristics of a negative sort: General Golozadov (Barebottom), or Governor Pucheglazov (Popeye). He assigns to his characters of very high rank—princes, counts, generals—names that create a comic effect in conjunction with their titles: Strekoza (Grasshopper), Soliter (Tapeworm). Nor does Salytkov forget the lower classes, for he endows his rascally policemen and clerks with suggestive names like Zubotychin (Knock your teeth out) and Khvatov (Bribetaker). On occasion Saltykov's personages are characterized by their names alone.

The narrator, the "migrating" protagonists, and certain themes serve as unifying threads within cycles and between cycles. Some cycles, however, are not as closely structured as others. Thus the stories in *Provincial Sketches* are only loosely linked, whereas the bonds connecting the disparate parts of *History of a Town* are tight and multifaceted.

Aside from the cycles for which Saltykov is primarily remembered, he also wrote some individual short stories, such as "Dvorianskaia khandra" ("Gentry Blues," 1878), "Starcheskoe gore" ("Sorrows of Old Age," 1879), and "Bol'noe mesto" ("A Sore Point," 1881). Although the short story as such was never as important as his cycles, the stories do possess some merits in contrast to the grotesque fantasies of the cycles. The stories describe emotionally poignant situations and offer plausible psychological portraits. Each story contains a dramatic or even tragic summing up of the ordinary life of ordinary people: a character has worked conscientiously and unobtrusively all his life, only to confront suddenly a revelation that strips his past of all meaning. Saltykov tells us that it is not sufficient for a man to have worked well all his life; rather he must consider *what* he has done and what he has served so well.

In some ways "A Sore Point" anticipates Tolstoy's *The Death of Ivan Ilych.* The protagonist's single solace in his old age is his only son. The young man, who has attended the university and associates with people with clear ideas of good and evil, discovers that his father has served an ignoble cause all his life. Unable either to reconcile himself to his father's past or to break with him, the son kills himself. Behind each intimate family drama, the author implies, lies an abnormal society.

The old man falls victim to an inevitable retribution for the past in the form of the pitiless judgment of the younger generation, who will not accept evil passively. The awakening of the father's conscience ends this version of *Fathers and Sons.*

Saltykov's influence on the intellectual life of Russia in his day was considerable. His iconoclastic attacks on the fundamental institutions of society—family, property, religion, the administrative apparatus of the state—stimulated the appearance of younger voices who would echo his indignant protests.

The Radical Writers: N. Uspensky, Pomyalovsky, Reshetnikov, and Sleptsov

Nikolay Uspensky (1837–89) was the first writer to describe peasant life without illusions and yet without the ethnographical objectivity of a Vladimir Dal. He looks at the villages soberly, not advertising the supposed charms of rural life. The peasantry as he pictures it is a defenseless, bankrupt mass of people, sunk in slavery, unawakened from the torpor of centuries, and living in superstition and the lethargy of ignorance. "Zmei" ("The Snake," 1858), "Koldun'ia" ("The Witch," 1863), "Sel'skaia apteka" ("The Village Pharmacy," 1859), and "Bobyl'" ("The Landless Peasant," 1859) paint horrifying scenes. In "Proezzhii" ("The Traveler," 1861) a member of the gentry beats his innocent drivers and servants, but when his mood changes, he offers them vodka to sing for him and they do so with no thought of their dignity. The tavern keeper in "Kabatchik" ("The Tavern Keeper") does well for himself: every day is a holiday for him, since people drink for all possible reasons. Uspensky's Russian village is full of hopeless, savage peasants, who through their drinking lose all their possessions and then thank the tavern keeper for robbing them. In their drunkenness the peasants send off to the army a sick villager with many starving children instead of a thief who has bribed them with vodka.

In his stories Uspensky takes his readers into fields, peasant huts, taverns, village meetings, and country fairs. He shows the people as they go about their daily lives, revealing their thoughts and problems, the dark ignorance in which they live, the ugliness of their manners. Frowning autumn skies or murky winter clouds spread over all.

Dostoevsky particularly liked Uspensky's "Porosenok" ("The Piglet," 1858), which tells of a widow's attempts to bribe officials to recover a piglet stolen from her in the market. Not only does she receive no help; she is somehow made to feel so guilty that she hands over her money quite willingly. Beneath the good-humored surface of this tale of a simpleminded peasant woman the reader perceives the distortion of the most basic human values. "Starukha" ('The Old Woman," 1858) paints a picture of frightful poverty that compels a peasant woman to beg for a little cottage cheese for her starving children, for whom she cannot even provide a roof. His well-known story "Noch' pod svetlyi den'" ("Easter Eve," 1859) similarly depicts the inhumanity and disharmony of the contemporary world, in which Christ's commandments that we love one another and forgive others' sins have been forgotten.

The young hero of "Brusilov" (1860) asserts that work can heal a man's spiritual life and form his character. Although eager to work in order to maintain his status as a university student, he finally succumbs to disease and hunger. Even with his extraordinary thirst for knowledge he cannot overcome the problems of poverty.

In the course of time Uspensky's sketchlike stories become more like genuine tales, as he weaves together seemingly accidental or trivial but nonetheless homogeneous episodes from everyday life. In his longer story "Uezdyne nravy" ("Provincial Mores," 1878) Uspensky presents disparate scenes from the meaningless lives of provincial landowners, merchants, clerks, and artisans through the consciousness of a young teacher who yearns for intellectual and spiritual companionship but realizes that he cannot find a kindred soul. The hero's alienation is the index of the degree to which society as a whole departs from the elementary norms of human relationships. Even the members of the same family suffer from the loneliness Uspensky depicts. He creates a terrible picture of a society with no authentic bonds between people, who communicate only by inflicting pain upon one another.

In "Tikhaia pristan'" ("A Peaceful Haven") the initial naive expectations of an elderly woman who arrives at her son's home are more reasonable than the reality confronting her upon arrival. The mother, who had lived in poverty all her life, now sees at close quarters the "peaceful haven" of which her family has always dreamed. The son, a prosperous bureaucrat, is "judged by the mother," but at the same time Uspensky subtly reevaluates the dream itself. The reader must fill in the details of a plot whose outlines Uspensky barely indicates. He stresses objectivity and verisimilitude, which he considers the principal ideals of literature.

Uspensky bases the ideological center of the story "Izdaleka i vblizi" ("From Near and Far," 1870) upon an examination of the relationship between the intelligentsia and the people, that is, between the educated segment of society and the uneducated peasant masses. Members of the intelligentsia, separated from the people and oblivious of their needs, lead grossly parasitic lives. And the peasants, too, embittered by unbearably hard work, can be indifferent to the sufferings of others. Thus in "Uzhin" ("Supper," 1859) an orphan boy with flies on his tear-stained face and thin legs too weak to support him sits in filth and begs for bread—in vain.

Even among the peasants there are those who cheat their fellows, especially the rich peasants, or kulaks, who enslave the poor peasants anew after the Emancipation. In "Egorka-pastukh" ("Egorka the Shepherd," 1871) Uspensky shows the power of the kulaks. The rich peasants bribe with vodka the father of a young girl in love with a poor shepherd. After the bride is forcibly married, the husband is found murdered. The wife and the shepherd are arrested, and the story ends with a question: "What will the prosecutor say? How will the jury decide?"

The legion of oppressors and exploiters grows constantly in Uspensky's fiction: landowners, merchants, officials, priests, and tavern keepers most of all. But he also depicts the evil the peasants do to themselves. Though he discerns vulgarity, brutality, corruption, and violence in every segment of society, he controls his authorial intrusion, keeping the personality of the narrator in the background and never drawing attention to it through an emotional epithet or a lyrical digression. Chekhov once said that one does not need many words to describe the poverty of a poor woman: one need merely say that she is wearing a faded cloak. Uspensky too creates his story line economically, calmly, and in a subdued tone. His sketchlike stories contain no complex plots, no profound or moving psychological analysis, no brilliant wit, no elegance. He conveys instead the vulgar, drunken, argumentative speech and intonations of his peasant protagonists, the admixture of Church Slavic in the conversation of his priests, the comical voices of newly rich merchants trying to ape their betters. Uspensky gave the reading public a firsthand portrayal of peasant life, unadulterated by sentimentalism.

Nikolay Pomyalovsky (1835–63) received an ecclesiastical education since his father was a deacon; but he had no wish to follow in his father's footsteps and in 1859 began attending classes at St. Petersburg University. In those vital years just before the Emancipation, Pomyalovsky contributed to the common enthusiasm by teaching in a free

Sunday school for working people. Unfortunately, however, his alcoholism led to his untimely death when he refused attention for a sore on his leg. He died at twenty-eight.

Aside from two short novels published in 1861, Pomyalovsky is best remembered for *Ocherki bursy* (*Seminary Sketches*). The first sketch, "Zimnii vecher v burse" ("A Winter Evening at the Seminary"), appeared in 1862; the second, "Bursatskie tipy" ("Seminary Types"), also came out in 1862. This was followed by "Zhenikhi bursy" ("Seminary Suitors") and "Beguny i spasennye bursy" ("Runaways and Survivors"), both of which appeared in 1863.

The theme of education was very popular at the time, but this by no means diminishes the worth of Pomyalovsky's sketches. They are a stark condemnation of the seminaries' pedagogical philosophy, which was based upon the suppression of human dignity through brute force, rote learning, and the eradication of every original thought. Nor does Pomyalovsky idealize the savage behavior of the seminarians themselves, though he makes the point that they were not born savages, but were made that way by the seminary, which destroyed their natural talents and characters. Even the best teachers in his stories abuse the students both psychologically and physically. Pomyalovsky himself calculated that in the fourteen years of his life at a seminary he was whipped four hundred times. Moreover, the students live in filth and are fed a diet that keeps them at the edge of starvation.

The critic Pavel Annenkov at the time declared that *Seminary Sketches* went beyond the bounds of art. The teachers as tormentors and the seminarians as victims were equally disgusting, he thought, as was the author himself, with his "dry, unbearable objectivity toward both sides." Another critic felt that the author's exaggerations extinguished the reader's sympathy.

It may be true that the seminarians evoke no compassion, but Pomyalovsky shows that their grotesque behavior stems from three interrelated causes: the wretchedness of their lives, their sense of helplessness, and their instinct of self-preservation. Their mutual brutality, wild drinking, cheating, and lying are a consequence of the way they live. Like Dostoevsky, Pomyalovsky seems to say that suffering and humiliation simply lead to more suffering and humiliation. The system destroys the weak and corrupts the strong.

Pomyalovsky's view of childhood was far from that advanced by Leo Tolstoy or Sergey Aksakov, who created sensitive pictures of a child's psychological growth. Pomyalovsky knew that the sons of the Russian clergy did not grow up in surroundings of leisured luxury. His first story, "Vukol" (1859), describes the birth of consciousness in a child but demonstrates how his merriment and sincerity gradually disappear until he becomes an embittered loner under the constant threat of punishment. Unlike Tolstoy and Akaskov, Pomyalovsky was less interested in the child's emotional growth than in conveying the concrete circumstances of the environment that would destroy him. In *Seminary Sketches,* for example, Pomyalovsky has no central autobiographical hero. Karas is the closest to such a hero, but even he is the central protagonist only of the last sketch; he is a peripheral figure in the other three.

The works composing *Seminary Sketches* differ structurally from one another. In each of the first three the action takes place within the limits of a single day; but since Pomyalovsky wished to show the evolution of consciousness in a clever boy in a savage pedagogical system through the autobiographical figure of Karas, he expanded the temporal framework to four years. But even in this sketch Pomyalovsky neither equates himself with his hero nor presents reality through the child's perception.

Seminary Sketches seemingly moves on two levels. The first, the depiction of seminary types and mores, predominates in the first three sketches, while the fourth sketch is on another level centered around the development of an autobiographical personage in the seminary's stifling atmosphere. But the first level exists on its own, not for the sake of the second. Pomyalovsky seems consciously to have decided to set a stage larger than that common in the autobiographical literature of the 1850s. He uses scenes, impressionistic sketches, portraits of individual seminarians, and interpolated stories and reminiscences to create a broad vivid picture of seminary life. Pomyalovsky deliberately avoids motivation in the development of the work, emphasizing the merely mechanical links between episodes. Thus the plot is very simple: he juxtaposes his protagonists as types, and not as participants in a developing story. He also varies the moods of his scenes, so that a comic occurrence may directly follow a somber episode.

For the purposes of his unique fictional genre Pomyalovsky developed an idiosyncratic language based on the speech of the seminarians, where elements of Church Slavonic, liturgical quotations, and scriptural allusions alternate and clash cacophonously with colloquialisms, comic comments, and witticisms. He defended himself against critical accusations that he used coarse, vulgar language by arguing that the work would be inauthentic otherwise. And the language of the author himself, with its gusts of indignation and ironic comments, is an organic synthesis of literary language with journalistic elements, a synthesis that was characteristic of the plebeian writers of the 1860s. We must remember, however, that the language was designed to destroy, so far as possible, every obstacle between author and reader.

Contemporaries hailed *Seminary Sketches* as a new discovery, and many similar works about seminary schools appeared afterward. This was not simply imitation, for a great number of seminarians were active in the intellectual life of Russia in the 1860s. Pomyalovsky's work obviously touched a sensitive nerve.

Fedor Reshetnikov (1841–71) had little formal education as a result of his poverty and suffered from alcoholism and want all his life. Passages from his somber diary reveal the agony he experienced. "With vodka I feel happier," he confessed once. "I suffer terribly with each day. Life is becoming more difficult, more unbearable. There is nothing except suffering. I hate lies, filth, and slavery in life. I wish for something better." When literary critics complained of his lack of artistic polish, he responded, "If I had the money to live in my own room and did not need advances, I would write more calmly and better than I do now."

Reshetnikov wrote in order to reveal the inhuman conditions in which some people lived in Russia: he vicariously shared his protagonists' dreadful lives. The first part of his cycle *Podlipovtsy* (*People of Podlipnaya,* 1864) describes the slow death by starvation of the inhabitants of the village of Podlipnaya and the search of survivors for a better life; the second part describes the life of barge haulers. The totality of these impressions creates a tale whose hero is "the whole mass of the people," as Saltykov put it at the time, and whose plot centers about the fate of a single family whose experiences mirror in microcosm the historical processes that engulfed large numbers of peasants.

Thus part 1 tells the dramatic "love story" of Sysoyka and Aproska, her supposed death, and her genuine funeral. The burial of the nineteen-year-old Aproska by her father, Pila (there is a hint of incest in the story), and her fiancé, Sysoyka, can only be described as grotesque. Sysoyka keeps begging Pila not to close the coffin so that he can see Aproska, but these sentiments are interrupted shockingly when he claims he wants to bite off her nose, and begins a fight with Pila: profoundly tragic emotion is expressed in a comic, almost animal manner. After the burial the two men hear moans coming from the grave but run away in fear of sorcery, while the author intervenes to inform us that they have buried Aproska alive.

No one could describe better than Reshetnikov the inner drama of the common people's life. Pila makes superhuman efforts to help both his own family and his fellow villagers, who have been abandoned by the authorities and by nature itself. When their flour gives out, the villagers sicken and die from eating tree bark mixed with their bread, but the living lack the strength to bury the dead. "Food torments everyone," Reshetnikov writes. Unceasing hunger makes monstrous egotists of the peasants; for the most part they lie ill and apathetic, with the only sounds being curses, cries, and quarreling. They suffer from a mass psychosis of passive indifference to their own fate.

These drunken, stupid, hungry peasants leading a primitive existence could not be less like the idealized muzhiks of earlier Russian literature. Reshetnikov does not attempt to explore the psychology of his protagonists or their spiritual life. He is interested only in the inhuman conditions that create inhuman feelings. The reader feels immersed in an entirely unfamiliar world, rendered all the more strange by the peasants' language: when Reshetnikov's characters speak in something more than grunts or monosyllables, they employ a peculiar Ural dialect.

The work's narrative structure exemplifies Reshetnikov's historical perspective. His protagonists belong to their family and clan, and by extension to their class. This leads Reshetnikov to the larger problem of society as a whole and the social changes occurring at this particular time. *People of Podlipnaya* is essentially about the struggle for existence. Pila and Sysoyka, two survivors, leave to seek their fortune in the city, where they quickly learn who exercises power: but they are simply fictional examples of the thousands of real-life peasants who abandoned their native villages and wandered about Russia.

The second part of the cycle describes the two men's lives as barge haulers. By the end of the narration all the protagonists are dead, although the reader is told about the situation of Pila's two sons, who have survived and found a foothold in the new, industrialized Russia.

In a slightly different vein, Reshetnikov's "Nikola Znamenskii" (1867) describes the arrival in a village of a young priest full of energy and desire to serve the people. But his speech, his gestures, all his ways, seem foreign to the peasants, and they gradually stop attending church. After a vain struggle the priest gives up and begins to live the dissolute, drunken life of his parishioners. His successor, who has been ordained thanks to a bribe, is totally lacking in both secular and religious knowledge.

Reshetnikov, in his other stories and sketches—such as "Na palube" ("On Board," 1863), "Skladchina" ("The Pooling," 1863), "Lotereia" ("The Lottery," 1863), "Maksia" (1864), "Gornozavodnye liudi" ("The Miners," 1863), and "S Novym godom" ("Happy New Year," 1864)—uses the same gray colors to paint a picture of the desperately impoverished masses. Reshetnikov had a one-track talent, which constituted both his strength and his weakness.

Vasily Sleptsov (1836–78) was the only man of gentry origin among the "plebeian" writers, although his life was also shadowed by poverty and insecurity. He was a fervent feminist for a time and associated with leading nineteenth-century feminists, although after he was arrested in 1866 he seemed to lose interest in the issue. His contemporaries unanimously described him as extraordinarily handsome and elegant, and that same elegance may be observed in his prose, in the refinement of detail with which he created a character. He was an extremely well-balanced writer, realizing artistically the conclusions of a serious intellect in a tersely constructed work. The events in his stories usually occur within a few days or a few hours and are set in locations with a multitude of people: a village inn, a busy street, a city square, a railway coach. In short, in the 1860s Sleptsov stood head and shoulders above his fellow democratic writers. In the 1890s Tolstoy would speak of him as an "unjustly forgotten writer."

In 1860 the Imperial Geographic Society sent Sleptsov to Vladimir province to collect folk songs, tales, and proverbs. The result of this expedition was the cycle of sketches entitled *Vladimir i Kliaz'ma* (*Vladimir and Klyazma,* 1861), a work written literally as he was on his way from Moscow to Vladimir to provide a firsthand description of what he had learned. The sketches exhibit the distinctive features of his prose fiction: they are as harmonious, as laconic, as artistically perfect as his most mature works. Sleptsov never moralizes or bursts into angry tirades: he seems solely concerned with depicting what he has observed with the greatest accuracy. *Vladimir and Klyazma* recalls Aleksandr Radishchev's great eighteenth-century classic *Journey from St. Petersburg to Moscow* in its form and approach.

Pis'ma ob Ostashkove (*Letters on Ostashkov*) appeared in 1862–63. After the press had published accounts of the extraordinary progress recently made in the cultural and social life of Ostashkov, including descriptions of its theater, library, bank, and school for girls, Sleptsov visited the town himself and wrote sketches exposing the superficiality of these cosmetic changes. Although the sketches at first glance appear insignificant, even accidental, in their entirety they present a picture of desolation, hunger, cold, slavery, illness, violence, and crime. The author seems detached from his subject, as if he did not realize how his reader must react to the horrors he describes in these free-flowing sketches. Saltykov remarked that behind the mass of apparently insignificant pictures with no statistics there lies the life of an entire town with its external smoothness and inner poverty.

Sleptsov's first short story set in an urban environment, "Ulichnye stseny" ("Street Scenes," 1862), is done in the sketch tradition that emerged from the natural school of the 1840s. The small scenes he presents, and even the neutral nature descriptions, are permeated with elements of social and political significance. A story that on the surface recounts the innocent amusements of city dwellers thus acquires additional overtones.

Sleptsov created a new form that may be best described as dramatized physiological sketches. In the established tradition of the sketch, these works have no effective external plot development. But they are marked by a predominance of dialogue over description and remarkable renditions of the characters' speech: Sleptsov has few equals in Russian literature in his sensitivity to the spoken language. Unlike Nikolay Leskov, however, he has no interest in verbal play: he employs dialogue as a direct or indirect demonstration of social contradictions. Indeed, the predominance of auditory over visual depiction was characteristic of the narrative manner of the 1860s, as may be seen from the writing of Pomyalovsky and of both Nikolay and Gleb Uspensky.

One of Sleptsov's more harrowing stories, "Pitomka" ("The Fosterchild," 1863) describes a peasant woman's conversations with people she encounters on a journey through the countryside. By his use of syntactic parallelism—"the peasant woman [baba] turned off the road," "the peasant woman bowed," "the peasant woman went on walking in silence," with the increasing repetition of the word *baba*—Sleptsov emphasized the movingly emotional tragedy of a mother whose child has been taken from her.

Sleptsov's art and life reached their culmination in 1863. Aside from "The Fosterchild" and "Stseny v bol'nitse" ("Hospital Scenes," 1863), in or before that year he produced his best stories, "Nochleg" ("Lodging for the Night," 1863) and "Spevka" ("Choir Practice," 1862), which display the structural elegance and refinement of detail observable in his best work. The Soviet critic Korney Chukovsky speaks of them as polished on a lathe in the harmony of their parts and faultless taste in the reproduction of dialogue. "V trushchobakh" ("In the Slums," 1866) and "Stseny v politsii" ("Scenes at the Police Station," 1867) round off Sleptsov's sketches on urban themes.

The essence of Sleptsov's literary approach lies in his protest against the violation of human rights. He returns constantly to the theme of the trampling of human dignity: none of his characters believes there are any such things as justice, compassion, selflessness, or goodness. Sleptsov's peasants know that authority exists only to steal, damage, and destroy.

Some of Sleptsov's contemporaries misinterpreted his narrative approach as cold or skeptical; his use of condensed colors and extravagance in "Mertvoe telo" ("The Corpse," 1866) earned him an unwarranted reputation as a "comic" writer who heartlessly mocked Russian life.

Gleb Uspensky and the Populists

Gleb Uspensky (1843–1902), the cousin of Nikolay Uspensky, lived a life of hardship and financial want before entering an insane asylum where he spent the last decade of his life. Uspensky once wrote that, for the working class, life's drama, which no moralizing can resolve, derives from its sufferings, deprivations, torments, illnesses, psychological pain, and crimes. The "psychological pain" of which he spoke seems to have affected him personally in a monstrous way: while mentally ill he saw himself as a disgusting porcine creature with a snout, and imagined that he had poisoned his children with strychnine.

Uspensky had an enormous influence on the democratic youth of the 1870s and 1880s, who looked to him constantly for guidance. He took his vocation very seriously, believing that a writer by telling the truth about the life of the common people could awaken the consciousness of the working class and inspire the masses. In his comments on the second edition of his works in 1888 he remarked, "Actually I have written very little fiction, and conversely, many observations that I convey I put in a nonfictional form."

Uspensky characteristically describes terrible events without explicit anger or condemnation. Though he was often accused of being an unmitigated pessimist, he could see both the comic and the tragic side of things. He explained what he termed the "unfinished character" of his work as the result of external conditions and of his own spiritual loneliness and lack of faith in his capacities.

Though Uspensky worked in the form of the sketch, the content of his prose is dense—nothing is extraneous. There are no loving nature descriptions, psychological subtleties, or peripheral characters in Uspensky. His stories are always compact, sometimes excessively so, and somewhat schematic. The narrator's comments, also more laconic than eloquent, have been compared to a concentrated broth undiluted with water. Uspensky is an ascetic aesthete: he rejects anything superfluous, anything that does not lead directly to his goal or that detracts from the point he seeks to make at the moment. At times he may have enough material for a novel—as in the short story "Neizlechimyi" ("Incurable," 1857), for example—but his work remains bare-boned because he sacrifices architectural harmony on the altar of his idea.

Uspensky's works of the 1860s are numerous, varied in subject, and artistically uneven. He took his material from his wanderings throughout Russia and into the corners and slums of the two capitals. He portrays the life of the urban proletariat, the petty bourgeoisie, the mores of little clerks. His very earliest stories—"Gost'" ("Guest," 1861), "Star'evshchik" ("The Junkman," 1863), "Pobirushka" ("The Beggarwoman," 1864), "Zimnii vecher" ("A Winter Evening," 1865)—exhibit the basic features of his writing: his skill at catching essential details and reproducing conversational speech, his mild humor, and his sympathy for the little man.

"Nuzhda pesenki poet" ("Poverty Forces One to Perform," 1866) tells the poignant tale of a magician and a couple named Ivanov who are entertainers. In order to obtain the two hundred rubles needed to buy a replacement to save the husband from the military draft, they hire themselves out to a local merchant who is giving a party. The pregnant wife, weeping and dressed in a "Turkish turban" and gypsy shawl, dances for the rowdy guests while her husband clowns. The little drama is saved from maudlin sentimentality by being narrated in the comic and grotesque vocabulary of the magician. Sketches like "Skandal" ("Scandal," 1865) and "Na begu" ("In a Hurry," 1863) describe paradoxical or caricatured situations. In one of his stories Uspensky defines a young provincial man as "something between a matchmaker or bonnetmaker and a newspaper feuilleton"; in another he compares a young man with a city education to a bad pâté.

Uspensky could convey the external and internal essence of a man, social event, or object with one or two sharply defined details. "Tryntrava" ("It's All the Same," 1867) contains a marvelous description of old "auntie," who, though once quite generous, now seems to have lost all reason: she keeps her money under her mattress in which she has ordered her servants to breed fleas and lice to keep thieves away. The fact that she herself cannot sleep because of the vermin is of no consequence.

One of Uspensky's most famous works is "Budka" ("The Sentry Box," 1868). Its central personage, the policeman Mymretsov, became a very popular figure among Russian revolutionaries (Lenin refers to him several times in his writings). Mymretsov's most famous sayings are: "Drag him off!"—as a result of which one is dragged off by the collar to a place one does not wish to go—and "Don't admit him!"—which means that one is forbidden to enter when one very much wants to. Mymretsov is so adept that eventually he perceives only collars, not real people. And who owns these "collars"? A laundress who trembles in fear as she tries to assert her independence from her "bloodsucker" husband; an alcoholic tailor; an old beggar starving along with his grandchildren; or a worker who throws himself into a barrel of boiling water rather than be drafted into the army. Throughout all these confrontations we hear Mymretsov shouting: "Where is my stick?" A stupid, ignorant man on the lowest bureaucratic rung, Mymretsov is the ideal servant of the autocracy. In his person he embodies the tsarist system.

Uspensky's first longer work was *Nravy Rasteriaevoi ulitsy* (*The Mores of Rasteryaev Street,* 1866), an innovative cycle of sketches painting a broad picture of life in post-Emancipation Russia. Rasteryaev Street, a microcosm of the larger world, corrupts man, disorients him, renders him helpless. Drink provides the only escape from unbearable conditions that show that the Great Reforms have not benefited the poor. Predators like Prokhor Porfirovich symbolize the money men, the builders of a nascent capitalism. Uspensky's portrait gallery also includes the somber figure of Tolokonnikov, a sanctimonious torturer who enjoys observing his subordinates' humiliation, and Drykin, a tyrant and money grubber. Uspensky's attitude is sad, almost tender, when he describes talented little people like Ignatych who are crushed by need, ignorance, and exploitation and who end up as alcoholics. The structure of the sketches is based on contrasts and juxtapositions between exploiters and their victims. Rasteryaev Street is a zoological world incompatible with human dignity, where people cannot change.

The trilogy *Razorenie* (*Ruin,* 1869–71) also offers a general canvas of post-Reform Russia, concentrating on the environment's crippling effects on individuals. The title refers to the destruction of the established pre-Emancipation way of life. One of the cycle's major threads is the disintegration of the Ptitsyn family: the episodic figure of old Ptitsyna, guardian of one of the old family strongholds, is brilliantly characterized by the simple slogan she repeats constantly to her family: "Put as much as you can in your pockets." On the other hand, the worker-rebel Mikhail Ivanovich, who constantly protests against injustice and oppression, proves incapable of reaching any of his goals: for all his talk, his plan of starting a new life in St. Petersburg comes to nothing. Nadya Ptitsyna strives to escape the shackles of her family and dreams of a better, more enlightened life, but her vague yearnings also bring no result. The people she meets turn out to be consumed by self-centered and petty concerns, just like everyone else.

The cycle's second part, "Tishe vody, nizhe travy" ("Lying Low"), contains the confession of an intellectual named Vasily Petrovich, who has returned to his family in a provincial town. His feelings of helplessness are reinforced by the apathy of the townspeople and his contacts with his downtrodden sister, his mother, and a teacher afraid of offending her colleagues, until in the end he flees in fear. The final part of the trilogy, "Nabliudeniia odnogo lentiaia" ("Observations of a Lazy Man"), depicts the life of the lower classes. The image of the "lazy man," the narrator, forms the background of this series of episodes showing the moral chaos, exploitation, and misery of the peasants and workers.

In *Ruin* Uspensky's artistic approach is more sophisticated than before: he no longer relies on obviously satirical and comically exaggerated portraits. Instead we observe the characters' inner emotions, desires, and hopes; we follow their actions, their conflicts, their arguments. Though the plot is not especially compact, in the ideological and thematic sense *Ruin* is a well-organized work.

One should not imagine that Uspensky worked with polymorphous semifictional and semijournalistic short-story cycles because he could not handle the larger form of the novel. He was far from indifferent to questions of genre: he examined thoughtfully the genres he thought were declining and those he believed were in the ascendancy. In connection with *Ruin* he wrote to Nikolay Nekrasov about his indecision over whether to work within the traditional short-story genre or to write superficially disparate sketches with a hidden inner unity. He made a conscious choice of form to enable his reader to enter into direct contact with the material under the direction of the author and narrator. Thus, while *Ruin* is composed of three independent stories, each is part of a larger artistic depiction of reality. In view of this, there is no doubt that Uspensky was a major reformer of Russian literary prose. His impact is felt even today in the didacticism of Soviet writing.

The cycle *Novye vremena, novye zaboty* (*New Times and New Problems,* 1873–78) is so saturated that it makes for difficult reading as Uspensky tries to depict the new disharmony of life. In "Na starom pepelishche" ("On Old Home Grounds") the heroine, Verochka, is introduced to "new ideas" and acquires a new vocabulary including such words as *labor, equality,* and *independence.* She even comprehends these concepts, but it takes her a long time to break through the restrictions of her heritage. When she finally does, however, she is unable to continue living and poisons herself. In a similar way a deacon in "Incurable" realizes that the new ideas are destroying his hitherto harmonious existence: he suffers greatly after having eaten of the fruit of the tree of knowledge. The new victims of conscience Uspensky describes are powerless.

But then Uspensky also creates images of the new man in Russian society. Thus Petr Vasilevich, in "Khochesh' ne khochesh'" ("Willy-Nilly"), abandons his former depraved life, his family, and his wealth to live anonymously in his former village and teach peasant children. Only then does he gain spiritual equilibrium. Uspensky also favored serious work. The hero of "Perestala" ("She's Stopped"), Mikhaylo, protects his wife by keeping her from working. A doughnut seller scolds both of them: the wife is vigorous, she says, and the husband is depriving her of the work she requires. "The harder the merrier," she argues: work brings true joy.

"Dokhnut' nekogda" ("No Time to Breathe") displays Uspensky's imagination, rich humor, clear exposition, and artistic finish at their best. In this story, however, work is a source not of spiritual peace but of eternal anxiety: there is such a thing as harmful work, which leads to tragedy. Each of the characters works so much he scarcely has time to breathe, but each works at senseless, unnecessary things only in order to obtain the means of existence. Uspensky has no cogent advice to offer for the amelioration of the genuine unhappiness of his characters.

In the 1870s Uspensky turned to the peasant theme in such works as *Iz derevenskogo dnevnika* (*From a Village Diary,* 1877–80), *Krest'ianin i krest'ianskii trud* (*The Peasant and Peasant Labor,* 1880), and *Vlast' zemli* (*The Power of the Earth,* 1882–83). *Power of the Earth* in particular is an example of a new genre combining fictional elements with journalistic rhetoric so skillfully other populists of the day could not match it.

In *From a Village Diary* Uspensky offers the reader a rare example of a peasant "in the full sense of the word," a man indissolubly linked to the earth in heart and mind, a patriarchal peasant who does not know how to be cunning or to cheat. Here Uspensky finds a purity of morals based on conscience and on certain principles that prevail, in his view, in unspoiled peasant families. In *The Peasant and Peasant Labor* Ivan Ermolaevich resorts to active labor as the only possible defense against the perils of capitalism. In the poetry of agricultural work that permeates Ivan Ermolaevich's life Uspensky detects the fullness of existence, the "wholeness" and "harmony" that make him an exemplary human being.

In *The Power of the Earth* Uspensky commences an investigation of the meaning of this power in the peasant's life. He re-creates an epic hero of Russian folklore, comparing him to the Russian peasant as he eulogizes agricultural work and the strong communal feelings of the peasantry. For the peasant the land is not merely a source of food: it also inspires him with unexpected strength, defines his entire view of the world, takes on a transcendent spiritual value. Uspensky insists—and almost believes—that the peasant instinctively knows everything that he needs to know. Ivan Bosykh earns a comfortable thirty-five rubles a month for easy work with the railroad, and yet he is dissatisfied. Life was hard back in the village, but at least he knew his work was both necessary and fulfilling. Ivan misses the harmony of life. Now he has become simply a cog in a huge mechanism whose purposes are distant from him.

Uspensky was a central figure in populist thought of the nineteenth century. He sought to discover methods by which the harmony of peasant life might be preserved; he appealed to the intelligentsia to accept the lofty mission that saints and holy men had accepted in the past. By the 1880s the image of the "intellectual toiler," an analogue to the righteous men of the past, began appearing in his works. Referring to the humanizing role of ancient Christianity in his phrase "the intelligentsia of the holy men," Uspensky argued that righteous men of old did not retreat to caves and forests but rather lived among and with the people. In his sketch "Narodnaia intelligentsiia" ("The Intelligentsia of the People"), from *The Power of the Earth,* Uspensky introduces the legend of Nikolay and Kasyan. When they both returned to give an account of their work among men, Nikolay wore dirty, torn clothes, while Kasyan was dressed like a dandy. Thus God decided that Kasyan had only talked of helping people, while Nikolay had worked at it, and ordered that the church celebrate Nikolay at least twenty times a year and Kasyan only once every four years. Uspensky's conception of the positively good man combines religious moral principles, religious images, ideas, and phraseology, with images and vocabulary from Russian folklore.

Uspensky's esthetic and ethical views coalesce in a curious sketch of 1882 entitled "Razgovory s priiateliami" ("Conversations with Friends"), which sets forth a rather androgynous ideal. There is a discussion of a picture depicting a young woman in a simple dress, with short hair and wearing a man's hat. The narrator comments that there is something extraordinarily attractive about her "purely feminine, virginal features that are endowed with . . . a presence of bright masculine thought." He perceives an organic linkage between male traits and feminine charm, which creates "a newly born and hitherto unknown radiant type." In "Vypriamila" ("She Straightened Up," 1885) Uspensky pens enthusiastic pages about the famous statue of the Venus de Milo, denying that the sculpture represents feminine charm and insisting that, to the contrary, the artist took what he required to create this "stone enigma" from both male and female beauty without consideration of sex or even, possibly, of age. The Venus de Milo, he goes on, is an ideal in that it blends various human traits harmoniously. It should be said, though, that all Uspensky's models—holy men, intellectuals, women—have a detached feeling about them, a sense of an ideal not made of flesh and blood.

After Uspensky one of the best known populist writers was Nikolay Zlatovratsky (1848-1911), who continued the tradition of idealizing the rural commune and poeticizing the peasant. Not surprisingly, he worked in the form of the sketch or cycle of sketches, unifying his episodes not by plot but by theme and seeking to create an integrated picture of the life of the people. This is the structure he employs, for example, in an original story of 1875 entitled "Muzhiki-prisiazhnye" ("The Peasant Jury"), which deals with the election of peasants to the jury according to the Reform Laws of 1864, their preparations for departure from the village, their journey to the town on foot, their life there as members of the jury, and their return to the village. "V arteli" ("In a Collective," 1875), a story of a peasant collective that travels to St. Petersburg to seek employment, has no plot, no conflict, and no resolution as it attempts to imitate real life in its natural flow. After the Emancipation the peasants entered on a new life; no longer tied to the land, they could move freely to the city. But Zlatovratsky thought the urban environment would destroy the peasant's healthily natural qualities: in this story he describes both the corrupting influence of urban life and the steadfastness of the peasant character, with its sense of group comradeship, mutual assistance, and responsibility. This idealized view of the village commune suggests that those peasants who remain with the collective are superior to the helpless city worker who must live as an individual. And it is true that Zlatovratsky's idealized view of the integrated peasant commune contrasted with the cruel city recalls Nikolay Karamzin's sentimentalist effusions on the peasantry from the end of the eighteenth century.

One might mention as well the names of a few other populist writers of the time. Filipp Nefedov (1838–1902), for instance, wrote sketches like "Nashi fabriki i zavody" ("Our Factories and Plants," 1872) and "Krest'ianskoe gore" ("Peasant Sorrow," 1872), which were used by the populists for propaganda purposes. Works by Nikolay Naumov (1838–1901), such as "Derevenskii torgash" ("The Village Shopkeeper," 1871) and "Krest'ianskie vybory" ("Peasant Elections," 1873), were influential in the "going to the people" movement of the 1870s, when young people sought to agitate and organize the peasantry for political purposes.

Of course the populists were not the only writers in the 1870s who dealt with contemporary issues. Others, though different stylistically or ideologically, did so as well. One characteristic representative of literature of the 1870s in this category was Petr Boborykin (1836–1921). The hero of his tale "V usad'be i na poriadke" ("On the Estate and among the Peasantry") is an acutely sensitive young man who can discover no normal life either within his own circles or among the peasants. Everywhere he finds only disorganization and self-interest. The evil the estate owners do is mirrored in the peasantry: the hero's mother lives openly with her lover, and his peasant foster mother does the same thing. The only man of energy in the entire neighborhood is a German. Eventually the hero decides to leave this "nightmare" of an environment.

Banartsev, the hero of "Rannie vyvodki" ("Early Broods," 1877), is a weak-willed, passive personality. He thinks of volunteering for the Russo-Turkish War, which was going on at the time, but does not; he wants something else, but again does nothing. He ends by leading a gray and boringly virtuous life.

"Dolgo li?" ("Will It Be Long?") is among Boborykin's most successful stories. Its hero, the writer Prisypkin, is spiritually flabby. He can barely earn a living; the woman with whom he is living and whom he once loved no longer appeals to him, and she finally leaves him for a man who promises marriage; his petty and insignificant colleagues think only of money. The author presents Prisypkin's apathy, his unwillingness and inability to change his life, as characteristic of an epoch when everything is so disorganized that no individual can better his lot in life by himself. The story's action develops consistently with its internal logic and without external effects.

Boborykin anticipates Chekhov to a certain degree. His stories of insignificant lives are cast in muted tones. Everything is simple and pedestrian: therein lies the very horror of life.

Women Writers and the Woman Question

The woman question was one of the burning issues of the day for nearly the entire period 1850–80, but authors approached it in different ways.

In the literature of the 1860s and 1870s are works that display compassion for the profound emotions of modest and truly feminine characters, contrasted with impertinently glib female intellectuals who regard themselves as followers of George Sand. In *Bourgeois Happiness,* for example, Pomyalovsky contrasts a dedicated George Sandist, a rich widow, to a modest young lady, much to the latter's advantage.

In certain short stories by Aleksey Pleshcheev (1825–93) the very polemical theme of the career woman is intertwined with the woman question and the family motif to form a complex narrative structure. Literature of this type often deals with the tyranny of a depraved husband, the suffering of a sensitive and well-educated wife, her fears for her children, her "spiritual kinship" with a teacher, a thinking young man, and subsequent gossip about their relationship. In Pleshcheev's "Dve kar'ery" ("Two Careers," 1859) the hero tries his strength as a provincial teacher, but the story is complicated by the introduction of the theme of woman's position within the family and in society. The heroine, Sasha, is shown as trying to create a new and meaningful life for herself.

A young woman's moral odyssey is at the center of Pleshcheev's "Zhiteiskie stseny: Otets i doch'" ("Worldly Scenes: Father and Daughter," 1857). The heroine, a strong and loving woman, sacrifices her personal happiness for her father's sake: she decides against marrying the man she loves and is ready to take an unloved husband in order to save her father from disgrace. But her sacrifice fails to save him, and he chooses suicide.

Marko Vovchok (pseudonym of Maria Markovich, 1834–1907) delves further into women's situation in society and their discontent with their situation. The encounter between two psychological and moral forces manifested in the relationship of a couple in love, or of a husband and wife, was a frequent literary theme, and it was often reinforced by social problematics, the author's assessment of women's role in society, and the effects of that role on women's characters.

The heroine of Vovchok's "Chervonnyi korol'" ("King of Hearts," 1859) is an intellectually lethargic woman doomed by her upbringing to depend upon her husband. Vovchok, however, also perceives her heroine's capacity for all-encompassing love and self-sacrifice. Although her feelings emerge in a somewhat comical and old-fashioned way, her capacity for self-sacrifice sets her very much apart from the heartless milieu of the provincial gentry. The story is also interesting in its demonstration that a seemingly prosaic love without the expected romantic decor may discover profound depths of genuine feeling hiding behind silly provincial habits—in this instance fortune-telling with cards. Vovchok's sympathy for this "simple heart" of modest expectations and refined sensibilities is evident. In some ways this small work is comparable to the best of the psychological stories of the 1860s.

The situation in "Tri sestry" ("Three Sisters," 1861) is somewhat altered. Now the narrative focus is not on the meek Olga, who dreams of a happy marriage and accepts domestic tyranny uncomplainingly, but rather on the restless Varvara, who is searching for an escape from the vulgarity of provincial gentry life, and of Sofia, who eventually becomes a revolutionary along with her lover. The liberals and reactionaries almost engage in fistfights when they visit the sisters and argue over such issues as wealth and poverty, the Great Reforms, the responsibilities of landowners, and the social position of women. Young people seek and find each other among these passionate debates, which reflect both genuine spiritual yearnings and material self-interest, fear of the new forms of life and the realization that it is no longer possible to live as before.

Vovchok is not especially profound or original in examining the emotional experiences of her protagonists. She often idealizes her heroines because she is attracted to strong, active female characters who move from undifferentiated yearnings through definite intellectual conclusions to specific action.

Vovchok's interest in the problems of women led her to create an entirely different picture of a serf girl in "Igrushechka" ("The Little Toy," 1859) than does Tolstoy in the person of Natalya Savishna in *Childhood.* Both works describe a serf girl who is brought to the manor house to serve the young lady of the family but who is ultimately sacrificed to her master's whims. However, whereas Tolstoy's serf forgives her master for destroying her opportunity for personal happiness and sincerely dedicates herself to the service of her young lady, Vovchok's serf owners regard her heroine as their "little toy" for the entire course of her life. Even when the young girl she was to attend in the first place dies, she is not permitted to return to her mother. Exhibiting no Tolstoyan meekness and submission, Vovchok's serf fears and hates her masters; she rebels and dreams of freedom.

V. Krestovsky (pseudonym of Nadezhda Khvoshchinskaya, 1824–89) gave articulate expression to problems of daily family life. Most of her stories, traditional in structure, hearken back to the George Sandism of the 1840s, as we may see in such works as "Bratets" ("Brother," 1858), "Stoiachaia voda" ("Stagnant Water," 1862), and "Domashnee delo" ("A Domestic Matter," 1864). In this last story a wealthy and determined estate owner turns her unworthy husband out of the house, a seemingly positive action that, however, has tragic consequences when their sixteen-year-old daughter cannot bear the shame of her father's disgrace. Though Krestovsky acknowledges a woman's right to liberate herself from the yoke of the family when necessary, she rejects the dogmatic idea that a woman must have an unloving heart in order to be free and equal.

Krestovsky mounts a similar defense of her humane ideal against egotistical "emancipated" society women in portraying a follower of George Sand in "Vera" (1860), where she contrasts genuine independence and the willingness to disregard false social conventions with idle female chatter about such matters. "Za stenoi" ("Behind the Wall," 1862) is a more original work done in the spirit of the psychological realism of the 1860s. The narrator—a lonely, sick man of letters living in a St. Petersburg furnished apartment—becomes the involuntary witness of a cruel drama played out between his neighbor and his beloved. The narrator has never seen the woman, but he can guess at her sufferings and sympathizes with her wholeheartedly. Both the lovers are wealthy and independent members of good society. The man, a well-educated, refined aesthete, holds liberal views about women's rights and cannot understand why his beloved, a well-educated and intelligent widow, wishes to regularize their relationship. In his selfishness he cannot comprehend her anxiety lest her daughter suffer from social prejudice. What the man sees as strength and independence is simply a fear of losing his freedom. The woman, on the other hand, cannot tolerate falsehood and so suffers because she loves deeply. Although the story is not explicitly resolved, the reader may infer that the woman ends tragically.

In the 1870s Krestovsky dealt more frequently with the political topics of the day. A characteristic work of this time is "Schastlivye liudi" ("Happy People," 1876), which deals ironically with the decline of the social activism of the 1860s. The generation of that decade still retains its ideals, whereas the men of the 1870s are either businessmen or bureaucrats, but the former, not having been trained to do anything in particular and now deprived of opportunities for action, are simply waiting for the end. Krestovsky finds these developments intriguing and speaks of the "fathers," of whom "one fell and another retreated" and a third was unable to act. She reaches the bitter conclusion that the present generation has retained nothing of the inheritance of the 1860s.

In view of this, Krestovsky searches for an active hero who will justify the generation of the 1870s. "Uchitel'nitsa" ("The Teacher," 1880) describes a young woman who goes to a village to organize a school for the peasant children. Although she loses her job, thanks to the intrigues of a neighboring gentry family, she does not despair: in a village church she discovers a small allegorical picture that gives expression to the ideal she seeks. The depiction is of a small figure with a halo in the desert and another figure with a halo on a hill in the distance. The first figure stretches out its arms as it walks toward the second: when the two meet, the desert will cease to be a desert.

One final representative of women in literature at this time was Evgeniia Tur (pseudonym of Elizaveta Salias de Tournemir, 1815–92). Although she belonged to the liberal wing of the women's movement, her fiction reflected the aristocratic way of life to which she was accustomed. Her first story, "Oshibka" ("The Mistake," 1849), displays many parallels with Dostoevsky's later novel *Unizhennye i oskorblennye* (*The Insulted and Injured,* 1861). For example, the mother in Tur's story engages in intrigue much as does Dostoevsky's Prince Valkovsky, who shrewdly consents to his son's marriage to the modest poor Natasha in order to destroy her romantic aura of forbidden fruit and thus propel him into a union with a rich princess. In any case, Tur's stories and novels deal mostly with love adventures in high society. Although she was initially successful, her popularity later declined. She was also the author of moralizing books for children and young people.

Leskov

Nikolay Leskov (1821–95), a highly original figure, is nearly impossible to fit into any trend or school in Russian literature. His origins lay in three distinct social classes: the gentry, the merchants, and the clergy; similarly, his literary work in its entirety probably offers a better cross-section of nineteenth-century Russian society than that of any other writer of his day. He depicts not only the most varied social classes and professions but also the different regions of the country to achieve an unusual breadth of interest.

Technically Leskov made frequent use of the frame device, which permits different voices to be heard and also frequently evokes a confession, or story, from one of the protagonists without the author's interference. But Leskov is perhaps most famous for his language. He did not write, he narrated: his language is so incredibly alive that his characters seem to arise physically from his pages, speaking an extremely colorful language specific only to them. Leskov once explained that in his view the author must be able to take possession of the voice and language of each of his heroes in turn. "I tried to develop this ability in myself," he wrote, "and I think I managed to see to it that my priests talk like priests, my peasants speak like peasants. . . . I did not invent the language in my pages; I heard it from peasants, quasi intellectuals, holy fools, sanctimonious hypocrites, windbags." Leskov has never been surpassed as a stylist; he revived the art of the folk storyteller who makes us hear the tone of each speaker's voice.

Since an audience can retain only a few sentences at a time—unlike the reader of a text—the storyteller must hold its attention by piling incident on top of incident, surprise on surprise, so that even Leskov's shortest works are saturated with events. Leskov moreover shared popular taste for excess. He liked his people full-bodied: when they drank they became very drunk, and when they fell in love they were not prudent about it. A good example of this is provided by the heroine of "Ledi Makbet Mtsenskogo uezda" ("Lady Macbeth of the Mtsensk District," 1865), who, consumed by passion, murders her father-in-law, her husband, a nephew, and finally her lover's mistress before destroying herself. In short, as the Soviet scholar Boris Eikhenbaum has put it, "it seemed that in the 1860s Leskov decided to compete with all the major writers of the time, to juxtapose his experience and his extraordinary literary language to theirs."

Leskov was intrigued by the problems of the positive hero and proved more successful with them than most writers: he found them in places where Gogol, Turgenev, and Dostoevsky would not have dreamed of looking for them. Bogoslavsky (a name based on the word for *theologian*), the protagonist of "Ovtsebyk" ("The Musk-ox," 1863), searches for meaning in life all his days, but accomplishes nothing despite his intelligence and goodness. Though filled with revolutionary fervor, this Don Quixote has no language in common with the people.

One of Leskov's masterpieces, "Ocharovannyi strannik" ("The Enchanted Wanderer," 1872–73), describes the manifold adventures of one Ivan Flyagin. His life is full of dramatic conflicts and tense situations recounted in a narrative structure that blends elements of romanticism and realism. While a young serf, Flyagin saves his masters' lives but asks no reward: Leskov stresses that the notion of payment or reward has no importance for this very natural man. Among other adventures Flyagin is captured by the Tartars but manages to escape. His service with a prince ends in romantic tragedy when the prince's gypsy mistress becomes Flyagin's great love. After the prince abandons her, she implores Flyagin to help her end her life, and he complies by shoving her from a rock into the river. Flyagin tries his hand at everything: at one time or another he is nursemaid, soldier, clerk, actor, even medicine man. But above all else he is a folk hero, incorporating the finest Russian features into a personage bigger than life. This Russian Hercules of fantastic physical proportions lives an appropriately epic existence. Finally he enters a monastery, though on the story's last page we once more find him longing to take up arms. His broad nature can never find rest as his love for the people and his motherland drive him forward. His last words are: "I want so much to die for the people."

Domna Platonovna, the central figure of "Voitel'nitsa" ("The Battle-ax," 1866), an original personality and also a virtuoso in the "craft" of using lace peddling to obtain access to the upper classes, operates on another ethical plane, for in actuality she is a procuress of "live merchandise." Domna takes in an educated young woman named Lekanida who has left her husband and come to the city to live independently but has been evicted from her lodgings. Domna wants to make an arrangement for Lekanida with a wealthy general and cannot comprehend her spiritual refinement when Lekanida refuses to open the door to him. Eventually destitution and pressure force her to succumb. Once she is secure in her position, however, she reviles Domna, who in turn takes revenge by denouncing Lekanida to the general's family, as a result of which the general decides to obtain a new mistress. Of course, in this story we see things from Domna's point of view, and by her lights she is eminently kind and fair: she is involved in her occupation for the "art" of it rather than for profit.

The second portion of "The Battle-ax" tells of Domna's sad downfall after she falls in love with a twenty-year-old, a scoundrel who exploits her mercilessly. Domna sacrifices everything for him. When he is arrested she has nothing more to live for, falls ill, and dies.

Leskov's mastery of skaz (narration in the words of an uneducated character) in "The Battle-ax" is unsurpassed. Generally speaking, intellectuals make poor skaz narrators, since their language is too literary. Leskov achieves his unique effect by selecting a colorful character like Domna, who does not belong to the cultural elite and speaks the language of the lower classes. Domna Petrovna tries to imitate the speech of her upper-class customers, but she does not understand it entirely and so cannot reproduce it correctly. The result is a comical jumble of colloquialisms, bookish language, and distortions of foreign words. In its absurdity and linguistic virtuosity this discourse is almost impossible to translate into another language, as Leskov works in the tradition of stylistic exhibitionism developed by Gogol and Veltman.

Leskov uses more standard language in "Lady Macbeth of the Mtsensk District," a title that counterposes a Shakespearean archetype with a specific Russian contemporary milieu. Katerina Izmaylova represents the merchant class, but her exuberant nature will not fit the empty existence offered her. Her sexuality cannot be contained, and she readily resorts to murder to achieve her objective of being with her lover. Incidentally, this highly charged story provided the material for Dmitry Shostakovich's opera *Katerina Izmaylova.*

"Zapechatlennyi angel" ("The Sealed Angel," 1873) combines two areas of Leskov's expertise: the Old Believers, or religious schismatics, and icon painting. The narrator is an Old Believer who employs a very unliterary language. Trapped in a storm, a group of travelers congregates at an inn where sleep is impossible; when the conversation turns to guardian angels, the narrator tells his story, a tale of Russian officials' seizing and sealing a magnificent icon and the Old Believer community's desperate efforts to recover it. Those efforts end in a miracle when the schismatic leader is crossing the Dnepr River at night under extraordinarily difficult conditions: the seal falls from the icon to reveal the angel's pure face. Although the author offers a possible realistic explanation of this occurrence, the reader is left with a strong impression of the goodness of the Old Believers and the beauty of the icon.

Several of Leskov's later stories center around Russia's "righteous men" (*pravedniki*). These crop up in unexpected places as Leskov's gallery of such types grew: the hero of "Odnodum" ("Singlethought," 1879) is a policeman; the hero of "Pigmei" ("Pygmy," 1880) is a prison official; the hero of "Pavlin" (1874) is the doorman at a large apartment house. Though, paradoxically, their exteriors are forbidding, these righteous heroes seek the truth of life in Christian ideals and concepts of good and evil. Their harmonious natures are distinguished by spiritual beauty, wholeness, healthy individualism, blood ties with the common people, and total loyalty to their motherland. The hero of "Pavlin" is the fanatically conscientious agent of an evil landlord who evicts a family of three women on only the second day after they have failed to pay their rent. Pavlin carries out the eviction order, after which the grandmother and the mother die, leaving the little girl an orphan. Pavlin adopts her, raises her, and eventually marries her, only to learn that she has accepted his proposal merely in order to become the mistress of the owner's son. He arranges a fictitious death for himself and forces the young man to marry the pregnant Luba. The husband is killed, Luba repents, and both she and Pavlin retire to a monastery. Ryzhov, the hero of "Singlethought," a former postman now a policeman, lives in a world of bribes, rank consciousness, and fear. At the end of his career this little man exhibits the moral strength necessary to oppose the bureaucratic system within which he works. In similar fashion the hero of "Pygmy" tries to save a man from an unjust sentence even though he as a loyal police official considers his own conduct treasonous.

Leskov did not write only about representatives of the Russian people: he produced some stories on the theme of foreigners in Russia—for example, "Iazvitel'nyi" ("The Mocker," 1863) and "Melochi arkhiereiskoi zhizni" ("Little Things in a Bishop's Life," 1870). The best of these works is "Zheleznaia volia" ("Iron Will," 1875), which contrasts two national archetypes, the Russian and the German. The latter is represented by a German engineer, a paragon of self-discipline who with his iron will is so rigid he cannot adjust to the realities of life.

He pushes his willpower to absurd lengths: he endures countless wasp stings without flinching, drinks gallons of strong tea, and commits other self-destructive acts rather than admit his own weakness. Perhaps his most inhuman act is his decision to delay consummating his marriage until he has saved ten thousand rubles, but his wife abandons him before that happens. At the end the German's iron will leads to his own destruction and the Russians prevail, even though they are portrayed as incompetent and unreliable—but also human.

Leskov occupies a special place in Russian literature because of his mastery of skaz, an area in which he had a number of followers, including Aleksey Remizov, Mikhail Prishvin, Mikhail Zoshchenko, and Isaak Babel.

Eva Kagan-Kans

THE RUSSIAN SHORT STORY 1880–1917

The Setting

The years 1880 to 1883 marked a historic turning point for Russian prose. It was then that the authors who had built the impressive edifice of the realist novel in the middle of the nineteenth century either died or turned away from earlier patterns. Fedor Dostoevsky and Aleksey Pisemsky died in 1881, Ivan Turgenev died in 1883, and Leo Tolstoy was undergoing a spiritual crisis that resulted in his renunciation of secular art. With the passing of this generation, the literary scene in Russia seemed barren, as few writers of ability emerged to point literature in fresh directions. This dearth of talent was particularly conspicuous in the larger prose forms like the novel. As a result, the short story became the most important medium for innovative prose fiction toward the end of the nineteenth century.

Several factors combined to produce this literary vacuum. For one thing, the incessant demands voiced by the progressive utilitarian critics during the 1860s that literature carry an obligatory social message had effectively vitiated any inclination among beginning writers to focus on questions of form or aesthetics in their work. As a result, the literature produced by the generation succeeding Dostoevsky, Turgenev, and Tolstoy tended to be ill formed and monotonous.

Moreover, the early 1880s were a time of palpable malaise among the intelligentsia. During the 1870s many young people had been inspired by the populist movement and its idea of transforming the social consciousness of the Russian people and spreading democratic concepts in the countryside. This movement soon collapsed, however, under the pressure of mass arrests and persecution by the authorities. Several of the radicals then resorted to terror, which led to further persecution and repression.[1] This cycle of terrorist activity culminated with the assassination of Tsar Alexander II in 1881; the wave of political repression that followed fueled feelings of disillusionment and apathy among the intelligentsia.

The best writer of this generation, Anton Chekhov (1860–1904), characterized the spirit of his age very well in a letter of 1892 in which he remarked of his contemporaries: "We truly lack a certain something: if you lift up the skirts of our muse, all you see is a flat area. . . . We have neither immediate nor remote goals, and there is an emptiness in our souls. We have no politics, we're not afraid of ghosts, and I personally am not even afraid of death or blindness."[2] Chekhov then comments on his own mood: "I won't throw myself down a flight of stairs the way Garshin did, but neither will I flatter myself with thoughts of a better future."

Garshin

Chekhov's reference to the death of Vsevolod Garshin (1855–88) is significant, for Garshin was one of the few young prose writers of that day with a compelling new voice. This voice, however, resonated with the strains of pessimism characteristic of the period as a whole. The son of a military officer, Garshin was educated in St. Petersburg. When war broke out with the Turks in 1877, he volunteered for duty as an enlisted man and was wounded in combat, an experience that inspired his first important literary work, the short story "Chetyre dnia" ("Four Days," 1877). A first-person narrative, "Four Days" records the impressions of a volunteer wounded in battle and forced to spend four days next to the decaying corpse of a Turkish soldier he himself has killed. The work makes a striking statement about the senselessness of war. Particularly noteworthy is the way Garshin counterposes a nuanced account of his hero's psychological suffering with graphic descriptions of the Turk's decaying body. The writer also charges the scene with symbolic overtones: as the Turk's flesh rots away, a deeper reality emerges before the soldier's eyes, and he perceives in the horrible skull the face of war itself. Garshin's compressed narrative, with its terse, simple sentences, established the young writer's reputation.

Garshin's subsequent work included other military tales, such as "Trus" ("The Coward," 1879) and "Denshchik i ofitser" ("The Orderly and the Officer," 1880), allegorical fables, and several stories depicting the travails of sensitive young intellectuals. Two of these—"Proisshestvie" ("An Incident," 1878), and "Nadezhda Nikolaevna" (1885)—feature prostitutes as central protagonists, and one may detect echoes of Dostoevsky in Garshin's portraits of people who are acutely aware of the baseness of their condition but who take morbid pride in their very wretchedness.

Perhaps the most effective of Garshin's psychological stories is "Krasnyi tsvetok" ("The Red Flower," 1883). In it he describes a mental patient's attempt to eradicate what he believes is the personification of all evil in the world—three red poppies growing in the asylum's garden. Garshin himself had been in a mental institution, and he provides haunting descriptions of the gloomy asylum and the patient's incredible nervous energy as he fluctuates between lucidity and madness. The ending of the story is ironic. With an extraordinary expenditure of effort, the patient succeeds in tearing out the last poppy blossom. Returning to his bed, he dies with an expression of "proud happiness" on his face, certain that he has vanquished the roots of evil in this world. This conclusion aptly reflects Garshin's complex worldview. While wanting to believe in the possibility of meaningful change in life, the writer remained very much aware of the limitations of individual initiative.

This combination of ideas appears in Garshin's allegorical works, too, as the tale "*Attalea princeps*" (1880) illustrates. A tropical plant growing in a northern greenhouse, *Attalea princeps* rebels against her captivity. Rejecting the skepticism of the other plants, she successfully struggles to break through the dirty panes of glass covering the greenhouse. As she lifts her head high in freedom, however, she finds nothing but a grim autumn landscape in which sleet and snow mingle before a driving wind. The story ends as the greenhouse workers destroy the proud tree.

Although Garshin's works are occasionally marred by moments of rhetorical excess, he combined a sensitive understanding of human psychology with an appreciation of the suggestive potential of symbolic imagery, creating a body of work that distinguishes him from the majority of his contemporaries.

Saltykov, Leskov, and Tolstoy

The greatest writer to emerge in the 1880s was Anton Chekhov, but before we consider his contribution to Russian literature, we must mention several other writers who did not begin their literary activity during this decade but rather continued established careers. The most important of these were Mikhail Saltykov (1826–89), Nikolay Leskov (1831–95), and Leo Tolstoy.

Saltykov, who wrote under the name of N. Shchedrin, was born into a noble family and pursued a career in government administration for much of his life. Known as one of Russia's sharpest satirists, Saltykov's most interesting short fiction in the 1880s was a series of allegorical fairy tales, or skazki. In Saltykov's hands, the genre became a medium for mordant observations about contemporary social issues and the quirks of human nature.

A prime target of Saltykov's fairy tales was a simplistic view of society and its ills. Although convinced that social conditions had to be improved, Saltykov doubted that such change could easily occur. In "Liberal" ("The Liberal," 1885) he shows how a liberal dreamer must make ever-increasing compromises to have any effect on those around him, until in the end he is left with nothing but "rubbish." The title character of "Karas'-idealist" ("The Idealist Carp," 1884) waxes eloquent about the powers of truth and virtue, but his concept of equal rights for all fish perishes when he is swallowed up by an astonished predator. In some stories, such as "Bednyi volk" ("The Poor Wolf," 1883), Saltykov's vision is unrelievedly dark: a rapacious wolf relentlessly kills other animals, but although he knows his behavior is loathsome, he realizes that this is his inescapable nature; for him, death by a hunter's bullet comes as a relief.

The language of Saltykov's tales merits attention. He blends folk formulas with colloquial slang, the language of abstract philosophy, and foreign terms to fashion an unusual mix of styles that highlights the folly or wisdom of his characters. Perhaps the best practitioner of Aesopian language in Russian literature, Saltykov encourages his audience to read beyond the surface meaning of his works to discover their more topical message.

Like Saltykov, Nikolay Leskov established his reputation with works published in the 1860s and 1870s. The son of a government official from a family of priests and merchants, Leskov received little formal education, but he traveled widely and developed a keen eye for colorful human personalities. The radical critics regarded his first novels as attacks on the progressive movement, and their censure was largely responsible for the fact that Leskov's art did not receive the recognition it deserved during his lifetime.

Leskov's narrative gifts are best displayed in his short fiction. Many of his stories are fast-paced tales in which a swift succession of adventures is described in a richly expressive idiom. One such tale is "Levsha" ("The Lefthander," 1881), a story of one-upsmanship on a grand scale. Impressed by a marvelous piece of British craftsmanship—a small steel flea that does an intricate dance when wound with a minute key—the Russian tsar Nicholas I orders the famed craftsmen of Tula to come up with something even finer. And they do: they forge shoes for the flea and mount them with tiny nails. Nicholas sends the flea and one of its makers to England, but the stalwart Russian finds British women pretentious and their alcohol, suspect. On his voyage home he becomes completely drunk and dies unattended in a charity hospital. The most impressive feature of the story is Leskov's language. Written in a narrative mode termed skaz (in which the syntax and lexicon of the narrative voice mimic that of oral speech), the tale contains several examples of ingeniously corrupted borrowings from Western languages. Thus a *microscope* is called a *melkoskop* (from the Russian root *melk,* "shallow, petty"), and *barometer* becomes *buremeter* (from *buria,* "storm").

Leskov's skill at suspenseful narration stands out in other tales such as "Grabezh" ("The Robbery," 1887) and "Tupeinyi khudoznik" ("The Toupee Artist," 1883). The latter work, a chilling account of a despotic landowner's maltreatment of his serfs, consists of swiftly alternating scenes of imminent danger and sudden rescue: just as the heroine and her beloved seemingly escape one hazard, they are plunged into new peril. The story ends on a somber note, with a final glimpse of the heroine, now an elderly nanny, drinking furtively at night to still the wrenching memories of her shattered life.

Leskov's sympathy for the downtrodden and the good inspired him to create a series of stories devoted to the depiction of righteous individuals. These stories—which in the 1880s included "Pugalo" ("The Bogeyman," 1885), "Figura" (1889), and "Chelovek na chasakh" ("The Sentry," 1887)—reveal Leskov's comprehension of the little man's innate decency. The last work, for example, shows how government officials can sacrifice their subordinates for the sake of their careers. Based on a real incident, the story concerns a palace sentry who leaves his post to save a drowning man. But another man takes credit for the feat and is rewarded by the emperor, and the poor private is thrown into solitary confinement and then lashed for deserting his post. This gentle soul, however, bears no grudge against his superiors; he is merely relieved that his punishment was not more severe.

Leskov's humanitarian impulses found support in the 1880s in the ethical teachings of Leo Tolstoy, whom he deeply admired. His own imagination, however, led him to create more elaborate and exotic tales about Christian life than those written by Tolstoy, and during the 1880s he composed an entire series of colorful works based in part on the Russian *Prolog* (*Prologue*), a medieval compendium of saints' lives and religious matter.[3] Although some of these stories are flawed by an excessive didacticism, others, such as "Skomorokh Pamfalon" ("Pamfalon the Clown," 1887), are truly effective: in this tale Leskov's lively narrative carries the message that one must save one's soul not through asceticism but through service to one's fellowman.

As Leskov's late works indicate, Leo Tolstoy continued to exert a decisive influence on his contemporaries in the 1880s. Although by 1880 he had rejected his previous mode of writing as immoral, he did not abandon literature for long, and he produced thereafter a diverse body of work, from nonfictional pamphlets to a novel. Tolstoy's literary output in the 1880s was marked by an intense concern with morality and religion. Having undergone a profound spiritual crisis during the late 1870s, Tolstoy adopted a new, personal concept of Christianity according to which the conscience and Christ's basic teachings should guide one in a life of goodness, simplicity, and nonviolence. Outlined in his rhetorical work *Ispoved'* (*A Confession,* 1879–80, published 1884), Tolstoy's quest for a set of beliefs to live by and the insights gleaned from that quest formed the nucleus of his subsequent literary activity.

In addition to works expounding his religious beliefs—for example *V chem moia vera?* (*What I Believe,* 1882–84)—Tolstoy wrote a number of short instructional tales often derived from popular legends or early Christian writings and cast in a simple style based on colloquial Russian. Frequently ending with aphoristic sayings or scriptural quotations such as "Unless you become like children, you will not enter the kingdom of heaven" ("Devchonki umnee starikov" ["Little Girls Are More Clever Than Old Men," 1885]), the tales illustrate basic Tolstoyan truths. Thus the story "Mnogo li cheloveku zemli nuzhno" ("How Much Land Does a Man Need?" 1886) points out the folly of greed. Lured by the promise of as much land as he can encircle in a day's walk, an avaricious peasant strides around a huge tract, only to collapse in mortal exhaustion as he returns to the point of departure. Instead of vast holdings, the man now needs only six feet of earth—just enough for his grave.

In addition to these simple tales, Tolstoy also wrote stories for more sophisticated readers. Although they contain transparent messages, they also display the writer's remarkable understanding of human nature. Perhaps the most skillfully crafted of these works is *Smert' Ivana Il'icha* (*The Death Of Ivan Ilyich,* 1886), a penetrating study of the psychology of dying. This work's narrative structure is noteworthy. Tolstoy begins by describing the egocentric reactions of Ivan Ilyich's colleagues and family to the man's death and only then provides an account of Ivan's life, which shows how this character becomes caught up in the pursuit of material well-being and career advancement. Finally, he introduces the reader directly into the psychology of the dying man himself, and the reader becomes an intimate witness to the invalid's painful struggle with the inexorable approach of death.

At each stage in his story Tolstoy peels back the layers of hypocrisy and convention with which everyday society cloaks itself. As he describes Ivan's life, Tolstoy enriches his chronicle with symbolic detail, and we realize that Ivan's preoccupation with material things is not a sign of a healthy life, but rather a harbinger of death. Tolstoy's impressive handling of the dying man's psychology provides a detailed analysis of Ivan's hopes and fears, and especially of the way the prospect of death forces Ivan to examine the way he has lived his life. As long as he clings to the belief that he has lived properly, he finds the approach of death pure torture. Only at the end of the tale, when he suddenly admits to himself that his life has been a sham and that there could be another, more selfless way to live, does he discover that there is no death, only joyous light. Tolstoy's concern with the problem of death and the moral questions it poses for life also informs "Khoziain i rabotnik" ('Master and Man," 1895), which describes the internal transformation of a self-centered merchant named Brekhunov trapped with his servant in a raging blizzard. Brekhunov sacrifices his own body warmth and his life to save his workman from dying. Like Ivan Ilyich, he discovers that when one ceases to cling selfishly to life, death represents liberation.

Tolstoy's preoccupation with death may have stemmed from a longstanding appreciation of life and its physical pleasures, but still his late fiction reveals a nagging distrust of physical urges, particularly sexual desire. Two stories of 1889—"Kreitserova sonata" ("The Kreutzer Sonata") and "D'iavol" ("The Devil")—portray this force in the darkest colors. In "The Devil," a married man's obsession with a former lover, a peasant woman working on his estate, destroys his life. Tolstoy left two endings to the story. In one, the protagonist kills himself; in the other, he kills the object of his desire. "The Kreutzer Sonata" also links sex with murder in the story of a man named Pozdnyshev who has killed his wife in a jealous rage over her affair with a musician. Pozdnyshev delivers an impassioned diatribe on the dangers of the sexual urge and of society's futile attempts to sanitize it through the conventional institution of marriage. Sensuality, he asserts, is so dangerous that it would be better for the human race to practice celibacy. Pozdnyshev's monologue has more the character of a didactic lecture than a dramatic illustration of human weakness, and this monochromatic quality undermines the artistic value of the piece. Nevertheless, upon its publication in 1891 "The Kreutzer Sonata" triggered a strong reaction among the reading public. Russian literature had remained remarkably chaste during the nineteenth century, but this work led the way to an open treatment of sexuality in literature. Over the next two decades Russian writers would develop this subject extensively.

Several other of Tolstoy's late stories, such as "Otets Sergii" ("Father Sergius," 1890–98, published 1911), "Fal'shivyi kupon" ("The False Coupon," 1902–04), and "Alesha Gorshok" ("Alyosha the Pot," 1905), display genuine artistic merit and prove that Tolstoy's creative powers remained strong in his later years. His fiction made a tremendous impression on the writers who followed him, and the memoirs of such writers as Chekhov, Gorky, and Bunin bear witness to their enormous respect for his genius.

Chekhov: The Beginnings

The very best short-story writer in the generation that followed Tolstoy was, of course, Anton Chekhov. Through his innovations in narrative structure and technique he endowed the genre with new elasticity and depth. Despite the magnitude of his contribution, he has remained an elusive subject for literary critics. Unlike a Tolstoy or a Dostoevsky, Chekhov did not use his fiction as a pulpit for tendentious sermonizing. His outlook on life and the means he used to convey it were more subtle than those of his major nineteenth-century predecessors, and he resisted attempts to categorize him. In the closest thing to an artistic credo one finds in his writing, Chekhov declared that his "holy of holies" was "the human body, health, intelligence, talent, inspiration, love and the most absolute freedom imaginable, freedom from violence and lies, no matter what form the latter two take."[4]

This love of freedom and aversion to falsehood determined the thrust of Chekhov's writing. Declaring the aim of art to be "unconditional and honest truth,"[5] he exposed hypocrisy and deception in all their forms, including self-deception. Nor did he restrict his attack to any one class or group. Indeed Chekhov brought so many types of people within the reach of his analytical lens that he was regarded by some of his contemporaries as a thoroughgoing pessimist.[6] Thus the philosopher Lev Shestov (1866–1938) wrote that Chekhov was a "poet of helplessness" who stubbornly and monotonously for twenty-five years "did one thing only: . . . he killed human hopes."[7] Such a view is entirely too simplistic. Although it is true that Chekhov peoples his works with characters living lives of delusion, frustration, and futility, his treatment of these lives implies that a better way of living is both possible and preferable. Moreover, Chekhov is not at all callous in his approach to his characters' flaws. He may hold out little hope of redemption for his heroes, but he depicts their plight with sympathy and understanding. Only from the arrogant and the insensitive does he withhold this ameliorating warmth.

Trained as a doctor, Chekhov believed that a writer "must be as objective as a chemist,"[8] and he denied that his objectivity implied an "indifference to good and evil, the absence of ideals and ideas."[9] Chekhov agreed that "it would be nice to combine art with sermonizing," but claimed that for him personally, "this is extremely difficult and almost impossible because of considerations of technique." To inject his own viewpoint into his narrative would be to dilute his images and destroy the compactness of his tale. "When I write," he said, "I rely fully on the reader, presuming that he himself will add the subjective elements missing in my story."

Chekhov's observation points to a fundamental principle of his narrative art: by declining to mold his reader's attitudes through traditional methods of authorial omniscience, he requires the reader to work at extracting meaning from his stories. Structurally, Chekhov eliminated much of the expository material that earlier writers used to establish a background for their characters and plots. Paring descriptions of people and settings to a minimum, Chekhov relied on the use of a few details chosen for their suggestive potential. In many stories an initial conflict or situation engenders expectations that are never met. Chekhov's plots have been compared to gradual curves that start out in one direction and gently arc to end up in an entirely unexpected place. Often, instead of a dramatic denouement that releases the tension built up over the course of the story, the writer provides no denouement at all. Such "zero endings" have since become a staple of the modern short story.

Chekhov's predilection for understatement emerges in his choice of language and imagery. Tolstoy was one of the first readers of Chekhov to call his descriptive manner "impressionist."[10] Instead of trying to re-create a naturalistic scene in all its comprehensive detail, Chekhov tried to evoke the emotional atmosphere of a given moment, blending a few important details with subtle dashes of color and allusive sounds; some of his passages are rhythmic or melodic. To underscore the subjective nature of a character's perception of a scene, he often uses impersonal constructions such as "it seemed" or "it appeared."

This impressionistic style took years to develop, for Chekhov's work evolved substantially over the course of his career. The son of a grocer and the grandson of a serf, he was raised in the town of Taganrog. After moving to Moscow in 1879, he enrolled in medical school and received his degree in 1884. While still in school Chekhov made his literary debut with frequent contributions to popular humor magazines like *Strekoza* (Dragonfly) and *Oskolki* (Fragments). Although these pieces fall far short of the later works on which Chekhov's fame is based, certain traits—for example, an emphasis on concision—would subsequently be refined. The subject matter for these sketches was often determined by the needs of the periodical and had to do with current events or seasonal topics. Chekhov was prolific in these early years: from 1883 to 1885 he published some two hundred short works, most of which he considered unworthy of reprinting when he later prepared his collected works.

A distinctive feature of Chekhov's early work is his ear for language. Parodies of legal jargon, ecclesiastical terminology, and street vernacular fill his sketches, and he often combines the language of several stylistic levels to humorous effect. Chekhov also parodied popular literary genres, including the horror tale ("Krivoe zerkalo" ["The Crooked Mirror," 1883]), detective stories ("Shvedskaia spichka" ["The Safety Match," 1883]), and the romantic tale after Victor Hugo ("Tysiacha odna strast', ili Strashnaia noch'" ["A Thousand and One Passions, or A Terrible Night"]).

Another genre had important antecedents in earlier Russian literature: tales from the lives of petty officials. Following a tradition going back to Gogol and Dostoevsky, Chekhov wrote a number of stories emphasizing the insecurity and consciousness of rank that plagued the lowly bureaucrat. "Tolstyi i tonkii" ("Fat and Thin," 1883), describes the way an amicable meeting between two former schoolmates degenerates into a humiliating scene of self-abnegation when one learns that the other holds a higher rank than he. Another civil servant dies from horror when his attempts to apologize for sneezing on a high-ranking official are dismissed by the latter as insignificant ("Smert' chinovnika" ["The Death of a Bureaucrat," 1883]). A third character is forced to wait outside his apartment while a series of superiors visit his wife; his colleagues console him by claiming that this will help his career ("Na gvozde" ["On the Nail," 1883]). In these sketches one can detect a clear evolution in Chekhov's narrative stance. In his very earliest work he adopted an intrusive approach, addressing the reader with direct commentary. He gradually moved away from this subjective manner to a more neutral position, finally arriving at the impressionistic style described above, in which the characters' perceptions become the work's central perspective.[11]

Interspersed among Chekhov's humorous tales are a few works more serious in tone (for example, "Barynia" ["The Lady," 1882] and "Tsvety zapozdalye" ["Late-Blooming Flowers," 1882]). Not until 1885–86, however, did Chekhov begin to write stories that clearly indicated his future course. One such work is "Eger'" ("The Huntsman," 1885), a brief account of a meeting between a lonely peasant woman and a huntsman to whom she has been married for twelve years but who has never loved her and does not live with her. Chekhov's evocative use of selected detail and his understated handling of his characters' emotions in this story testify to his growing talent.

A pivotal work in Chekhov's career is the lengthy "Step'" ("The Steppe," 1888), which has almost no plot and consists of a series of descriptive vignettes tracing the journey of a boy named Egor from his native village to the town where he will attend school. Much of the story describes the journey itself, conveying predominantly through Egor's eyes the sights he encounters as he travels with his uncle and a group of peasant carters. Egor's passage through the steppe assumes the character of an initiation into the mysteries of existence. At Chekhov's hands the natural world comes alive and is imbued with an atmosphere of vague mystery and suspense. A recurring element in this mysterious realm is random violence and death: for example, a grasshopper devours the belly of a fly, which then flies off to feed on a horse.

Against this broad background the world of man seems trivial. Egor's uncle and an old priest chatter idly about the virtues of education, while other characters seem absorbed in their own sorrows or needs. The real hero is the realm of nature itself; its mysterious processes underscore man's ignorance. "The Steppe" is not a perfect work of art: Chekhov's attempt to tie the tale together through Egor's character and through a series of interweaving motifs is not wholly successful. Nevertheless, it marks a turning point in the writer's career, for Chekhov now leaves the humorous sketches of his early years to concentrate on the problem of existence itself.

Chekhov: The Mature Work

The first of the major existential stories to appear after "The Steppe" bears the ironic title "Skuchnaia istoriia" ("A Boring Story," 1889). A first-person narrative, the work presents the thoughts of an aging medical professor who realizes that he will soon die. The narrative exposes the professor's profound emotional paralysis and spiritual emptiness. He takes no comfort in his work, feels alienated from his family, and cannot escape his own self-consciousness. Asking himself why he experiences such distress, he surmises that his life lacks a central focus. In all his thoughts and feelings, he says, he cannot find anything that could be called "a general idea or the god of the living man."

Some of Chekhov's readers have seized upon this statement as the key to the professor's plight and have hastened to supply him with that missing "general idea." The writer Dmitry Merezhkovsky declared that the professor's problem stems from his scientific orientation and his lack of spiritual values, and Soviet critics see the professor's difficulties deriving from his failure to be involved in progressive social movements. Such solutions are too facile. The professor has in fact one overarching belief, and even now he still believes that science is the most important, beautiful, and necessary thing in the life of man. Yet this conviction brings him no comfort, and one must look beyond the lack of a "general idea" to explain the man's malaise. The professor's description of his relations with his family offers an important clue. His dealings with his wife and daughter are stilted and formal, and he feels estranged from them. The severity of that estrangement becomes clear when he is unable to comfort his emotionally distraught daughter on one occasion.

The professor's alienation emerges even more sharply in his relationship with his ward, Katya, the one person he truly loves. In the story's concluding scene Katya comes to him in tears and begs him to help her shape her life. His response reflects his own emotional isolation: "What can I say . . . I can't tell you anything." Disillusioned, she turns to leave, and the professor's last thoughts reveal his invincible self-concern: "So does this mean that you will not be at my funeral?" Thus it is not merely the lack of a general idea in his life that plagues the professor. He is emotionally crippled, unable to reach out and communicate with others, even his loved ones.

"A Boring Story," with its portrait of human isolation and alienation, reveals Chekhov's growing technical mastery. The narrative begins in the third person, with a detached description of a man who has become a symbol of success to the world at large. Only at the end of the paragraph does the professor reveal that he is the one described, and it is not until several paragraphs later that he moves beyond his "name," his social image, to reveal his true personality. By this device Chekhov hints at the professor's essential weakness: to the outside world he is merely a hollow shell; the inner man is hidden away and cannot break through that shell. Even the specter of death, which triggers such a dramatic moral revelation for Tolstoy's hero in *The Death of Ivan Ilyich,* cannot draw him out of his self-imposed isolation. Indeed, Tolstoy's story provides a striking contrast to "A Boring Story."

Chekhov would return to this type of character in later years, but in 1889–90 his exploration of the human condition assumed a broader scope. In 1890 he traveled to a penal colony on Sakhalin Island, and his exposure to the barbarous conditions there heightened his awareness of the cruelty of life itself. That experience stripped Chekhov of some of the idealist leanings of his youth. Formerly a great admirer of Tolstoy and his ideas of moral improvement through hard work and nonviolent resistance to evil, he then rejected Tolstoy's simple remedies for the problem of evil in the world.

One of the first works reflecting Chekhov's experiences on Sakhalin Island is "Gusev" (1890), a short piece that describes two men dying on a ship returning from the Far East. One, an intellectual named Pavel Ivanych, is an unpleasant, almost Dostoevskian character. Declaring himself to be "protest personified," he rails against social injustice and vilifies people like Gusev, whom he considers too passive. Although his concern with justice is commendable, the virulence of his diatribe undermines his effectiveness. Yet as impotent as Pavel Ivanych's words may be, Gusev's stolid placidity has scarcely more appeal. Although he accepts adversity without complaint, there is something animallike in his impassivity: for instance, staring at a Chinese man, he thinks: "It would be good to bash that fat fellow in the neck."

Significantly, the debate between the two men has no result, and they both meet the same end: they die and are buried at sea. Chekhov views the cosmos as a realm of blind, rapacious forces when he follows Gusev's canvas-wrapped body into the depths where a large shark rips the bag apart. The author offers no easy solution to the depredations of life. Instead, in his final scene he describes the sea and sky, focusing on the beautiful play of light at sunset, and concludes, "Looking at this magnificent, enchanting sky, the ocean at first frowns, but soon it also takes on tender, joyful, and passionate colors difficult even to name in human words." This scene carries symbolic implications. Like the realm of the sea, the human realm—the world "below"—is dark and disordered. Neither vehement protest nor apathetic resignation offers a clear path to fulfillment or peace. Rather, one must absorb the mute lessons of nature. Only through wordless communion with the natural world can one transcend the limitations of the self and attain a modicum of tranquillity and joy.

Chekhov's expository method in "Gusev" deserves comment. In contrast to the monological approach he took in "A Boring Story," the writer explores philosophies of life in the form of a debate between two contrasting points of view. He does not take sides overtly, but rather allows the reader to judge for himself the merits and drawbacks of each approach. Above all stands the world of nature, a silent commentary on the limited vision of the average mortal. This strategy of opposing two viewpoints in a single work appears repeatedly in Chekhov's fiction at this time, most notably in "Duel'" ("The Duel," 1891) and in "Palata No. 6" ("Ward Six," 1892), one of his finest works.

"Ward Six" contrasts Ivan Gromov, an inmate at a provincial mental asylum, with Dr. Andrey Ragin, who is in charge of the institution. Gromov is an intelligent young man somewhat reminiscent of Pavel Ivanych in his critical attitude toward the boorish ignorance of the rural town in which he lives. Hypersensitive to potential injustices in life, he becomes obsessed with the paranoid fear that he will be arrested by mistake, and eventually he can no longer function in the outside world. Consequently he is placed in the mental ward, a filthy place ruled by a loutish guard, Nikita. Dr. Ragin is also an intellectual, but he takes a different approach to the harsh realities of life: instead of worrying about them, he tries to shut them out of his mind. Although physically strong, he is emotionally weak, and although he recognizes the inadequacies of the medical facilities he oversees, he does not try very hard to correct them. Instead, he resorts to such easy rationalizations as "why hinder people from dying if death is the normal and legitimate end of us all?"

The confrontation between Gromov and Ragin forms the ideological core of the story. To Ragin's argument that one can find peace of mind anywhere, even in prison, Gromov replies that men are made of flesh and blood and that to reject the pains of the flesh is to reject life itself. He accuses Ragin of having only a theoretical knowledge of life and perceives in Ragin's theories a philosophy of mere expedience. This perception is borne out when Ragin himself is institutionalized after antagonizing the townspeople by his erratic behavior. Now Ragin undergoes a chilling conversion. As he stares out the asylum window he sees the blank stone walls of a prison and the dark flames of a bone mill: "There is reality!" he realizes. Shaken, he tries to leave the ward, but receives a beating from Nikita instead. The next day he dies of a stroke. Of the two men, Gromov may appear more sympathetic: his cry "I desperately want to live!" rings with conviction. Nevertheless, he, like Ragin, finds it much easier to talk about life than to live it. Neither man has the strength to play an active role in the world. Chekhov's decision to use a mental asylum as the setting for his tale was ingenious. In so doing, he not only follows the tradition of Garshin in "The Red Flower" in exposing the ignorance that frustrates treatment of the mentally ill; he also endows the asylum with symbolic import. Gromov complains that scores of madmen are walking free outside the asylum, while people like him are imprisoned. Ragin agrees, saying that it is all a matter of chance who is put inside the walls. These comments, taken together with the character sketches of other people Ragin encounters in his town and on a trip to Moscow and St. Petersburg, enable one to see how Leskov could maintain that Ward Six is Russia itself.[12] Chekhov's perception of the world as mental asylum made a significant impression on later writers such as Fedor Sologub and Leonid Andreev.

Chekhov created a very different image of mental illness itself in "Chernyi monakh" ("The Black Monk," 1894), an intriguing study of the solace found by a man visited by a spectral monk who tells him that he is one of the elect of the world. The discovery of fleeting moments of happiness in the midst of hardship also figures in the lyric sketch "Student" ("The Student," 1894). Here Chekhov depicts the shift in mood of a theology student who initially despairs over the seemingly endless miseries of life but is inspired with joy when he realizes that human empathy can be timeless as well.

Aside from these specialized studies of personal psychology, Chekhov's work in the mid-1890s falls into two general subject areas: stories dealing with social issues and stories illuminating individual life-styles, particularly those of stunted or unfulfilled people. Even in the first group, the social theme is often subordinate to a more intimate human drama. This is the case in "Dom s mezaninom" ("The House with a Mezzanine," 1896), another story in which Chekhov contrasts two character types—a dreamy artist who narrates the tale and an energetic teacher named Lida. Whereas Lida is an austere social activist who believes that man's highest calling is service to his neighbors, the narrator asserts that one's energies should go not into the construction of schools but into nurturing the spiritual potential of the human race. The conflict between Lida and the narrator, however, is less a struggle over ways to help the common folk than a struggle for ascendancy over Lida's impressionable sister Zhenya. In this contest, the strong activist bests the passive idealist: Lida succeeds in spiriting Zhenya away, and the narrator characteristically makes no effort to retrieve her. The hero's passivity and the tone of elegiac sadness pervading the narrative recall Turgenev. Neither Lida not the narrator is entirely sympathetic. Striving to avoid simple black and white portrayals, Chekhov indicates the limitations of both the dreamer and the activist, and thereby encourages the reader to consider a middle path. Ideally, one should be able both to work with a sense of purpose and to remain open to the full range of human emotions, including love.

Chekhov turned his attention to the common people in stories such as "Muzhiki" ("Peasants," 1897). An extended work with only a minimal plot, "Peasants" traces the experience of the family of Nikolay Chikildeev, a waiter from Moscow who returns home to his native village after falling ill. From the outset Chekhov emphasizes the misery of peasant life, contrasting Nikolay's fond recollection of a "bright, cozy, comfortable" place with a reality that is "dark, crowded, and dirty." Chekhov's exquisite nature descriptions accentuate the disparity between the beauty of the natural world and the squalor of human life. As the story unfolds, vignettes of rampant ignorance, violence, and petty greed follow one after another in numbing succession, and Chekhov provides no sign that assistance is forthcoming from any quarter. The secular authorities' activities seem limited to tax collection; representatives of the gentry class sweep into the village to fight a fire and then sweep out again without lasting effects; and even the religious figures provide no consolation for the villagers: as Chekhov notes, "there were few who believed, few who had any understanding." Just once a year, during the procession of a holy icon, are the peasants inspired with any hope of salvation. Yet even this mood soon passes as they subside into their normal routine of holiday drunkenness. Only Nikolay's wife Olga displays any deep spiritual impulse, although it derives less from an informed understanding of Christian teachings than from an instinctive appreciation of the concepts of charity and love. As the story ends, Olga and her daughter Sasha are leaving the village after Nikolay's death: in the final scene Sasha begs for alms "for Christ's sake." The peasants' hope for Christian mercy is the only source of consolation available to them.

Chekhov's narrative suggests that the peasant himself is responsible for the drunkenness and corruption of village life, but he is evenhanded in his approach, and Olga concludes: "Yes, to live with them was terrible, but all the same they are people . . . and there is nothing in their life for which one could not find justification." Chekhov avoids either sweeping accusations or justifications. He is content to depict life as he perceives it and to let others argue over its verisimilitude. Understandably, "Peasants" provoked considerable debate among its readers.

If Chekhov's portrait of peasant life on the land is dark, his examination of the peasant turned merchant in "V ovrage" ("In the Ravine," 1899) is even gloomier. Whereas the characters in "Peasants" live in a beautiful natural setting, the protagonists of this work live in town, in a milieu polluted by industrial wastes. Chekhov's study of human greed and callousness culminates in cold-blooded murder. Angry that her sister-in-law's baby may become an heir to the family business, a grasping woman named Aksinya scalds the child with boiling water. The only noble character in the family is the baby's mother, Lipa. Like Olga in "Peasants," she displays an instinctive warmth and compassion that raise her above the brute figures who devour one another in their lust for material gain.

Chekhov's antipathy toward lives wasted in pursuit of selfish or petty ends informs many of his works of the mid-1890s. At the center of this cycle are three stories written in 1898 and collectively called "the little trilogy"—"Chelovek v futliare" ("The Man in a Box"), "Kryzhovniki" ("Gooseberries"), and "O liubvi" ("About Love"). Each story is a frame tale presenting a vivid illustration of a squandered life. The first, narrated by a teacher named Burkin, centers on a Gogolian character named Belikov, a narrow-minded teacher of Greek whose permanent retreat from life is symbolized by his constant wearing of an overcoat and galoshes. Belikov has an oppressive impact on those around him. Forever imposing his own distrust of spontaneity and freedom onto others, he intimidates his fellow teachers into following his lead. His sullen life comes to an unexpected end when he dies, apparently of humiliation, after being laughed at by a lively girl whom he had been seeing in town. Unfortunately, Belikov's passing brings the townspeople only temporary release. Soon life drops back into its familiar rut and is once more ruled by other "men in boxes."

Burkin's interlocutor, Ivan Ivanych, narrates the next story describing his brother, another Gogolian character. The man had dreamed of owning a country estate and after years of obsessive privation finally succeeded in buying some land. From Ivan's perspective, this dream come true is more like a nightmare: instead of a beautiful pond one finds a polluted stream, and the crown jewel of his dream—a set of gooseberry bushes—produces only sour fruit. But the brother is supremely happy, and as he piggishly stuffs the gooseberries into his mouth, he exclaims "How tasty!" Ivan is both depressed and angered by all this. In an implicit allusion to Tolstoy's story "How Much Land Does a Man Need?" he rejects the idea that a man needs only six feet of earth. Man needs not six feet, not an estate, but "the whole world, all of nature," so that he can exercise his power without constraint.

The narrator of the last piece, a miller named Alekhin, relates a personal anecdote about the love that he and a neighbor's wife felt for each other but never expressed until it was too late. Once more, people in Chekhov's world squander their lives by following convention, missing any chance to find personal fulfillment.

Each story of the little trilogy is framed by a brief but polished nature description that serves as a silent commentary on the stories enclosed within. Chekhov contrasts the spacious freedom of nature with the closed and stultifying world of everyday life.

Instances of youthful hope deteriorating into lives of banality figure in other stories of this period such as "Uchitel' slovesnosti" ("The Teacher of Literature," 1894) and "Ionych" (1898). Several works investigate the relationship between the sexes as the arena in which dramas of failed expectations occur. In three stories of 1895—"Supruga" ("The Wife"), "Ariadna" ("Ariadne"), and "Anna na shee" ("Anna on the Neck")—Chekhov singles out domineering females as the source of misfortune for the men who love them. Some critics think these stories marred by misogyny,[13] but Chekhov's narrator in "Ariadne" suggests that a woman's predilection for manipulating men stems from faulty upbringing: when men and women are raised as true equals, this disparity in their behavior will disappear.

Although Chekhov featured fractured relationships in his stories of the mid-1890s, as the decade drew to a close he portrayed more often people pursuing dreams of emotional fulfillment. His most famous work of this period, "Dama s sobachkoi" ("The Lady with a Lapdog," 1900), illustrates this idea. A masterpiece, the work contains a characteristically Chekhovian plot curve. When Dmitry Gurov first sees the married woman with whom he will become involved, Anna Sergeevna von Dideritz, he foresees only a casual fling with her in Yalta, where they are both vacationing. But the affair proves much more serious. After returning home to Moscow, Gurov finds that he cannot forget Anna. Impetuously he goes to her provincial hometown and confronts her at the theater. Horrified yet thrilled, she agrees to meet him in Moscow, and thus Gurov enters upon an agonizing double existence. Outwardly he lives a normal life of routine, while his real life lies within, hidden from the world. The conclusion of the story provides a fine example of the zero-end technique. The two lovers continue to meet despite all obstacles, but they have no idea how to change their situation. Thus they remain suspended in an excruciating state of radiant joy and enervating anxiety. Chekhov attains a high level of artistic refinement in this tale through his evocative handling of setting, gesture, and character. By describing two people who are by no means distinguished or special, he illuminates the unique power of love to transform even the most ordinary lives.

Chekhov's command of the short story remains powerful in the final works of his career. In "Nevesta" ("The Bride," 1903), he provides a last look at a character able to perceive the traps of routine existence and to break free in search of a better life. In "Arkhierei" ("The Bishop," 1902) he comes to terms with the inevitability of human mortality and the boundlessness of nature's immortality. The latter work in particular displays the extraordinary skill Chekhov achieved in his late years. This intensely lyrical tale focuses on the impressions of an aging bishop in the last days of his life. Like the professor in "A Boring

Story," the bishop is irritated by the formality and detached respect with which those around him, including his mother, treat him. Unlike the earlier character, however, the bishop manages to break through this barrier because his illness exposes him as an ordinary human being, frail as a child. Death, when it comes, does not portend an icy void, but rather acts as an agent of release. Chekhov's narrative technique here is extremely complex, almost symphonic, as is evident from the opening paragraph, a description of the Palm Sunday service in which sound, rhythm, and even phrasing reflect the movements of the liturgy and the impressions of the old priest conducting it. In such works as "The Bishop" Chekhov attains a degree of artistic perfection seldom matched by other short-story writers.

Korolenko and Gorky

A contemporary of Chekhov's was Vladimir Korolenko (1853–1921). Born in the Ukraine, Korolenko was educated in St. Petersburg and Moscow, where he became inspired by populist doctrines and took part in protest movements. After several confrontations with the authorities Korolenko was arrested in 1879 and sent into exile, ending up in Siberia. His first literary works grew out of his prison experience. "Chudnaia" ("The Strange One"), for example, written in a transit prison in 1880, records an encounter between a proud political prisoner and the sympathetic guard accompanying her to her place of exile.

Korolenko's most famous early work, however, treats a very different subject: "Son Makara" ("Makar's Dream," 1883) depicts the hard life of a primitive Siberian peasant who dies after becoming drunk on cheap vodka and losing his way in the snowy taiga. The concluding portion of the story records his experiences after death, when he travels to meet the great Toyon ("master" in Yakut), who passes judgment on his life. "Makar's Dream" displays Korolenko's characteristic blend of light humor and warm compassion for human travail. Seeing the scales of judgment tip against him, Makar tries to prop up the pan containing his sins with his foot. Sentenced to punishment as a cart horse, Makar launches into an impassioned speech about the hardship he has suffered in life. His story of pain, degradation, and loneliness leaves Toyon in tears, and the scales tip back in Makar's favor.

Korolenko's experiences in Siberia also inspired a series of sketches and stories on the lives of simple folk who roam the region (for example, "Sokolinets," 1885, and "Cherkes," 1888). Many of them describe the rugged beauty of the land in lyric passages reminiscent of Turgenev (for example, "Les shumit" ["The Forest Rustles," 1886] and "Reka igraet" ["The River Plays," 1891]). In 1896 Korolenko moved to St. Petersburg to become an editor of the populist journal *Russkoe bogatstvo* (Russian wealth), and within the next few years his work became more publicistic in orientation. He wrote several stories championing the rights of minorities and excoriating the authorities for political repression (for example, "Bytovoe iavlenie" ["An Everyday Occurrence"], an attack on the numerous executions carried out after 1905).

Although Korolenko was perhaps the most artistically successful of the populist writers of the 1880s and 1890s, numerous others reflected populist ideas in their works, from Nikolay Zlatovratsky (1845–1911) and Aleksandr Ertel (1855–1908) in the 1880s to Nikolay Garin (pseudonym for N. Mikhailovsky, 1852–1906) and Petr Yakubovich (1860–1911) in the 1890s. But the writer whose critical vision of the social order gained the widest recognition at the turn of the century was Maksim Gorky (1868–1936). Born in Nizhny Novgorod on the Volga River, Gorky (the pseudonym of Aleksey Peshkov) was raised by his grandparents in an atmosphere of poverty, abuse, and avarice. Forced to earn his keep from an early age, Gorky held a succession of jobs, from picking rags to working as a baker in Kazan. Eventually the life of material hardship and his perception of inescapable poverty in the world took its toll when he tried unsuccessfully to kill himself in 1887.

Gorky's first literary triumph came with the publication of "Makar Chudra" in 1892. A short narrative about the fatal passion felt by a gypsy bandit named Loyko Zobar for a dazzling woman named Radda, the story exhibits Gorky's early fascination with a romantic spirit of independence and boldness. Though deeply in love with each other, both Loyka and Radda value their freedom more than their love. To escape this trap, Loyko stabs Radda and is in turn stabbed by her father. The story is related by Makar Chudra, an old gypsy, who begins by discussing a prominent theme in Gorky's early fiction—the disparity between the masses of people who live lives of dreary toil and the special few who cherish their proud independence.

Gorky returned to this topic in "Chelkash" (1895), in which he draws a sharp contrast between the freedom-loving title character—a vagabond thief—and a slavish peasant named Gavrila whom Chelkash enlists in a smuggling operation. Gorky underscores the differences between the two through such devices as comparing their attitudes toward the sea: Chelkash feels an elemental kinship with the sea, "boundless, free, and powerful," whereas Gavrila cowers in fright before its force. The portrait of Chelkash is nuanced: he understands Gavrila's attachment to village life because he recalls with nostalgia the security of his own peasant childhood. Yet though now a rootless criminal, he proves nobler and more compassionate than Gavrila. After the latter tries to kill him to steal the money they have made in smuggling, Chelkash gives him the money anyway, feeling nothing but contempt for the depths to which greed can take a man. Gorky's dismay over the way relentless toil debases the human spirit informs the description of the bustling activity on the docks in the opening pages of the story. In such passages, Gorky tends toward the hyperbolic. His descriptions lack subtlety and grace by comparison with Chekhov's, but their raw energy impressed later writers, and early Soviet literature owes much to Gorky's highly charged style.

During the mid-1890s Gorky wrote feuilletons, reviews, and stories for papers in Samara and Nizhny Novgorod; among the better known works of this period are "Starukha Izergil'" ("Old Izergil," 1895), "Na plotakh" ("On the Rafts," 1895), "Pesnia o sokole" ("The Song of the Falcon," 1895), "Konovalov" (1897), and "Mal'va" (1897). Here Gorky illuminates the hardships of the working poor and the undying aspiration for a life free of oppression. Several works draw on folklore traditions to create striking allegorical images, such as the heroic Danko who tears out his heart and uses it as a beacon to guide his people out of a dark forest ("Old Izergil"), or the wounded falcon who strives to return to the sky at the cost of his life ("The Song of the Falcon"). Gorky also resorted to allegory in his brief sketch "Pesnia o burevestnike" ("The Song of the Stormy Petrel," 1901), a work popular with the revolutionary movement because of its central image of a brave bird, "the prophet of freedom," flying courageously into the storm.

Gorky's portraits of bold *bosiaki* (tramps) who scorn the restraints of conventional life appealed to a reading public tired of impoverished landowners, downtrodden peasants, and unhappy intellectuals in fiction. When his stories appeared in a two-volume edition in 1898, they reached an astonishing circulation of 100,000 copies, a figure rivaled only by Tolstoy. Gorky became something of a cult figure, and his work became increasingly critical of social injustice. For him, human unhappiness was not an existential problem but instead had definite origins in social exploitation and material deprivation. His writing documented specific features of these conditions and conveyed a message of hope for eventual improvement. This combination of graphic analysis and lyrical emotion became his hallmark.

"Dvadtsat' shest' i odna" ("Twenty-six Men and a Girl," 1899) provides a fine example of Gorky's approach. He begins with a description of a bakery located in a cellar and operated by twenty-six men, "living machines" crammed into an airless room dominated by a huge oven that Gorky depicts as the deformed head of a fantastic monster staring pitilessly at the slaves laboring before it. When the men begin to sing, however, the walls seem to recede, and the song itself becomes a wide road beckoning them all to freedom. Unfortunately, such transcendent moments are short-lived. The only other source of joy for the bakers is a young woman named Tanya who comes every day to collect pretzels. The men worship her like a goddess, but in a stroke of foolish pride, they endanger their happiness by betting a newcomer that he cannot seduce her. When the newcomer succeeds in seducing Tanya one rainy day, the men forfeit their last repository of beauty and grace.

After 1900 Gorky directed his creative drive toward plays and novels, and he is better known for such works as the play *Na dne* (*The Lower Depths,* 1902) and the novel *Mat'* (*Mother,* 1907) than for his short fiction. In the 1910s, however, he wrote a number of stories and sketches—including the cycle *Po Rusi* (*Through Russia,* 1912–16)—that convey his impressions of Russian life in effective colors.

In addition to his own literary creation, Gorky was a central participant in cultural discussion groups, such as the Wednesday Circle, and in collective publishing ventures, the most famous of which was the Znanie (Knowledge) publishing house. Founded in 1898, Znanie became under Gorky's direction a leading publisher of domestic and foreign fiction and poetry. Gorky and several other writers published by Znanie held leftist political views, but a broad range of writers contributed to a series of miscellanies Znanie issued from 1904 through 1913. The most prominent of these were Chekhov, Leonid Andreev, Ivan Bunin, and Aleksandr Kuprin. Among the lesser lights of the Znanie circle, the following may be mentioned: Vikenty Smidovich (1867–1945), who used the pseudonym Veresaev, wrote about the changing attitudes of the intelligentsia at the turn of the century; Aleksandr Popov (1863–1949), better known as Aleksandr Serafimovich, wrote tales about the working class; Nikolay Teleshov (1867–1957), who ran the Wednesday Circle, and Evgeny Chirikov (1864–1932) chronicled life in the provinces; Semyon Yushkevich (1868–1927) and David Aizman (1869–1932) portrayed conditions of Jewish life; Sergey Gusev-Orenburgsky (1867–1963) wrote about the provincial clergy; and Stepan Petrov (1869–1941), who used the name Skitalets, emulated Gorky in writing about tramps. Several of these writers later achieved prominence in the Soviet period. Gorky himself attained a position of unique influence under the Soviets, becoming something of a minor deity in his lifetime.

Bunin

Other writers pursued a different course. One of these was Ivan Bunin (1870–1958), perhaps in this period the finest craftsman of the Russian short story after Chekhov. Born into a family of impoverished nobility, he had only four years of formal education but read avidly. He began his literary career as a poet, attaining recognition for his original poems and his translations from English. His early prose was influenced by Chekhov. Sketches such as "Na krai sveta" ("To the Edge of the World," 1894), which depicts the migration of a village populace from their native home to new territory, recall "The Steppe" with their lyrical animation of nature.

Bunin discovered his personal literary voice around 1900, when he wrote a series of "mood paintings"[14] recording the changing social conditions in the Russian countryside. The best of these is "Antonovskie iabloki" ("Antonov Apples," 1900), a sensual evocation of the disappearing life-style of the great landowners of the past. Beginning with the words "I remember," Bunin's narrator takes his reader on a nostalgic journey from the distant past to recent times in a movement through time accompanied by the narrator's aging. The two movements together underscore Bunin's perception of time's inexorable passage.

Although Bunin had developed a remarkable facility for evocative description, his work reached an impasse around 1903. He could evoke the imminent passing of an entire social order in lyrical imagery, but his sketches lacked depth. At this crucial juncture Bunin sought to broaden his horizons by traveling to the Middle East in 1903 and again in 1907. After visiting the sites of the great cultures of the past—Greek, Roman, Egyptian—Bunin returned to Russia with a deeper understanding of national character and the ineluctable rise and fall of civilizations. Beginning in 1909 he wrote a series of works that illuminate the Russian soul and the changing conditions of life in the country. The most famous of these was the novella *Derevnia* (*The Village,* 1909–10), a dark examination of savagery and ignorance among the peasantry that caused a sensation upon its publication. Bunin's shorter fiction also dramatized the tendency toward violence that erupts among the peasantry when severed from its traditional roots by the forces of industrialization or famine. Works such as "Nochnoi razgovor" ("A Nocturnal Conversation," 1911), "Ermil" (1912), "Ignat" (1912), and "Vesennii vecher" ("A Spring Evening," 1914) contain incidents in which a peasant commits an act of violence, sometimes without provocation. On the other hand, Bunin did not always present the peasant as a callous brute; works such as "Sverchok" ("Cricket," 1911) and "Veselyi dvor" ("A Gay Farmhouse," 1911) offer moving depictions of selfless love among the peasantry.

Nor did Bunin single the peasant out as the only inhabitant of the countryside moved by dark spiritual forces. One of the finest works of his career, the novella *Sukhodol* (sometimes translated as *Dry Valley,* 1911), reveals that a deep streak of irrationality can grip peasant and landowner alike. Bunin devoted a cycle of stories to the extraordinary dimensions of the Russian soul, including "Zakhar Vorob'ev" (1912), "Ioann Rydalets" ("Ioann Weeper," 1913), "Ia vse molchu" ("I Keep Silence," 1913), "Sviatye" ("Saints," 1914), and "Aglaia" (1916), a sketch revealing the writer's interest in the genre of saints' lives.

At the same time in the mid-1910s Bunin's investigation of the dynamics of human behavior became increasingly broad. A major topic of his concern was romantic love. One of his most compelling works of the period, "Legkoe dykhanie" ("Light Breathing," 1916), is a terse depiction of a young girl's discovery of the power of her own sexuality and her unexpected death at the hands of a jilted lover. Bunin's handling of the girl's psychology is characteristic of him. Unlike Tolstoy, who records in minute detail the thought processes of his protagonist, Bunin is more reserved. He suggests a psychological state through evocative detail and gesture, relying on this method even more than Chekhov to create an emotional mood. His manipulation of narrative structure in the tale is also characteristic of him. He begins with a description of a cemetery and focuses on the picture, attached to a cross, of his protagonist Olya, "a high school girl with joyful, strikingly lively eyes," thereby arousing the reader's curiosity about the girl and her untimely end and creating a somber background against which the girl's exuberance stands out in relief. He returns to the cemetery at the end of the story, but now focuses on a visitor to the grave who turns out to be a new character, Olya's former teacher, drawn to the grave by her fascination with Olya's fate. The teacher recalls Olya's comment that the most telling marker of beauty was "light breathing." Bunin concludes his tale with the words: "Now this light breathing was once again dispersed in the world, in this clouded sky, in this cold spring wind." This image lifts the reader out of the confines of the graveyard and creates an aura of transcendence. Together with the figure of the teacher who keeps Olya's memory alive, Bunin uses this image to fracture the closed symmetry of the cemetery scenes framing Olya's life and to suggest the boundless continuity of the cosmos itself. Through his expansion of plot and textual boundaries Bunin enhanced the narrative capacity of the short-story genre in general.

Bunin's interest in the power of passion was a hallmark of his mature fiction, although stories such as "Light Breathing," "Grammatika liubvi" ("The Grammar of Love," 1915), and "Syn" ("The Son," 1916) reveal that passion is transitory and often ends in pain or death. This combination of intense power and tragic brevity permeates most of Bunin's subsequent treatments of the theme, and it is particularly evident in the work he wrote as an émigré from the 1920s through the 1940s.

Absorbed in the mid-1910s with the transience of human happiness, Bunin found a stimulating explanation for this problem in the Buddhist doctrine that all suffering stems from desire and that true peace comes only with its cessation.[15] The stories "Brat'ia" ("Brothers," 1914) and "Sny Changa" ("The Dreams of Chang," 1916) deal directly with this concept; to a lesser degree it also informs his most famous work of the period, "Gospodin iz San-Frantsisko" ("The Gentleman from San Francisco," 1915). The story has only a minimal plot: a rich American businessman travels to Europe with his family, dies of a heart attack, and returns home in a coffin. On the bare bones of this plot Bunin constructs an elaborate narrative densely textured with subtle counterpoint and evocative detail. The work has often been viewed as an indictment of Western capitalism, but it is more than that. Through the anonymous title figure Bunin illustrates a pervasive problem in modern society—a tendency toward unbridled egocentricity that leaves one indifferent to the outside world, to nature, and to God.

Bunin's narrative points up the shallow insensitivity of the gentleman. After arriving in Italy, for example, he and his family slip into a torpid routine involving such standard activities as visits to churches, where "the same thing is found everywhere: . . . vast emptiness, silence . . . slippery gravestones under the feet and someone's *Deposition from the Cross,* invariably famous." The images of death here foreshadow the gentleman's own impending fate, but they do not move him any more than do the religious objects themselves. Even the image of

Christ's crucifixion, a central mystery of Christianity, is only a museum piece whose fame is to be noted, and nothing more.

Bunin does provide a counter to this vision of self-indulgence, but holds it in reserve until his main character has passed from the stage. Death strikes the gentleman down suddenly on Capri, and without anything like the moral revelation that visits Tolstoy's Ivan Ilyich. Redemption is unlikely in the gentleman's world. Instead, Bunin turns his attention to two peasants descending Monte Solaro as they relish the beautiful natural vista spread out before them. When they stop at a statue of the Madonna in the rocks, they offer "naive and humbly joyful praise" to the Madonna, to God, and to nature. Their simplicity, humility, and closeness to nature contrast sharply with the gentleman's narrow world.

Bunin returns to that world at the end of his narrative, as he describes the ship carrying the gentleman's body back to America. This description is deeply symbolic. Ruled by the mysterious figure of the captain, a kind of pagan idol to the passengers, the ship is a mighty manmade edifice that crushes the resistance of the natural world raging at it in a storm. Bunin's narrative closes with a mournful image of the coffin resting in the ship's hold, a naked emblem of the corruption at the core of the selfish modern world.

The writer's apprehension over the course the modern world was taking seemed justified with the outbreak of World War I in 1914 and the Russian Revolution in 1917. Bunin viewed the Revolution with antipathy, and so left Russia in 1920. Settling in France, he continued his writing, composing numerous short stories, memoirs, and an autobiographical novel entitled *Zhizn' Arsen'eva: Istoki dnei* (*The Life of Arsenyev: The Well of Days*). In 1933 he became the first Russian author to receive the Nobel Prize for literature.

Kuprin and Andreev

Another writer who entered literature along with Bunin and also became an émigré for a time was Aleksandr Kuprin (1870–1938). Born in southern Russia, Kuprin grew up in Moscow, where he attended a military high school and a military academy. While still in school he wrote poetry; he published his first story, "Poslednii debiut" ("The Last Debut"), in 1889. For two years he served in garrisons in the Ukraine, an experience that inspired several short stories and his most famous novel, *Poedinok* (*The Duel,* 1905). After leaving the army in 1894,

Kuprin held a number of jobs, from journalist to carpenter. His familiarity with various occupations is manifest in his fiction, with its colorful portraits of a motley crew of character types.

In his early work Kuprin was fascinated by unusual psychological states. Some stories of the time—including "Psikheia" ("Psyche," 1892) and "Vpot'makh" ("In Darkness," 1893)—are marred by a tendency toward melodrama. More accomplished was "Doznanie" ("The Inquiry," 1894), a tale of a sensitive young officer's disillusionment with the harshness of army life, which anticipates *The Duel.* A series of sketches of the mid-1890s published under the general title *Kievskie tipy* (*Kievan Types*) reveals Kuprin's penchant for sketching the life-styles of various social groups, from thieves to choir singers. This interest also surfaces in his collection *Miniatiury* (*Miniatures,* 1897), containing some twenty-five short stories. One of the better known of these is "Allez!"—a simple tale about a young circus performer's lack of control over her life. Built on the repetition of the command "Allez!" the story follows the girl as she is ordered about by adults—first to perform circus acts and then into and out of an affair with a star clown. The story ends when she is rejected by her lover and leaps to her death from a hotel window in response to an inner voice commanding "Allez!" Kuprin also wrote a series of sketches on industrial settings culminating in his long tale *Molokh* (*Moloch,* 1896), an indictment of capitalist exploitation as seen from an engineer's perspective.

At the turn of the century Kuprin worked on the popular St. Petersburg journals *Zhurnal dlia vsekh* (Journal for all) and *Mir bozhii* (God's world) and continued writing short fiction. Though few in number, his stories of this time—like "V tsirke" ("At the Circus," 1902), "Boloto" ("The Swamp," 1902), "Konokrady" ("Horse Thieves," 1903), "Trus" ("The Coward," 1903), and "Zhidovka" ("The Jewess," 1904)—demonstrate Kuprin's growing artistic proficiency. "At the Circus," for example, describes the death of a wrestler in a match that his doctor had urged him to cancel because of a heart ailment. Kuprin's narrative points up the irony of the way a mighty human can be felled by a weak heart, and his treatment of the wrestler's psychology conveys his compassion for the plight of one driven to sacrifice his life for pride and money. Also noteworthy is Kuprin's skill at re-creating the unique atmosphere of circus life, a realm of glitter, suspense, and practicality. "At the Circus" drew praise from Chekhov and Tolstoy alike.

Kuprin depicted many other social groups, from degenerate aristocrats ("Zhrets" ["The Priest," 1905]) to Jewish smugglers ("The Coward"). In "The Jewess," written at a time when pogroms were at their height, he ponders the beauty and enduring strength of the Jewish people as reflected in the face of an innkeeper's wife. In his subsequent fiction Kuprin occasionally accomplished successful fusion of political sentiment and description of everyday life. "Gambrinus" (1907), for example, begins by examining the life-style of the sailors, fishermen, and dockworkers who frequent a tavern in Odessa, though the central protagonist is a Jewish fiddler named Sasha, who plays tunes that echo current events. During the Boer War he plays the "Boer March"; during the Franco-Russian festivities he plays the "Marseillaise." After the Russo-Japanese War, however, Odessa witnessed the rise of a revolutionary spirit and a corresponding reaction of pogroms. When asked to play the national anthem by a bully, Sasha refuses, and his defiance results in his arrest and the crippling of his hand. He triumphs nevertheless. Unable to play the violin, Sasha plays a small pipe instead, and Kuprin concludes: "It's possible to cripple a man, but art will endure and conquer all."

This spirit of idealistic emotion informs several stories Kuprin wrote about love, from "Sulamif'" ("Sulamith," 1908), an opulent tale about the passion between King Solomon and the vineyard keeper's daughter Sulamith, to "Granatovyi braslet" ("The Bracelet of Garnets," 1911), a tale of exceptional but unrequited love. The latter work, which displays Kuprin's characteristic emotionalism and skill at creating suspense, centers on the inability of an aristocratic married woman to respond to the ardent but concealed devotion of a man named Zheltkov. After Zheltkov has committed suicide, the woman recognizes her loss and, in the end, is reconciled with the spirit of the dead man. Kuprin's other pieces of this period also demonstrate that his artistic strength lay in depicting unusual characters and situations rather than in communicating weighty philosophies. "Izumrud" ("Emerald," 1907) is a marvelous portrait of the sensual and emotional perceptions of a superior racehorse. Kuprin's skill at conveying the animal's simple love of nature overshadows the darker message that the horse has been exploited and destroyed merely to satisfy some human's monetary greed.

The output of Kuprin's later years is uneven in quality. On the one hand, he composed a fine series of sketches on the life of Greek fishermen entitled *Listrigony* (*The Laestrygones,* 1907–11), but on the other, he wrote a tendentious novel on the evils of prostitution called *Iama* (*The Pit,* 1909–15). After leaving Russia in 1919, Kuprin had difficulty supporting himself through his writing. Impoverished and ill, he returned to the Soviet Union in 1937 and died a year later. Although less subtle and poetic than Bunin and less forceful than Gorky, Kuprin has earned a definite niche in the annals of the Russian short story.

A very different kind of storyteller was Leonid Andreev (1871–1919). Imaginative, talented, and volatile, Andreev sought to explore such dimensions of the human experience as madness, sexuality, the workings of fate, and the mystery of death. In treating these subjects he revealed a distinct fondness for the sensational. Born into a lower-middle-class family in Orel, Andreev was sensitive and self-conscious. After the age of sixteen he made at least three suicide attempts and often tried to escape from nervous depression in heavy drinking. Although he took a law degree at Moscow University, he did not practice law for long and soon became a journalist and writer. An important step in his career was the publication of the story "Bargamot i Garas'ka" ("Bargamot and Garaska") in 1898. Written in the sentimental tradition of Easter tales, this story of the reconciliation between a tough policeman and a habitual drunkard attracted Gorky's notice by its vivid description of life in a rough urban district and its lightly ironic tone. Gorky introduced Andreev to the members of the Wednesday group and later published his work through Znanie. Though many writers in this circle adopted a realist approach in their writing, Andreev took a pronounced interest in the riddles of the psyche and its penchant for the symbolic, so that his fiction bore certain similarities with the work of the symbolists, although Andreev personally felt no camaraderie with that group.

Andreev's early fiction concentrates on people striving to find happiness while battling feelings of isolation from others. A typical example is "Molchanie" ("Silence," 1900), in which a stern priest insists that his daughter tell him what sorrows she bears within her soul. When she refuses, he stops talking to her. A week later she commits suicide. Much of the story deals with the growing weight of the silence that surrounds the priest after his daughter's death; even his wife now stops speaking to him. The tale concludes: "And the whole, dark, empty house was silent." Suicide and sudden death occur in other early works of Andreev's. "Rasskaz o Sergee Petroviche" ("The Story of Sergey Petrovich," 1900) details the labyrinthine mental process by which a student fascinated with Nietzsche's superman decides to kill himself to affirm his freedom from nature and necessity. In "Bol'shoi shlem" ("The Grand Slam," 1899) a man who has dreamed all his life of making a grand slam at cards dies of a heart attack just before his dream comes true. Both stories reveal the folly of insulated lives.

Andreev repeatedly depicted human beings in thrall to forces beyond their control. In 1902 he wrote two stories—"Bezdna" ("The Abyss") and "V tumane" ("In the Fog")—that expose the weakness of civilized man when confronted by one such inner force—the sexual drive. "The Abyss" illustrates the point graphically. It begins with a young couple named Nemovetsky and Zina taking an evening walk in the woods. The scene has the air of a romantic idyll: the two talk about the immortality of love and are themselves described as young and pure. Imperceptibly, though, the mood shifts. As the sun sets, the environment becomes threatening. They encounter a band of three men who attack them, beating Nemovetsky into unconsciousness and raping Zina. When Nemovetsky comes to, he is disoriented and finds Zina lying naked and unconscious nearby. As he attempts to revive her, he feels himself stirred with overwhelming desire. The narrator concludes: "For a single instant flaming horror lighted up his mind, opening before him a black abyss. And the abyss swallowed him."

This image may strike the modern reader as melodramatic, but Andreev's vision of a civilized youth yielding to his bestial instincts gained him widespread contemporary notoriety. The publication of "In the Fog" increased his fame. Here again the protagonist, Pavel Rybakov, is a well-bred youth, but this time he has already surrendered to his sexual drive and has contracted a venereal disease. Andreev's portrayal of the boy's anguish is moving, and the reader feels the complex of emotions tearing at him, including shame, desire, and alienation. Andreev creates an atmospheric tale out of recurring images of darkness: the dingy fog enveloping the city streets is emblematic of the gloom in Pavel's soul. The story concludes with a dramatic confrontation. After getting drunk with a surly prostitute, Pavel ends by stabbing her and then himself. Andreev's readers conducted a spirited debate over the work. Some—Tolstoy's wife, for example—attacked the writer for his sensationalism, but others applauded his frank approach to a serious issue. It is ironic that Tolstoy's wife should have entered the debate, for it was her husband's treatment of sexuality in works such as "The Kreutzer Sonata" that paved the way for responses like Andreev's.

With the outbreak of the Russo-Japanese War and the ensuing political unrest of 1905–06, Andreev's work assumed more topical dimensions. His impressionistic depiction of the horrors of war in

"Krasnyi smekh" ("Red Laughter," 1904) again aroused controversy. Beginning with the words "Madness and horror," narrated in a series of fragments by a first-person observer, "Red Laughter" generalizes the experience of war, with the image of red laughter itself standing for the monstrous destructiveness of the militaristic impulse. Some war veterans criticized this Goyaesque evocation of the devastation of war as unrealistic, but the work proved popular with the public.

Andreev's liberal sympathies led to a brief incarceration in 1905. At this time he wrote several works on political themes, including "Gubernator" ("The Governor," 1906) and "Tak bylo" ("Thus It Was," 1905). His most famous political piece was the long tale "Rasskaz o semi poveshennykh" ("Seven Who Were Hanged," 1908), an interesting gathering of psychological portraits of political prisoners condemned to death for plotting the assassination of a government official. Like Tolstoy's pamphlet *Ia ne mogu molchat'* (*I Cannot Be Silent*), Andreev's story stemmed from the numerous executions that followed the political struggles of 1905 and 1906. As Andreev analyzes the prisoners' personal reactions to impending death, he discloses a whole range of emotions from terror and alienation to resignation, peace, and even transcendent joy. Andreev's concluding scene emphasizes the grotesqueness of the execution itself, and he leaves the reader with a searing picture of the prisoners' corpses lying in the snow at dawn.

Andreev's fascination with death emerged in numerous treatments of the subject. Among the most striking is "Eleazar" ("Lazarus," 1906), a work that describes the petrifying effect Lazarus had on his fellowman when restored to life by Christ after three days in the grave. Andreev's own "horror of the Infinite" informs the story, and he describes in elaborate detail the terror that overcomes those who gaze into Lazarus's eyes. He inserts an affirmative note into the tale with an encounter between Lazarus and the Roman emperor Augustus: although Augustus too finds his life force ebbing under Lazarus's gaze, he recalls the multitudes of citizens depending on him for leadership and regains his composure. To ensure that Lazarus destroys no more lives, he orders him blinded. The final scene describes Lazarus wandering in the desert, vainly reaching out toward the warmth of the setting sun.

Such works as this demonstrate why Andreev was so popular in the century's first decade and why he seems so dated now. He treated controversial subjects with a flair that impressed his contemporaries as daring and novel. Yet this very tendency to play up the sensational aspects of an issue, to depict in hyperbolic emotional terms that which might be better treated more subtly, now makes his work seem gaudily pretentious at times. Andreev's popularity peaked in 1908 and steadily diminished thereafter.

Symbolism and the Short Story

By 1908 the symbolist movement was at the height of its influence. Developing in Russia in the mid-1890s, it became the dominant literary current within a decade. One of the first writers to anticipate this phenomenon was Dmitry Merezhkovsky (1866–1941), who in 1893 published a long essay entitled *O prichinakh upadka i o novykh techeniiakh sovremennoi russkoi literatury* (*On the Reasons for the Decline and on the New Currents in Contemporary Russian Literature*). Discussing the causes for what he sees as a sterile atmosphere in contemporary Russian literature, he reproaches the utilitarian critics for failing to promote a climate favorable to literary creation. He then notes two opposing impulses in the literature of the day, which he views as extreme and passionate "idealistic" outbursts of the spirit. Until the present, he writes, the prevailing taste of the crowd had been oriented toward realism and materialism. Now, however, he sees a reaction forming. Among the writers whose work expresses a new striving toward idealism and symbolism in literature are Garshin, Chekhov, and the poets Konstantin Fofanov (1862–1911) and Nikolay Minsky (pseudonym of N. M. Vilenkin, 1855–1937).

Merezhkovsky's essay is of value less for its evaluations of particular writers than for its identification of a general mood among the reading public. Many readers were tired of endless accounts of the wretchedness of rural life; they were eager for literature that would speak to their emotions and their dreams. The symbolist movement seemed to respond to that desire. Drawing on the examples of the mature symbolist movement in France as well as on material from native Russian sources such as the poetry of Fedor Tyutchev and Afanasy Fet, Russian symbolism offered a new approach to the depiction of the human condition. The symbolists were not interested in describing the world objectively. Rather, they sought to articulate a more personal perception of human experience and to convey the hidden emanations of their psyches. Rejecting the notion that the intellect could comprehend the world and its mysteries through reason, they aimed at exploring existence through the emotions and intuition. This emphasis on the primacy of the emotions over reason recalls the aspirations of the early nineteenth-century romantic writers, and the symbolists have been called neoromantics.

A recurring concept in symbolist literature is the notion that the everyday world is only a surface concealing a more essential reality. Objects in the visible world are merely external signs of that deeper reality. Only in rare moments of insight can the writer gain intimations of the higher reality, and he cannot describe such experiences directly. Following Tyutchev's dictum "A thought uttered is a lie," the symbolists tried to evoke particular sensations through a careful selection of allusive images. Embracing Paul Verlaine's words "la musique avant toute chose," they stressed rhythms and sounds in their work and achieved a high degree of technical craftsmanship.

After first arising as a movement in poetry, symbolism soon encompassed prose and drama, and its spirit can be seen in the other arts in Russia, too, as well as in the activities of the *Mir iskusstva* (World of art) journal edited by Sergei Diaghilev. The movement went through two main stages in Russian literature. The first has often been termed *decadence* because the works of this phase resonate with the theme of civilization's decline as its writers soberly probe such subjects as the glorification of the ego, aesthetics, amoralism, sexual license, and death. The writers of this group—which includes Valery Bryusov (1873–1924), Konstantin Balmont (1867–1942), Fedor Sologub (1863–1927), and Zinaida Gippius (1869–1945)—tended to view symbolism primarily in aesthetic terms, as a method of artistic expression. For the second generation, however, symbolism was more than an aesthetic phenomenon. It took on profound philosophical meaning and became a way of interpreting human experience itself. For the writers of this generation—Vyacheslav Ivanov (1866–1945), Andrey Bely (1880–1934), and Aleksandr Blok (1880–1921)—the creation of symbolist art could be a quasi-religious act that not only expressed elusive emotions but laid bare the essential beliefs and myths of humanity. This later generation of symbolists was influenced by the writings of Vladimir Solovev (1853–1900), one of several thinkers whose work responded to a rising interest in philosophical inquiry in Russia at the turn of the century (other important philosophers of the day included Shestov, Nikolay Berdyaev, and Vasily Rozanov).

Although critics often distinguish between the symbolists and the realists in Russian literature, the differences were not always clear-cut. Some writers, such as Andreev and Bunin, had something in common with both groups, and many realists shared with the symbolists a predilection for allegorical images and the creation of palpable moods through evocative and rhythmic prose.

The foremost representative of the early symbolist movement in Russia was Valery Bryusov. The son of a wealthy Moscow merchant family, Bryusov came to the attention of the literary world in 1894 with a series of poetry collections entitled *Russkie simvolisty* (*The Russian Symbolists*), which shocked the reading public both by their unusual subject matter (including necrophilia) and by their unorthodox form. Bryusov subsequently became a leader of the symbolist movement as much through his activities with the publishing house Skorpion and the journal *Vesy* (The scales) as through his own literary output, which included prose, poetry, and critical essays. He published two collections of short stories: *Zemnaia os'* (*The Axis of the Earth,* 1907) and *Nochi i dni* (*Nights and Days,* 1913). In the preface to the second edition of *The Axis of the Earth* (1910) he explained the central theme of his early stories: they probed the idea that "there is no defined boundary between the real and the imagined world, between 'dream' and 'waking,' 'life' and 'fantasy.' That which we ordinarily consider imaginary is perhaps the supreme reality of the world, while the reality which we all acknowledge is perhaps the most terrible delirium."

Bryusov's early short stories illustrate this theme in a manner reminiscent of Edgar Allan Poe, whom Bryusov admired and translated. In his "Teper', kogda ia prosnulsia . . ." ("Now That I Have Awakened . . . ," 1902) a deranged man relates how he used to take pleasure in dreams of rape, torture, and murder until one day he dreams that he has killed his wife but cannot wake up: the murder was not a dream but reality. Another individual dreams that he is a prisoner in a medieval German fortress. After awakening, however, he is troubled by the question: "What if I am sleeping and dreaming *now,* and will suddenly awaken on the straw in the dungeon of the castle of Hugo von Reisen?" ("V bashne" ["In the Tower," 1902–07]). Other stories deal with the theme of the double. The narrator of "V zerkale" ("In the Mirror," 1903) becomes so captivated by the idea that mirrors contain alternate realities that she thinks she is imprisoned in one of them, while her place in the real world has been usurped by the double she saw in the mirror.

Although these stories are not very complex, they demonstrate Bryusov's skill as a prose writer. Utilizing a first-person narrator to create a feeling of immediacy and suspense, he writes in a style that recalls Pushkin's by its leanness and precision, although he stylizes the language of some works to reproduce the atmosphere of a different era—for example, "V podzemnoi tiur'me" ("In an Underground Prison," 1901–05). Bryusov also conveys an antiutopian vision in two works—"Respublika iuzhnogo kresta" ("The Republic of the Southern Cross," 1904–05), a chronicle of a psychological plague that destroys a new Antarctic nation, and "Poslednie mucheniki" ("The Last Martyrs," 1906), a grim account of the persecution of a cult of religious aesthetes by a band of brutal uncultured revolutionaries. Bryusov's second collection, which is less exotic, has as one of its major topics troubled love. An interesting tale is "Za sebia ili za druguiu" ("For Myself or for Another," 1911), which also uses the theme of doubles. A man is tormented by a woman who, he believes, is his former lover, but who keeps him in doubt as to her real identity. At the end of the story she informs him that she has tortured him to avenge his mistreatment of his lover years ago, but she refuses to divulge whether she is taking revenge "for myself or for another."

Several other symbolist writers also wrote short stories of distinction, although they were often better known as poets or novelists. Fedor Sologub (pseudonym for Fedor Teternikov) is perhaps best remembered today for his novel *Melkii bes* (*The Petty Demon,* 1907), but he was a prolific short-story writer too: between 1894 and 1917 he wrote more than eighty stories as well as a number of fairy tales. These works incorporate a fundamental theme of Sologub's fiction: the inescapable tension between the author's awareness of the coarseness of everyday life and his dream of an alluring yet inaccessible realm of beauty and peace. Confronted with a world of cruelty, Sologub's characters often try to escape into the universe of private fantasy, and this at times leads to madness or death.

Although Sologub's work underwent a definite evolution,[16] the opposing poles of grim reality and alluring dreams coexist in all his fiction, beginning with his first published short story "Teni" ("Shadows," 1894). The protagonist of "Shadows" is a sensitive boy dismayed by the roughness he encounters at school. Intrigued by a pamphlet showing how to cast shadows on the wall with one's hands, the boy soon takes refuge in the world of shadow play and eventually becomes entirely immersed in it. In an interesting plot twist, the boy's mother, who at first tries to keep him away from the shadow world, is caught up in it as well. At the end of the story both mother and son are throwing shadow figures on the wall: "In their eyes shines madness, blissful madness."

Sologub's subsequent work provides ample instances of ways in which the trials of everyday life can destroy the sensitive. A young girl in "Cherviak" ("The Worm," 1896) is literally consumed by anguish at the thought that she has been led to swallow a worm as punishment for breaking an adult's cup. A group of adolescents in "V tolpe" ("In the Crowd," 1907) is crushed to death at a holiday fair by a crowd of people whose veneer of civilization is stripped away to reveal the beasts within.

In many of Sologub's works children play a leading role. For him children were a symbol of purity and innocence not often found in the jaded world of adult experience, and they hold out the tenuous possibility of a transformation of life.[17] Yet in many of Sologub's early works children fare badly. They seem ill suited for earthly life, and in several stories they are driven to suicide by revulsion at the coarseness of reality and the attraction of a better life in a realm beyond death—for example, "Uteshenie" ("Consolation," 1899) and "Zhalo smerti" ("The Sting of Death," 1903). This impulse to escape life's cruelty in death affects some adults as well as children. Suicide beckons as the ultimate refuge for alienated characters such as the protagonists of "Golodnyi blesk" ("The Glimmer of Hunger," 1907) and "Ulybka" ("The Smile," 1897), and it offers an escape to those who long for a world of beauty but must live amid vice, as in "Krasota" ("Beauty," 1899).

Sologub's dark view of human existence softened somewhat around 1908. In several stories written at this time he offered examples of salvation not through death but through faith. Some of them have a religious tenor. "Alchushchii i zhazhdushchii" ("The Hungry and the Thirsty," 1908) depicts a band of crusaders lost in the desert on their way to Damascus. Dying of hunger and thirst, they call on their leader to save them. He sardonically mimics Moses' gesture of finding water by striking a rock with his staff and then drags the staff through the sand as if scraping up grain. Half of his followers believe that he has indeed worked a miracle. They eat the sand and drink the imagined water, and their faith saves them. They make their way to Damascus alive, while those who were unable or unwilling to see the miracle perish in the desert. Similar images of miracles touching only those who believe in them occur in "Pretvorivshaia vodu v vino" ("The Woman Who Turned Water into Wine," 1908) and "Mudrye devy" ("The Wise Maidens," 1908).

In his later years Sologub moved away from symbolism. During World War I he wrote stories on patriotic subjects and afterwards nearly ceased writing short stories altogether. His best work is written in a style that echoes his dualistic worldview. Lyrical and poetic when he moves in the realm of fantasy, his prose becomes concrete and plastic when he treats everyday life. Sologub's precision has struck some observers as more typical of Western writing than Russian,[18] but his debt to Chekhov, for example, is unmistakable, particularly in his manipulation of subjective point of view and in his mood-setting passages with their rhythmic phrasing and evocative detail. Yet Sologub's prose is more hypnotic than Chekhov's, and he seems almost to weave a spell through the repetition of key words and phrases.

The short stories of Zinaida Gippius are rather more abstract. The wife of Dmitry Merezhkovsky and an influential figure in the symbolist movement through her St. Petersburg salon, Gippius wrote prose, poetry, plays, and critical articles. She viewed art as a way to initiate the reader into the supreme truths of existence, truths primarily spiritual and religious in nature. Her prose fiction, which consists of several volumes of short stories and novels such as *Chertova kukla* (*The Devil's Doll,* 1911), presents a complex exposition of the battle between skepticism and faith, darkness and light. Her early stories—published in the collections *Novye liudi* (*New People,* 1896) and *Zerkala* (*Mirrors,* 1898)—center on solitary thinkers who have turned their backs on conventional morality in search of personal fulfillment. In these and subsequent works Gippius exposes the sterility of disembodied intellect and knowledge. Thus the female protagonist of "Sud'ba" ("Fate," 1906) finds life a tedious burden. Having been shown by a soothsayer all the events and emotions of her future, she must now live out that life deprived of the joy of mystery and anticipation.

Against this melancholy background Gippius offers some signs of hope. The story "On belyi" ("He Is White," 1912) describes the visitation of the Devil to a dying student. The Devil explains that his mission on earth is to create dark shadows so that the radiance of God will be visible to humanity. Ultimately the Devil too will be redeemed through his suffering and will then return to heaven. Like Dostoevsky, Gippius believes that suffering can play a positive role in life, but she provides no easy path to salvation, and her work emphasizes the difficulty of finding peace on earth. Thus, in "Strannichek" ("The Pilgrim," 1908), a religious pilgrim's facile words about the inevitability of suffering bring no consolation to a peasant woman who has just lost her child; she reacts with all the fury of a grieving mother when he suggests that the child's suffering and death were a punishment for his sins. Even love provides only partial comfort unless it represents a genuine fusion of the deepest emotions and the flesh. The narrator of "Nebesnye slova" ("Heavenly Words," 1906) realizes that his attachment to his mistress is empty because it has not transcended the physical. Yet when physical love is informed by genuine emotion and conscious faith, it can assume religious dimensions and thus attain its highest potential. Filled with such ideas as these, Gippius's stories often seem more like philosophical tracts than narrative tales, but at their best they provide a penetrating perspective on the human condition.[19]

A final symbolist worthy of note is Andrey Bely (pseudonym of Boris Bugaev). Best known for his novel *Peterburg* (*Petersburg,* 1913–14), Bely also wrote poetry, essays on symbolism and on Gogol, and valuable memoirs. His short stories reveal an interesting dimension of his creative imagination. Some seem to serve as preliminary sketches for his novels. "Svetovaia skazka" ("A Luminous Fairy Tale," 1904), for example, anticipates the novel *Kotik Letaev* in its handling of evolving human consciousness. The story traces a first-person narrator's birth, childhood, and adolescence, but Bely's handling of the subject is far from naturalistic. Beginning with a kaleidoscopic description of the dawn of the universe, he connects his narrator's developing consciousness with cosmic images of fireworks, spirals, and ethereal waves. A commingling of levels—physical, metaphorical, and metaphysical—is characteristic of the author's symbolist method.

Even more complex in its use of symbolic imagery is "Kust" ("The Bush," 1906), a work that Bely's second wife called a turning point in his prose because of its poetic density and concentrated imagery. A study of visionary madness, the story traces a man's belief that a bush in the countryside has separated him from his soul. At sunset the soul comes in the form of a beautiful maiden to caress the bush. After he tries to woo the girl away from the bush, the man engages in combat with the plant. The man falls unconscious and subsequently awakens in a mental hospital, which he, however, sees only as a dream. The story concludes with his renewed vision of the bush and the maiden. Bely's narrative is rich with possible meaning and contains many religious, political, literary, and autobiographical associations. Thus, for example, the struggle between the hero and the bush for the maiden's favor may be seen as a reflection of Bely's rivalry with Aleksandr Blok for the affection of Blok's wife, Lyubov.[20]

In Bely's later stories the metaphysical and religious spheres are paramount. "Adam" (1908) is an ironic study of a man who believes himself to be a kind of new Messiah, but who proves foolishly ineffectual;

"Iog" ("The Yogi," 1918) explores the attainment of higher states of being through meditation and dreams; and "Chelovek" ("A Man," 1918) is an elliptical exploration of the spiritual condition of the world culminating in a vision of human communion in a new dawn. Although none of these works has the depth or range of Bely's masterpiece *Petersburg,* they remain intriguing minor works of a prose master.

Kuzmin, Remizov, and Others

The impact of the decadents and symbolists on narrative prose fiction in Russia was considerable, both in terms of enlarging the thematic repertoire of the period and in terms of restoring vitality to the literary language. The openness with which the decadents treated such subjects as sexuality, death, and religious striving influenced their contemporaries: soon societies devoted to the exploration of ideas on free love, mystical inspiration, and demonology sprang up in St. Petersburg and Moscow. Many writers responded to this intellectual fashion and, with the relaxation of censorship at the time, became more daring in their approach to such subjects as sexuality and free love. Among those who achieved some notoriety in this field were Anatoly Kamensky (1876–1941), Evdokiya Nagrodskaya (1866–1930), Nikolay Oliger (1882–1919), Anastasiya Verbitskaya (1861–1928), and Mikhail Artsybashev (1878–1927).

Another writer whose work reflects the liberal mood of this time, though with a higher degree of artistry, was Mikhail Kuzmin (1872–1936). A poet, playwright, composer, and novelist, Kuzmin first gained public notice with his novel *Kryl'ia* (*Wings*) in 1906. With its frank treatment of homosexuality and its support for natural sensuality *Wings* provoked a lengthy controversy in the press. Yet the novel does not strive for sensational effects; it is written in the fluid, direct style that became Kuzmin's hallmark in his subsequent prose fiction.

Kuzmin's best works are deftly crafted tales depicting emotional relationships; they highlight nuances of feelings as characters fall in love, find various distractions, and begin new relationships. Kuzmin's treatment of these intrigues is often ironic and detached, his touch generally light, not somber. Love triangles appear frequently in his writing, as do homosexual or bisexual loves. In "Kartonnyi domik" ("The House of Cards," 1907), for example, the artist Demyanov loves the poet Myatlev, who has broken off relations with an actress named Ovinova and soon does the same with Demyanov. Kuzmin enriches his simple plot by surrounding his characters with details of stylish bohemian life, from the trappings of domestic theatricals to such props as a bottle of Piper Heidsieck champagne.

Kuzmin's familiarity with the theater is evident in the structure of his stories. He uses dialogue extensively, and his stories unfold in a rapid succession of brief scenes. At times the theatrical approach provides unique perspectives, as in "Kushetka teti Soni" ("Aunt Sonya's Sofa," 1907), a first-person narrative related by a piece of furniture. Privy only to what occurs within its auditory range, the sofa describes a triangle involving a brother and sister who are both charmed by the same man.

Although Kuzmin could appear lightly cynical about the relationship between the sexes, he could also depict deeper, more obsessive forms of love—such as "Dvoinoi napersnik" ("The Double Confidant," 1908)—and his own experience with tragic affection (his lover Vsevolod Knyazev committed suicide in 1913) left an imprint on his work. Some of Kuzmin's writings delve into the supernatural and exotic; the brief story "Flor i razboinik" ("Florus and the Bandit"), for example, is constructed with an exquisite classical flavor. The wealthy Florus in a vivid dream sees himself apprehended for theft at the same time that a real thief is caught in the city. Later Florus dies in his sleep and is found with a bruise on his neck at the very moment the thief is hanged. Such stories as these reveal that Kuzmin was as proficient at re-creating the atmosphere of exotic settings as he was at handling contemporary Russian ones.

Whereas Kuzmin's prose is distinguished for its refined elegance of expression, the work of Aleksey Remizov (1877–1957) displays great stylistic and lexical complexity. Born into a family of Moscow merchants, Remizov attended Moscow University for two years before being arrested at a student demonstration, expelled from school, and imprisoned. Exiled to Siberia, Remizov returned to St. Petersburg in 1905, where he lived until he emigrated from Russia in 1921.

In the early part of his career Remizov channeled his literary output into two broad areas: stories and novels depicting contemporary Russian life, and shorter works such as fairy tales, fables, folk dramas, and historical tales based on Russian folk sources and on medieval religious lore. Certain of his short stories—for instance, "V plenu" ("In Captivity," 1898–1903), "Serebrianye lozhki" ("Silver Spoons," written 1903), and "Po etapu" ("In Transport," 1909)—reflect the writer's experiences as a prisoner. Others, such as "Neuemnyi buben" ("The Incessant Tambourine," 1909) and "Chertik" ("The Little Devil," 1906), vividly portray the stifling life of rural Russian towns. The protagonist of the former story, a solid Philistine named Stratilov, recalls the creations of Gogol and Saltykov-Shchedrin. For forty years he has worked as a clerk in a court office and has carried the same blue bag and worn the same galoshes. This life of routine finally ends when Stratilov marries a young bride who then abandons him; Stratilov dies from shock. Remizov's rambling narrative is humorous and ironic, and he relates his tale in a colloquial skaz style reminiscent of Gogol and Leskov. "The Little Devil," by contrast, is a fine example of a suspenseful tale of the supernatural, and Remizov's colloquial manner heightens the aura of sinister mystery emanating from the evil character of a demented cockroach exterminator. Remizov's works often underscore the role of fate in life, and the author shows his empathy for human suffering in a way that recalls Dostoevsky.

On the other hand, Remizov shared with Nikolay Leskov a fascination with Russia's folktales and religious legends and published many works based upon this material. One of the first of these, *Posolon'* (1907), is a collection of short narratives arranged in four sections to correspond to the four seasons. Inspired by popular legends, games, and songs, the narratives present a wide range of subjects and styles in a picture of the world as a fabulous kingdom full of wondrous events. Also in 1907 Remizov published the first edition of his collection *Limonar',* an anthology of religious tales and apocrypha, and he followed this with numerous collections of Russian folklore both before and after emigrating from Russia.

Remizov's love of things Russian and his remarkable narrative style are noteworthy in all these collections. His innovative approach to language was perhaps his greatest contribution to Russian literature. Intent on infusing the literary language with the natural vitality of spoken Russian, Remizov created an original prose style marked by several features: a rich lexicon combining expressions from colloquial speech with neologisms and archaisms; complex syntactic structures; and a tendency toward rhythmic phrasing. Remizov's innovations in narrative prose influenced the rising generation of writers. Along with Bely, he is considered one of the creators of the ornamental prose style made popular in the early 1920s, especially in the work of Evgeny Zamyatin, Boris Pilnyak, and Vsevolod Ivanov.

Although these last three writers wrote their best work after 1917, each made his literary debut in the period from 1908 to 1917, and

Zamyatin in particular impressed the reading public with his early tale "Uezdnoe" ("A Provincial Tale," 1913). Written in a modified skaz style, "A Provincial Tale" presents a sobering view of the coarseness of rural Russian life as embodied in the hulking figure of a bully named Anfim Baryba, a lazy schoolboy who rises to the position of town policeman. Zamyatin's tale is noteworthy for its use of unusual images to convey the essence of a character: thus the widow Chebotarikha's doughy flesh suggests her gluttonous nature, and Baryba's iron jaws underline his primitive stolidness. Zamyatin's ear for language and his eye for salient detail point to the influence of Remizov and Sologub on his early work.

The view of human experience expressed in Zamyatin's early fiction is disquieting: his characters find their aspirations for love or fulfillment constantly thwarted. In "Chrevo" ("The Womb," 1915), for example, a woman's desire for a child results only in a miscarriage after her husband beats her; she subsequently murders him and is then tormented by guilt. The boredom, insensitivity, and cruelty of life in a military garrison lead to drunkenness and suicide in "Na kulichkakh" ("To the Ends of the World," 1914). The themes of human folly and ignorance found in these tales also appear in the fables Zamyatin wrote in the pre-Revolutionary period—for example, "D'iachek" ("The Deacon")—and the irony in his earlier work becomes a prominent feature of his post-Revolutionary fiction, where it is employed to expose the dangers of rigid thinking and the timelessness of human irrationality.

Although Zamyatin wrote his finest works after 1917, his early stories developed in what he would later call a neorealist style, a narrative mode relying on bold, often exaggerated detail, fast-paced, even elliptical exposition, and colorful, rhythmic language to create vivid images of life. Zamyatin perfected this style in the post-Revolutionary period.

The decade of the 1910s encompassed the early careers of many other writers destined to achieve prominence after 1917. Mikhail Prishvin (1873–1954) achieved early success with his sketches of the nature, language, and life-style of the far North—for example, *V kraiu nepugannykh ptits* (*In the Land of Fearless Birds,* 1907). Vyacheslav Shishkov (1873–1945) also wrote about the North in tales about the hard lives of Siberian peasants ("Taiga," 1916). Aleksey N. Tolstoy (1882–1945) published colorful stories and novels about the life of provincial landowners—for instance, *Zavolozh'e* (*Beyond the Volga*). Sergey Sergeev-Tsensky (pseudonym of S. Sergeev, 1875–1956) concentrated on conditions in the Russian countryside—as in "Pechal' polei" ("The Sadness of the Fields," 1909). While these men eventually continued their careers in the Soviet Union, other promising young prose writers left the country permanently after 1917. Among them Boris Zaytsev (1881–1972) and Ivan Shmelev (1873–1950) stand out, Zaytsev for his impressionistic tales imbued with light spiritual nuances, and Shmelev for his penetrating descriptions of the life and mores of the urban poor.

When the Russian Revolution broke out in 1917, it engendered a wave of dislocation. As disruptive as this upheaval was for the literary community, however, it also found a generation of writers ready to record this experience in their work. The language of narrative fiction had been revitalized through the efforts of such writers as Remizov, Bely, and Zamyatin in prose (and by the futurists in poetry), and the very form of the short story had been reshaped and made more flexible by writers such as Chekhov, Bunin, and the symbolists. Thus the innovations in the short-story genre of the preceding two decades made it the perfect medium to capture life's swift pace and the dynamics of change in the immediate post-Revolutionary period. As a result, the short story flowered anew in the early 1920s.

Julian W. Connolly

THE RUSSIAN SHORT STORY 1917–1980

The Background

After the October Revolution of 1917, followed by years of Allied intervention, civil war with the tsarist armies, and a conflict with Poland, the Soviet regime seemed firmly in the saddle by 1921. When Lenin introduced in 1921 his New Economic Policy (NEP)—a moderate return to capitalist practices—the economy began to recover. Also at that time party policy in the area of literature permitted considerable freedom for nonaligned writers. Through the Central Committee resolution of June 1925 "Concerning the Policy of the Party in the Area of Belles-Lettres," the party came out against the "hegemony of proletarian writers" and advised tolerance of bourgeois writers. It refused to take sides in questions of style and form and advocated "free competition" among literary groups and trends. This "charter of liberty" remained in force for a while. But then NEP ended in 1927, and the moderately liberal people's commissar for education Anatoly Lunacharsky was forced to resign in 1929. The Russian Association of Proletarian Writers (RAPP) came to dominate literature more and more.

There had hardly been any proletarian literature before the Revolution. The dominant literary movements had been symbolism, futurism, and a variety of modernist and avant-gardist trends including acmeism and imagism. Indeed, most of them continued beyond 1917, which in literature was not at all the kind of watershed it was in politics. Literature became truly proletarian and party-minded only between 1929 and 1934, the time of Stalin's rise to power. In 1934 the founding congress of the Union of Soviet Writers took place, as a single organization replaced all previous groupings of writers. Socialist realism became the obligatory style of writing for all Soviet authors.

Revolution and Modernism

Evgeny Zamyatin (1884–1937), a born rebel, joined the Bolshevik party as a young man and was soon arrested (1905). After completing his education and teaching at the St. Petersburg Polytechnical Institute, he traveled to England in 1916 to supervise the building of ships ordered by the Russian government. After the Revolution he returned to Petrograd, gave up his technical work, and devoted himself entirely to literature. Maksim Gorky had just founded the World Literature publishing house and had been instrumental in setting up a House of the Arts, a House of Writers, and a House of Scientists, where needy intellectuals could at least find heated rooms and a place to work. Zamyatin had met Gorky in 1917 and became one of his closest collaborators. He participated in the administration of Gorky's enterprises, organized seminars, taught, arranged literary evenings, and read from his own work. Literature then was still dominated by writers of nonproletarian viewpoint, or fellow travelers, as Trotsky called them.

In those years Petrograd—formerly St. Petersburg, later Leningrad—represented for Zamyatin all that was positive in Russia. It was there that most of the formalists lived and the most important publishing houses had their seats. St. Petersburg had been the center of Russian symbolism and was known as very Western in attitude and outlook. Moscow, by contrast, had been the seat of the nationalist Slavophile movement of the nineteenth century, though it was also there that the Futurist Manifesto of 1912, which denounced all ties with tradition, had appeared. And Moscow was the seat of the new Bolshevik government, as well as the center of proletarian literature. Zamyatin's essay, "Moscow—Petersburg" (1933), defined the contrast between these two centers of intellectual activity.

Zamyatin himself, a representative of the best of the St. Petersburg liberal tradition, came under attack from the proletarian writers. He was briefly arrested in 1922; a year later Trotsky called him an internal émigré and elitist snob, starting a campaign of vilification that came to a head after the appearance of Zamyatin's utopian novel *My* (*We,* 1926). By 1931 he had been forced from all his positions. With Gorky's help and after a personal appeal to Stalin, he was permitted to emigrate to France. To this day he has not been rehabilitated in the Soviet Union.

Zamyatin realized the Revolution had ushered in a new age demanding a new style, a kind of neorealism that combined realism and the fantastic. Like Dostoevsky and the symbolists, he looked not for the realism of life but for the *realiora,* the essentially real. He emphasized the disfigured, the slanted, the nonobjective, the dynamic as revealed to the eye under a microscope. His style has been described as elliptic, cinematographic, dynamic, excited, and subjective, and has been linked to futurist stylistic experiments. Irony and satire are its natural components. Zamyatin had an acute sense of his time, clearly foresaw the dangers inherent in Bolshevik plans for Russia, and defended freedom.

After the Revolution Zamyatin turned to his immediate environment, the city of Petrograd. In "Peshchera" ("The Cave," 1922) he draws a parallel between Ice Age man and an elderly couple in the frost-ridden city. The images blur and a Petrograd apartment actually seems to turn into a cave dominated by a "god—the short-legged, rusty-red, squatting, greedy cave god—the little cast-iron stove." Zamyatin's expressive language re-creates the mood of utter despair that reigned in the city in the year after the civil war.

In "Mamai" (1922) we are confronted not just with the fate of an individual, as in "The Cave," but with the collective life of the inhabitants of a six-story tenement building in Petrograd that is compared to a ship drifting at night along the "heaving, rocky ocean of the streets." During the day it lies at anchor in port, but at dusk it steams out into the ocean again. People are reduced to the essentials of life as they battle the elements and live under primitive conditions, all the while plagued by memories of their former comfortable, civilized existence. The confusion created by the upheaval of the Revolution is also re-created in the grotesque situations of the tale "X" from the collection *Nechestivye rasskazy* (*Unholy Tales,* 1926).

The Serapion Brothers

Zamyatin lectured in the Petrograd House of Arts from November 1919 to January 1921. Among his listeners were several young writers and formalist literary theoreticians such as Viktor Shklovsky and Boris Eikhenbaum. They first met as a group in February 1921 and decided to adopt the name Serapion Brothers, derived from E. T. A. Hoffmann's collection of short stories (1818–21) about the hermit Serapion, who lived entirely in a world of fantasies. The Russian Serapion Brothers sought "to preserve the clarity of the hermit's visions." Their acknowledged leader Lev Lunts described their program as follows: "We need a literature of dizzying tempos, a dynamic literature of adventures and stormy passions corresponding more closely to the new epoch!" They stressed the irrational roots of art and its independence from ideology as well as its closeness to the concrete details of life, calling themselves *bytoviki*—describers of everyday reality. Their works, written in an ornamental but colloquial prose, contain powerful yet terse descriptions of the concrete and often cruel details of life; they also display a formalist concern for plot structure. Their antitraditionalism had an avant-garde quality that was appropriate to the 1920s. A characteristic device is that of estrangement, which gives their stories a touch of the grotesque and even absurd as they view ordinary occurrences in such a manner as to make them appear unusual. The plot is sometimes artificially rearranged and cut up into brief units. Only select glimpses of reality are provided, so that the reader must fill in the rest himself.

Most Serapions were avowed Westernizers: Lunts warned his colleagues against "Muscovite glory, Muscovite criticism, Muscovite royalties." Yet the Muscovite tradition proved attractive to at least some of the Serapions, in particular Konstantin Fedin, Vsevolod Ivanov, and Nikolay Nikitin, who held the Muscovite writer Boris Pilnyak in high esteem and sympathized with Aleksandr Voronsky's literary group Pereval (the mountain pass), founded in an attempt to win the fellow travelers over to the side of the Bolsheviks. In general, the Serapions kept their distance from the party: Fedin even left it when he joined the brotherhood. Lunts died in 1924, and the other members of the group began each to go his own way by the mid-1920s.

Among the Serapions Venyamin Kaverin (1902–) was closest to Hoffmann, although he reacts to him in his own manner. Kaverin's first collection of fantastic tales—*Mastera i podmaster'ia* (*Masters and Apprentices,* 1923)—tells of monks, devils, alchemists, students, artisans, and others. They are delightfully absurd stories, yet contain a deeper meaning. Kaverin, a great enthusiast for German romanticism, wore a dark cloak when attending literature classes. He uses medieval German settings in order to create an imaginary world where he can experiment playfully with characters and plots. Kaverin himself formulates his motivation in "Purpurnyi palimpsest" ("The Purple Palimpsest") thus: "Lobachevsky had parallel lines meet in space. What then prevents me from having two parallel plots meet not only in space but also in time?" In "The Purple Palimpsest" Mr. Wurst (sausage) and

Mr. Kranzer (Kranz means "wreath") travel in opposite directions and meet at night when their coaches collide. By mistake they exchange coaches to continue their journey, and each returns to his own hometown. However, part of each man's personality seems to have continued the journey in the other coach and to have superimposed itself on the other. Mr. Wurst becomes interested in bookbinding, actually Mr. Kranzer's profession, while the latter develops an interest in old manuscripts, Mr. Wurst's hobby. Mr. Wurst discovers an ancient palimpsest containing two stories superimposed on each other and repeating the plot of Kaverin's story. In the end the two men meet and their characters merge, like the texts on the palimpsest.

Mikhail Slonimsky (1897–1972) came from a cultured Jewish family. The outbreak of the Revolution found him a soldier writing war sketches. In 1918 he settled in Petrograd, where he soon joined the House of Arts. His first collection of stories appeared in 1922 as *Shestoi strelkovyi* (*The Sixth Rifle Regiment*), which depicted the horrors of war and revolution. Zamyatin's influence and formalist concerns emerge in Slonimsky's predilection for the exaggerated and grotesque, his impressionistic style, and the loose structure of his stories. An outstanding example of his work is "Mashina Emeri" ("The Emery Machine," 1923), set in the NEP period. A church in a salt-mine settlement is to be decorated with murals depicting the workers' march to the promised land of communism and then is to serve as a workers' theater seating 450 miners. The manager's description of the six proposed mural scenes encapsulates the utopian ideology of the day, which envisioned machines replacing human labor and ushering in a communist paradise. The artist hesitates, for he would prefer to paint "nature, flowers, young couples in love, ships, exotic countries." He also recognizes the essential flaw in the utopian conception of the future when he asks: "Only won't the workers think: if there is not going to be any *me* in this future—then what good is it?"

Oleynikov's order for the murals is delivered in a pathetic speech full of clichés, which contrasts sharply with the contents of a letter he has just received from an old friend who tells him that he intends to shoot himself and asks him to marry his sister. The letter describes in retrospect the war and the Revolution, re-creating the mood of that time. Here is its summary of the civil war: "1919—Civil war. We shot, smashed, destroyed everything that even faintly recalled the past. We leapt thousands of years ahead, and between us and the ones we killed was an abyss a thousand years across. . . . I did not move along the line of man, but along the line of mankind." Now the letter's author regrets what has happened, saying: "I feel sorry for people—the whites, the communists, everybody. I want everything to have been achieved by now and everyone to be happy." Oleynikov is the exact opposite of his friend. He wishes "to mechanize everything in human beings except thought: all our feelings, sensations, desires." He would like to measure them with a machine like the emery machine that determines the force necessary to break an iron bar.

Vsevolod Ivanov (1895–1963) and Nikolay Nikitin (1897–1963) wrote highly colorful and starkly naturalistic stories. Nikitin's prose is both lyrical and erotic, yet marked by violence. Both writers use a colloquial, elliptic language colored by provincialisms, an earthy idiom that captures well the atmosphere of the years after 1917. For a time Ivanov belonged to a group of proletarian poets, who expelled him when he refused to leave the Serapion Brotherhood. Ivanov published his first book of stories in 1919, after working as a sword swallower, a fakir, and a typesetter (he set his book himself). Only thirty copies were printed. His ornamental style was eminently adapted to the description of the terror and violence of the Revolution, which he rendered in all its naturalistic detail. Ivanov's collections *Tsvetnye vetra* (*Colored Winds*) and *Golubye peski* (*Blue Sands*) appeared in 1923, followed in the same year by Nikitin's collections *Bunt* (*The Revolt*), *Russkie nochi* (*Russian Nights*), and *Veshchi o voine* (*Pieces about the War,* 1924). The texts of these stories are usually broken up into brief segments numbered like chapters. Paragraphs are short, often consisting of single sentences; dialogue predominates. A good example of Ivanov's approach is the story "Polaia Arapiia" ("Hollow Arabia"). Russia is suffering from a drought, and the peasants are starving. A whole village sets out on a journey to a mythical land of milk and honey, but one by one they die. As the story ends, three men and a woman are preparing to kill another man who is just about to die, with the obvious intent of using him for food.

Konstantin Fedin's (1892–1983) prose differs considerably from that of his fellow Serapion Brothers. He is by far the most obviously realistic writer among them: his epic style recalls Chekhov and Bunin. Fedin's first volume of tales, *Pustyr'* (*The Desert*), came out in 1923. From 1934 on he held leading positions in the Writers' Union; after 1971 until his death he was its president.

Fedin's first collection of stories contains seven works dealing mostly with characters and problems of old Russia. The first story, "Sad" ("The

Orchard," 1920), depicts the remnants of the old society. An old gardener at an estate now turned into a home for children cannot adapt to his changed situation and in the end sets fire to house and garden. In "Tishina" ("The Silence") Fedin describes an old landowner who has been expropriated but still lives on his former property. The mood of these stories is rather melancholy. There are no great passions, no singular events. They describe rather the quiet flow of insignificant occurrences, yet enveloped in a tragic mood of cruelty and despair. In style and presentation Fedin continues the traditions of nineteenth-century Russian prose.

The Serapion Brothers had in their ranks one satirist of note, Mikhail Zoshchenko (1895–1958). He became famous with his collection *Rasskazy Nazara Il'icha gospodina Sinebriukhova* (*The Stories of Nazar Ilich, Mr. Bluebelly,* 1922, 1926). The narrator, a soldier fighting the Germans in World War I, narrates events in true skaz manner, using colloquial, idiomatic Russian. The soldier obviously understands neither the events of the February Revolution nor those of the October Revolution. This permits the author to depict the absurdities of life as experienced by a simple man, while employing a fine irony based on the discrepancy between the soldier's naive perception of events and their true dimensions, known to the reader. Zoshchenko's stories are mostly based on actual incidents. His style can be aphoristically brief and concise, or else conversational, as the author addresses his readers and reflects on his age and his craft. "Strashnaia noch'" ("A Terrible Night," 1925) begins with the words: "There you go writing and writing and what for—only the devil knows——." Zoshchenko begins a polemic with his readers who may think that he writes for money, and then complains of the discrepancy between his readers' demands and reality:

> Where should one take the headlong rush of fantasy from, when Russian reality is so different? . . . How, I am asking you, should one achieve scientific exactitude and the correct ideology, if one comes, as I do, from a bourgeois family and is still unable to suppress the bourgeois interests within himself, this quaint acquisitiveness and love of flowers, for instance, of curtains and cushioned chairs? Oh, dear reader! One might as well cry, so poorly are Russian writers doing.

Some passages sound prophetic now, when we know what happened in the 1930s:

"What do you want," said the old man, smiling wickedly and without reason. "Everything in our life changes in this manner. Today they abolish calligraphy, tomorrow drawing, and the day after tomorrow they will perhaps knock at your door."

The old man is a former teacher of calligraphy, now out of a job. His remarks frighten the musician Kotofeev, the hero of "A Terrible Night," who imagines that he, too, might become superfluous one day.

Pereval

The Serapions were the most prominent, but by no means the only group of nonproletarian writers in the 1920s. Zamyatin had spoken of two traditions in Russian literature identified with the two capital cities. It was in Moscow that the Marxist critic Aleksandr Voronsky edited one of the earliest Soviet thick journals, *Krasnaya nov'* (Red virgin soil, 1921–27), and successfully attracted bourgeois writers by offering them a publication outlet. In 1923 Voronsky published an essay entitled "Na perevale" ("On the Mountain Pass") concerning the transition from the present state of things to the presumably much richer fields of communism. The name *Pereval* stuck, and several miscellanies containing stories of writers identifying with Voronsky and his journal appeared under this title from 1924 until about 1930. Pereval authors—as well as some who did not formally belong to the group but were close to it in spirit—might be conveniently classified under three headings: (1) fellow travelers, whose critical attitude led to their eventual arrest and repression; (2) adherents of a romantic escape to nature, the exotic and distant, the adventurous; and (3) conformists who adapted to the needs of the day and escaped unharmed from the terrorism of the thirties.

The most fascinating prosewriter in the first group certainly is Boris Pilnyak (pseudonym of Boris Vogau, 1894–1934), chairman for a time of an independent organization of fellow travelers. In 1923 he wrote: "I am no communist and don't see why I should be obliged to write like one. . . . Insofar as the communists are for Russia, I am for them, too."

After the demise of the Pereval group in 1932, Pilnyak created a small literary society or salon in his house in Moscow consisting mostly of former Pereval writers; he called it simply the Thirties. There he and his friends drank and held endless discussions about the uncertain future of Russian literature. In 1936–37 he became one of the earliest victims of Stalinist terror, arrested as an alleged Japanese spy. Today we know that Pilnyak was sentenced in 1937 to twenty-five years of hard labor and then was shot in September 1941 for a variety of "crimes" including espionage, sabotage, Trotskyism, and terrorism. Following Stalin's death he was rehabilitated (1956), and a collection of his works appeared in 1978.

Pilnyak, who had already published before the Revolution, created his own peculiar style, a continuation of Andrey Bely's, known as "Pilnyakism." Pilnyak sees life and history as a biological process that is beyond human control. The life he describes in impressionistic scenes is set usually far away from urban centers in distant exotic provincial regions of the country. For him, revolution is like an elementary natural catastrophe: "Olga thought that the revolution was like a snowstorm and people were like snowflakes in it," a character says in "Metel'" ("The Snowstorm," 1923). This is a recurring image in Pilnyak's prose. Like Bely, Pilnyak employs sound symbolism—particularly such new Soviet abbreviations as GAU and GLAVBUM—to recall the blasts of a storm or the rumbling of thunder rolling through all of Russia.

Pilnyak's first collection of stories, *S poslednim parokhodom i drugie rasskazy* (*With the Last Steamer and Other Tales,* 1918), was followed by the miscellany, *Byl'e* (*The Past,* 1920), which made him famous.

One of his most characteristic stories is "Tysiacha let" ("A Thousand Years," 1919). In it Pilnyak creates an almost magic sense of Russia's thousand-year history from the Varangians to the Revolution. Two brothers who trace their family to one of Russia's earliest rulers walk through rural Russia, somewhere in the provinces, realizing that their time has passed, that all Russia's history is gone. But outwardly little has changed: people still believe in forest spirits and pagan rituals; they live in poverty and hunger as before; they are still uncouth, sick with typhoid fever, and unaware of what is happening around them. Pilnyak describes the chaos of the Revolution in "Ivan and Maria" (1921). Here his style is almost telegraphic. The writer can hardly catch his breath: events, people, strange new terms created by the new regime stream forth without much regard to plot structure and logical order. Pilnyak's main concern is Russia, that archaic, ancient, "holy animal" Russia.

Before long Pilnyak did two unforgivable things. First, he criticized Stalin in his story "Povest' o nepogashennoi lune" ("The Tale of the

Unextinguished Moon," 1926), a literary version of the events surrounding the mysterious death of one of the most famous military leaders of the 1920s, General Mikhail Frunze. The general died following an operation undertaken needlessly at Stalin's order, who wanted him removed. In Pilnyak's story Stalin himself appears as the "unbendable man" in the "Number One" house who pulls the strings behind the scenes and intrigues against Commander Gavrilov. Pilnyak's second sin was the publication of "Krasnoe derevo" ("Mahogany," 1929) in Berlin after this long story, which had been scheduled for publication in the Soviet Union, was turned down by the censor. Yakov Skudrin, a survival of the old days who has outlived all the Russian tsars including Lenin, as he puts it, develops a counterrevolutionary thesis on the coming demise of the proletariat. Akim, Yakov's son, is a Trotskyite romantic. Upon publication of "Mahogany" Pilnyak was attacked from all sides and expelled from all literary associations.

Yuri Olesha (1849–1960) came from the sunny south of Russia, the Black Sea port of Odessa, to Moscow in 1922. In the late 1920s he began to contribute to Voronsky's journal. As his initial enthusiasm for the new regime faded (Olesha for a time wrote propaganda verses), he became more and more critical. One of his main concerns is the role and position of the individual set against surrounding reality, as in "Liompa" (1927), where in the fantasies of a dying man the objects about him assume human shape and begin to talk to him. Olesha describes the relationship between man and the objects of his world at a point when objective reality starts to disappear, to dissolve into nothingness. In "Liubov'" ("Love," 1928) Shuvalov waits in a park for his girlfriend Lelya. A young man sits down beside him. What is green to Shuvalov is blue to the man, who is color-blind. This contrast points up the imaginary character of Shuvalov's own perception of things. Because he is in love, his perceptions have become almost surrealistic: "flies on the wings of love," as an onlooker comments. Thus Olesha shows that love changes man's perception of the world of objects and may even alter the laws of nature, thus subtly criticizing the concepts of Marxism. In "Vishnevaia kostochka" ("The Cherrystone," 1929) the narrator formulates the main concern of his story thus: "So I create in spite of everybody, despite order and society, a world which is not subject to any laws except the fantastic laws of my own sensations."

After 1936 the political situation was such that Olesha could no longer publish. He lived in great poverty and was subject to arrest. Nevertheless he outlived Stalin, and in the course of the 1950s he was rehabilitated.

Another writer who suffered under Stalin was Isaak Babel (1894–1941), who came from a Jewish merchant family in Odessa. He grew up in the Jewish quarter of the town, where he studied Hebrew, the Bible, and the Talmud. His early life left lasting impressions, which he incorporated into his stories. When Gorky printed Babel's first Russian story in 1916, he advised him to "go to the people" to gather more experience. From 1917 to 1924 Babel did exactly that, serving with the infamous Cheka (the communist secret police) and with Budenny's famous First Red Cavalry Regiment. His first stories after the Revolution appeared in 1924 in Vladimir Mayakovsky's journal *LEF* and were later collected in *Konarmiia* (*Red Cavalry,* 1926), *Evreiskie rasskazy* (*Jewish Tales,* 1927), and *Odesskie rasskazy* (*Tales from Odessa,* 1931). Babel was arrested in 1939 and is reported to have died in a forced labor camp in 1941. In contrast to many other writers, Babel belonged to no literary group. He cherished his independence, but his views resembled those of the Pereval group.

Babel's tales can be arranged under three headings: civil war stories such as "Smert' Dolgushova" ("Dolgushov's Death") from *Red Cavalry;* the *Tales from Odessa* devoted to the Odessa underworld of Jewish criminals around the uncrowned king of crime Benya Krik, a living legend; and autobiographical stories, including accounts of his travels. Babel's language is terse and compact, yet also dynamic and varied. He developed an ornamental style with a distinct leaning toward the exotic. Scenes of stark naturalism are juxtaposed with lyrical and reflective passages; caricature and grotesque add further color. The story "Korol'" ("The King") describes the wedding in Odessa of Benya Krik's sister. A new commissar in town avails himself of the festivities to arrest Krik's gang, but Krik outsmarts him. In "Istoriia moei golubiatni" ("The History of my Dovecote") Babel describes his childhood in 1904–05, relating the fate of a Jewish boy who had to get top marks to gain entry into high school at a time when there was a 5 percent quota for Jewish students. Babel also describes a pogrom, of which there were many at the time.

Mikhail Bulgakov (1892–1940) was another major figure among the fellow travelers of the 1920s and 1930s. He studied medicine and worked as a doctor for a few years, but after 1919 lived as a writer and journalist. Always something of an outsider, Bulgakov came under pressure toward the end of the 1920s and could not publish any more, though upon a personal appeal to Stalin he was appointed assistant director of the Moscow Art Theater. After 1955 his work began to be published again, though even now not all of it is accessible.

Together with Zoshchenko, Bulgakov is one of the outstanding humorists of the 1920s. His main theme is the conflict between old and new, the absurd consequences of traditional habits and attitudes within the new context of Soviet life. Above all, it is the inadequacies of Soviet life that furnish subjects for his grotesque stories.

In one work a distracted librarian advises a worker who wants to prepare for university admission to read an encylopedia so as to broaden his education. The worker promptly does this, but after the fifth volume he shows clear indications of going mad. Bulgakov's longer texts—for example, the five stories of his first book *D'iavoliada* (*Diaboliad,* 1925)—attack crucial weaknesses of the system. The title story describes the confusion created by an inept bureaucracy and a learned inventor whose invention is exploited by inept assistants. As a consequence, Russia is threatened by an invasion of huge crocodiles, snakes, and ostriches. The government is helpless. Nature finally puts an end to the peril through an early fall freeze that kills the monsters. The story implies that the Soviet state might have perished through its bureaucratic abuse of academic research in pursuit of short-term political goals. Nature alone can save the country from the disaster caused by a combination of political, administrative, and personal incompetence. The implications of "Pokhozhdeniia Chichikova" ("Chichikov's Adventures"), a "poem in ten chapters with a prologue and an epilogue," are even more far-reaching. Chichikov and other characters from Nikolay Gogol's novel *Dead Souls* come alive in the Moscow of the early 1920s. The author indicates that his tale is actually a dream, but the adventures of Chichikov *redivivus* are described realistically. By exploiting the Soviet bureaucracy, Chichikov soon establishes himself as a flourishing "nepman," producing iron from sawdust and feeding all of Moscow with sausages made out of spoiled meat. Yet just as in Gogol's novel his enterprises soon collapse and Chichikov vanishes. Thus the story implies that the Soviet administrative system is easily corruptible, and a modern Chichikov would find far greater opportunities than Gogol's original hero had a hundred years earlier.

Ivan Kataev (1902–1939) joined the Red Army in 1919 as a volunteer and soon became a party member. In the 1920s he studied economics and worked as a journalist. In the middle 1920s Kataev joined Pereval and became one of its leading members. After the Writers' Union was founded, he served on its board, but he was attacked for his Pereval activities and was arrested in 1939. His further fate is unknown, though he was rehabilitated in 1955.

Kataev is best known as the author of short prose works collected in his miscellany *Serdtse* (*The Heart,* 1928), followed by another collection in the 1930s. The title story describes a new communist hero who dreams of the future communist society and works tirelessly for the material well-being of the people. Kataev's deeply humanistic attitude shows clearly in the allegorical tale "Avtobus" ("The Bus," 1929). The driver who bears responsibility for the passengers crowding his bus, who "thinks of them all" and displays "a smile of kindness and happiness" as he successfully avoids all the dangers of the road, may symbolize the new proletarian power leading the masses towards a new and happy life.

In the 1930s Kataev wrote a series of stories on the heroes of Stalin's five-year plans. Nevertheless, he was accused of a sentimental attitude toward class conflict when he published "Moloko" ("Milk," 1930), which deals with the collectivization of agriculture. Kataev adopted a humane attitude toward the kulaks, or rich peasants, who were most fiercely persecuted at that time, and was therefore vehemently criticized by the party. In "Leningradskoe shosse" ("Leningrad Road," 1933) Kataev exhibits his mastery of descriptive prose in drawing a memorable picture of Moscow of the early 1930s.

Soviet Romantics

Every Soviet child reads the stories of a particular group of writers who turned away from reality, politics, and ideology and withdrew to an exotic land, which they either created in their imagination or discovered in the distant regions of rural Russia. They include Aleksandr Grin (who said of himself in 1925, "I write about storms, ships, love requited and unrequited, fate, the secret ways of the soul and the meaning of chance"); Mikhail Prishvin; and Konstantin Paustovsky. All of them today belong to the classical tradition of Soviet writing.

Aleksandr Grin (1880–1932) is sometimes disparaged as a "seafaring desperado who skillfully plagiarized the work of western adventure writers," but that is a popular misconception. The son of a participant in the Polish uprising of 1863 who was banished to Russia, Grin read adventure stories from his earliest days. In his kitchen garden in Vyatka his imagination created the subtropical "Grinlandia," a combination of the forests of America, the jungles of Africa, and the taiga of Siberia: "The words Orinoco, Mississippi, and Sumatra rang like music in my ears," Grin recalled. At fifteen Grin set off for Odessa to become a sailor and he sailed the Black Sea for two years. After he drifted about for some time trying various occupations, a socialist revolutionary regional leader discovered Grin's talent as a writer when he composed socialist proclamations. His first book appeared in 1908. The years before and during World War I were among his most prolific. Grin was profoundly impressed by the October Revolution: yet he greeted it with mixed feelings, hoping for greater justice and happiness than it seemed to provide. At the end of the 1920s, Grin came under pressure from the Russian Association of Proletarian Writers (RAPP) and could no longer publish freely. Suffering from tuberculosis and cancer, he died in 1932 and was buried in accordance with the rites of the Orthodox church.

Grin's imaginary world has concrete names and topographical features. The sea is always nearby, with picturesque ports, like Zurbagan, San-Riol, and Liss where adventurous smugglers and sailors live, and women are either "angels or furies." Captain Duke, Captain Robert Estamp, Captain Renior, and Captain Chinchar discuss pirates and plan their secret enterprises. The story "Korabli v Lisse" ("Ships in Liss") contains a detailed description of the port city of Liss, set in the midst of tropical vegetation. In "Propavshee solntse" ("The Missing Sun," 1923) Grin describes a cruel experiment performed upon a little boy, Robert, by a millionaire named Hoggay. Robert has been brought up in artificial light, never seeing the sun. At fourteen he is shown the sun just once, and then told that it will now disappear forever. Hoggay and his friends talk about the results of this test: some bet that the boy will go mad, others that he will die. Yet Robert instinctively believes in the sun and its return and suspects that he has been tricked. The millionaire's cruel game is thus exposed as self-defeating.

A story with a philosophical background is "Vozvrashchenie" ("The Return," 1924), in which a Norwegian sailor of peasant stock takes his first journey south. Unaccustomed to the tropics, he falls ill and is taken to a hospital in a tropical port. His ship leaves. Suffering from consumption, he eventually returns home, realizing that his desires have diverged from reality. The South could have been paradise for him, but it is now too late. "The Return" is paradigmatic for Grin, exhibiting as it does an irrepressible yearning for the exotic and faraway, for life as paradise, for endless adventure.

Mikhail Prishvin (1873–1954) grew up in a country village near Eletsk in a family of middle-class merchant background and in a liberal atmosphere influenced by populist ideas. At ten he tried to run away from home to Asia or America, with only the vaguest idea of either.

As a young man he took an interest in Marxism and was briefly arrested for translating Marxist literature. He then went to Leipzig to study. In 1907 he published his first book, *V kraiu nepugannykh ptits* (*In the Land of Fearless Birds*). His travels thereafter took him as far as Norway, Asiatic Russia, and the Crimea. Prishvin rejected the Bolshevik Revolution as a manifestation of chaos and violence. Afterward he worked briefly as a teacher and librarian before dedicating himself completely to writing, hunting, and observing nature. Among his major concerns were the protection of valuable natural reserves and the establishment of nature parks to protect the most valuable land. At his son's prompting Prishvin joined Pereval in 1927, and later the new Writers' Union. Yet he always kept his distance, remaining uncommitted and apolitical.

Among Prishvin's works are novels, sketches based on his hunting trips (one of them shows Lenin hunting), descriptions of life among simple people, and even fairy tales like "Kladovaia solntsa" ("Storehouse of the Sun," 1945), which deals with treasures buried in a huge bog and children who lose their way there and almost perish. Their closeness to nature and animal life, however, helps them survive. In his introduction to *Vremena goda* (*The Seasons of the Year*), which describes the changing forms of natural life in a series of sketches, Prishvin says of his motivations:

> I try to catch the passing moment with my word. . . . breathing freely I begin to write my notes in nature . . . to create my own daily myth. And that is how my microgeography began, which entirely corresponds to the human need to make oneself at home in one's homeland.

Generations of Soviet people have developed a love of nature and the outdoors by reading Prishvin's sketches and tales. He is unique among Soviet writers in this respect.

Konstantin Paustovsky (1892–1968) was of Turkish and Polish blood. He grew up in Kiev and went to school with Mikhail Bulgakov. Paustovsky first studied botany and then law in Moscow. During the Revolution and the civil war he was in Odessa, hoping for "a great spiritual revolution, a rebirth and creation of the human soul," and maintaining contact with Babel, Olesha, Ilya Ilf, and Eduard Bagritsky. Back in Moscow Paustovsky published seafaring stories between 1925 and 1928. In 1931 he traveled to the Caspian Sea to study industrial projects and used the material for his book *Kara Bugaz* (1932), whose documentary realism made him famous as a master of socialist realist style.

Paustovsky's stories are devoted to nature, especially the natural setting of central Russia. He has said of the landscape there: "I do not know any region which has such an immensely lyrical and touchingly picturesque force—in all its sadness, silence and depth—as the central belt of Russia." Paustovsky also excelled in the historical-biographical tale.

During World War II Paustovsky was a war correspondent, and his tales of that time reflect the events and the atmosphere of the war in southern Russia. After 1945 he wrote fairy tales and worked as a teacher of literature at the Gorky Institute of World Literature in Moscow. He spent his last years in Tarusa (Kaluga) in central Russia, which he considered his second home, writing his voluminous memoirs and short prose works.

Paustovsky's technique of rendering minute details from life in short, precise formulations lends his prose a documentary quality. A fine example is "Zheltyi svet" ("Yellow Light," 1936), which describes the coming of fall in the central Russian region and records the author's talks with a simple fisherman whose philosophy derives from his daily life close to nature. This work has the exquisitely lyrical quality of a poem in prose. In "Staryi cheln" ("The Old Boat," 1939) Paustovsky tells of passengers on a train forced to stop in the woods during a thunderstorm. A forest ranger traveling south and a young girl, Natasha, are the only passengers who feel at ease; all the others, city people, are frightened by the storm. By chance a local peasant passes by, recognizes the forest ranger as a former friend, and asks him to use the involuntary stop to inspect the forest that they once planted together. Natasha comes along and experiences a beautiful night by a forest lake. When the train continues next morning, it is as if she has returned unexpectedly from a strange but wonderful world. The enforced stop serves as a frame emphasizing the contrast between life in nature and the artificial, civilized life of the train, where people are well dressed but unhappy.

Conformists

Up to this stage we have discussed two groups of writers: the fellow travelers, who at some point came under political pressure and were either liquidated or encountered various difficulties, and the so-called Soviet romantics, who escaped any repression. Still another group of writers in the early Soviet period consists of those who adapted to the needs of the time. They began as fellow travelers but eventually became fully recognized Soviet writers who are today numbered among the pillars of Soviet literature.

Leonid Leonov (1899–1983), the son of a minor writer, grew up in a Moscow suburb among merchants like his grandfather. By the age of fourteen he was writing poems. He completed school in 1918 and then joined his father in exile in Archangel, where he worked as a journalist. In 1920, after the British expeditionary forces had left northern Russia, he joined the Red Army and edited an army paper. He later settled in Moscow.

Leonov's early tales of 1920 and 1923 have little to do with contemporary life. They deal with romantic and fantastic topics, are set in an irrational dream world, and recall the tales of Edgar Allan Poe. He wrote about fishermen of the North plagued by a devil that assumes the form of a monk in "Gibel' Egorushki" ("The Downfall of Egorushka") and Tartar rulers of the distant past in "Tuatamur." If Leonov refers to the great events of the time at all, he does so only indirectly, from a village perspective or that of a small merchant in a provincial town. Like the Serapions, he tended to divide his stories into brief chapters and short paragraphs, sometimes consisting only of a line or a phrase and several dots. In the story "Bubnovyi valet" ('The Jack of Diamonds"), for instance, the entire fourth chapter reads: "Toward fall the eyes become sad. So it was with Lenochka . . ."

Leonov's style is colloquial and seems so genuine that critics of the 1920s thought that he had used material from real life. Indeed in 1928 he published a cycle of stories from peasant life called *Neobyknovennye rasskazy o muzhikakh* (*Unusual Stories about Peasants*). Leonov's early stories are in the tradition of avant-gardist, modern prose. As a Soviet critic has said, they display a "romanticism far removed from life." The hero of "Konets melkogo cheloveka" ("The End of an Ordinary Man," 1924) is a world-famous paleontologist Likharev, who continues his research on Mesozoic fossils despite such hardships as lack of food and heat. He falls ill and is visited by the Devil. He sees a vision in which all those whose lives have been upset by the Revolution meet to discuss the situation. Before Likharev dies, he burns the manuscript of his magnum opus. The end is total: both his scientific life and his physical life end at the same time. Likharev is of no use to the new society. In *Unusual Stories about Peasants* Leonov describes the cruelty and evil inherent in life. The only smith in a village steals a horse but escapes punishment because the villagers need his skills. The village, however, has several carpenters, and one of them, though innocent, is killed instead of the real thief—because justice must be done. The problem of a just society lies at the heart of most of Leonov's early tales.

Mikhail Sholokhov (1905–83) came from a middle-class cossack background and did odd jobs in Moscow in the early 1920s. From 1926 on he lived in the Don area. His first two collections of stories appeared in 1926 under the titles *Donskie rasskazy* (*Tales from the Don*) and *Lazurevaia step'* (*Blue Steppe*). Both autobiographical and written in a naturalistic style, they depict the class struggle among the cossacks. *Tales from the Don* describes the work of the Bolsheviks among the cossacks and the deep rifts caused by conflicting ideologies, as in "Prodkomissar" ("The Requisitioning Commissar"), where a son sentences his father to death when the latter refuses to hand over his grain reserves to the Red Army. Love, class antagonism, patriotism, and betrayal intertwine in highly emotional tales. But Sholokhov is always firmly on the side of the new order, maintaining a "clear class standpoint."

Aleksey Tolstoy (1883–1945) wrote some ten volumes of short prose, including novellas or short novels. His early stories, which appeared long before World War I, usually describe unusual people, individualists deeply rooted in the earth and full of the zest of life. When Tolstoy returned to Russia from exile in 1923, he quickly adapted his literary approach to life there. His stories treat a great variety of themes, but they invariably include the conflict between party ideology and the old bourgeois and capitalist attitudes. In a typical story, "Soiuz piati" ("The Union of the Five," 1925), Tolstoy depicts attempts by American business tycoons to use science in order to gain power over the entire world. Eventually they control four-fifths of the world's wealth and have assumed political power as well. Yet something peculiar happens to people then. Once everything has been taken from them, they care about nothing. The more oppressive the power of the five dictators becomes, the more skillfully do people evade it. Ignaty Ruf, who has masterminded the march to power, summarizes the situation in the end:

> I forbade music in public places—the whole city walks about whistling. I closed taverns and theaters—and they have begun to meet in private apartments and entertain themselves for free in the city. We are a mirage; we are gods to whom nobody wants to sacrifice any more. I ask you: should we decide to bury ourselves in our gold up to the neck or blow ourselves up in front of this fireplace out of pride, enthusiastic about the fact that we have such power as the earth has never seen before? I ask you: what is the practical conclusion from all our might?

Tolstoy believes it is easy to destroy an authoritarian government: do not take it seriously, and it will collapse.

An attempt to glorify party loyalty and the spirit of civil war communist fighters is very obvious in Tolstoy's "Gadiuka" ("The Viper," 1925), dealing with a woman member of the Red Cavalry. Olga Vyacheslavovna's strength is in her tenacity, which earns her the nickname "the viper." She serves along with her protector, the commanding officer Emelyan, whom everyone considers her husband. But he scrupulously avoids coming near her: "During the campaign they spent the night in the same hut and often were in the same bed: he facing in one direction, she in another, each covering himself with his own fur coat." Both are true heroes. He dies attacking the enemy; she is badly wounded and receives a strange decoration: a brooch of pure gold with an arrow and a heart. The decree reads: "Zotova [her surname] is to be awarded the golden brooch—an arrow, but the heart, being a bourgeois emblem, is to be removed." Unable to adjust to normal life after the war, Zotova eventually turns criminal, killing people who slander her.

Aleksey Tolstoy's stories are too numerous to be done justice in a brief survey. They are always eminently readable and full of adventurous action, although ideologically correct. Tolstoy frequently indulges his penchant for science fiction and utopian perspectives.

Ilya Erenburg (1891–1967), born in Kiev, attended school in Moscow and early in life became involved in revolutionary activity. Eventually he emigrated to Paris, where he spent a considerable part of his life working as a journalist and writer and living as a bohemian. A treatment of the Russian short story of the 1920s would not be complete without mention of his collection *Trinadtsat' trubok* (*Thirteen Pipes*, 1923). Erenburg's style is close to that of the Serapion Brothers; like them he experiments with language and form. Each story in *Thirteen Pipes* is linked to a different kind of pipe, with the pipe generally symbolizing the author's cosmopolitan attitude. These stories span continents and describe the fates of contemporary individuals.

Another fellow traveler who has adapted to Soviet ideology is Valentin Kataev (1897–). Kataev, the son of a teacher, began publishing poetry at thirteen. His early stories were written during the Revolution and the civil war, when the author was working as a journalist. Kataev eventually joined the Communist party in 1958, and for many years he served on the board of the Writers' Union.

Kataev's early story "Opyt Krantsa" ("Kranz's Experiment," 1919, published 1922) is already remarkable for its accurate plot structure, philosophical depth, and psychological delineation of character. The setting is a provincial town in the hands of tsarist troops and their foreign allies, where the old "capitalist" order still flourishes. Kataev opposes Kranz, a German-born student of mathematics who wants to arrange his life according to logic, to the "people who . . . read novels and poems, fall in love and attend the theater." Kranz then develops in a manner recalling Hermann in Pushkin's "Queen of Spades" or Dostoevsky's Raskolnikov (*Crime and Punishment*).

In the late 1920s Kataev wrote lyrical tales of but a few pages, such as "Gora" ("The Mountain," 1927), describing an excursion to a Crimean mountain, or a humorous and satirical story like "Veshchi" ("Things," 1929) in which a girl, Zhurka, is in love with love. When her husband dies soon after their marriage she immediately transfers her love to another man.

Proletarians

In 1918 the poet Mikhail Gerasimov said at a conference of the Organization of Proletarian Culture (Proletkult): "Proletkult is an oasis where our class will crystallize. If we want our furnace to flame, we will throw coal, petroleum into the fire, but not the peasant straw or the intelligentsia shavings, which will produce only smoke, no more." On the other hand, Evgeny Zamyatin said in the mid-1920s that "it is time to understand that in truth there are in Russia no or almost no talented communist writers." These quotations illustrate very well the essential conflict of Soviet literature: the struggle between an ideologically motivated and an artistically motivated literature.

There are, indeed, very few writers of the 1920s who could be called "proletarian" and whose work has endured. One of them is Maksim Gorky (1868–1936), who began writing romantic tales around the turn of the century. His pre-Revolutionary work has been discussed in the preceding chapter, and thus our attention will be focused here on his stories written after 1917. These were collected in a volume entitled *Rasskazy* (*Stories,* 1922–24), which opens with "Otshel'nik" ("The Hermit," 1922), describing a former sawmill worker and vagabond now living in a cave and comforting people who come to him for advice. He carries an exuberant love for all creatures in his heart and a kind of fantastic understanding of God, who, he says, "has dissolved in our tearful lives like sugar in water. . . . he is everywhere and lives in every soul as its spurious spark and it is our duty to search for God in man, to reunite him into one whole."

It is significant that Gorky placed precisely this story at the beginning of a collection that goes on to deal with various topics of the time. Gorky takes up the question of the border between fiction and reality in "Rasskaz ob odnom romane" ("The Story of a Novel"). The relationship between art and reality is also the subject of "Repetitsiia" ("The Rehearsal"), which describes a break in the rehearsal of a play during which the actors discuss the role of literature and the theater and the function of the imagination. In "Rasskaz o neobyknovennom" ("A Story of the Unusual") Gorky writes: "The soul must grow wings. . . . the main thing is the freedom of the soul, one cannot be human without a soul." This story describes an orphan who grew up in Siberia and was helped along by a kind doctor. He lives through the turmoil of war and revolution; on one occasion he is almost shot. His experiences cause him to dislike politics and political parties. "Politics aims at control and force," he says, "Every party member will prove that he is cleverer than the other. . . . they want power, but we want freedom for the soul." The civil war brings general brutalization in its train, and Eliazev, the hero, recognizes that cruelty and power go together and that the salvation of man lies "in simplicity": "The 'unusual' [the great] has been devised by Satan to ruin man. That's it, brother."

Andrey Platonov (pseudonym of Andrey Klimentov, 1899–1951) was a true proletarian. His father was a locksmith for the railways, his mother the daughter of a watchmaker. He was born in a suburb of Voronezh, which still looked like a village, and attended the electrotechnical section of the railway polytechnical school, which he finished in 1922 as an electrician and mechanic. By that time he was both writing poetry and lecturing on electrification. Platonov was among those who greeted the Revolution enthusiastically, believing it would transform the world with the aid of science and technology: "Science is the head of the Revolution, its heart—it is the sense of truth inherent in man" (1920). Influenced by certain minor proletarian poets, he worked for five years as a technician on various electrification projects, all the while continuing to write. In the late 1920s he joined Pereval. Then his description of forced collectivization, particularly some of its negative aspects, in the story "Vprok" ("The Advantage," 1931) led to repression and banishment, until in the late 1930s he was able to publish again. In 1946 he fell victim to devastating criticism for his story "Sem'ia Ivanova" ("Ivanov's Family"). Although Platonov soon lost his trust in the party, he always remained a staunch defender of basic human values. His heroes are outsiders, peasants and workers whose simplicity is coupled with a keen sense of right and wrong. This choice of hero permitted him to reflect naively on the absurd aspects of Soviet life.

In "Epifanskie shliuzy" ("Epifan Locks," 1927) Platonov returns to the time of Peter the Great to tell the story of an English engineer hired by Peter to build a waterway. He fails because of poor planning by his predecessors, and Peter sentences him to die. The story of his work in Russia parallels the story of his equally unhappy love for an English girl in far-away Newcastle. The text conveys a sense of utter helplessness in the face of an autocratic ruler whose wishes are as unpredictable as the whims of nature and a harsh climate.

Platonov's "Reka Potudan'" ("The Potudan River," 1937) is one of the strangest love stories in world literature. A young soldier returns from the civil war to join his lonely carpenter father. When he meets the local teacher's daughter, Lyuba, now in training to become a medical doctor, he helps her cope with life and eventually comes to love her. The two marry after her graduation. Though he is an uneducated and naive man, he is full of respect for his wife and fearful of hurting her feelings. The relationship then develops in an almost absurd manner as Platonov composes a surrealist story in a setting of utter realism and truthful detail. More interesting is "Usumnivshiisia Makar" ("Makar the Doubtful," 1929), a story that aroused considerable criticism. The hero Makar (the proverbial name for a man of the people) is a peasant worker who has "clever hands" but an "empty head," as comrade Lev Chumovoy points out, and who "because of his intelligence supervises the people's progress in a straight line toward the common weal." Makar is used to taking everything he hears or sees literally. So it is no wonder that he causes trouble and eventually leaves the village for Moscow. Although he has no ticket, he reasons that his weight increases the momentum of the train he is riding, thus helping it reach Moscow, and so his presence is justified. Makar has a technical mind, no matter how primitive, and constantly tries to improve the technical aspects of the work going on around him. At a construction site he is told that "an eternal building out of iron, concrete, steel and bright glass" is being erected. He suggests the use of a "construction hose" to pump concrete upward and simplify the building process, a proposal that brings him a ruble from the workers' union. The story then meanders on in this same way. Still, we should mention two passages that caused critical controversy. In a dream Makar sees a gigantic "scientific man" on top of a hill gazing with horrible, dead eyes into the distance, silent and oblivious of Makar. When Makar climbs the hill and touches the figure, it collapses, for the man is dead. The symbolism of the dream emphasizes the contrast between utopian expectations and the individual. The second passage in question contains "quotations from Lenin" read by Makar's friend Peter at a mental hospital: "Our administrative offices are crap . . . our laws are crap. We are good at giving instructions, but bad at carrying them out. . . . some of our comrades have turned into pompous courtiers and are doing their work like nincompoops." The mentally disturbed listen avidly, for, we are told, "they had not known until then that Lenin knew everything." Makar and Peter next go to the Worker and Peasant Inspection Office and become Soviet officials. However, Platonov informs us, "soon people stopped coming to Makar's and Peter's office because their way of thinking was so simple that the poor themselves were able to think and make decisions the same way, and so the working people began to think for themselves in their own rooms."

The 1930s

The 1930s saw the forced collectivization of agriculture and the continuation of the five-year plans begun in the 1920s. In 1934 the new Union of Soviet Writers replaced all previous organizations, as we have seen: from then on the method of socialist realism became mandatory for Soviet writers. The second half of the decade was a time of purges, arrests, trials, and executions. Hundreds of writers disappeared in Stalin's camps, and literature was restricted to topics more or less prescribed by the party. Experimentation with literary form was no longer possible.

A good example of the plight of Soviet literature in these years is Ivan Kataev's story "Pod chistymi zvezdami" ("Under Clear Stars," 1936), which could not be published because the author was arrested in 1937 and disappeared into the dark world of the gulag. It came out only in 1956, in the almanac *Literaturnaia Moskva* (Literary Moscow). The story's subject is straightforward: Kataev's impressions of a day and night he spent in the fields with collectivized peasants in a work brigade led by Apollinaria Lesnykh, a young woman famous for her successful fulfillment of work plans. The scene is set in a most attractive landscape in the Altai mountains in the South of the Soviet Union. The author arrives with a group of friends on horseback and witnesses a competition between Apollinaria and Timka, a peasant lad. Each of them tries to finish a haystack first with the aid of a team. Timka wins and the rest of the evening is spent in preparing food, joking, and viewing a movie dealing with the civil war. That night the author by chance overhears a conversation between Timka and Apollinaria that supplies a serious background for the story. The two are in love, and in fact Apollinaria is expecting a child by Timka. The work in the brigade is too limiting for Timka, who wants to go to town to study and improve his situation. She wants to keep him on the farm, but he feels that he has strength and the world is open to him if he only will risk it. The story, which had to be optimistic in accordance with the Soviet literary canon of the time, shows the immense strength of people dedicated to work and self-improvement. It embodies an exuberant glorification of life and faith in the future that the people are creating. At the end of the story it seems that Apollinaria and Timka will stay together after all.

Other writers of the 1930s include Yuri German (1910–67), who in his *Rasskazy o Felikse Dzerzhinskom* (*Stories of Feliks Dzerzhinsky,* 1938–47) depicted the first head of the Soviet secret police as a person entirely devoted to the people and always objective in his judgment; and Nikolay Virta (pseudonym of Nikolay Karelsky, 1906–76), winner of Stalin prizes, who wrote stories illustrating the notion of "no-conflict literature," the idea that Soviet society was no longer subject to conflicts generated in a bourgeois society, a theory he still defended explicitly as late as 1952.

In addition, Valentin Ovechkin (1904–68) wrote stories about the early years of collectivization, which appeared as *Kolkhoznye rasskazy* (*Kholkhoz Tales,* 1935). They were designed to show the development of new socialist relationships among people, while satirizing the ancient peasant ways of life that were slowly yielding to the exigencies of collectivism. Vasily Grossman (1905–64), a chemical engineer, published his first story, about the life of Soviet miners (Grossman himself worked in the Donbass mining region), in 1935. His stories of the 1930s describe people who, after fighting the tsar and winning the civil war, confronted the task of building a socialist economy. In the West today Grossman is better known as the author of later works criticizing the Soviet system quite relentlessly.

Literature and War

On June 22, 1941, German troops attacked Russia. During the war years, literature became part of the struggle against the aggressor, who quickly drove to the very heart of Russia. Patriotism, the heroism of the Soviet army, and the ruthlessness of Hitler's soldiers became dominant themes in the literature of the 1940s, a purposefully tendentious literature that taught the Soviet citizen love and dedication to his homeland, as well as pride in its historical past. A certain literary schematicism was understandably necessary at the time.

Many works of that decade are based on the personal recollections of the authors; as, for example, Konstantin Simonov's (1915–80) volume of 1946 containing a section "Iz voennykh dnevnikov" ("From My War Diaries," 1941). The story "Tretii ad"iutant" ("The Third Adjutant") opens the collection. One main figure is a commissar who maintains that courageous people die more rarely in war than do cowards. That theory is tested when one night he sends his third adjutant ahead to join the soldiers in the front line. Next day he learns that the Germans have overrun the outpost. The commissar himself leads the counterattack and retakes the post. It turns out that all the soldiers at the outpost are dead, while the adjutant has fallen about a hundred meters behind the post, as if he had tried to flee. But he is still alive and recovers. Later it develops that the German attack had begun before he even reached the front-line post. The commissar's theory is thus confirmed: courageous soldiers do not die easily!

Like many of his colleagues, Valentin Kataev was a war correspondent for *Pravda* and *Red Star,* the army newspaper. His "Flag" (1942) is one of the better stories of that time. Written in a terse style, it vividly conveys the tragic mood of inescapable defeat and unavoidable death as the price of final victory. The Soviet commander of a fort built into the rocky shore of an island in the Baltic Sea has just fired his last shell and has provisions for only one more day. He is surrounded by German ships, and the German commander demands unconditional surrender to be signaled by a white flag on top of the steeple of a little church. During their last night thirty Soviet soldiers sew together a huge red flag and hoist it up the steeple. In the morning the Germans mistakenly think that it is the sun that makes the flag seem red. They enter the island fortifications and are promptly blown up in a huge explosion. The Soviet soldiers around the church defend the red flag to the last man. One by one they are killed, but only after each has first killed several Germans. In the end the banner flies over thirty dead Russians surrounded by "hundreds of dead Germans." The flag assumes symbolic significance, flying high "as if an invisible giant flagbearer were carrying it steadfastly through the smoke of battle forward toward victory."

Vadim Kozhevnikov (1909–), who joined the Communist party in 1943 and became editor of the literary section of *Pravda* in the late 1940s, is known as a true servant of the party. His war stories, written in the spirit of the Stalinist personality cult, celebrate heroes of nearly superhuman strength and intelligence who always prove far superior to their enemies. In "Mart-aprel'" ("March-April," 1942) he tells of Captain Zhavoronkov, a hero who has already been captured once and almost executed by the Germans. Though half dead, he crawls twenty kilometers (!) back to Soviet lines in the course of one night. He and a girl radio operator are dropped behind enemy lines on a special assignment. While returning to their own lines they discover a German airfield and call in Soviet planes. Despite arctic temperatures and wounds suffered in the course of the air attack, they manage to reach their own lines. There is also a partisan in the story who once had been a peaceable beekeeper incapable even of cutting the neck of a chicken. "But now I have cut the throat of so many Hitlerites!" he exclaims. "I am an evil, insulted man!" Kozhevnikov's tales exemplify the trend toward exaggeration and a blatantly black-and-white representation of reality.

Aleksey Tolstoy's cycle *Rasskazy Ivana Sudareva* (*The Tales of Ivan Sudarev,* 1942) came into being as a result of the author's conversations with partisans and a platoon of soldiers who had been fighting in the rear of the German army. In "Strannaia istoriia" ("A Strange Story") Tolstoy shows the Russian population united by hatred of the German occupation. Its hero is an elderly peasant, Petr Filippovich, once a kulak, who has just returned from ten years in a Soviet labor camp. The Germans have occupied his village and, assuming that he is an anticommunist, have appointed him its mayor. Petr Filippovich secretly sneaks into the woods to meet the Soviet partisans and offer to collaborate with them. Guided by his information, the partisans blow up trains and ammunition depots. "Russkii kharakter" ("The Russian Character," 1944), added to Tolstoy's collection later, appeared in several periodicals at the time, including *Pravda.* It was one of Tolstoy's most popular war stories, and among the last he would write. Egor Dermov, who commands a tank and after many brave deeds almost burns to death when his tank is hit, is left with a badly disfigured face. When he returns home he pretends to be a friend of Dermov's so as not to frighten his parents. He sees his fiancée Katya and then leaves for the front without having told anybody of his true identity. Yet his mother has recognized him nevertheless and comes to visit him at the post where he is stationed, bringing along Katya, who declares her love for him. This story, simple though it is, has a warm emotional appeal.

Once the war had ended, Stalin saw to it that the more liberal spirit of wartime was quickly terminated. In August 1946 the party central committee attacked two Leningrad journals, *Krasnaia zvezda* (*Red Star*) and *Leningrad,* for having published "slanderous and empty" works, particularly by the revered poet Anna Akhmatova and the humorist Mikhail Zoshchenko. Zoshchenko had been writing children's stories for the past two years. Under the heading *Novye rasskazy dlia detei* (*New Stories for Children*) he published his "Prikliucheniia obez'iany" ("Adventures of a Monkey") in *Krasnaia zvezda,* of which he had just become editor. It took a paranoid Stalinist to classify this work as anti-Soviet. A monkey escapes from the zoo and is finally caught by a Red Army man, who presents it to a little boy. Zoshchenko erred in causing the monkey to think "that it is better to live in a zoo than at liberty" and that "in a cage one breathes more easily than among Soviet people." However, the condemnation of this otherwise innocuous story, whose context precludes any anti-Soviet interpretation, led to Zoshchenko's expulsion from the Writers' Union.

The next seven years, until Stalin's death, were characterized by timidity and a return to the strict precepts of socialist realism and a limited number of themes. In addition the cold war again isolated Russia from the West and Western literature.

The Thaw

Stalin died on March 5, 1953. The next few years witnessed the emancipation of literature and art from the shackles of the "personality cult," to use a phrase coined by Nikita Khrushchev in a famous speech to the 20th Party Congress in February 1956. The thaw, named after a novel by Erenburg, began in December 1953 when Vladimir Pomerantsev, a minor writer, in an article for the journal *Novyi mir* (*New world*) pleaded for greater sincerity in literature. His call met with immediate resistance from established Stalinists, so that by the closing months of 1953 the foundations had already been laid for the fateful struggle among the party, the conservatives (Stalinists and neo-Stalinists), and the liberals (nonconformists) that would define the intellectual life of the country for the next two decades.

Major events among the liberals were the founding in 1955 of the monthly *Yunost* (Youth), which became the focal point for a new generation of writers, and the establishment of the monthly *Druzhba na-*

rodov (Friendship of peoples). However, it was *Novyi mir,* edited by Aleksandr Tvardovsky, that was to become the most respected liberal journal. The conservative reaction against liberal successes gained ground in the late 1950s. In 1958 a conservative Russian Writers' Union was founded; its new organs *Literatura i zhizn'* (Literature and life [from 1963 on Literary Russia]) and *Moskva* began to preach the dogma of party-mindedness once again. Optimism and simplicity of form, the conservatives held, were essential to literature.

The 22nd Party Congress of 1961 brought another step in Khrushchev's de-Stalinization campaign, leading to the so-called second thaw and the publication of Alexander Solzhenitsyn's *Odin den' Ivana Denisovicha* (*A Day in the Life of Ivan Denisovich*) and similar works dealing with deportations and forced labor camps. But then Khrushchev's fall from power in October 1964 led to a steady strengthening of conservative forces. Writers were again arrested and sentenced to hard labor, and yet the wave of new writing that began in the middle and late 1950s continued into the 1970s producing a considerable number of impressive literary texts.

The year 1956 witnessed a notable attempt to give literature a new direction and steer it away from Stalinist norms. Konstantin Paustovsky edited a literary almanac in two volumes, *Literaturnaia Moskva* (*Literary Moscow*), which might be called a manifesto of the post-Stalin era. The second volume is of particular interest, for its authors pursue a program of literary sincerity and de-Stalinization much more openly than do the authors of the first volume. The contributions to the second volume include "Svet v okne" ("Light in the Window"), a parable of the Stalinist personality cult and its effects on society by Yuri Nagibin; "Derevenskii dnevnik" ("Rural Diary") by Efim Dorosh (1908–72), a chronicle of life in the country; "Rychagi" ("Levers") by Aleksandr Yashin (1913–68), an investigation of Communist party politics in rural Russia; and "Poezdka na rodinu" ("A Trip Back Home") by Nikolay Zhdanov, the very title of which defines a theme that would become common in the village prose of subsequent years.

In 1961 Paustovsky brought out another almanac, *Tarusskie stranitsy* (*Leaves from Tarusa*), which supported the tendency among writers of the time to turn away from the public sphere and toward the private life and feelings of ordinary Soviet citizens. For instance, Bulat Okudzhava's (1924–) long story "Bud' zdorov, shkoliar!" ("Stay Well, Scholar!") describes a Soviet teenager during World War II who, as a close witness of war, rather like Hemingway recounts "how I made war, how the war tried to kill me, and how I turned out to be lucky." Such notions as "heroism," "duty," "fatherland" are debunked, reduced to their actual meaning for the individual who seeks only to survive amidst the horrors of war.

Young Prose

Beginning with the 1950s Russian prose displayed a great variety of trends. The earliest of these trends, known as "young prose" (*molodaia proza*), features adolescent heroes modeled on literary figures from the work of J. D. Salinger, Jack Kerouac, and similar Western authors. The preferred genre is the short story or short novel. Out of young prose would develop "urban prose" or "everyday prose" (*gorodskaia, bytovaia proza*) as one of the two leading trends in the literature of the 1960s and 1970s (the other was "village prose"). Two subtrends within urban prose were what we might call the "female theme" or "emancipatory prose," writing dealing with contemporary Soviet women and their problems in a society still dominated by male prejudices and habits, and "science prose," that is, prose set in the world of research institutes and universities.

It was on the pages of *Yunost* that the negative hero, clad in jeans, using American slang, and reading Salinger's *Catcher in the Rye,* came forward—the representative of a new kind of sensibility, an intellectual and idealist, unadapted to reality, full of youthful protest.

Yuri Kazakov (1927–82) studied music and played in an orchestra before his first publication came out in 1953. That was followed by study at the Gorky Institute of Literature. Since then several collections of his stories have appeared. Kazakov's prose stands in the classical tradition of Bunin, Chekhov, and Paustovsky. It is lyrical and musical, intensely personal and individualistic, and usually narrated in the first person. It is free of ideology and politics. Kazakov deals with individual experiences of everyday people, particularly negative experiences such as loneliness and disappointment, as in "Osen' v dubovykh lesakh" ("Fall in the Oak Forest," 1961) or "Dvoe v dekabre" ("Two in December"), a story of two young people. He has just graduated in law, and she is still studying. The story describes their trip to his villa near Moscow. However, their love is marred by the inability of each to make a commitment to the other. The concluding sentence reads: "as always they took leave of each other with a cursory smile and he did not walk her home."

Vasily Aksenov (1932–), trained as a doctor, began his literary career in *Yunost* and eventually became one of its editors. In 1979 he was a key figure in compiling the modernist almanac *Metropol,* which brought him into conflict with the authorities and led to his emigration to the United States in 1980. In the 1960s he was known as the "leader of the fourth generation," that is, the post-Stalin generation. The hero of his stories and novels is a kind of Soviet beatnik or James Dean, a *stilyaga* (young man in stylish clothes). His hero breaks away from conventional life, escapes from his parents' tutelage, and travels somewhere far away to the sea in search of a free and bohemian life. The motif of the journey is particularly characteristic of the stories and novels of Aksenov's generation. His long story "Na polputi k lune" ("Halfway to the Moon," 1962) is set on board a jetliner which flies between the Soviet Far East and the Crimea. A young chauffeur in love with a stewardess repeats that journey enough times to match the distance from the earth to the moon, just in order to be near the woman he adores. "Pobeda—rasskaz s preuvelicheniiami" ("Victory—A Story with Exaggerations"), set on an express train, contrasts two ways of life, two ways of thinking: the direct, unsophisticated aggressiveness of a chess fan and the complex, reflective mood of a grandmaster. A mind concentrated entirely on the present is opposed to one that integrates past and present into an intricate view of life. The grandmaster loses the game.

Andrey Bitov (1937–), the son of a Leningrad architect who studied at an engineering college, began to publish at the end of the 1950s and immediately attracted favorable attention. Bitov has written psychological studies of the motivation of individual actions—for example, "Sad" ("The Garden," 1960–63), in which he minutely analyzes the thoughts of a young man given to excessive reflection who is in love with a married woman. Spurred by his passion, he commits a theft. Like Kazakov, though more subtly, he turns from the public sphere and concentrates entirely on the private lives of his heroes. "Uletaiushchii Monakhov" ("The Departing Monakhov," 1976) extends this kind of analysis, possibly referring back to Dostoevsky's character Alesha Karamazov, a novice in a monastery, by his choice of the hero's name (Alesha Monakhov) and his hero's intellectual propensities. Monakhov travels to Tashkent to investigate an accident on a building site, which led to the death of two people. But he also has two other aims in mind: to visit his aged parents and the girl with whom he once had an affair. Thus the official reason for the journey is actually a pretext for an intensely personal confrontation with the past. The essence of the story is contained in the reflections and observations of the main character, which cannot easily be summarized. Monakhov's journey is not only a journey into the past but simultaneously one into the depths of his soul. Bitov attempts to capture an essential feature of life: people's spiritual interdependence, a theme quite central to Boris Pasternak's novel *Doctor Zhivago.*

The 1960's and 1970's also saw the revival of satire and humor. Vladimir Voinovich (1932–), for example, who has been living in the West since 1980, is the author of the satirical novel *Zhizn' i neobychainye prikliucheniia soldata Ivana Chonkina* (*Life and Memorable Adventures of the Soldier Ivan Chonkin,* Paris, 1975). During his last six years in the Soviet Union he labored under great hardships and could not publish after his expulsion from the Writers' Union in 1974. Voinovich began appearing in the early 1960s and was much praised for his first story "My zdes' zhivem" ("We Live Here," 1961). But his realistic and satirical, often hilarious, descriptions of Soviet reality soon led to difficulties. "V kupe" ("In the Sleeping Compartment," subtitled "A Scene") is a good illustration of Voinovich's method. The plot is anecdotal, based on a bureaucratic mishandling of train tickets. A male traveler purchases a ticket for a two-person sleeping compartment only to discover that his fellow traveler is a prudish, aggressive lady, the embodiment of official Soviet morality. She protests his presence and stays up all night, even keeping the door open, which makes life difficult for her innocent companion. The humor stems from the situation and unfolds in the dialogue, which is realistic and yet absurd, as it is based on the incommensurability of triviality and pathos.

Fazil Iskander (1929–), a journalist and editor from Abkhazia, published his first prose works in the mid-1960s. One of his earliest stories is the "Sozvezdie Kozlotura" ("Constellation of the Goatabix," 1966), a satire on the frequent Soviet campaigns to raise production levels in agriculture. An editor of the paper *Red Subtropics* hears about some sensational cross-breeding experiments in Moscow: a Moscow professor has supposedly crossed an ordinary goat with the abkhazian ibex to obtain a "goatabix." A campaign for the propagation of the new animal is begun right away and goes to absurd lengths. There is a "goatabix movement," an article is published on "The Goatabix—A Weapon in Antireligious Propaganda," and a choir of tobacco workers sings an ode in honor of the nonexistent animal. The campaigns are abruptly halted after a critical article appears in one of the central papers. The chief editor of *Red Subtropics* exposes the folly of his agricultural editor. The latter is immediately replaced, every mention of the strange animal is promptly removed from all publications, and the ode is transformed into an instrumental piece. In a word, the nonexistent goatabix suffers the fate of many former public figures in the Soviet Union, including writers, who, however, at least actually existed at one time.

Anatoly Gladilin (1935–) comes from Moscow. Like Voinovich, he is of working-class origin and was an electrician before studying at the Gorky Institute of Literature in 1954–58. His first publications appeared in 1956, and in 1976 he too emigrated to the West.

Gladilin articulates the fears of many Russians when he has Stalin rise from the dead and cause havoc at a party meeting in "Repetitsiia v piatnitsu" ("Rehearsal on a Friday," 1975). His story "Poezd ukhodit" ("The Train Is Leaving," 1961) is in the tradition of literature of the absurd as practiced in the early 1950s but suppressed at that time. The hero, an ordinary Soviet citizen who leads a perfectly normal life, is married to a woman who "serves him warmed-over fish at night and cold tea . . . who does the washing when he has his free evening. . . . his figure fitted perfectly into the suits of the Moscow textile trust." Yet this well-adapted product of Soviet reality suddenly develops a dream "of a train about to leave," a train that would fulfill everybody's romantic desires. His romantic inclinations show through in his appearance: "One of his eyes was orange-colored, the other violet, the eyebrows were green, his hair the color of raspberries, the nose was dotted." One day he hears on the radio that the Blue Dream express train is about to leave town "for the first time in the last 2,000 years." Anyone may choose any partner of the opposite sex and board the train, knowing that his family will not suffer thereby. Gladilin uses this tale to expose the conventionality of married life in the Soviet Union and the secret wishes of numberless husbands and wives who dream of escaping their dreary everyday existence. But the man whose insistent dream has called the train into being misses its departure.

Urban Prose

One Soviet critic in 1971 defined urban prose thus:

> Writers depict the "private life" of contemporary urban people, choosing as their heroes those who are markedly ordinary, not distinguished in any way, [and] place them in situations which correspond entirely to everyday reality and do not disturb the general course of events.

Soviet writing returned to the eternal themes of love, death, and conflicts between individuals. In a pointed formulation paraphrasing a statement of the nineteenth-century writer Aleksandr Herzen, Yuri Trifonov opposes this new writing to the didacticism of earlier Soviet literature, saying: "we are not the doctors, we are the pain." The author assumes the position of his hero, avoids passing judgment, and lets his characters speak for themselves. First-person narration, direct speech, free indirect speech, and stream-of-consciousness narration are among the key features of this prose, which tries to take up where modernist literature of the 1920s was forced to leave off. These stories investigate the meaning of *byt,* the *realia* of everyday life, which Trifonov defines as follows: "Our element is the modeled, complicated structure of *byt* at the intersection of a multitude of connections, outlooks, friendships, acquaintances, antagonisms, psychologies, ideologies. Anyone who lives in a large city senses every day, every hour, the magnetic streams of that structure."

Yuri Trifonov (1925–81) was a locksmith by profession who eventually graduated from the Gorky Institute of Literature. Trifonov is known best for his novels and novellas, not his short stories, although they are among the best Soviet literature has to offer. In his stories Trifonov can compress an entire life into the space of some ten pages. The events of "Byl letnii polden'" ("It was Midday in Summer," 1966), for example, take place in 1958, yet through dream, memory, and recollection, Trifonov takes the reader back to the turn of the century. Private life and historic events—the Revolution, civil war, Stalinist camps, the denigration of former revolutionaries and their rehabilitation in the 1950s—are painted on a broad historical canvas in a few spare but well-placed strokes. As in his *Moscow Novellas,* Trifonov focuses on the fate of an individual, providing carefully selected details that are left ambiguous because they are presented entirely from his main figure's point of view. The reader obtains a description of a typical Soviet family and a nutshell history of the Soviet Union. "V gribnuiu osen'" ("An Autumn Full of Mushrooms," 1968) illustrates Trifonov's use of the stream of consciousness. Nadya, a middle-aged, rather stout woman separated from her alcoholic husband, lives with her two young boys, her mother, and a lover, who also has a great liking for vodka. The story deals with the sudden death and burial of the mother; its attraction derives from the juxtaposition of the utterly trivial lives of Nadya's friends and her family with her genuine pain at her mother's unexpected death.

Although Valentin Rasputin is known as a major representative of village prose, he has also written stories that belong to urban prose. One of its finest love stories is Rasputin's "Rudolfio" (1965), set in a suburb of Moscow. She is a schoolgirl of fifteen or sixteen; he is twenty and married. The two meet regularly in a streetcar they both ride. He does not really wish to become involved with her but jokingly goes along as she keeps telephoning and even visiting him, all in a delicate but persistent manner. Finally, as they are taking a long walk together, she tells him that nobody has ever kissed her. He kisses her on the cheek. When she asks him to kiss her on the lips, he replies that is only for people very close to each other. Deeply wounded, she runs off, and only then does he realize how much the girl loves him.

While we are on the subject of love stories, we must not omit the one story that Louis Aragon has called the most beautiful love story in world literature—Chingiz Aitmatov's (1926–) "Dzhamilia" (1958). It is told by Said, a fifteen-year-old boy, and the stepbrother of Dzhamilia's unloved husband whom she betrays with her lover, a shy and dreamy ex-soldier. The Kirghiz community condemns her for her infidelity and Dzhamilia flees with her new lover. Said alone does not condemn her, for he himself adores her. An artist, he will preserve her image in his paintings.

The Woman Question

This trend is sometimes mockingly termed the "ladies' tale" (*damskaia povest*). It might more appropriately be called "emancipatory prose." Its authors are mostly, though by no means exclusively, female; their main concern is the position of Soviet women in today's society, particularly as it has to do with the more intimate sphere of family life. Vera Panova, Irina Grekova, Irina Velembovskaya, Nadezhda Davydova, and Natalya Baranskaya are but a few of those who have sought to draw public attention to the plight of the average Soviet woman at home and in the professional sphere. In 1975 a Soviet sociologist pointed out that in major urban centers of the Soviet Union there are up to five hundred divorces for every one thousand marriages. Cramped living conditions, hooliganism, a rising crime rate, rampant alcoholism, and an inefficient bureaucratic system all contribute to the decay of the family. A patriarchal male attitude on the one hand and exaggerated expectations on the woman's part create additional problems. Behind the concern for the family stands a fundamental realization that, at least in the Soviet context, is new: it is not the party or the state that is the center of attention for the individual, but rather the "thou"—the person with whom one has chosen to share one's life. So says Vladimir Tendryakov (1923–84), another major representative of urban prose, who wrote mostly novellas and short novels, in his long story "Zatmenie" ("Eclipse"): "HE and SHE—the most important link, the solidity of which guarantees that we will not die, . . . with it, all our relationships begin." And Trifonov points to the problem behind it when he says in his novella *Drugaia zhizn'* (*The Other Life*): "But why do we, poor fellows, try so hard to understand others when we cannot understand ourselves? Let us understand ourselves, my God, as a beginning!"

Natalya Baranskaya (1908–) published her first story, "Nedelia kak nedelia" ("Just Another Week"), in 1969. It depicts the plight of a working wife in the Soviet Union. A husband, two children, a household, and a job exert almost unbearable pressures upon her. Olga, the heroine, works in a chemical laboratory, but can hardly manage because of her other responsibilities. At home she is nervous and exhausted. The household makes demands she can hardly cope with, and her husband refuses to help at home. Baranskaya presents her material in the form of a diary, making it clear that there is no way out for Olga, that her life will continue this way "week after week."

Since her first publication Baranskaya has published a book of short stories, *Zhenshchina s zontikom* (*Woman with an Umbrella,* 1981), that mostly develops the female theme. The title story tells of a lonely woman of sixty, Sofya Koretskaya, a teacher of biology, who once was married and spent the two happiest years of her life with her husband on the lake where she is now vacationing (the author hints that her husband disappeared during Stalin's purges of the 1930s). The theme of the lonely, aging woman recurs in "Potselui" ("The Kiss"). Nadezhda Mikhaylova, a philologist employed at the Academy of Sciences, is an "ordinary woman past forty," already a grandmother. Leaving a late-night party, she takes an elevator with Viktor, a young man she hardly knows, who embraces her with a kiss that lasts all eleven floors down. The next day Viktor begs to see her. Nadezhda goes shopping, sets the table, takes a bath, and dresses. Then she looks at herself in the mirror, collects the food she has just purchased, and goes off to visit her daughter and grandchild. With a minimum of words Baranskaya succeeds in transmitting the woes and cares of a whole generation of lonely women who lost their husbands to war, forced labor camps, or separation and divorce. This is their last attempt to capture something of that happiness they either never experienced or lost all too soon.

Irina Velembovskaya (1922–) completed the Gorky Institute of Literature in 1964 and started publishing in the early 1960s. Her first stories center around typically female problems: her "Sladkaia zhenshchina" ("Sweet Woman," 1973) created a stir and was made into a film. The young and attractive Anya Dobrokhotova, the "sweet woman" of the title, works in a candy factory and its smell exudes from her clothing. Yet there is more to her sweetness: she is one of those women who attract men almost automatically. After several affairs and the birth of a son, she finds a husband, Nikolay Egorovich, who agrees to adopt her son. The marriage lasts for fifteen years, though not without problems, as Anya continues to have more love affairs. Eventually, Nikolay leaves her for another woman, and Anya finds comfort in an affair with a divorced man.

The "ladies' tale" became stereotyped in the 1970s. A young and talented woman, dissatisfied with family life, overcomes all obstacles to realize her academic or artistic aspirations. Nevertheless the pressures brought to bear by husband and/or mother-in-law lead her to sacrifice her worldly ambitions for her family's sake. In the end the best work of art for her is the carpet, the best book the cookbook, the best music the clanking of pots and pans in the kitchen sink, as in Tatyana Gorbulina's story "Krug" ("The Circle").

"He and she" plots are another standard version of the trend in the literature of the 1970s and early 1980s. A frequent plot is the following: he is a geologist (journalist, engineer, brigadier) who in the course of a professional excursion meets her, usually a plain country girl or a frustrated village teacher. Their love lasts for the duration of his trip, and ends with his return home. A variation on this plot is the "love on the job" story. He and she work in the same place. She has loved him for a long time, but he is too involved with his work to notice. He is married. She suffers. The basic plot then develops in various ways. He may eventually return to his wife, leaving her with an illegal offspring, or else he may leave his wife and children for her.

Science Prose

Science prose has little to do with actual scientific research, but analyzes the intellectual and emotional conflicts among people in academe, a strictly hierarchically ordered universe lending itself easily to intrigues and personality conflicts, even though intellectually somewhat freer than society at large.

One of the best representatives of writers in this genre is Daniil Granin (1919–), himself an engineer employed in industry and research institutes. Granin is interested in the ethical and scientific problems arising out of academic research. In "Kto-to dolzhen" ("Somebody Has To," 1970) he investigates the opposition of easy success and risky innovation, a topic with a long tradition in Soviet literature. The thaw began with Vladimir Dudintsev's short novel *Ne khlebom edinym* (*Not By Bread Alone,* 1956), dealing with the conflict between the ethical responsibility of a brilliant scientist and *apparatchiks* who guard the bureaucratic structures and have no use for a man of talent. "Variant vtoroi" ("The B-Variant," 1949), one of Granin's earliest stories, describes the difficulties of research assistants in getting their dissertations approved. A young scientist, Aleksandr, has developed a new type of electric rectifier. After completing his research, he discovers that another assistant, who had died during the war, had developed another variant of the same model with much more advanced features—the B-Variant. When by chance Aleksandr obtains the dead man's research papers, he solves the ethical problem that arises by reporting his dead colleague's invention at the defense of his own dissertation.

Granin's story "Sobstvennoe mnenie" ("One's Own Opinion," 1956) again poses questions like those raised in Dudintsev's famous novel, as it questions the entire hierarchical structure of Soviet academic life. The secretary to the prospective director of a research institute formulates the essential problem as follows: "I write as you want it so that I may later write the way I see fit." Minaev, the prospective director, declines to publish an article by a talented young colleague in which he attacks a famous scientist and member of the Academy of Sciences. Minaev fears that he might not be confirmed in his position if he publishes the article. He wants to help, but would like to postpone publication as long as possible until he is firmly entrenched in his new position as director. The story ends without any resolution to the conflict.

Another popular author is Irina Grekova (pseudonym of Elena Ventsel, 1907–), herself a noted mathematician and university professor, who began writing quite late in life. In her work she combines features of young prose and urban prose with those of the feminine theme and science prose. The critics attacked her in 1966, when her collection *Pod fonarem* (*Under the Streetlamp*) appeared. In 1980 she published another collection, *Kafedra* (*The Academic Chair*), containing three novellas. The title story provides impressive proof of her status as a major representative of science prose.

Village Prose

Village prose is a complex phenomenon. In the 1950s it concentrated on the official aspects of life in the villages, the collective farm organization, and administration; later it shifted focus more and more to the private daily lives of individual peasants and the conflict between urban and rural life. Two subtrends may be distinguished within village prose: a distinctly Russophile trend best represented by the stories of Vasily Belov, who draws loving pictures of a fast disappearing world founded on ancient traditions, and a tendency toward a more distant, at times critical, view of today's village. The latter emerges in romantically colored prose recalling Paustovsky and Prishvin, as in many stories by Fedor Abramov and in psychological and sociological analyses of various types of peasants, especially those undergoing urbanization (the stories of Rasputin and the starkly realistic prose of Vasily Shukshin). Another noteworthy trend is prose promoting ecological concerns, as, for instance, the works of Vladimir Soloukhin and, more recently, Rasputin, both of whom have publicly fought for the preservation of nature.

Solzhenitsyn contributed to the early history of village prose with his moving story "Matrenin dvor" ("Matrena's Homestead," 1963). His depiction of a misunderstood, rejected peasant woman who had "worked for others for no reward, . . . had buried all her six children, had stored up no earthly goods" has since become almost paradigmatic for the genre. Matrena is Mother Russia and simultaneously the soul of the earth of pagan mythology: "None of us who lived close to her perceived that she was the one righteous person without whom, as the saying goes, no village can last. Nor any city. Nor the world itself." A former inmate of Stalin's forced labor camps returns from Siberia to central Russia in the summer of 1953, wishing "to lose himself in the innermost heart of Russia." And it is indeed in old Matrena's hut that he experiences a kind of moral regeneration. Vladimir Soloukhin expressed the essence of Solzhenitsyn's concerns in an interview of 1984 in which he commented that "the Russian village was never only an economic or sociological phenomenon; it has always been a spiritual phenomenon." And yet the traditional village is endangered. In 1976 Fedor Abramov complained that the old village with its thousand-year history today ceases to exist. This means that fundamental pillars are destroyed, that the age-old soil disappears on which our entire national culture has thrived—its ethics and aesthetics, its folklore and literature, its wonderful speech. . . . there, in the village, is our origin, are our roots.

Sergey Zalygin, whose formative years coincided with Stalin's rise to power and the collectivization of rural Russia, became first an engineer and then a university professor in Omsk and later Novosibirsk. Zalygin is considered one of the early representatives of village prose in post-Stalinist times. He is interested in the administrative aspects of life as they affect the individual and determine his ethics and morals. In "Funktsiia" ("The Function") he sets the daily cares and problems of a collective farm chairman against bureaucratic routine. The milkmaid Kosya puts the question to the chairman directly: "Well then, try to feed the cows with your arguments! And I will see how many liters of milk you get, and what percentage of fat!"

Vasily Shukshin (1929–74), an actor, director, and writer, was one of the most prolific and significant representatives of the genre. His stories contain a veritable gallery of unusual types who often combine features of urban and village psychology. Shukshin is particularly interested in the specific problems of that intermediate environment that can no longer be classified as rural but has not yet become entirely urban either. In 1967 he wrote of himself that basically he was not an urban man and yet no longer a villager: he had "one leg on shore, the other in the boat." Shukshin grew up in the country but left his Siberian village to work in factories and on building sites in various central Russian localities. After navy service he became a teacher at a school for adults in a village. In the 1950s he studied film in Moscow and graduated from the film academy in 1960. His first book of stories appeared in 1963 under the programmatic title *Sel'skie zhiteli* (*The Villagers*).

In "Mikroskop" ("The Microscope," 1969) Shukshin tells of the simple carpenter Andrey Erin, who spends 120 rubles on a microscope in order to investigate "microbes." For one week Andrey "studies" microbes and develops his own theory of their effect on human life expectancy. The microscope lends him more elevated status, and for a time he realizes an inner need, his cherished dream. When his wife discovers that he has wasted money on a microscope, she sells it. Andrey goes out and gets drunk.

The conflict between the peasant and the urban mentality is illustrated in the story "Srezal" ("Fooled," 1970). Gleb Kapustin, who has made it his specialty to test educated people from town and puncture their pretensions, has a discussion with the son of a peasant woman who has become a scientist. Kapustin's arguments are false or muddled, but he presents them with such self-assurance that it is difficult to counter them. In the villagers' eyes Kapustin emerges victorious from the debate because he has fooled his opponent. Shukshin has defined a potentially dangerous phenomenon: the impact of too much information provided by modern mass media on minds unequipped to cope with it.

Many of Shukshin's stories exhibit a touch of the comic without losing their underlying seriousness. This is particularly true of "Veruiu!" ("I Believe!" 1971), whose hero, the villager Maksim Yarikov, suffers from "ennui"; his "soul hurts." He questions the meaning of life and his own existence. One day he hears that a village priest has arrived on a visit and decides to ask him whether the "souls of believers also hurt." The priest admits they do and explains *his* understanding of good and evil, of God and Christ, in a strange mixture of Marxist dialectics and Christian doctrine. God is equated with life. God is both good and evil. There is no world beyond, no hell or paradise; everything is of this world, and "how all this will end, I don't know." The conversation eventually becomes a wild singing and dancing party as both get drunk and shout:

> I be-lie-ve! . . . in aviation, in chemicalization, in the mechanization of agriculture, in the scientific re-vo-lution! In space and weightlessness! Because it's all ob-jective! Together! After me! . . . I believe that soon everyone will gather in huge stinking cities! I believe that they will suffocate there and rush back to the open fields.

The priest's final advice to Maksim is: "live, my son, cry and dance, and dance to your tears."

In 1956 Fedor Abramov (1920–) wrote a critical article on "The People of the Collective Farm Village in Postwar Prose," in which he came out against the idealization of village life under Stalin. Abramov came from a peasant family, studied at Leningrad University, served in the army in World War II, and eventually joined the Communist party in 1945. Between 1956 and 1960 he was professor of Russian literature in Leningrad. In 1982 a three-volume collection of his works appeared.

In one of his early stories, "V Piter za sarafanom" ("Going to St. Petersburg for a Sarafan," 1961), Abramov's heroine, an old peasant woman, tells of her journey on foot to the capital city to purchase a beautiful "sarafan," or sleeveless peasant dress, with which she hopes to find a husband. The simple story is told in the peasant idiom of northern Russia and illustrates the naive, unspoiled, natural, yet forceful character of rural people. In "Posledniaia okhota" ("The Last Hunt," 1962) an old huntsman fights a duel with a wolf. Despite the loss of three fingers and a leg crippled by frost, he continues the hunt, which turns out to be his last. Abramov depicts the *byt* of the northern village which is still largely intact, although changes are imminent, as old Solomida indicates in "Iz kolena Avvakuma" ("From the Tribe of Avvakum," 1970): "It's three years since they closed the store here, and soon, people say, they'll close the village, too. It's a new way of doing things—they bury the living earth." Old Solomida is an Old Believer, regarded as a witch by the local people. Actually she is a deeply religious person with the gift of healing. It is moving to read the story of this Soviet peasant who, in her own words, "passed through life with the word of the Lord on her lips." This story exhibits one of the major attractions of village prose for writers and readers alike: withdrawn from public life and ideology into the distant nooks of rural Russia, it allows both more freedom than they might otherwise enjoy.

Vasily Belov (1932–) is particularly interested in rural Russia's folklore traditions, its peasant architecture, various feasts and superstitions, its ancient crafts and legends, and the earthy wisdom and racy speech of the peasant. Time and again Belov refers back to the crucial events in the history of the Russian peasantry: the collectivization campaign, the years of warfare, the creeping urbanization of the countryside, the mechanization of agriculture.

Belov began to publish in 1961 and was widely acclaimed for his story "Privychnoe delo" ("That's How Things Are Done," 1966) which describes a villager who seeks work in town but decides to return, only to discover that his grieving wife has just died of a heart attack. In 1968 followed *Plotnitskie rasskazy* (*The Carpenter Tales*), a cycle narrated from the point of view of a city man returning to the village in search of his roots. In 1969 Belov published *Bukhtiny vologodskie* (*Vologda Whimsies;* the Russian word *bukhtiny* denotes a mixture of legend, joke, and nonsense), a series of fantastic tales told by Kuzma, a professional fairy-tale narrator with features of a pagan shaman. It includes a grotesque account of a visit to the netherworld, where Kuzma learns that "in an amalgamation of departments, heaven and hell have been united into one amoral world." Belov's lyrical descriptions of nature and his accounts of random meetings with local people—such as truck drivers ("Gogolev," 1974) or a ninety-four-year-old peasant who tells of witches in "Utrom v subbotu" ("A Morning on Saturday," 1975)—recall the mood of Turgenev's *Hunting Sketches.* With skill and sympathy he converts the sights, smells, and objects of the village into earthy language.

Valentin Rasputin (1937–) comes from a village on the Angara River near Irkutsk, where he still lives. Before 1966 he traveled all over Siberia as a journalist, but then his long story "Den'gi dlia Marii" ("Money for Maria," 1967) made him famous throughout the country. Maria, the wife of a collective farmer, is in charge of the village's only store. When an inspector checks her books, he finds that she is a thousand rubles short. Maria must refund the money within a week. Most of the story is told in retrospect. Her husband, Kuzma, is on the way to town after trying unsuccessfully to raise the money in the village. In Kuzma's recollections and dreams—some reaching back to World War II and even further—events are perceived entirely from the narrator's point of view, partly in free associations, in a very modernistic manner. Rasputin draws a rather sinister picture of a village where neighborly concern is minimal.

Rasputin's short story "Ne mogu-u" ("I Ca-an't," 1982) can leave a shattering impression on a reader. Two travelers on a train come across a poorly dressed fellow in a state close to delirium tremens who cries out in pain and constantly repeats "I ca-an't." His fellow passengers condemn him, suggesting he be thrown off the train, or demand "the authorities," or say he should be given another glass of wine to lessen his pain. Eventually he is given more wine. After gulping down half a bottle, the fellow tells of his wife and son, both, as he says, alcoholics. After a brief bright spell, he reverts to his previous state. He claims to be from Moscow, but does not know where he is going. The alcoholic in a train traveling to nowhere and crying out with pain all along emerges from the expanses of the Russian countryside, a lost son of his silent mother: "There, behind the window, behind the playful net of endless wires, spread Mother Russia."

The story "Vasily and Vasilisa" (1967) recalls Gogol's "Old World Landowners" in its good-humored opening. Rasputin describes an old couple and their grown-up children and grandchildren somewhere in a Siberian village. Both are true Russian peasants, still firmly rooted in the soil and village traditions. Vasily lives in a shed, Vasilisa in the main hut. Step by step the reader is introduced to the complex emotional background that hangs over the family's otherwise idyllic life and lends it more than a touch of tragedy. Vasily had once, under the influence of alcohol, threatened his wife with an axe, and Vasilisa never forgave him. As the story ends, Vasily is on his deathbed. Only then does Vasilisa enter his shed for the first time, and with a few short words the two take leave of each other. With no words or gestures beyond holding hands, they are finally reconciled. The story concludes: "He smiles, he lies there and smiles. The day is quiet, just as before a rain. On such a day it's good to drink homemade beer—not very cold and not very warm—and look out the window to see what is going on in the streets." Life returns to normal, death loses its sting, when harmony between people close to each other has been restored.

In "Vniz po techeniiu" ("Down the Stream," 1972) the village where Victor, the hero, spent his childhood has disappeared under the water dammed up to be used for a new hydroelectric plant. His parents' new home depresses him as he recalls his early years in the village. Victor realizes that the former way of life was based on spiritual values that have subsequently vanished.

Vladimir Soloukhin (1924–), who comes from a village in the north of Russia, obtained a technical education, participated actively in World War II, and finally attended the Gorky Institute of Literature in Moscow, writing poetry and working as a journalist. His lyrical prose appeared in *Vladimirskie proselki* (*Paths in Vladimir,* 1957) and *Kaplia rosy* (*A Drop of Dew,* 1960), both of which brought him fame. Soloukhin's interest in the art of the icon is linked to a positive attitude toward the Christian tradition.

The authors of village prose like to describe eccentrics (*chudaki*), individualists unadapted to society. Such people have preserved the traditional values of peasant life more than others. However, the chudak may also have retained precisely those character traits that contradict communist ethics. A good example of this may be found in Soloukhin's "Pasha" (1978), where the author describes his unusual vacations in a country house in his native village of Olepino. Old "Pasha," now in her seventies, is a chudak who dreams of having her own hut in the village. When asked why she did not work on the collective farm (she worked in a Moscow factory), she replies: "I say: assign me a number [of rubles, i.e., a salary]. But they cannot do this. . . . I'm a worker, I'm supposed to get a number. What am I to do with workdays?" (On collective farms, wages were calculated at the end of the year on the basis of actual workdays, so that no peasant knew in advance how many rubles he might earn in a given year.) The narrator suggests she enter a home for the aged, where she could live in material comfort, though at the cost of her meager pension. Pasha reacts violently. She won't give up her pension, and she has an intense dislike for the rules of such a home: "There everything would be according to a schedule. Breakfast on schedule. Lunch on schedule. Dimitry Kuzmich [chairman of the collective farm] already told me once: join us, Pasha, in the collective farm." There could not be a more obvious parallel between the inhabitants of the home for the aged, deprived of their individuality and pension money, and the peasants organized in a collective farm. Still, the criticism is veiled and indirect, for the story's protagonist is a whimsical old woman whose views may be considered atypical in the context of Soviet life.

Soloukhin's ecological concern comes through in the essaylike story "Med na khlebe" ("Honey and Bread," 1978), which could be classified almost as a poetic treatise on bees, honey, and their healing powers, as well as on the need to keep honey pure. Soloukhin views the earth as an ecological system in which every component is linked to every other. The story closes with a lament that today's honey and bread are not the same as in the days of the author's grandfather.

Urban prose, like village prose and its subgenres, seems to have reached an epigonic stage. The 1980s may lead to stagnation, or else another wave of liberalization may energize the immense creative potential that undoubtedly exists in Soviet literature. But the signs of the time do not point in that direction. The literary flowering of the 1960s and 1970s now seems a matter of the past.

Rudolf Neuhäuser

Notes and References

Introduction: Pushkin and the Russian Short Story

1. Peter Brang, *Studien zu Theorie und Praxis der russischen Erzählung 1770–1811* (Studies in the theory and practice of the Russian short story 1770–1811) (Wiesbaden: Otto Harrassowitz, 1960), 262.

2. Ibid., 24–27.

3. Ibid., 49–52.

4. Karl D. Kramer, *The Chameleon and the Dream: The Image of Reality in Čexov's Stories* (The Hague and Paris: Mouton, 1970), 16–17.

5. Ibid., 14–15.

6. *Moskovskii telegraf* (Moscow telegraph), no. 22 (November 1831), 255–56. It is noteworthy that even at this early date American authors set the international standard for the short-story genre.

7. Vissarion Belinskii, "O russkoi povesti i povestiakh g. Gogolia" (On the Russian tale and the tales of Gogol), in *Estetika i literaturnaia kritika v dvukh tomakh* (Aesthetics and literary criticism in two volumes) (Moscow: Gosudarstvennoe izdatel'stvo khudozhestvennoi literatury [State Publishing House of Artistic Literature], 1959), 1:118–65.

8. Boris Eikhenbaum, "O. Genri i teoriia novelly" (O. Henry and the theory of the short story), in *Literatura: Teoriia, kritika, polemika* (Literature: Theory, criticism, polemics) (Leningrad: Priboi [Breakers], 1927), 171.

9. M. A. Petrovskii, "Morfologiia novelly" (Morphology of the short story), in *Ars poetica* (Moscow: Gosudarstvennaia akademiia khudozhestvennykh nauk. Literaturnaia sektsiia—Trudy [State Art Academy, Literary Section—Works], 1927), 1:70.

10. A. P. Chekhov, Letter of 10 May 1886, in *Sobranie sochinenii* (Collected works), 12 vols. (Moscow: Gosudarstvennoe izdatel'stvo khudozhestvennoi literatury, 1960–63), 11:92.

11. Letter of 1 April 1890, in ibid., 11:411–12.

12. A. Ninov, *Sovremennyi rasskaz: Iz nabliudenii nad russkoi prozoi (1956–1966)* (The contemporary short story: Observations on Russian prose [1956–1966]) (Leningrad: Khudozhestvennaia literatura, 1969), 44.

13. Maksim Gor'kii, *Sobranie sochinenii* (Collected works), 30 vols. (Mos-

cow: Gosudarstvennoe izdatel'stvo khudozhestvennoi literatury, 1949–56), 27:220.

14. Eikhenbaum, "O. Genri," p. 171.

15. A. N. Tolstoi, "Chto takoe malen'kii rasskaz" (What is the short story?), in *Sobranie sochinenii* (Collected works), 10 vols. (Moscow: Gosudarstvennoe izdatel'stvo khudozhestvennoi literatury, 1958–61), 10:416. The article was first published in 1955, but the date of its writing is uncertain.

16. Ibid., 417.

17. Introduction to *Russkie lguny* (Russian liars) in A. F. Pisemskii, *Sobranie sochinenii* (Collected works), 9 vols. (Moscow: Pravda [Truth], 1959), 7:339.

18. Deming Brown, "The Očerk: Suggestions toward a Redefinition," in *American Contributions to the Sixth International Congress of Slavists: Prague, 1968,* vol. 2, *Literary Contributions,* ed. William E. Harkins (The Hague and Paris: Mouton, 1968), 29–41.

19. Ninov, *Sovremennyi rasskaz,* 29, 37.

20. Remarks by Zoshchenko, in *Kak my pishem* (How we write) (Leningrad: Izdatel'stvo pisatelei v Leningrade [Publishing House of Leningrad Writers], 1930), 56.

21. Ninov, *Sovremennyi rasskaz,* 47.

22. Lev Tolstoi, *Sobranie sochinenii* (Collected works), 20 vols. (Moscow: Khudozhestvennaia literatura, 1960–65), 20:174.

23. Zoshchenko in *Kak my pishem,* 58.

24. Konstantin Paustovsky, "Reminiscences of Babel," in *Dissonant Voices in Soviet Literature,* ed. Patricia Blake and Max Hayward (New York: Pantheon, 1962), 47.

25. Shalamov's stories cannot be published inside the Soviet Union, but John Glad has translated a powerful selection of them in Varlam Shalamov, *Kolyma Tales* (New York and London: W. W. Norton, 1980).

26. John Bayley, *Pushkin: A Comparative Commentary* (Cambridge: Cambridge University Press, 1971), 318.

The Russian Short Story 1830–1850

1. V. V. Vinogradov, "Romanticheskii naturalizm (Zhiul' Zhanen i Gogol')" (Romantic naturalism [Jules Janin and Gogol]), in *Evoliutsiia russkogo naturalizma: Gogol' i Dostoevskii* (The evolution of Russian naturalism: Gogol and Dostoevsky) (Leningrad: Academia, 1929), 153–205.

2. Other examples of Russian physiological sketches: "Vodovoz" ("The Water Hauler") by Aleksandr Bashutsky (1841); "Znakhar'" ("The Faith Healer") and "Armeiskii ofitser" ("An Army Officer") by Grigory Kvitka (1842); "Barynia" ("A Lady") by Ivan Panaev (1841). For more information

on the Russian physiological sketch and its Western sources, see A. G. Tseitlin, *Stanovlenie realizma v russkoi literature* (*Russkii fiziologicheskii ocherk*) (The formation of realism in Russian literature [The Russian physiological sketch]) (Moscow: Nauka [Science] 1965).

3. As per A. G. Tseitlin, *Povesti o bednom chinovnike* (*K istorii odnogo siuzheta*) (Tales of the impoverished civil servant [The history of a theme]) (Moscow, 1923).

4. *Skaz* is a Russian literary term meaning a narrative conducted not in the author's own voice but in a voice marked as belonging to a person who is socially, educationally, or otherwise distinct from the author.

5. B. M. Eikhenbaum, *Stat'i o Lermontove* (Articles on Lermontov) (Moscow: AN SSSR [USSR Academy of Sciences], 1961), 200.

6. Paul Debreczeny, *The Other Pushkin: A Study of Alexander Pushkin's Prose Fiction* (Stanford: Stanford University Press, 1983), 232–38.

7. Walter Schamschula, *Der russische historische Roman vom Klassizismus bis zur Romantik* (The Russian historical novel from classicism to romanticism) (Meisenheim am Glain: Anton Hain, 1961), 84.

8. An attempt at a revival was made by Valerian Pereverzev in the 1930s. Recently, Iurii Akutin has republished some of Veltman's works with introductory essays and commentaries. See Aleksandr Vel'tman, *Povesti i rasskazy* (Tales and stories) (Moscow: Sovetskaiia Rossiia [Soviet Russia], 1979). With an introduction by Iurii Akutin.

9. See Vinogradov, "Naturalisticheskii grotesk (siuzhet i kompozitsiia povesti Gogolia 'Nos')" (Naturalistic grotesque [Plot and composition in Gogol's "Nose"]), in *Evoliutsiia russkogo naturalizma,* 18–40.

10. F. C. Driessen, *Gogol as a Short Story Writer: A Study of His Technique of Composition* (The Hague: Mouton, 1965), 194.

11. After Boccaccio's story "The Falcon" in *The Decameron,* used generically by Paul Heyse and other nineteenth-century theorists of the short story.

12. *Raznochinets,* plur. *raznochintsy,* literally "a person from other [than the noble] class," hence "a commoner." Raznochintsy came from the low clergy, the urban working and merchant class, or from manumitted peasant families.

13. See Rudolf Neuhäuser, *Das Frühwerk Dostoevskijs: Literarische Tradition und gesellschaftlicher Anspruch* (Dostoevsky's early work: Literary tradition and social demand) (Heidelberg: Carl Winter, 1979), 176–89.

14. See Gary Rosenshield, "Point of View and the Imagination in Dostoevskij's 'White Nights,'" *Slavic and East European Journal* 21 (1977):191–203.

15. For a catalogue of women writers prior to the 1830s and a general discussion of Russian women writers, see V. G. Belinskii, "Sochineniia Zeneidy R-voi" (The works of Zeneida R.), in *Polnoe sobranie sochinenii* (Complete works), 13 vols. (Moscow: AN SSSR, 1953–59), 6:648–57.

The Russian Short Story 1880–1917

1. For a discussion of this process, see Franco Venturi, *Roots of Revolution* (New York: Grosset & Dunlap, 1966), chaps. 18 and 20.

2. Anton Chekhov, *The Letters of Anton Chekhov,* trans. Michael Heim (New York: Harper & Row, 1973), 243.

3. For a discussion of Leskov's work and the *Prolog,* see Stephen S. Lottridge, "Nikolaj Leskov and the Russian *Prolog* as a Literary Source," *Russian Literature* 3 (1972):16–39.

4. Chekhov, *Letters,* 109.

5. This appears in a letter from Chekhov to M. V. Kiseleva of 14 January 1887. See A. P. Chekhov, *Pis'ma* (Letters) (Moscow: Nauka {Science}, 1975), 2:11.

6. Robert Louis Jackson provides a sampling of critical opinions in this vein in his introduction to *Chekhov: A Collection of Critical Essays,* ed. R. L. Jackson (Englewood Cliffs, N.J.: Prentice-Hall, 1967), 8.

7. *A Shestov Anthology,* ed. Bernard Martin (Athens: Ohio University Press, 1970), 94.

8. Chekhov, *Pism'a,* 2:12. For a discussion of the impact of Chekhov's medical training on his approach to literature, see Simon Karlinsky's excellent introduction to Chekhov, *Letters,* 27, and Leonid Grossman's essay, "The Naturalism of Chekhov," in Jackson, ed., *Chekhov: A Collection of Critical Essays,* 32–48.

9. This and the subsequent quotations in this paragraph are from a letter to Suvorin of 1 April 1890. See Chekhov, *Pis'ma,* 3:54.

10. Many critics have written about Chekhov's impressionistic style. See, for example, Peter M. Bitsilli's detailed discussion in *Chekhov's Art: A Stylistic Analysis,* trans. Toby W. Clyman and Edwina Jannie Cruise (Ann Arbor: Ardis, 1983), and the essays of Charanne Carroll Clarke, Savely Senderovich, and Thomas Winner in *Chekhov's Art of Writing: A Collection of Critical Essays,* ed. Paul Debreczeny and Thomas Eekman (Columbus, Ohio: Slavica, 1977).

11. This process is described in detail in the seminal study by Aleksandr Chudakov, *Chekhov's Poetics,* trans. Edwina Jannie Cruise and Donald Dragt (Ann Arbor: Ardis, 1983).

12. See A. P. Chekhov, *Sochineniia* (Works) (Moscow: Nauka, 1977), 8:458.

13. See, for example, Donald Rayfield, *Chekhov: The Evolution of His Art* (New York: Barnes & Noble, 1975), 145.

14. This term was used by Thomas Winner, "Some Thoughts about the Style of Bunin's Early Prose," in *American Contributions to the Sixth International Congress of Slavists,* vol. 2, *Literary Contributions* (The Hague: Mouton, 1968), 370.

15. For a brief discussion of this topic, see Julian W. Connolly, "Desire and Renunciation: Buddhist Elements in the Prose of Ivan Bunin," *Canadian Slavonic Papers* 23, no. 1 (1981):11–20.

16. This evolution is discussed by Carola Hansson, *Fedor Sologub as a Short-Story Writer* (Stockholm: Almqvist & Wiksell International, 1975), 8–16.

17. For a detailed discussion of the significance of children in Sologub's fiction, see Stanley Rabinowitz, *Sologub's Literary Children: Keys to a Symbolist's Prose* (Columbus, Ohio: Slavica, 1980).

18. See, for example, Yevgeny Zamyatin, "Fyodor Sologub," in *A Soviet Heretic: Essays by Yevgeny Zamyatin,* ed. and trans. Mirra Ginsburg (Chicago: University of Chicago Press, 1970).

19. A detailed analysis of Gippius's worldview is given by Temira Pachmuss, *Zinaida Hippius: An Intellectual Profile* (Carbondale: Southern Illinois University Press, 1971).

20. Ronald E. Peterson discusses these works and their autobiographical elements in *Andrei Bely's Short Prose,* Birmingham Slavonic Monographs, no. 11 (Birmingham: University of Birmingham Press, 1980).

Bibliography

This bibliography is intended to be a helpful supplement to the study of the history of the Russian short story, a guide for the reader who wishes to delve more deeply into one of its facets. I have placed primary emphasis upon English-language publications (and within them upon books and articles published in the United States), but I have also included a number of Russian writings and some items in French and German that are clearly relevant to a topic. Because of the amount of literature on the Russian short story, I have had to be selective in choosing items.

The first and smaller of the two major subdivisions of this bibliography corresponds chronologically to the chapters of the book. These are, in turn, arranged under several rubrics:

1. Anthologies of short stories in English. This listing, which is fairly complete for American publications, contains many anthologies published in Great Britain and a few that have appeared in the Soviet Union. In the annotations I provide some notion of the compiler's objectives in designing each collection.

2. Anthologies of short stories in Russian, for those who wish to read the originals. I have excluded all short-story collections wherever published, however, that are intended wholly or primarily as aids to the teaching of the Russian language.

3. General studies discussing the development of the Russian short story in general or over particular periods. Most of these are Russian studies published in the Soviet Union, but some have appeared in Western languages.

It should be noted that the chronological periods covered by the anthologies in particular usually do not coincide with the periods chosen for the chapters of this book. Thus, for example, many of the anthologies listed under the period 1830–1850 include writers active in 1850–1880 and/or 1880–1917. At the end of this section, I have listed two bibliographies of help for the study of the Russian short story.

I am indebted to Elizabeth O. White for her assistance in compiling this subdivision of the bibliography.

The second subdivision, focusing on individual writers important for the history of the Russian short story, is arranged in alphabetical rather than chronological order. Though most writers listed here did not confine themselves to the short-story genre alone, the bibliography concentrates upon this aspect of their writing.

Under each author I have listed in nearly all instances a convenient and relatively accessible edition of his collected works in which his short stories are to be found (Russian writers always have had their works published in collected editions much more frequently than have American authors). This is followed by a reference to an English edition of the collected works, where it exists, and then to selected or complete editions of the writer's short stories.

Individual volumes of short stories are usually less important in Russian literature than in American writing, but cycles of short stories, and once in a while even an individual short story, can be prominent. Thus the entry under an author *may* include information on the publication dates of major collections, cycles, and individual stories, followed by English translations and then critical studies of these works.

Finally, I have included under nearly every author a listing of critical and biographical literature on the writer himself. These include major general studies, which will ordinarily deal with his short stories among other things, and studies of his short stories in particular or of the author as a short-story writer. This portion of the bibliography is highly selective in many instances.

In all cases in which a Soviet edition is listed as published in Moscow without indication of the publisher, then the publisher is Goslitizdat, the State Publishing House for Artistic Literature, under the various names it has borne over the years.

Charles A. Moser

I

General Anthologies in English Translation

Graham, Stephen, ed. *Great Russian Short Stories.* 1929. Reprint. New York: Liveright, 1975. A curious selection from a large number of authors from Zhukovsky to Kataev, including some unexpected and minor writers. A strange preface.

Richards, David, ed. *The Penguin Book of Russian Short Stories.* Middlesex: Penguin Books, 1981. One story each by twenty authors from Pushkin to Solzhenitsyn. Well selected, with translations by various specialists.

Russian Short Stories. London: Faber & Faber, 1943. Generally prominent stories by writers from Pushkin through Leonov. Produced under wartime conditions, it misspells certain writers' names (for example, 'Mikhail Pzishvin').

A Treasury of Russian and Soviet Short Stories. Greenwich, Conn.: Fawcett, 1971. Eighteen stories by authors from Pushkin to the contemporary Vasily Belov. Compiled with the assistance of the Soviet press agency.

The Russian Short Story 1830–1850

Anthologies in English

Daniels, Guy, ed. *Russian Comic Fiction.* New York: New American Library, 1970. Humorous tales by six nineteenth-century authors: Ivan Krylov, Gogol, Dostoevsky, Saltykov, Chekhov, and Tolstoy.

Houghton, Norris, ed. *Great Russian Short Stories.* New York: Dell, 1958. A standard selection of mostly nineteenth-century works from Pushkin to Andreev.

Kamen, Isai, ed. *Great Russian Stories.* 1917. Reprint. New York: Random House, 1959. Samplings of one, two, or three stories from each of ten major writers from Pushkin through Bunin. A standard selection.

Korovin, Valentin, ed. *Russian 19th-Century Gothic Tales.* Moscow: Raduga (Rainbow), 1984. An interesting selection of tales from the Gothic genre by Somov, Senkovsky, Odoevsky, Gogol, Pushkin, and others.

Lavrin, Janko, ed. *A First Series of Representative Russian Stories, Pushkin to Gorky.* 1946. Reprint. Westport, Conn.: Greenwood Press, 1975. One or two stories each by Pushkin, Lermontov, Gogol, Turgenev, Dostoevsky, Tolstoy, Garshin, Chekhov, and Gorky, with a sensible introduction.

———. *Russian Humorous Stories.* London: Sylvan Press, 1946. Comic stories from Pushkin's "Undertaker" through Leskov and Zoshchenko down to Ilf and Petrov.

Proffer, Carl, ed. *From Karamzin to Bunin.* Bloomington: Indiana University Press, 1969. The very best stories of some of Russia's finest writers from the early nineteenth to the early twentieth century. An intelligent selection.

———. ed. *Russian Romantic Prose.* Translated by David Lowe. Ann Arbor, Mich.: Translation Press, 1979. Classic stories of the romantic period by Pushkin, Odoevsky, Veltman, Bestuzhev-Marlinsky, Lermontov, Somov, Gogol, and Sollogub.

Schweikert, Harry, ed. *Russian Short Stories.* 1919. Reprint. Freeport, N.Y.: Books for Libraries Press, 1972. A somewhat old-fashioned collection, with works from Pushkin through Kuprin.

Seltzer, Thomas, ed. *Best Russian Short Stories.* New York: Modern Library, 1925. Twenty-two stories, generally well selected, by writers from Pushkin to Bunin.

Townsend, R. S., ed. *Short Stories by Russian Authors.* 1924. Reprint. New York: Dutton, 1960. Ten stories by writers from Pushkin to Gorky, in an uneven selection.

Yarmolinsky, Avrahm, ed. *A Treasury of Great Russian Stories, Pushkin to Gorky.* New York: Macmillan, 1944. A substantial volume with a relatively small representation of writers, but good selections. A large group of stories by Chekhov is included.

Anthologies in Russian

Kostelianets, B., and **P. Sidorov,** ed. *Russkie ocherki* (Russian sketches). 3 vols. Moscow, 1956. An extensive and well-chosen selection of the literary sketch from Radishchev to the early twentieth century, with a lengthy theoretical introduction on the genre overall.

Meilakh, Boris, ed. *Russkie povesti XIX veka 20–kh–30–kh godov* (Russian tales of the 1820s and 1830s). 2 vols. Moscow, 1950. A nicely chosen selection of stories (especially by Odoevsky) with a helpful introduction.

Scholarly Works

Meilakh, Boris, ed. *Russkaia povest' XIX veka: Istoriia i problematika zhanra* (The Russian tale of the nineteenth century: History and theory of the genre). Leningrad: Nauka, Leningradskoe otdelenie (Science, Leningrad Division), 1973. A major collective history of the genre of the povest', which largely overlaps with the short story in the century's first decades.

Mersereau, John, Jr. *Russian Romantic Fiction.* Ann Arbor, Mich.: Ardis, 1983. Not limited to the short story, but deals extensively with that genre because of its prominence during the romantic period.

O'Toole, L. Michael. *Structure, Style and Interpretation in the Russian Short Story.* New Haven and London: Yale University Press, 1982. A series of interpretive approaches in a "Neo-Formalist" mode (narrative structure, point of view, fable, character, and so on) applied to particular short stories of the nineteenth century.

Städtke, Klaus. *Zur Geschichte der russischen Erzählung (1825–1840)* (On the history of the Russian short story [1825–1840]). Berlin: Akademie-Verlag, 1975. The third chapter (pp. 29–128) delineates the chief subgenres of the short story of the 1820s and 1830s (historical tale, society tale, *Kunstlererzählung,* and so on), and the final two chapters deal with Pushkin and Gogol.

The Russian Short Story 1850–1880

Anthologies in English

Lavrin, Janko, ed. *A Second Series of Representative Russian Stories, Leskov to Andreyev.* London: Westhouse, 1946. A good selection from Leskov, Korolenko, Bunin, Remizov, Kuprin, and several other writers. Intended to present "works typical of Russian realism between the period of its triumph and the revolution of 1917."

Strahan, John W., ed. *Fifteen Great Russian Stories.* New York: Washington Square Press, 1965. Stories from Dostoevsky through Zoshchenko, with short introductions to each author.

Anthologies in Russian

Meilakh, Boris, ed. *Russkie povesti XIX veka 40–50–kh godov* (Russian tales of the 1840s and 1850s). 2 vols. Moscow, 1952. A collection of important short works of the period difficult to obtain in modern editions.

———. *Russkie povesti XIX veka 60–kh godov* (Russian tales of the 1860s). 2

vols. Moscow, 1956. Sometimes quite lengthy works by relatively obscure writers of the decade.

The Russian Short Story 1880–1917

Anthologies in English

Luker, Nicholas, ed. *An Anthology of Russian Neo-Realism: The "Znanie" School of Maxim Gorky.* Ann Arbor, Mich.: Ardis, 1982. Representative works, primarily short stories, by Andreev, Bunin, Kuprin, Mikhail Artsybashev, and Gorky, with biographical sketches of the authors.

Anthologies in Russian

Buchkin, S. V., ed. *Pisateli chekhovskoi pory: izbrannye proizvedeniia pisatelei 80–90–kh godov* (Writers of the Chekhov era: Selected works by writers of the 1880s and 1890s). 2 vols. Moscow, 1982. Representative works by now largely forgotten writers of the final two decades of the nineteenth century and the early years of the twentieth century.

Meilakh, Boris, ed. *Russkie povesti XIX veka 70–90–kh godov* (Russian tales of the 1870s–1890s). 2 vols. Moscow, 1957. Most of the authors included in this collection are no more than footnotes in the history of Russian literature.

Scholarly Works

Grechnev, Viacheslav. *Russkii rasskaz kontsa XIX–XX veka (problematika i poetika zhanra)* (The Russian short story of the late nineteenth and twentieth centuries [Problems and poetics of the genre]). Leningrad: Nauka, 1979. A scholarly study of the short story's development from 1880 to 1900, followed by chapters on Bunin, Andreev, and Gorky.

The Russian Short Story 1917–1980

Anthologies in English

Atarov, Nikolai, ed. *Anthology of Soviet Short Stories.* 2 vols. Moscow: Progress, 1976. A large number of prominent writers represented by one story each and translated by various hands. Only a few non-Russian Soviet authors are represented.

Azure Cities: Stories of New Russia. New York: International Publishers, 1929. A valuable collection by Soviet writers of the 1920s of considerable prominence, with an enthusiastic foreword by Joshua Kunitz.

Bearne, C. G., ed. *Modern Russian Short Stories.* 2 vols. London: MacGibbon & Kee, 1968–69. Volume 1 contains seven stories by postwar writers from Vasily Aksenov to Sergey Zalygin. Volume 2 has six works by prominent authors of the 1920s, including Babel, Platonov, and Zamyatin.

Cournos, John, ed. *Short Stories Out of Soviet Russia.* New York: Dutton, 1929. A good selection of works of the 1920s, including items by Babel, Aleksey Tolstoy, and Vsevolod Ivanov.

Dodson, Daniel Boone, ed. *Eight Great Russian Short Stories.* 1959. Reprint. Greenwich, Conn.: Fawcett, 1962. Eight stories of the nineteenth and twentieth centuries by writers purposely chosen because they are little known, forming the "vast and almost entirely neglected terrain behind the monuments of nineteenth century Russian literature." These include Aleksey Apukhtin, Aleksandr Ertel, and Evgeny Chirikov, in addition to Leskov and Pilnyak.

Dukas, Vitas, ed. *Twelve Contemporary Russian Stories.* Rutherford, Madison, and Teaneck, N.J.: Fairleigh Dickinson University Press, 1977. A selection of recent stories by contemporary writers.

Fen, Elisaveta, ed. *Soviet Stories of the Last Decade.* London: Methuen, 1945. Stories written from 1933 to 1943, several by authors no longer of much importance in the history of Soviet literature.

———. *Modern Russian Stories.* 3d ed. London: Methuen, 1943. Eight works of the 1920s mostly by authors still well known, including Babel, Leonov, Pilnyak, Fedin, Zoshchenko, and Aleksey Tolstoy.

Flying Osip: Stories of New Russia, ed. 1925. Reprint. Freeport, N.Y.: Books for Libraries Press, 1970. Stories from the first years of the Revolution and war. Some of the authors represented are no longer prominent in the history of Soviet literature.

Guerney, Bernard Guilbert, ed. *New Russian Stories.* New York: New Directions, 1953. Sixteen writers of the Soviet period—some famous, some obscure—represented by one story each.

Kapp, Yvonne, ed. *Short Stories of Russia Today.* Boston: Houghton Mifflin, 1959. One story each by some nineteen Soviet authors composed from the mid-1930s to the mid-1950s.

MacAndrew, Andrew, ed. *Four Soviet Masterpieces.* Toronto and New York: Bantam, 1965. "The Ore," by Georgi Vladimov; "I'd Be Honest If They'd Let Me," by Vladimir Voinovich; "Halfway to the Moon," by Vasily Aksenov; "The Kabiasy Imps," by Yuri Kazakov. Kazakov is now dead, the others in emigration.

Orga, Margarete, ed. *The House on the Fontanka: Modern Soviet Short Stories.* London: William Kimber, 1970. Limited to works published between 1966 and 1969 and not easily available. Includes two early works by Mikhail Bulgakov (died 1940) first published only in 1966.

Owen, U. N., ed. *Soviet Eight: Contemporary Russian Short Stories.* New York: Pageant, 1963. Eight stories by for the most part quite obscure contemporary authors.

Pomorska, Krystyna, ed. *Fifty Years of Russian Prose: From Pasternak to Solzhenitsyn.* 2 vols. Cambridge, Mass.: MIT Press, 1971. Volume 1: from Pasternak to Viktor Nekrasov, with the emphasis upon experimental prose. Volume 2: from Nagibin to Kazakov, with Solzhenitsyn well represented. An able group of translators.

Proffer, Carl, ed. *The Barsukov Triangle, The Two-Toned Blond, and Other Stories.* Ann Arbor, Mich.: Ardis, 1984. A group of Soviet Russian stories published from 1961 to 1984, by both prominent and less well-known authors.

Reavey, George, ed. *Fourteen Great Short Stories by Soviet Authors.* New York: Avon Books, 1959. Works by twelve writers of the Soviet period from Gorky to Pasternak, selected to show that "not all literature in the new Russia is written according to plan or formal prompting."

———. *Modern Soviet Short Stories.* New York: Grosset & Dunlap, 1961. Twenty-five stories by well-known authors written between the early 1920s and the late 1960s.

Reeve, Franklin, ed. *Great Soviet Short Stories.* New York: Dell, 1962. Representative short stories by a considerable number of Soviet Russian authors from 1917 to 1957, but with emphasis on the 1920s.

Rooker, John, ed. *Soviet Anthology.* London: Jonathan Cape, 1943. A number of fairly short works or excerpts mostly by reasonably prominent authors.

Soviet Short Stories, 1942–1943. London: Pilot Press, 1943. A series of small books done mostly for wartime purposes.

Wasser, Selig O., ed. *Treasury of Russian Short Stories.* New York: F. Fell, 1968. From Andreev's "Nippie" of 1900 to Anatoly Rubinov's "The House Guest" of 1966, but with concentration on literature of the 1950s and 1960s in which the "voice of protest . . . strikes with the force of a prayer."

Yarmolinsky, Avrahm, ed. *Soviet Short Stories.* 1960. Reprint. Westport, Conn.: Greenwood Press, 1975. Stories by eighteen Soviet writers of varying fame, from Evgeny Zamyatin to Israel Metter.

Anthologies in Russian

Rasskaz (Short story). Moscow: Sovremennik (Contemporary). Individual volumes have been issued each year at least from 1977 through 1982.

Rasskazy—goda (Short stories of the year——). Moscow: Sovetskii pisatel' (Soviet writer). Begun in 1951–52, the series continued with a volume a year at least through 1962.

Scholarly Works

Kovalev, V. A., ed. *Russkii sovetskii rasskaz: Ocherki istorii zhanra* (The Soviet Russian short story: An outline history of the genre). Leningrad: Nauka, 1970. A substantial collective history of the development of the short story in Soviet Russia from the Revolution through the 1960s. Unfortunately it lacks an index.

Ninov, A. *Sovremennyi rasskaz: Iz nabliudenii nad russkoi prozoi (1956–1966)* (The contemporary short story: Observations on Russian prose [1956–1966]). Leningrad: Khudozhestvennaia literatura, Leningradskoe otdelenie (Artistic Literature, Leningrad Division), 1969. The first chapter provides a quick but very helpful overview of the development of the Russian short story from its nineteenth-century beginnings before the author goes on to discuss writers of the 1950s and 1960s.

Ognev, Aleksandr. *O poetike sovetskogo russkogo rasskaza* (The poetics of the Soviet Russian short story). Saratov: Izdatel'stvo Saratovskogo universiteta (Saratov University Press), 1973. Contains only two large chapters: one on the narrator, the other on the problem of time in literary works.

———. *Russkii sovetskii rasskaz 50–70-kh godov* (The Soviet Russian short story from the 1950s to the 1970s). Moscow: Prosveshchenie (Enlightenment), 1978. A detailed look at the contemporary Soviet short story within the limitations of ideological interpretation.

Shubin, Eduard. *Sovremennyi russkii rasskaz: Voprosy poetiki zhanra* (The modern Russian short story: Problems in genre poetics). Leningrad: Nauka, Leningradskoe otdelenie, 1974. Chapter 2 (pp. 16–59) offers a survey of the short story's development in the nineteenth century. Later chapters deal with problems of theory and practice in the contemporary Soviet Russian short story.

Zamorii, T. *Sovremennyi russkii rasskaz* (The modern Russian short story). Kiev: Naukova dumka (Scholarly thought), 1968. A critical discussion of some major Soviet Russian short-story writers of mid-century.

General Bibliographical Works

Groznova, N. A., and **E. A. Shubin**, comps. *Russkii sovetskii rasskaz: Teoriia i istoriia zhanra: Bibliograficheskii ukazatel', 1917–1967* (The Soviet Russian short story: A bibliography of the theory and history of the genre, 1917–1967). Leningrad: Biblioteka Akademii nauk SSSR, 1975. Over nine hundred entries listing critical literature on the Soviet Russian short story arranged in modified chronological order, but at least with an index of names.

II

Andreev, Leonid

Povesti i rasskazy (Tales and stories). 2 vols. Moscow, 1971.

The Seven That Were Hanged and Other Stories. New York: Modern Library, 1958.

Kaun, Alexander. *Leonid Andreev: A Critical Study.* 1924. Reprint. New York and London: Benjamin Blom, 1969. A biography followed by a critical discussion of Andreev's fiction.

Woodward, James. *Leonid Andreyev: A Study.* Oxford: Clarendon Press, 1969. An analysis of Andreev's writing in chronological order, with appropriate attention to his short stories.

Babel, Isaak

Izbrannoe (Selected works). Moscow, 1966.

Konarmiia (Red Cavalry), 1925:

Ehre, Milton. "Babel's *Red Cavalry:* Epic and Pathos, History and Culture." *Slavic Review* 40, no. 2 (1981):228–40. A stimulating study of Babel's major work, with an epic sweep.

Luplow, Carol. *Isaac Babel's "Red Cavalry."* Ann Arbor, Mich.: Ardis, 1982. Investigates narrative, style, structure, and other elements of this major cycle.

Terras, Victor. "Line and Color: The Structure of I. Babel's Short Stories in *Red Cavalry.*" *Studies in Short Fiction* 3, no. 2 (Winter 1966):141–56. An excellent treatment of Babel's achievement in the short-story genre.

Falen, James. *Isaac Babel: Russian Master of the Short Story.* Knoxville: University of Tennessee Press, 1974. The best and most detailed overall study of Babel.

Mendelson, Danuta. *Metaphor in Babel's Short Stories.* Ann Arbor, Mich.: Ardis, 1982. Perhaps more concerned with metaphor as an entity in itself, the author in the second part of her study discusses its uses within the genre as Babel developed it.

Belov, Vasily

Izbrannye proizvedeniia (Selected works). 3 vols. Moscow: Sovremennik, 1983–84.

Hosking, Geoffrey. "Vasilii Belov, Chronicler of the Soviet Village." *Russian Review* 34, no. 2 (April 1975):165–85. A good general treatment of Belov's career down to a turning point around 1975.

Bestuzhev-Marlinsky, Aleksandr

Sochineniia (Works). 2 vols. Moscow, 1958.

Leighton, Lauren. *Alexander Bestuzhev-Marlinsky.* Boston: Twayne, 1975. A good general introduction to Bestuzhev's life and work, including his stories.

Bryusov, Valery

Sobranie sochinenii (Collected works). 7 vols. Moscow, 1973–75.

The Republic of the Southern Cross and Other Stories. 1918. Reprint. Westport, Conn.: Hyperion, 1977.

Rice, Martin. *Valery Briusov and the Rise of Russian Symbolism.* Ann Arbor, Mich.: Ardis, 1975. A concise life and works that deals with Bryusov primarily as a poet.

Bely, Andrey [Bugaev, Boris]

Complete Short Stories. Ann Arbor, Mich.: Ardis, 1979.

Mochulsky, Konstantin. *Andrei Bely: His Life and Works.* Ann Arbor, Mich.: Ardis, 1977. An overall study of the man and author, translated from the Russian.

Peterson, Ronald. *Andrei Bely's Short Prose.* Birmingham Slavonic Monographs no. 11. Birmingham: Department of Russian Language and Literature, University of Birmingham, 1980. A pioneering study of Bely's short stories with primary attention to their links with his novels.

Bulgakov, Mikhail

Izbrannoe (Selected works). Moscow, 1980.

Diaboliad and Other Stories. Translated by Carl Proffer. Bloomington and London: Indiana University Press, 1972.

Natov, Nadine. *Mikhail Bulgakov.* Boston: Twayne, 1985. A good brief introduction to Bulgakov's writing, with appropriate attention to his short stories.

Proffer, Ellendea. *Bulgakov: His Life and Work.* Ann Arbor, Mich.: Ardis, 1984. A detailed and judicious study.

Wright, A. Colin. *Mikhail Bulgakov: Life and Interpretation.* Toronto: University of Toronto Press, 1978. A thorough treatment of Bulgakov as writer and man, with an extensive bibliography.

Bunin, Ivan

Sobranie sochinenii (Collected works). 9 vols. Moscow, 1965–67.

The Gentleman from San Francisco. Translated by Bernard Guilbert Guerney. 1934. Reprint. New York: Octagon, 1981.

In a Far Distant Land: Selected Stories. Translated by Robert Bowie. Ann Arbor, Mich.: Heritage, 1983.

Connolly, Julian. *Ivan Bunin.* Boston: Twayne, 1982. An overview of Bunin's life and work, including his stories written in emigration.

Poggioli, Renato. "The Art of Ivan Bunin." In *The Phoenix and the Spider.* Cambridge, Mass.: Harvard University Press, 1957, 131–57. A study of Bunin's prose, including both his short stories and his longer works.

Woodward, James. *Ivan Bunin: A Study of His Fiction.* Chapel Hill: University of North Carolina Press, 1980. A detailed analysis of Bunin's prose, with full attention accorded his short stories.

Butkov, Yakov

Povesti i rasskazy (Tales and stories). Moscow, 1967.

Hodgson, Peter. *From Gogol to Dostoevsky: Jakov Butkov, a Reluctant Naturalist in the 1840's.* Munich: Wilhelm Fink, 1976. The pioneering study of this minor but characteristic figure of the 1840s.

Chekhov, Anton

Sobranie sochinenii (Collected works). 12 vols. Moscow, 1960–63.

The Oxford Chekhov. Translated by Ronald Hingley. 9 vols. London, New York, and Toronto: Oxford University Press, 1965–80.

Anton Chekhov's Short Stories: Texts of the Stories, Backgrounds, Criticism. Selected and edited by Ralph Matlaw. New York: W. W. Norton, 1979.

The Stories of Anton Chekhov. Edited by Robert Linscott. 1932. Reprint. New York: Modern Library, 1959.

Simmons, Ernest J. *Chekhov: A Biography.* Boston and Toronto: Little, Brown, 1962. A large detailed biography, but pays very little attention to Chekhov's writings as artistic works.

Chekhov, A. P. *Letters on the Short Story, the Drama and Other Literary Topics.* Edited by Louis S. Friedland. New York: Minton, Balch & Co., 1924.

A nicely arranged selection of Chekhov's own views on literature.

Chudakov, A. P. *Chekhov's Poetics.* Translated by Edwina Cruise and Donald Dragt. Ann Arbor, Mich.: Ardis, 1983. A study of Chekhov's techniques in both his plays and prose.

Hahn, Beverly. *Chekhov: A Study of the Major Stories and Plays.* London and New York: Cambridge University Press, 1977. A considerable portion of this study deals with the short stories.

Hulanicki, Leo, and David Savignac, eds. and trans. *Anton Čexov as a Master of Story-Writing: Essays in Modern Soviet Literary Criticism.* The Hague: Mouton, 1976. A collection of essays by prominent Soviet critics concentrating on the short story, with a bibliography of further works in English.

Kramer, Karl. *The Chameleon and the Dream: The Image of Reality in Čexov's Stories.* The Hague: Mouton, 1970. A well-defined but very broad topic of investigation within Chekhov's prose fiction, which leads to sometimes unpersuasive but always stimulating observations on the short stories.

Welty, Eudora. "Reality in Chekhov's Stories." In *The Eye of the Story.* New York: Random House, 1978, 61–81. A perceptive essay, based on wide reading, on Chekhov's "constructive revolution" within the genre of the short story.

Dal, Vladimir

Povesti, rasskazy, ocherki, skazki (Tales, stories, sketches, fairy tales). Moscow and Leningrad, 1961.

Baer, Joachim T. *Vladimir Ivanovic Dal' as a Belletrist.* The Hague and Paris: Mouton, 1972. After a short biographical chapter, the book offers a very close reading of Dal's numerous and influential short stories, with many parallels to the works of other Russian authors.

Dostoevsky, Fedor

Polnoe sobranie sochinenii (Complete works). 30 vols. Leningrad: Nauka, 1972–.

The Novels. Translated by Constance Garnett. 12 vols. London: Heinemann, 1912–20. A collected edition including the short stories.

The Best Short Stories of Dostoevsky. Translated by David Magarshack. New York: Modern Library, [1954].

The Short Stories of Dostoevsky. Edited by William Phillips. Translated by Constance Garnett. New York: Dial, 1946.

Leatherbarrow, W. J. *Fedor Dostoevsky.* Boston: Twayne, 1981. A remarkably stimulating critical study of such a prolific writer within a restricted format.

Mossman, Elliott. "Dostoevskij's Early Works: The More than Rational Distortion." *Slavic and East European Journal* 10, no. 3 (Fall 1966):268–78. Examines an important link between Gogol's work and Dostoevsky's stories of the 1840s.

Schmid, Wolf. *Der Textaufbau in den Erzählungen Dostoevskijs* (Text structure in Dostoevsky's short stories). Munich: Wilhelm Fink, 1973. A study of the "interference between the narrator-text and character-text" in Dostoevsky's short stories as a step toward understanding Dostoevsky's contribution to the novel form.

Terras, Victor. *The Young Dostoevsky (1846–1849): A Critical Study.* The Hague and Paris: Mouton, 1969. Since most of the young Dostoevsky's writings were short stories, this thorough critical study deals primarily with that genre.

Garshin, Vsevolod

Polnoe sobranie sochinenii (Complete works). Moscow: Academia, 1934.

The Signal and Other Stories. Translated by R. Smith. 1915. Reprint. Freeport, N.Y.: Books for Libraries Press, 1971.

Yarwood, Edmund. *Vsevolod Garshin.* Boston: Twayne, 1981. A general introduction that necessarily deals at length with the short stories.

Stenborg, Lennart. *Studien zur Erzähltechnik in den Novellen V. M. Garšins* (Studies in the narrative devices in the short stories of V. M. Garshin). Uppsala: Acta Universitatis upsaliensis, 1972. A technical literary study of Garshin's works.

Gogol, Nikolay

Polnoe sobranie sochinenii (Complete works). 14 vols. Moscow: Akademiia nauk SSSR (USSR Academy of Sciences), 1937–52.

The Collected Tales and Plays of Nikolai Gogol. Edited by Leonard J. Kent. New York: Pantheon, 1964.

Vechera na khutore bliz Dikan'ki (Evenings on a farm near Dikanka), 1831–32:

Holquist, J. Michael. "The Devil in Mufti: The *Märchenwelt* in Gogol's Short Stories." *Publications of the Modern Language Association of America* 82 (October 1967):352–62. Traces a very important fantasy element through the corpus of Gogol's shorter works.

Mirgorod, 1835:

McLean, Hugh. "Gogol's Retreat from Love: Towards an Interpretation of *Mirgorod.*" *American Contributions to the Fourth International Congress of Slavists.* The Hague: Mouton, 1958, 225–45. Argues that Gogol's attitudes toward erotic love became more primitive as time passed.

"Shinel'" (The overcoat), 1842:

Eichenbaum, Boris. "How Gogol's 'Overcoat' Is Made." In *Gogol from the Twentieth Century: Eleven Essays*. Edited by Robert Maguire. Princeton: Princeton University Press, 1974, 267–92. The classic formalist essay on "The Overcoat."

Trahan, Elizabeth, ed. *Gogol's "Overcoat": An Anthology of Critical Essays*. Ann Arbor, Mich.: Ardis, 1982. Five essays by Soviet and Western writers on aspects of "The Overcoat."

Erlich, Victor. *Gogol*. New Haven and London: Yale University Press, 1969. A good brief survey of Gogol's life in its entirety.

Gippius, Vasily V. *Gogol*. Edited and translated by Robert Maguire. Ann Arbor, Mich.: Ardis, 1981. The best treatment of Gogol written by a scholar in the Soviet Union.

Driessen, F. C. *Gogol as a Short-Story Writer: A Study of His Technique of Composition*. The Hague: Mouton, 1965. Some general remarks and systematic analyses of Gogol's principal short stories by a Dutch scholar.

Woodward, James B. *The Symbolic Art of Gogol: Essays on His Short Fiction*. Columbus, Ohio: Slavica, 1981. Careful studies of five of Gogol's major short stories, including "The Overcoat." Has a good bibliography.

Gorky, Maksim

Polnoe sobranie sochinenii. 25 vols. Moscow: Nauka (Science), 1968–76.

Collected Works. 10 vols. Moscow: Progress Publishers, 1978–82.

A Book of Short Stories. Edited by Avrahm Yarmolinsky and Moura Budberg. 1939. Reprint. New York: Octagon, 1973.

Kaun, Alexander. *Maxim Gorky and His Russia*. New York: Jonathan Cape & Harrison Smith, 1931. A detailed biography published several years before Gorky's death.

Weil, Irwin. *Gorky: His Literary Development and Influence on Soviet Intellectual Life*. New York: Random House, 1966. The standard "life and works" study of Gorky in English.

Borras, F. M. *Maxim Gorky the Writer: An Interpretation*. Oxford: Clarendon Press, 1967. Chapter 2 (pp. 59–94) analyzes Gorky's short stories as a component part of his work.

Kataev, Valentin.

Sobranie sochinenii (Collected works). 9 vols. Moscow, 1968–72.

Russell, Robert. *Valentin Kataev.* Boston: Twayne, 1981. A good introduction to Kataev's life and works. Includes a chapter on his short stories.

Kazakov, Yuri

Going to Town and Other Stories. Translated by Gabriella Azrael. Boston: Houghton Mifflin, 1964.

The Smell of Bread and Other Stories. Translated by Manya Harari and Andrew Thompson. London: Harvill Press, 1965.

Arcturus: The Hunting Hound and Other Stories. Translated by Anne Terry White. Garden City, N.Y.: Doubleday, 1968.

Kramer, Karl. "Jurij Kazakov: The Pleasures of Isolation." *Slavic and East European Journal* 10, no. 1 (Spring 1966):22–31. A careful study of the important theme of isolation from society in Kazakov's stories.

Orth, Samuel. "The Short Stories of Jurij Kazakov: Old Russia and the Soviet World." *Russian Language Journal* 32, no. 112 (Spring 1978):177–83. A brief study of a central theme of national nostalgia in Kazakov's short stories.

Korolenko, Vladimir

Sobranie sochinenii (Collected works). 10 vols. Moscow, 1953–56.

Makar's Dream and Other Stories. 1916. Reprint. Freeport, N.Y.: Books for Libraries Press, 1971.

Bialyi, Grigorii. *V. G. Korolenko.* Leningrad: Khudozhestvennaia literatura, 1983. A study of Korolenko's life and works by a leading Soviet scholar.

Kuprin, Aleksandr

Sobranie sochinenii (Collected works). 9 vols. Moscow, 1970–73.

Gambrinus and Other Stories. 1925. Reprint. Freeport, N.Y.: Books for Libraries Press, 1970.

Sentimental Romance and Other Stories. New York: Pageant Press, 1969.

A Slav Soul and Other Stories. 1916. Reprint. Freeport, N.Y.: Books for Libraries Press, 1971.

The Duel and Selected Stories. Translated by Andrew MacAndrew. New York: Signet, 1961.

Luker, Nicholas. *Alexander Kuprin.* Boston: Twayne, 1978. An introduction to Kuprin's writings with proper attention to his short stories.

Kuzmin, Mikhail

Selected Prose and Poetry. Translated and edited by Michael Green. Ann Arbor, Mich.: Ardis, 1980. Contains eleven short stories.

Lermontov, Mikhail

Sobranie sochinenii (Collected works). 4 vols. Moscow and Leningrad: Akademiia nauk SSSR, 1961–62.

A Hero of Our Time. Translated by Vladimir Nabokov, with Dmitry Nabokov. New York: Doubleday, Anchor Press, 1958.

Mersereau, John, Jr. *Mikhail Lermontov.* Carbondale: Southern Illinois University Press, 1962. Dedicated almost entirely to a discussion of *Hero of Our Time,* despite the general title.

Garrard, John. *Mikhail Lermontov.* Boston: Twayne, 1982. A general introduction that spends much time on Lermontov's poetry as well as his prose.

Leskov, Nikolay

Sobranie sochinenii (Collected works). 11 vols. Moscow, 1956–58.

Satirical Stories of Nikolai Leskov. Translated by William B. Edgerton. New York: Pegasus, 1968.

Selected Tales. Translated by David Magarshack. New York: Noonday Press, 1961.

Lantz, K. A. *Nikolay Leskov.* Boston: Twayne, 1979. Provides a brief biography, followed by an overall critical study of Leskov's writings.

McLean, Hugh. *Nikolai Leskov: The Man and His Art.* Cambridge, Mass., and London: Harvard University Press, 1977. The definitive study of Leskov in any language.

Benjamin, Walter. "The Storyteller: Reflections on the Works of Nikolai Leskov." In *Illuminations.* New York: Harcourt, Brace & World, 1968, 83–109. A general essay on the short story as an oral and written genre, with fairly frequent references to Leskov.

Odoevsky, Vladimir

Sochineniia (Works). 2 vols. Moscow, 1981.

Russian Nights. Translated by Olga Koshansky-Olienikov and Ralph Matlaw. New York: E. P. Dutton, 1965.

Karlinsky, Simon. "A Hollow Shape: The Philosophical Tales of Prince Vladimir Odoevsky." *Studies in Romanticism* 5 (1966):169–82. A sympathetic and intelligent general article, with emphasis on *Russian Nights.*

Matlaw, Ralph. Introduction to *Russian Nights.* Translated by Olga Koshansky-Olienikov and Ralph Matlaw. New York: E. P. Dutton, 1965, 7–20. A brief general discussion of Odoevsky, with major attention paid to *Russian Nights.*

Pilnyak, Boris

Sobranie sochinenii (Collected works). 8 vols. Moscow: Gosizdat, 1929–30.

The Tale of the Unextinguished Moon and Other Stories. Translated by Beatrice Scott. New York: Washington Square Press, 1967.

Mother Earth and Other Stories. Translated by Vera Reck and Michael Green. New York and Washington: Praeger, 1968.

Reck, Vera. *Boris Pil'niak: A Soviet Writer in Conflict with the State.* Montreal and London: McGill-Queen's University Press, 1975. Not a full biography but an account of Pilnyak's major clashes with the Soviet literary establishment.

Pisemsky, Aleksey

Sobranie sochinenii (Collected works). 9 vols. Moscow: Pravda, 1959.

Moser, Charles A. *Pisemsky: A Provincial Realist.* Cambridge, Mass.: Harvard University Press, 1969. A general study of the life and works with a detailed bibliography including Pisemsky's short works.

Platonov, Andrey

Izbrannye proizvedeniia (Selected works). 2 vols. Moscow, 1978.

Collected Works. Ann Arbor, Mich.: Ardis, 1978.

The Fierce and Beautiful World. Translated by Joseph Barnes. New York: E. P. Dutton, 1970.

Pomyalovsky, Nikolay

Sochineniia (Works). 2 vols. Leningrad: Khudozhestvennaia literatura (Leningradskoe otdelenie), 1965.

Seminary Sketches. Translated by Alfred Kuhn. Ithaca, N.Y.: Cornell University Press, 1973.

Kuhn, Alfred. Introduction to N. Pomyalovsky, *Seminary Sketches,* pp. xi–xxxvii. One of the very few works on Pomyalovsky in English, with emphasis, of course, on the *Sketches.*

Pushkin, Aleksandr

Polnoe sobranie sochinenii (Complete works). 10 vols. Moscow: Nauka, 1962–66.

Complete Prose Fiction. Translated by Paul Debreczeny. Stanford: Stanford University Press, 1984.

Povesti pokoinogo Ivana Petrovicha Belkina (Tales of the late Ivan Petrovich Belkin), 1831:

Bethea, David, and Sergei Davydov. "Pushkin's Saturnine Cupid: The Poetics of Parody in *The Tales of Belkin.*" *Publications of the Modern Language Association of America* 96 (1981):8–21. In part a response to the Gregg article below. The authors emphasize, among other things, the literary and parodic facets of the cycle.

Gregg, Richard. "A Scapegoat for All Seasons: The Unity and the Shape of *The Tales of Belkin.*" *Slavic Review* 30 (December 1971):748–61. A stimulating analysis of the *Tales* as a unified cycle.

"Egipetskie nochi" (Egyptian nights), 1835[?]:

O'Bell, Leslie. *Pushkin's "Egyptian Nights": The Biography of a Work.* Ann Arbor, Mich.: Ardis, 1984. A close study of one of the most prominent fragments in nineteenth-century Russian literature.

"Pikovaia dama" (The queen of spades), 1834:

Bocharov, S. G. *"The Queen of Spades." New Literary History* 9, no. 2 (Winter 1978):315–32. Translation of a close reading and discussion of the story, by a Soviet critic in a relatively good Soviet critical tradition.

Simmons, Ernest J. *Pushkin.* New York: Vintage, 1964. The standard biography of Pushkin in English.

Bayley, John. *Pushkin: A Comparative Commentary.* Cambridge: Cambridge University Press, 1971. See in particular the seventh chapter, on Pushkin's prose, for intelligent remarks on the writer's literary achievement.

Debreczeny, Paul. *The Other Pushkin: A Study of Alexander Pushkin's Prose Fiction.* Stanford: Stanford University Press, 1983. Includes readings of the short stories that draw upon the extensive scholarship on Pushkin now in existence.

Lezhnev, Abram. *Pushkin's Prose.* Translated by Roberta Reeder. Ann Arbor, Mich.: Ardis, 1974. Analysis of Pushkin's prose in close conjunction with that of his contemporaries.

Remizov, Aleksey

Izbrannoe (Selected works). Moscow, 1978.

Selected Prose. Ann Arbor, Mich.: Ardis, 1985.

The Clock. Translated by J. Cournos. London: Chatto & Windus, 1924.

Saltykov-Schchedrin, Mikhail

Polnoe sobranie sochinenii (Complete works). 20 vols. Moscow and Leningrad: Gosudarstvennoe izdatel'stvo khudozhestvennoi literatury, 1933–41.

Fables. Translated by Vera Volkhovsky. 1931. Reprint. Westport, Conn.: Hyperion, 1977.

Sanine, Kyra. *Saltykov-Chtchédrine: Sa vie et ses oeuvres* (Saltykov-Shchedrin: His life and works). Paris: Institut d'études slaves (Institute of Slavic Studies), 1955. A large detailed study, in the best tradition of French Slavists.

Sholokhov, Mikhail

Sobranie sochinenii (Collected works). 8 vols. Moscow, 1980.

Short Stories. Translated by Robert Daglish. Moscow: Raduga Publishers, 1984. Vol. 1 of projected *Collected Works* in eight volumes in English.

Ermolaev, Herman. *Mikhail Sholokhov and His Art.* Princeton: Princeton University Press, 1982. Concentrates primarily on *The Quiet Don.*

Stewart, D. H. *Mikhail Sholokhov: A Critical Introduction.* Ann Arbor: University of Michigan Press, 1967. Also emphasizes *The Quiet Don.*

Shukshin, Vasily

Izbrannye proizvedeniia (Selected works). 2 vols. Moscow: Molodaia gvardiia (Young Guard), 1975.

Snowball Berry Red and Other Stories. Translated by Donald Fiene et al. Ann Arbor, Mich.: Ardis, 1979.

Roubles in Words, Kopeks in Figures, and Other Stories. New York: Marion Boyars, 1984.

Hosking, Geoffrey. "Vasily Shukshin." In *Beyond Socialist Realism: Soviet Fiction since Ivan Denisovich.* New York: Holmes & Meier, 1980, 162–79. A general discussion of the man and his work.

Sleptsov, Vasily

Sochineniia (Works). 2 vols. Moscow and Leningrad: Academia, 1932–33.

Sologub, Fedor [Teternikov, Fedor]

Sobranie sochinenii (Collected works). 12 vols. St. Petersburg: Shipovnik, 1909–12.

Rasskazy (Short stories.). Edited by Evelyn Bristol. Berkeley: Berkeley Slavic Specialties, 1979.

The Kiss of the Unborn and Other Stories. Translated by Murl Barker. Knoxville: University of Tennessee Press, 1977.

Hansson, Carola. *Fedor Sologub as a Short-Story Writer: Stylistic Analyses.* Stockholm: Almqvist & Wiksell International, 1975. Detailed discussions of certain of Sologub's short stories.

Leitner, Andreas. *Die Erzählungen Fedor Sologubs* (Fedor Sologub's short stories). Munich: Otto Sagner, 1976. A very systematic description (dissertation) and analysis of Sologub's stories.

Soloukhin, Vladimir

Sobranie sochinenii (Collected works). 4 vols. Moscow, 1983–84.

White Grass. Moscow: Progress Publishers, 1971.

Solzhenitsyn, Aleksandr

Sobranie sochinenii (Collected works). 6 vols. Frankfurt: Posev (Sowing), 1969–70.

Stories and Prose Poems. Translated by Michael Glenny. New York: Bantam, 1972.

Matryona's House and Other Stories. Harmondsworth, England: Penguin, 1975.

Kodjak, Andrej. *Alexander Solzhenitsyn*. Boston: Twayne, 1978. A short biographical chapter followed by discussion of Solzhenitsyn's writings down to about 1975.

Scammell, Michael. *Solzhenitsyn*. New York: W. W. Norton, 1984. A mammoth biography of the writer, reliable and detailed, but with little attention given to the writings as such.

Peppard, Victor. "The Structure of Solženicyn's Short Stories." *Russian Language Journal* 32, no. 112 (Spring 1978):165–75. A brief but concentrated study of the structural coherence of Solzhenitsyn's shorter works.

Žekulin, Gleb. "Solzhenitsyn's Four Stories." *Soviet Studies* 16, no. 1 (July 1964):45–62. A compact study of Solzhenitsyn's four short works of the early 1960s, with *One Day in the Life of Ivan Denisovich* considered a story rather than a novel.

Tolstoy, Leo

Sobranie sochinenii (Collected works). 20 vols. Moscow, 1960–65.

The Centenary Edition of Tolstoy. 21 vols. Translated by Louise and Aylmer Maude. London: Oxford University Press, 1929–37.

Great Short Works of Leo Tolstoy. Edited by John Bayley. New York: Harper & Row, 1967.

Simmons, Ernest J. *Leo Tolstoy*. London: John Lehmann, 1949. Probably the best biography of many in existence, full of detail but not excessively so.

Christian, R. F. *Tolstoy: A Critical Introduction*. Cambridge: Cambridge University Press, 1969. Penetrating critical remarks on the entire scope of Tolstoy's writing.

Heim, Michael. "'Master and Man': 'Three Deaths' Redivivus." In *American Contributions to the Eighth International Congress of Slavists*. Vol. 2, *Literary Contributions*. The Hague and Paris: Mouton, 1978, 260–71.

Trifonov, Yuri

Izbrannye proizvedeniia. 2 vols. Moscow, 1978.

The Long Goodbye: Three Novellas. Translated by H. P. Burlingame and Ellendea Proffer. Ann Arbor, Mich.: Ardis, 1978.

Hosking, Geoffrey. "Yuri Trifonov." In *Beyond Socialist Realism: Soviet Fiction since Ivan Denisovich.* New York: Holmes & Meier, 1980, 180–95. A good general treatment of the man and his work.

Turgenev, Ivan

Polnoe sobranie sochinenii i pisem (Complete works and letters). 28 vols. Moscow and Leningrad: Akademiia nauk SSSR, 1960–68.

The Novels of Ivan Turgenev. 15 vols. Translated by Constance Garnett. London: Heinemann, 1894–99. Includes his stories.

First Love and Other Tales. Translated by David Magarshack. New York: W. W. Norton, 1960.

The Hunting Sketches. Translated by Bernard Guilbert Guerney. New York: Signet, 1962.

Peters, Jochen-Ulrich. *Turgenevs Zapiski ochotnika innerhalb der očerk-Tradition der 40er Jahre: Zur Entwicklung des realistischen Erzählens in Russland* (Turgenev's *Hunting Sketches* and the sketch tradition of the 1840s: On the development of the realistic short story in Russia). Berlin-Wiesbaden: Otto Harrassowitz, 1972. Includes a treatment of the physiological sketch and an attempt at defining the term *ocherk* (sketch) before turning to the *Hunting Sketches.*

Shapiro, Leonard. *Turgenev: His Life and Times.* New York: Random House, 1978. A very thorough biography by a careful scholar who has made excellent use of his sources.

Yarmolinsky, Avrahm. *Turgenev: The Man, His Art and His Age.* 1959. Reprint. New York: Collier, 1962. Still a very good shorter treatment of Turgenev's life and work.

Brodianski, Nina. "Turgenev's Short Stories: A Revaluation." *Slavonic and East European Review* 32, no. 78 (December 1953):70–91. A wide-ranging and very stimulating investigation of Turgenev's approach to the short story generally.

Ledkovsky, Marina. *The Other Turgenev: From Romanticism to Symbolism.* Wurzburg: Jal-Verlag, 1973. A study of Turgenev's "nonrealism" that emphasizes his shorter works and, more specifically, his "mysterious tales."

Natova, Nadine. "O 'misticheskikh' povestiakh Turgeneva" (On Turgenev's "mystical" tales). *Transactions of the Association of Russian-American Scholars in U.S.A.* 16 (1983):113–49. A close reading of certain of Turgenev's stories, particularly "Klara Milich."

Uspensky, Gleb

Sobranie sochinenii (Collected works). 9 vols. Moscow, 1955–57.

Zamyatin, Evgeny

Sochineniia (Works). 2 vols. Munich: A. Neimanis, 1970, 1982.

The Dragon and Other Stories. Translated by Mirra Ginsburg. Harmondsworth, England: Penguin, 1975.

Shane, Alex M. *The Life and Works of Evgenij Zamjatin.* Berkeley: University of California Press, 1968. The standard work on Zamyatin, divided into biography and a chronological study of his writing.

Zoshchenko, Mikhail

Izbrannoe (Selected works). 2 vols. Leningrad: Khudozhestvennaia literatura, Leningradskoe otdelenie, 1978.

The Woman Who Could Not Read and Other Tales. Translated by Elisaveta Fen. 1940. Reprint. Westport, Conn.: Hyperion, 1973.

The Wonderful Dog and Other Tales. Translated by Elisaveta Fen. 1942. Reprint. Westport, Conn.: Hyperion, 1973.

Nervous People and Other Satires. Translated by Maria Gordon and Hugh McLean. 1963. Reprint. Bloomington: Indiana University Press, 1975.

Chudakova, M. O. *Poetika Mikhaila Zoshchenko* (Zoshchenko's poetics). Moscow: Nauka, 1979. A very thorough study that deals with much more than the "authorial word" (as the author puts it) as the key to Zoshchenko's writing.

Titunik, Irwin R. "Mikhail Zoshchenko and the Problem of *Skaz.*" *California Slavic Studies* 6 (1971):83–96. Examines the question of skaz with particular application to Zoshchenko; concludes one can make "no safe assumptions" on the subject.

Index